IN WINTER'S SHADOW

'Well cousin, by now you have heard that your
father is dead, and you know that I am his successor
to the lordship of our clan . . .

'When last we spoke, you told me I spoke like a
beggar, and commanded me not to mention this
subject to you again. But I am a chieftain now . . .
Those lands I spoke of would be the easiest thing in
the world for you to win for us. Your husband the
Emperor dotes on you – or so they say – and you
have only to get him to mention the matter to our
King for Ergyriad to give us all we ask, were it lives
instead of lands.

'Accept that you are one of us, do what I ask, and
I will forget the past. But if you prefer the imperial
purple to your own blood you must suffer for it . . .'

GILLIAN BRADSHAW

In Winter's Shadow

METHUEN LONDON LTD

A Methuen Paperback

IN WINTER'S SHADOW
ISBN 0 417 06740 2

First published in Great Britain 1982
by Eyre Methuen Ltd

Copyright © 1982 by Gillian Bradshaw

This edition published 1982
by Methuen London Ltd
11 New Fetter Lane, London EC4P 4EE

Made and printed in Great Britain by
Richard Clay (The Chaucer Press) Ltd,
Bungay, Suffolk

To Robin

for Akko and the Adirondacks,
Cambridge, Caesarea, and Chartres
and much more.

'Brief as the lightning in the collied night,
That, in a spleen, unfolds both heaven and earth,
And ere a man hath power to say, "Behold!"
The jaws of darkness do devour it up:
So quick bright things come to confusion.'
A Midsummer Night's Dream

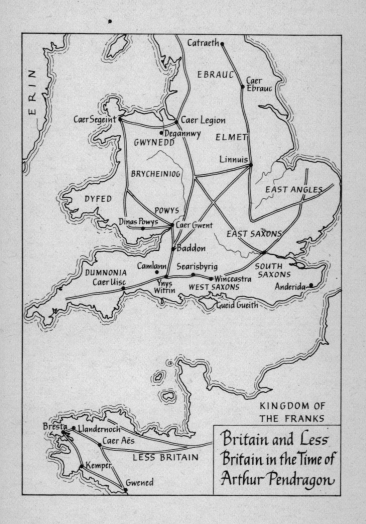

Britain and Less Britain in the Time of Arthur Pendragon

One

'To Gwynhwyfar daughter of Ogyrfan, Augusta, Empress of Britain,' the letter began, 'from Menw son of Cynan, lord of the noble clan of the sons of Maxentius, many greetings. Well, cousin, by now you have heard that your father is dead, and you know that I am his successor to the lordship of our clan. You must not expect that I will, as he did, humour you and let our own fortunes take whatever course they will. I mean to better them, as you, for all your protestations of love and virtue, never have.

'When last we spoke, you told me that I spoke like a beggar, and commanded me not to mention this subject to you again. But I am a chieftain now, and lord of your own flesh and blood, and, though you have married above us, now I can demand this of you, and need no longer beg. Those lands I spoke of would be the easiest thing in the world for you to win for us. Your husband the Emperor dotes on you – or so they say – and you have only to get him to mention the matter to our king for Ergyriad to give us all that we ask, were it lives instead of lands.

'If you refuse us this service, do not trouble to write again. I will know that you have chosen to be no part of your clan, and, if I have any power here, I will see to it that you are treated accordingly. You are no better than us, however high you may have risen in the world, and you have no right to keep to yourself riches and honours which ought to be shared with your family. Accept that you are one of us, do what I ask, and I will forget the past. But if you prefer the imperial purple to your own blood you must suffer for it.'

I set the letter down on the table and stared at it, then pressed the palms of my hands against my eyes, as if that would ease the dull burning there. If I could sit still, if I could not think or feel, even for a little while, perhaps the rage and grief would not crush against my heart so closely.

I remembered the time I had told my cousin Menw that he spoke like a beggar. Three years before, I had accompanied my husband on a visit to the northern kings, and had stopped at my clan's holding, meaning to stay for a

11

week or so. It was the first time I had been home since I married Arthur and went south to hold his fortress for him; my father had ridden out miles to meet me, and treated me like the blessed mother of God the whole time I was there. He had always enjoyed spoiling me – I was his only child, and my mother had died giving birth to me, so he had no one else to spoil. Menw was right when he said that. And yet, it was not to the point. He should be able to see that.

When I had been home two days, Menw had offered to escort me to the house of an òld friend whom I wished to visit. I might have taken some of Arthur's warriors instead, but I was touched that my cousin offered, and agreed at once. He had been something of a bully when we were little, and I thought he wished to make amends. But no sooner had we ridden from our holding than he began to speak pointedly of the power I must have as wife of the Emperor, and I grew uneasy. I had heard that tale from too many petitioners, as preface to too many pleas for justice, money or revenge, not to recognize it immediately. And sure enough, on the way back, Menw reined in his horse on a hill and looked out over the land in a calculating fashion.

'Pretty!' he observed.

I nodded. The dusk lay purple across the hills, and the soft summer stars were coming out eastward over the holding. To the north the Roman Wall leapt into the sunset behind us, scaling the boundaries of the old Empire.

'That land there,' Menw went on, pointing southeast, 'is the only part not ours.' His tone gave particular significance to the words 'not ours', and when I looked at him sharply I saw that he had a sly, insinuating smile. Menw was a big man, with thick dark hair and heavy eyebrows, and the smile suited him very badly.

'Is there something you would say?' I asked, hoping that my coldness would discourage him.

But he seemed pleased, and frankly proposed a scheme for obtaining his neighbours' lands by official fraud and deceit. 'No one would be surprised,' he told me. 'Through you we are not only noble and Roman-descended, but the Emperor's kin as well. The sons of Hueil are scarcely more than peasants, and rebellious ones at that – you know they fought in Bran's rebellion? And they are dishonest, and give short measure when they trade, and are of no use to anyone. We have more right to the land than such as they.'

'But what have they done that is criminal enough to deprive them of their fathers' lands?'

He looked startled. 'What do you mean, what have they done? It is what they are, and what we are, that matters.'

'The laws are clear, Menw. I cannot help you.'

He began to glower. 'You mean you do not wish to help us.'

I shook my head. But it was no use trying to pretend I had misunderstood him and thought he wanted legal advice. He knew I understood, and began angrily to claim that I was indifferent to my family's welfare. It was no use to tell him of the ties of justice and the laws: he did not wish to understand anything more than the tie that binds each to his own clan. Eventually I simply turned my mare and rode on towards the holding, but he refused to leave the subject and rode after me, shouting that we needed the land. It was then that I told him that he spoke like a beggar. At that he forced his horse against mine and seized my arm, his face dark with anger, and I had to stop my mare for fear of being pulled from her back.

'You selfish vixen! What do you want with all those riches and honours? Great lady you may be, but you've no children to pass them on to. If I were your husband I would divorce you and marry any slut that could give me an heir. I'd divorce you at once, do you hear? And if he divorces you, you'll need your kin. Better think who you call a beggar, "noble lady"!'

I struck him across the face, jerked my arm free, then, not trusting myself or him to say anything more, spurred my horse to a gallop. He galloped after me, shouting, but my horse was faster than his, and he arrived at the holding several minutes after I pulled my mare to a halt in the yard. I waited for him to dismount, then dismounted myself. I tossed him the mare's reins as though he were a groom, said, 'Never mention this subject to me again,' and left him holding the sweating horse, glaring at me, his eyes bright with a powerless hatred.

And now my father was dead and Menw was chieftain of our clan. *Father*, I thought, still trying to understand it. I had only heard of his death the week before, and I still did not really believe in it. It is hard to believe that someone is dead when they have lived far away. They form no part of the pattern of one's life, and are not missed in the common things. It seemed as though, if I could only go home, he would be waiting there, as young and strong as in my earliest memories, and not even bent and feeble as he had been on that disastrous last visit. Only my father was not, never again would, be waiting for me at home. And now, after this, I could not go home at all.

I took my hands from my eyes and stared at the letter. Home. That was a strange name to give that remote holding in the North which I had left eleven – no, twelve – years before to come to this fortress of Camlann. I tried to remember it. The house had been built by my great-grandfather's grandfather, who had received his lands from the Emperor Theodosius, the last of the Roman emperors to die with the Empire still whole. That ancestor – the Maxentius we named ourselves after – had been a military official of the British province of Valentia. He had fought bravely for Theodosius the first time the province had nearly been overrun by the Saxons, and our lands had been his reward. He had built the house of grey fieldstone, partly in the Roman, partly in the British fashion. His Roman atrium had been thatched over by my great-grandfather to make a central hall, and that same grandfather had also dug up the mosaic floor of the atrium and built a firepit instead. The firepit still had a rim of patterned tiles: I could remember playing on them when I was small, while the older members of the clan sat by the fire and talked. My father once told me that the mosaic had been of a man driving a fiery chariot through the stars, and I used to try to imagine that picture. The idea stirred me. I was not sure what a chariot looked like – sometimes I pictured it as a cart, at other times as a kind of wheelbarrow – but I could always imagine it riding in fire across the wide sky and along the winds of heaven, brushing the stars. I played at driving the chariot when I rode my pony out into the hills, or when we took a cart from our holding south to fetch grain.

The land around our house was wild, if beautiful, and sparsely settled. The nearest holding was three miles away, and the nearest town – Caer Lugualid on the coast – a full day's ride. Once there had been other towns closer to us. The Roman Wall passed about a mile from our holding, and at intervals along it were the ruins of towns and garrisons, all long abandoned. From the time I was old enough to ride any distance I used to go out with some of my cousins and look for treasure in the ruins, crawling under the fallen roofs and walking through the grass-grown streets. For a long time I accepted the ruins as simply as I accepted the hills, and only wondered over what I found in them – a broken glass bottle iridescent with age; a copper coin with the head of an ancient emperor; a tiny bronze statue of a god. But when I grew a little older I began to wonder what it had been like when those towns were full of people, how they could have lived in a land where so few lived now, and where they had all gone. One day I asked my father.

'They were protecting the Empire, my own darling,' he told me. 'They were soldiers like our father Maxentius, stationed on the Wall to defend Britain from the Saxons. As for how they lived, why, the Emperor had grain shipped to them from the south. Hundreds of ships brought it up the coast to Caer Ebrauc, where our king Caradoc lives now, and from there it was taken to all the people living on the Wall. And the ships didn't bring only grain, my girl, but those treasures you are always seeking. Glass, and gold, and silk and fine dyes, and spices from the East, carried all the way from Constantinople where the Emperor reigns.'

'But Uther Pendragon is the Emperor,' I pointed out, 'and he doesn't live at Con— at where you said, but at Camlann, in the South country.'

'Uther Pendragon is the Emperor of the provinces of Britain, true. He is king over the other kings of Britain, and to him chiefly falls the task of defending Britain against the Saxons. But once there was an Empire over the whole world, and all the provinces of Britain together were only its furthest western boundary. And the eastern part of the Empire is strong yet, and is ruled from Constantinople, which is so far away that a ship might sail from now to Michaelmas, and not reach it.'

'Why doesn't that Emperor still rule Britain, then? And what happened to all the people on the Wall?'

'He never used to rule from Constantinople; he ruled from Rome. The people on the Wall, Gwynhwyfar, left it and Britain and went to defend Rome, but they failed. And because they failed there is no emperor at Rome, only the

15

one in Constantinople and the one in Camlann.' And my father explained to me carefully about the fall of Rome. I was young: I had never heard that tale. But my father was a learned man, and owned books of history and philosophy, from which he knew something of the stretch of time and space beyond the small present we inhabited. It awed me. I had learned to read, along with my cousins, because we were noble and Roman-descended, and my father insisted that we ought to learn to read, but until then my knowledge of letters had been confined to crude messages and to accounts, with some stammering over a gospel imposed between the two. The idea of Rome struck me like a vision. I could not look at the Wall, or the tiles round the fire-pit, or my collection of bits from the ruins, without that vast Empire leaping up before my mind like the world revealed by a lightning-bolt. With my father's help I began to struggle through the cramped pages of his books till my eyes ached.

I suppose that that is one of my chief memories of home: my father's room with its wolfskin rug and copper lamp, myself sitting next to my father, his arm around me, and both of us bending over some book opened on the table before us, struggling with complicated Latin abbreviations and laughing at each other's mistakes. My father had been a lonely man until I showed an interest in his books. In a gentler age he might have been a scholar; had he been an unimportant member of the clan he might have left it to become a monk. But his father had designated him as his successor to the chieftainship; the clan had confirmed it, and he was left to do his best to meet the responsibility and to feel guilty when he spent time with his books. He had no one to talk to about them but me. My male cousins were not much interested in reading, beyond what was obviously useful. It was not surprising, really: we were noble, which meant that they were kept busy learning the arts of war, while at the same time they had to master the proper way of caring for our lands. Occasionally the older ones went off and fought for our king, Caradoc of Ebrauc, and came back boasting of their accomplishments and rousing the younger ones to envy. As for my female cousins, they had to learn to spin and weave and sew, to butcher and cook an animal or to heal it of various common ills, to make cheese and mead, to keep bees, keep house, manage servants, and see to the holding accounts. I had to learn the same things, but shamelessly ran off, especially from the cooking and housekeeping (I quite liked accounts, and, God help me! managing servants) and my father never punished me for it, though perhaps he should have. Sometimes he would reluctantly say, 'Gwynhwyfar, you ought to be helping with the poultry', but I would reply, 'Of course, Father, but first could you explain . . .' and two hours later he would still be explaining.

Sometimes I would feel ashamed of myself for avoiding the work, and yet more ashamed for manipulating my father in such a way, and I would resolve to be better in future, and work very hard at the things I most disliked. But always wonder or astonishment at the past would stir in me again, and I would go back to the books looking for an answer to one question, and stay to answer twenty while the day's concerns sank into the centuries.

Our clan was always fairly busy. Most of our land was only good for sheep, but we received wheat from dependent clans further south, and raised cattle and horses in the valley pastures. The lands my cousin Menw now coveted were good cattle lands. But we did not need them to make us wealthy. Our family had always been one of the most important in the north of Ebrauc. To the south and to the west, and even north across the border into Rheged, we were respected, honoured, feared. About the east we did not speak when I was young, for there lay the Saxon kingdom of Deira, from which, at any time, bands of raiders might march to burn down holdings and drive off cattle. An eastern dependency of ours suffered such a fate, one bad winter, and there was very little we could do to aid the survivors. Sometimes whispered accounts spread that such-and-such a holding had been taken, and with what deaths, rapes and brutalities the victims had suffered. Sometimes wretches would turn up begging at our holding, half-starved and desperate: they had lost lands and livelihood to the Saxons. It grew worse as I grew older. While Uther Pendragon remained Emperor there was some degree of order, but when he died the kings of Britain fought over who was to succeed him, and were too busy fighting to pay much heed to keeping out the Saxons.

Then, in the autumn of my twenty-first year, the new Emperor Arthur rode with his men from the east, leaving a Saxon army shattered behind him. He asked my father for hospitality and for a place to leave his wounded.

I was awed by it. I had been listening to reports of him for as long as I could remember. At first he had been the leader of the imperial warband under the old Emperor, then, when the civil war broke out, he had been the one man who continued to fight the Saxons. But after the war had dragged on for several years, and after a massive Saxon invasion in the South, Arthur claimed the imperial purple for himself, and defeated the other contenders to win the title of Emperor. He had no legal right to it. He was the Emperor Uther's son, true, but a bastard son by an unknown peasant mother, and a clanless man, an orphan raised out of charity at a monastery. At first all Britain was outraged by his usurpation. But he was an incomparable warleader. He not only defended the borders of Britain against Saxon invasions, but actually invaded the Saxons, and compelled their kings to become his tributaries and subjects of the Empire. Many of the British kings continued to hate him because of his birth, and the Church called him anti-Christ and devil because he taxed it to support his war against the Saxons, but my father said, 'I don't mind if he is a devil so long as he rules like an angel of God,' and began to support him. So, when Arthur turned up at our holding one grey morning with the whole of his warband after him, my father spared nothing and no one to make them welcome.

I was shaken awake by one of my aunts, given a babbled account of what was happening, and told to come and help. I went out into the dawn and found the yard full of armed men on tall horses, looming out of the mist. Their spears looked like a forest in winter. I saw my father in the centre of the yard and hurried over to him. He was talking to a tall, fair-haired man who glanced up as I came over; his eyes were the colour of the mist. 'Ach, there you are,' my father said. He sounded calm, but I could tell that he was very excited. 'This is my daughter Gwynhwyfar, your excellency. She is a sensible girl. You can give her charge of the wounded.' And, to me, in an undertone, 'This is the

18

Emperor, my girl. He has just defeated Fflamddwyn. Do you think we could put the wounded in the cow-byre? There's no room for them all in the house.'

I had expected Arthur to be middle-aged. I had pictured him as a grey, gaunt old warrior, wearing the imperial purple as clumsily as the crow in the fable wore its stolen peacock feathers. But he was barely thirty, with hair and beard the colour of wheat before the harvest, and his eyes seemed to have the sun behind them. When I stammered out that all we had for the wounded was a cow-byre, he smiled, said, 'It will do,' summoned various men out of the mist like a conjurer calling them from the air, and told me to tell them what to do. Of course, on the whole, they told me what to do, and Arthur strode in when it was half done and most of the wounded were cared for, to see them settled. He had already settled the rest.

I had seen wounded men before, the times being what they were, but not so many, fresh from a battle. I was confused, horrified, and could scarcely manage to tell Arthur's surgeons where the supplies were, or give reasonable orders to the servants. The world beyond our holding, the remnant of the Empire of my visions, had burst in upon us like a storm.

Arthur did not stay long, as he was eager to continue his campaign against the Saxons before the winter closed the roads. But he left his wounded with us, and asked if he might use our holding as one of his bases, promising (with a glint of dry humour) to find his own supplies and not borrow from us. That was essential. However welcome he was, his warband, the Pendragon's 'Family', numbered nearly seven hundred trained warriors, as well as doctors, grooms, armourers and a few servants, with more than twice their number of horses. It required a kingdom or two to support them all, and most of the kingdoms of Britain were notoriously reluctant to contribute to that support, with the result that, while the Family relied principally on plunder from the Saxons, it also tended to take supplies wherever it could find them. Most men in my father's position would have done their utmost to persuade the Emperor to take his Family elsewhere – one cannot refuse an Emperor outright – but my father hesitated only for a moment before agreeing to provide a base. It was plain that

Arthur was surprised by this, and more than a little pleased.

The Emperor was in and out of the holding at intervals over the next year, continuing his campaign against the northern Saxon kingdoms. He could not hurry the campaign because his force was far smaller than that which the Saxon kings could raise, so he did not dare meet them in pitched battles. Instead he tried to wear them out by raiding, and would turn up suddenly when they thought he was a hundred miles away and had sent most of their army home. When he judged that the time was ripe he would ask his British subject kings to raise their armies and risk a pitched battle against the Saxons, but for a long time they would be too strong for that. He had used these tactics against the southern Saxons with some success, but he told us that they were not defeated, as we had thought, but merely stalled. 'It will take another three or five years to settle them properly,' he said. He had time to talk to us on the later visits. He talked mainly about the Empire. Defeating the Saxons was, to Arthur, only the first step towards the goal of preserving the Empire. His monastic education had forced him to read books, and he knew that the Empire had once meant more than just a man in a purple cloak leading a force to crush the Saxons if they invaded too often. He had thought about the value of peace and of impartial justice, and could imagine what it might be like to live in a world that was not constantly at war with itself. He and my father were soon talking easily, eagerly. When Arthur spoke of the Empire his eyes shone, and when he thought out some new idea he would be unable to sit still, but would leap up and stride about the room, his purple cloak flapping, and stop suddenly when he understood what he wanted to say. I used to watch him and think of the man in the mosaic I had never seen, driving the chariot of fire. A chariot like Arthur's Empire, whirling precariously through the dark ruins of the West. I only prayed that it would not break among the winds.

If I had been a man I would probably have begged Arthur to allow me to join his warband. As it was, all I could do was try to see that our holding was a smoothly managed, effective base for him, and listen while he and my father talked – occasionally forgetting the modesty required of an unmarried woman, and joining in. Once, on his third visit,

Arthur and I found ourselves speaking alone together while my father watched us, and we stopped, embarrassed, and, on my part, suddenly afraid. We watched each other out of a great silence. Afterwards I saddled my mare and rode out to the Wall, recklessly alone in the grey afternoon. I walked the horse along the ruined fortification, trying to be reasonable. Why should the lord Arthur, Augustus, Emperor of Britain, take any notice of the daughter of an obscure northern nobleman? I would be sensible, I resolved, and eventually the constriction that had locked about my heart when he looked at me would go away.

But when I returned to the holding and turned my mare out to pasture – there was no room for her in the stables, which were full of Arthur's men – I met Arthur again. He saw me carrying my saddle back, and hurried over to me and took it from me. Then, arranging it over his arm he frowned, looked at me and said, 'You must have ridden some distance, Lady Gwynhwyfar: the saddle cloths are damp. That is no safe thing for a woman to do, in times such as these, and so near the border. You especially should not do it.'

'Why me especially, your excellency?' I asked, before I thought.

For a moment he stared at the saddle, then looked up suddenly and directly at my face. Without answering he turned away and took the saddle into the stables, returning it to its place. I stood outside, realizing that I had had no need to reason with myself, and feeling even more afraid.

We were married after the harvest, the year after Arthur's first visit. My father could not but be glad at the marriage. He had put my worth very high, which was why I was unmarried until I was twenty-two, an age when most women have two or three children. But now I was the wife of an emperor, and in a strange way it confirmed my father's love for me, and proved his devotion to the old Empire as well. He was proud and happy. But his grief went deeper than the gladness, for I left him alone. I went south to Camlann with an escort of wounded and cripples whom Arthur was sending home from the war, to hold Arthur's fortress for him and to find supplies while Arthur completed his campaign in the North.

Menw had spoken with bitter envy of the 'riches and

honours' I had received. But, God knows, honours were few those first years, and as for riches, I was hard put to it to find enough to keep the fortress and the army alive. Most of the kings of Britain still hated us as usurpers, and refused to pay the tribute, and our allies we had to conciliate with gifts. Arthur took plunder from the Saxons – cattle and grain, sheep and woollen clothing, arms, armour and cooking pots – which were very useful. Occasionally he sent me some uninjured men whom I could send to various kings to demand the tribute – but it was desperately hard! And I was at first an intruder in his fortress, a northerner among southerners, a woman of twenty-two suddenly put in authority over men who had served at Camlann since the Emperor Uther's time. Moreover, there had been a bad harvest that first year, and food was scarce. I remembered one of Arthur's grim letters to me, that first winter: 'The alliance with Urien wears badly. He begins to complain that he cannot support his own warband these days. I will need him to raise his army for me in a few months: make him a gift of six hundred head of cattle and something golden – I have given all my own plunder to Ergyriad. We have nothing to eat and are living off the land. The horses are sick. Ten men have the fever; I pray it does not spread. Beg Urien to send something, especially grain, to supply us at Yrechwydd, for I have told the men there will be food there. We will be there in three weeks.' And I, who had been making the servants at Camlann live on boiled cabbage, wrote madly to every king between Camlann and Caledon to produce those wretched cattle, and wrested a gold crucifix from a monastery. It worked. Arthur got the supplies, and his campaign was able to continue to its eventual success. But the cost of it, the cost! Kings and the Church offended, less tribute received the next year, and, at Camlann, a sullen anger poisoning everything. You cannot blame a man for being angry when he has lived on cabbage for a month, only to see six hundred head of fat cattle sent north, and not even to his own king, but to a wealthy ally. After one appalling day, when I really feared that half the servants would run off and rob the local farmers, I had to lock myself into the empty house and weep until I was sick. I was alone, distant from my family and from my new husband, and the people in Camlann appeared to hate me. I do not know how I survived that first winter, and the winter that followed was worse. That was the year I lost my baby, the only child I ever carried. Perhaps I had been working too hard, or perhaps my body had always been at fault, but I lost the child, a boy, in the sixth month, with a great deal of pain and blood, so that I was very sick for a month afterwards.

The war in the north ended; Arthur came back and campaigned in the south, all the second year of our marriage. That campaign took another four years, and ended at last in victory. We worked together on the peace, thinking that now all our hopes would be realized, believing that now all would be well. But the hope that had been dearest to me receded slowly, and when I was thirty I had at last to admit that something was wrong, that I would never conceive, that I was barren and would die so. It was just over a year later that Menw flung my childlessness in my face and I gave him the blow he regarded as a dishonour and would never forget.

Riches and honours. In these years of peace, there might be some things that Menw would recognize under that name. Most of those kings who had hated us were reconciled to us now, and even the Church was growing less vehement. The Saxons showed some signs that they began to feel part of the Empire, no longer sullen and conquered enemies. The tribute came in regularly, and we were able to set the warband to sweeping bandits from the roads of Britain and to protecting trade and good order. But even now there was little ease or comfort in wearing the purple. It was like trying to walk the edge of a sword. And there were new problems now, splintered alliances and, worse, internal quarrels, so that I sometimes wished we were back in the years of the war, when at least one had open enemies and a plain solution to the problems.

I had no time to sit staring at a letter. This very afternoon I must buy grain to feed the fortress – undoubtedly the grain-sellers were waiting for me to come and bargain with them. I had to arrange a feast for the emissaries from the kings of Elmet and Powys. I must allot some wool from the stores to the weavers of the fortress, if all the Family were to have their winter cloaks in time. Soon, if not today, I must find a new supply of iron for the smiths, as we had bought none for some time, and there might be a shortage soon. There would doubtless be some petitioners asking for a hearing. And there was the question of what our emissary must say to the king of Less Britain

Yet I sat staring at the letter, re-read it. *If you prefer the imperial purple to your own blood you must suffer for it.* It was typical of Menw to phrase it that way, I thought bitterly. An extreme sentence and a violent one.

I had never expected to go home. Even when I knew that I would never give Arthur a child, an heir, I knew that he would not divorce me. He had relied upon me in the long war with the Saxons, often for his very life. We had seen each other rarely while the war continued, and since the peace we had generally been too busy to talk of anything but the concerns of the Empire, but the bond between us went as deep as life itself. Arthur and I knew each other as only those who together have spent themselves to their limits can, and he would as soon cut out his heart as divorce me.

No, I had never expected to go home. But I had always had my home behind me, forever a possibility: the house and the hills, the Roman Wall leaping off into the west, the patterned tiles around the firepit. Though I had preferred the purple to my blood, and suffered for it, in a way it was my blood, my home, all that I had been, which had chosen the purple. To be cut off from it all was to have my father die all over again.

And if I refused Menw's demand I could never go home. I would be as good as kin-wrecked, exiled from my clan. Most of he clan agreed with Menw, and thought I ought to do more for them. Moreover, I had been gone a long time. They would not oppose him to support me.

Best to get it over with. I picked the letter up, rose from the desk, and dropped it in the fire. It uncurled slowly, wrapping itself around the coals, and the ink darkened even as the parchment went brown, standing out sharp, clear and absolute. Then the coals ate through, here and there, and it darkened to illegibility, while the air was full of its burnt leather stink.

My eyes stung and I wiped them with the back of my hand, finding that my hand shook. But it was over now, and the only thing I could do, done. I must get back to work, and not brood over it.

I picked up the light spring cloak which I had draped over a chair when I sat down to read the letter, then picked up my mirror to check that I appeared dignified and composed, as befitted an empress. I saw instead that I was crying. 'It's the smoke,' I told myself, aloud, but I had to set the mirror down and stand a moment, wrestling with myself. I went into the adjoining room, found the water pitcher and washed my face. The cold water was soothing against my hot eyes, and I felt calmer when I went back and checked the mirror again. Better. I could not afford to show weakness, not when Camlann was as tense as it was at present.

There was more white in my hair, I noted absently, when I looked to see that it had not come down when I washed my face. Well, red hair does not suit purple cloaks. I turned the purple border of my own cloak inwards so that it would not clash as much. If my hair were white I could stop worrying about that, at least. There, there was the picture of the woman I had to be: still looking younger than thirty-four, thick hair pulled back severely and piled behind her head, gold necklace proclaiming wealth; poised, controlled. My eyes were red, and I could not smooth the lines of tension on my face, though I smiled at the reflection, trying to lie to it. But probably no one would notice, if I acted assured. I took a deep breath and went out.

The house Arthur and I shared was next to the Feast Hall of Camlann, on its west. It had three rooms: an outer room for conferences, with a firepit; a bedroom, and a washroom. The servants who looked after it lived down the hill to the north, so that, though we had to fetch our own wood and water at night, we had privacy. The house faced north, looking over the most crowded part of the fortress: the road from the gates past the stables to the Feast Hall. The Hall covered the crown of the hill, set east of the centre of the walled enclosure. The hill slopes very steeply on the east, and the houses on that side cling to the slope at an angle. Standing in the door of the house I looked out at the huddled houses along the side of the road, with their chickens scratching in the dust around them; at the stables sprawling along the north slope, and some horses, being worked on a lead rein, circling in the sun of a practice yard.

The green patches between the houses grew larger further down the slope, and then the great grey bulk of the walls broke the pattern, firmly set stone with a wooden rampart above them. The gates were guarded by a single watch tower, but, because it was a time of peace, were left open. Beyond them the road stretched away, turning eastward across the patchwork of fields, fallow and pasture and ploughed land. It was April, and the swallows, returning from the remote south, were beginning to wing circles about the eaves of the Feast Hall, while dandelions flowered in the grass, and apple trees scattered here and there were budding. That morning it had rained, but now the sun was out, and everything glittered, the light so sharp it seemed to cut into the soul. Here was Camlann, here was my fortress, the strong heart of the visionary Empire. I took another deep breath, then turned from the view and walked along the west wall of the Hall to the south, where the storerooms were.

The fortress was generally short of grain by the end of the winter, and many farmers, finding that they had some surplus left, took advantage of this to sell the old grain at a high price. A number of them had arrived that morning, and I was expected to bargain with them for their produce. The steward could have done it, but he was a bad bargainer, and could make no use of the information we could obtain from them about the state of things in the countryside, which was invaluable to me. When it came to buying large amounts of goods, later in the year, the price paid by Camlann set prices for all the South, and the amount taken by Camlann checked availability everywhere, so it was very important for me to understand what was happening outside the fortress as well as what was happening within it.

There were half a dozen carts drawn up before the main storeroom, with their owners, all tight-lipped, independent clansmen, sitting in the carts in a row, looking sour because I was late. Normally I enjoyed bargaining with them because they enjoyed bargaining, and practised it as a great art. Now I found it maddening, and wished I could simply impose a reasonable price and have done with it. Instead, we worked through the preliminary stages of the poorness/richness of the previous harvest; the amount of seed corn available to the farmers; the amount the grain would sell for in an ordinary market; the relative scarcity/surplus of grain at Camlann and in the countryside; the value of the goods Camlann offered in return for the grain; the relative scarcity and value of these, and their cost in terms of products other than grain. We were finally approaching the vital question of whether the farmers wanted payment in cattle, woollen goods or metal, and how much, when the Family's infantry commander, Cei ap Cynryr, came storming along the wall of the Hall, saw me, and made his way towards us. Cei was a very big man, the largest in the Family. He had a great mass of sandy red hair, and wore large quantities of garish jewellery and brightly coloured clothing so that even when he was in a quiet mood it was impossible to overlook him. Now he was plainly in a temper. I braced myself.

'That golden-tongued, oily-mannered bastard!' he exclaimed, pushing aside a farmer. 'My lady, you must speak to Rhuawn and make him offer me an apology, or I will fight him, I swear it by my sword, and not spare him. And yet it is not his fault, but the fault of that weasel from the Ynysoedd Erch.'

I took his arm and hurried him aside. I knew who 'that weasel' was, but it would be better not to let the farmers, outsiders, know the details of quarrels within the Family – though by now most of Britain must be aware that Arthur's invincible, formerly indivisible force was torn in half by violent factions. The quarrel had been going on long enough to become notorious. Almost since 'that weasel' arrived in Camlann.

'What has Medraut done now?' I asked.

Cei spat. 'Ach, he has done nothing, not directly. Would you expect it of him? No, he will never confront a man to his face. He will leave some lying story behind his back, and let someone else fight for it.'

The farmers looked very interested at this, and I made hushing motions. Medraut ap Lot was the youngest son of Queen Morgawse of the Orcades Islands, which in British are called the Ynysoedd Erch, the 'Islands of Fear'. His mother was the legitimate daughter of the Emperor Uther, and Arthur's half-sister. Medraut had adored his mother, who had intended him to become king of the Islands on her

27

husband's death, though it was widely believed that he was not her husband's son, but born of an adulterous love affair. However, Morgawse was dead, murdered by her eldest son Agravain in revenge for another of her affairs and for a rumoured connection with her husband's death; and the royal clan of the Islands had chosen Agravain as its new king, despite the murder. The Queen had been reputed a witch and the clan had not loved her, though they were too much afraid of her to deny her anything. They were not so afraid of Medraut, and he had come to Camlann, while the new king, his brother, who had long fought for Arthur, returned and ruled in the Islands. Medraut was very bitter against Agravain. But the immediate cause of quarrels was generally his other brother, Gwalchmai, who was also at Camlann, and was one of Arthur's most trusted and valued followers. Gwalchmai seemed to be hated by Medraut even more than Agravain was, though he had had no part in the murder, and most of the quarrels were between his friends, of whom Cei was one, and Medraut's.

Cei glanced at the farmers and lowered his voice. 'Rhuawn has taken to blaming Gwalchmai for the death of that witch from the Ynysoedd Erch. He has been repeating that tale for years now, like a catechism, so that half the Family thinks that Gwalchmai murdered his mother – as though the witch deserved to live in the first place! Whose tale is that but Medraut's? Ach, but it is an old story; so old that I must listen to it in silence and say nothing. But when Rhuawn dared to say that Gwalchmai is hindering the negotiations with Less Britain, and deliberately obstructing the conclusion of a peace there, because of some imagined weak-mindedness – when I heard Rhuawn saying this to his friends, I went to him as he spoke and told him that it was he who was weak-minded, to believe such ravings. And Rhuawn leapt up with his hand on his sword, and called me a blind, stubborn fool who could not see what was before his eyes, and accused me of flattering the Emperor into believing falsehoods – and this in the presence of four others! My lady, I could ask Arthur to demand that Rhuawn apologize to me, but I do not wish to humiliate the man. You can persuade him to offer it: do so, for God's sake, or I will fight him tomorrow, and, though he is a fool, I do not wish to harm him.'

I nodded, feeling sick. The quarrel was typical. I had had to wheedle too many warriors into offering apologies, and I could not disguise the fact that my sympathies were entirely with Gwalchmai, which meant that it grew increasingly difficult for me to win over members of Medraut's party, which included Rhuawn.

Warriors tend to quarrel in the best of years. They are taught to regard an insult, or an admission of weakness, as a dishonour, and the only remedy for dishonour as the sword. They quarrel most in the winter, when they are kept in a narrow space together – the three hundred men who slept in our Hall had more space than most – and have little to do. In the summer they can go to war if there are any wars to be fought, or else fight bandits and form escorts, or, at the least, go hunting; and then they tend to be good-natured. But the quarrels at Camlann were more serious. They were not easing with the warm weather. For years they had been growing steadily worse, and the ordinary methods of soothing them – flattery and pleas on both sides – were working less and less well. I was afraid for the future.

'If Rhuawn apologizes,' I told Cei, 'you must beg his pardon for calling him weak-minded.'

'Must I, by God? He is weak-minded, to believe such slander!'

'The slander is Gwalchmai's affair. If anyone accuses him to his face, he can demand an apology, and we can see to it that he receives it, at least as far as the negotiations with Less Britain are concerned. But it is not your affair to fight Rhuawn on his behalf, noble lord. Let Gwalchmai guard his own honour. He is not exactly helpless.'

'He is too courteous. And no one will accuse him to his face if they must fight him: he either escapes the insults or turns them.'

'It is still his affair. And if you do not wish to fight Rhuawn, noble lord, you will have to apologize.' I said it more sharply than I meant, for I was growing impatient.

Cei again began to protest, but one of the farmers, also impatient, came over and suggested a price for his grain, asking if it was acceptable. It was too much, and I knew it, but I snapped 'Perhaps,' and went back to make arrangements. Cei hung about behind me like a large red thundercloud, waiting for me to finish.

When we had fixed on a price – and the price was still too high, since I was in no mood to bargain patiently, and these southern farmers are not to be out-bargained at the best of times – I was further distracted by a petitioner. A boy who had been sitting in one of the carts jumped out and knelt before me.

'What is it?' I asked wearily.

'M-most n-noble queen,' he began, then switched to a surprisingly good formal Latin. 'Your grace, I have come here hoping to find a place in the Emperor's service.'

I had expected some complaint about a neighbouring clan, and I looked at the farmer whose cart the boy had been sitting in, surprised. 'Isn't he your son?'

The farmer shook his head. 'No, noble lady. I only gave him a ride from Baddon. He is a good, biddable lad, though; listen to him.'

I sighed and brushed back a loose strand of my hair. Another petition for service at Camlann. People came all the time, offering to practise any imaginable trade, and many of them we accepted, and many we did not. I did not feel like weighing this boy's qualifications now, after the letter and with Cei looming behind me. But I reminded myself to be strong, be gracious, and smiled at the boy. Cei snorted impatiently.

'What manner of place, young man?' I asked, also in Latin, studying him. He looked about thirteen, of average height for that age, with a mass of pale hair above a thin face and a pair of surprisingly dark eyes. He was not a farm lad, I decided. His Latin was too good, and there was a nervous sensitivity to his face which argued some education.

'I . . . your sacred kindness, I am willing to do almost anything. But I wish to learn how to be a warrior.'

Cei snorted again. 'Boy, do not trouble the lady. Go back to your family and don't run away from it in future.'

The boy flushed deep crimson. 'I . . . I . . .' he stammered.

I smiled again to reassure him. 'What is your name?' I asked. 'And where is your family? You are young to seek service on your own.'

'They call me Gwyn,' he said. 'I don't know my father's name. And I have no family, except for my mother, and she

30

is in a convent in Elmet. Your grace, I am willing to do almost anything, if you will let me stay here and train to be a warrior. I know you must train boys to be warriors here. All the sons of the great warriors – like this lord here' (with a nervous, appeasing smile at Cei) '– they must become warriors as well. Surely it would be no trouble for one more to join them?'

'So he is a nun's bastard, raised at a nunnery,' said Cei. 'My lady, send him away. We have more servants than we can feed already, and don't need some half-grown dreamer of a nun's bastard.'

The boy had gone an even deeper red when Cei began, but went white at the end of his speech. He jumped to his feet, began to stammer a reply, then was quiet, blinking miserably. He evidently was a nun's bastard, and must be a dreamer, if he wished to be a warrior so badly that he was willing to leave what home he had, alone, and travel to Camlann to offer to do 'almost anything' to learn the arts of war.

'My lady,' Cei began again, going back to the subject which had been his sole concern all the while, 'how can I apologize to Rhuawn after his slanders?'

But I felt sorry for the boy now. 'You are too old to learn to be a warrior,' I told him gently, for a moment ignoring Cei and the farmers. 'Most boys begin their training between the ages of seven and nine.'

'But I did start then, noble lady, on my own!' he cried, slipping back into British. 'And a monk at the brother foundation to my mother's convent, he taught me, too – he used to be a warrior, you see. Only I need to know more.'

'Be quiet, boy,' Cei snapped, but I raised my hand for him to wait.

'Can you read, Gwyn?' I asked.

He nodded eagerly. 'Yes, noble lady. And I can write, book hand and cursive both. My mother wanted me to be a priest, and made certain that I learned how to write. She taught me herself.'

I looked at Cei, lifting an eyebrow. 'There is a shortage of servants who can read, even here,' I said. 'I could use a copy clerk to take down inventories and keep records for me.'

Cei shrugged. 'As you please, my lady. It is a waste of

time to teach some priestly little bastard from a convent the arts of war, but if you need a clerk, by all means keep him. Will you speak with Rhuawn?'

'You may stay,' I told the boy. 'Go to the Hall and ask for Gweir the steward; he will look after you, and tonight I will ask my lord Arthur to confirm you in a place as a servant. Yes, Cei, I will speak to Rhuawn, but I will promise him that if he apologizes you will as well. Good fellows,' to the farmers, 'if you will come with me I will arrange for you to receive the price of your grain.'

The farmers were satisfied, Cei grumbled agreement, and the boy Gwyn was overjoyed. The next matter, then, was to talk to Rhuawn – though while I was in the storerooms I ought to see about the wool for the weavers. And then there was the feast for that night.

I spoke with Rhuawn before the afternoon was half over, and eventually persuaded him to apologize to Cei. But I knew that neither of the warriors would be content. Their reconciliation was like the forcing together of two fragments of a broken dish, which might hold together for a little while if undisturbed, but which left the break as deep and unremedied as before. And at first Rhuawn had not listened to me, but only eyed me with a kind of suspicion and given polite, noncommital replies. By the end of our talk he had grown warmer, and told me how he regretted his harsh words, but that Cei's insult had been too much for any honourable man to endure, and so on and on.

Yet when walking back up the hill towards the Hall I kept remembering the way his eyes slid sideways from mine at the first. The mistrust was growing. I could scarcely bridge the gap between the two factions now, and if things continued as they were, Rhuawn and his friends would soon regard me as an enemy. Indeed, I was aware of rumours about me circulating, conversations suddenly hushed at my approach. Only up to now no rumours about me had been believed.

As I approached the kitchens, where I would check the arrangements for the feast to be given that night, my name was called and I found Arthur's second-in-command, the warleader and cavalry commander Bedwyr ap Brendan, hurrying towards me.

'My lady Gwynhwyfar!' he called again. 'My lord

32

Arthur asked me to find you. He wishes to have a conference upon the situation in Less Britain before the feast tonight.'

I stopped, trying to order my thoughts and rearrange my plans for the afternoon. 'Very well, lord,' I said, after a moment, 'but I must give some orders to the kitchens first or there will *be* no feast tonight.'

He nodded, smiling, and fell in step beside me. As Arthur's warleader, Bedwyr would naturally be at the conference as well, so he had nothing to do but wait for me.

Bedwyr was a complex man. He was Arthur's best friend, and Cei's as well. But he was as different from Cei as a man can be, and different from most other warriors as well. He dressed plainly, without any of the bright colours or jewellery they love. He had very dark brown hair, brown eyes, wore his beard close-trimmed, and his usual expression was one of quiet attention. Very little escaped his notice. He was a Breton, from the south-east of Less Britain, of a noble, Roman-descended family. He had had a Roman education, for the Roman ways are stronger in Gaul than in Britain, but he had not paid much heed to it. He joined the warband of Bran, the younger son of the king of Less Britain, who became Arthur's ally. There he quickly gained in fame and authority, for he was a dangerous cavalry fighter, and had the clarity of thought, the self-possession and the force of personality that make a leader in war. When his lord Bran crossed the sea to help Arthur in his struggle against the kings of Britain for the purple, Bedwyr was one of his captains. But he was wounded in the battle in which Arthur won the title, and lost his shield hand – he had since fought with his shield strapped tightly to his arm. This brush with death had put an end to his former ruthlessness, and he was converted to the philosophy he had read as a boy, and intended to return to Less Britain and become a monk. Instead he met Arthur, and after one conversation had decided that it was better to fight for God than to contemplate him in a monastery. Some dozen warriors had followed him in swearing the oath of allegiance to Arthur, and Lord Bran had ruefully remarked that he had come to Britain to help Arthur to a title, not to his own best warriors. But Arthur smiled and made Bedwyr his cavalry commander.

Yet even as commander of Arthur's cavalry, and later, when Arthur relinquished that position, as warleader, Bedwyr had kept a philosophic detachment. He was a very good man, who had never since his conversion had one base or cruel action reported of him, and he had a passion for honour, but when I first met him, that seemed his only passion. I found him cold. He was never discourteous, but he had had very little to say to me, and would not even look at me for long. After trying for some time to be friends with him and achieving nothing, I presumed that, like many philosophers, he had little use for women. I found this the more irritating because he was only four years older than I, and no grey-bearded sage. I was puzzled that so many others, whom I loved, loved him, and I began to return his coldness with an (equally courteous!) dislike.

When Medraut arrived in Camlann, however, and the quarrels began, I decided that the fortress could not afford this quiet enmity between the Emperor's wife and his war-leader, and once again set out to be friends with him. For a long time, again, I made no progress – and then, one after-noon over something quite trivial, Bedwyr smiled at me. His smile transformed his face in a way I had never noticed before, perhaps because I had never received a smile from him before. The dark eyes were warm and delighted, fixed on my face with an attention which had ceased to be quiet and considering and had become alive, eager. Then I saw that I had been wrong all along: he was not cold. His detachment was the protection of a proud and honourable mind against a passionate nature. He had once been ruthless and violent, swayed by impulse, and was now determined to trust his mind alone. And I decided that his philosophic honour had led him to avoid women, so that he scarcely knew how to speak to them, but that he had never con-sciously been an enemy to me. I began to like him then, and he had ceased to be cold and distant with me, so that I came to love and trust him as Arthur did. It was the one good thing that came out of Medraut's presence at Camlann.

Bedwyr waited while I gave some orders to the steward's wife about the feast, then escorted me out of the kitchens. 'My lord Arthur must have been waiting for us for some time now,' he commented, without anxiety. 'Where were you, my lady? I expected to find you at the storerooms;

34

indeed, I was told you had gone there.'

I sighed. 'I left the storerooms to visit Rhuawn – yes, another quarrel. With Cei!'

'Ach! And will Rhuawn apologize?'

'Yes. As will Cei. But God knows how long it will last.' And I thought again of Rhuawn's eyes slipping aside from mine, the distrust, the suspicion.

Bedwyr looked at me another moment, then said, 'And?'

'And? And I am concerned for the future. Soon I will be able to coax no more apologies from Rhuawn or from any of . . . his party. But for the quarrel itself, it was no worse than the other quarrels.'

'Well. And yet you look troubled, my lady, more than by the other quarrels.'

I walked on a few steps before looking at him. His eyes were on my face, waiting. 'I am troubled, yes,' I told him. 'But it is a personal matter.'

His expression cleared. 'Your father. Forgive me. I should have remembered and kept silent.'

'Even you cannot remember everything, noble lord. There is nothing to forgive.'

'You have heard from your clan since?'

He was trying to ease the grief of the death by reminding me that I had other family, trying to be kind, and I confused him when I stopped abruptly and clenched my hands together, struggling with myself. I was tired, I thought, or I would not weaken like this, not be so subject to my grief and anger. There had been too much to do in the past month, and the mood of the fortress had been so embittered that often I had been too tense to sleep.

'My lady?' Bedwyr had stopped, facing me, and was watching me with concern.

I waved him back. 'I had a letter from my cousin Menw. He . . . we quarrelled, years ago. He is now clan chieftain. He . . .' I stopped, because I was ashamed that Menw had demanded what he had, and ashamed to accuse him, my own cousin. I did not want to talk of that letter.

Bedwyr's jaw set. He turned and began to walk on, not looking at me, and I joined him. 'You should not allow small-minded men to distress you, my lady,' he said.

'More easily advised than done, Lord Bedwyr. Like most philosophic advice.'

He looked at me again, not smiling, not distracted by my attempt to divert him. Half unwilling, I began to tell him about the letter.

We arrived at my house before I finished. The spring sun was still high, although the afternoon was drawing on, and it fell warm and heavy upon our heads and sides. Inside the house someone was playing a harp, and the soft sound carried clear and liquid into the silence when we stopped and I hurriedly ended my account. Bedwyr and I looked at each other.

'It was bravely done, lady,' he said softly. 'It was no doubt a most bitter thing, to accept exile from your home, but it was bravely done. If there were time – but our lord is waiting.'

Arthur was indeed waiting, sitting and staring into the fire with his feet propped against the grate. Lord Gwalchmai ap Lot, who was to be the emissary to Less Britain, was also there: it was he who had been playing the harp. Arthur could not play, for harping is a noble skill not taught at monasteries such as the one where he was raised – but he loved to listen. When Gwalchmai saw us, however, he at once set the harp down and stood to greet us, and Arthur straightened, took his feet off the grate, and waved to us to be seated.

'My lady,' said Gwalchmai, bowing his head; then took my hand and smiled, at me, at Bedwyr. 'And Bedwyr; we thought you must have ridden clear to Ynys Witrin, so long have you been in arriving.'

'Lady Gwynhwyfar was resolving a quarrel between Rhuawn and Cei,' Bedwyr said quietly, taking his seat on Arthur's right.

The corners of Arthur's mouth drew down in pain and he looked at me. 'Another quarrel?'

I nodded and settled wearily into my own place at the desk, opposite Arthur. Gwalchmai resumed his seat, all smiles gone, and stared at the fire. He knew whom the quarrel must have concerned. I watched him for a moment as he sat very dark and still in his crimson cloak with his jewelled sword, his black eyes seeming to look through the flames into another world, as they always did when he was troubled. He had lost weight recently. Part of that had been in travelling – he had returned from Less Britain only the week before, and neither that embassy nor the voyage had been an easy one. But the situation at Camlann must have been almost unbearable for him. I longed to reach past that withdrawal and unearthliness and ease the hurt, to mother him. But it was impossible. He was only four years younger than I and difficult to mother. As Cei had said, he was too courteous. I must watch him suffer the enmity his brother had raised against him, and say nothing.

And it is only enmity to him, now, something in the back of my mind added. *Some day it will be enmity to me and even to Arthur. Medraut will turn the fortress against us. And soon, it will be soon.*

I looked at my husband, who was waiting for me to give an account of the quarrel. Already it hurt him as much as it hurt Gwalchmai, for he loved the Family even more than he loved his Empire, if such a thing were possible, and the division in it was a constant torment to him.

'Cei overheard a comment Rhuawn made to one of his friends,' I told Arthur, 'and he called Rhuawn a fool because of it. Rhuawn returned the insult. But there were no swords drawn and no blows given, and they have agreed to be reconciled.'

Arthur nodded, but his eyes were cold and bitter. 'What was the comment?'

I hesitated, looking at Gwalchmai.

'We will agree that I am not here,' Gwalchmai said, giving an ironic half smile. 'I never heard the comment and need fight no one because of it.'

I hesitated again – but, after all, it did concern the very problem we had come together to discuss. 'He accused you of deliberately obstructing the negotiations with Less Britain. I am sorry.'

Gwalchmai shook his head. He touched the hilt of his sword briefly, for reassurance rather than in anger, then locked his hands together on his knees, staring once more into the fire. He felt responsible for the quarrels and had once asked Arthur to send him away from the Family to avoid them. Arthur had refused.

'There is nothing more we can do to disprove that,' Arthur said, looking at his warrior. 'We are already sending you back to Less Britain. No one can say that I mistrust you.' Gwalchmai nodded, looking no happier.

'And the accusation will be the more firmly refuted if we can achieve a settlement with Macsen. So, to the matter at hand.' He fixed his eyes on Gwalchmai until the warrior looked up, smiled ruefully, and bowed his head in agreement. 'Tell us again what Macsen claims.'

Macsen was the king of Less Britain, in Gaul. His kingdom was originally colonized from Britain and was closely bound to it, subject to the same laws and enjoying the same privileges. While Macsen's younger brother Bran was king, all had been peaceful, for Bran was Arthur's ally, joining with him against most of the kings of Britain when Arthur first claimed the purple. But Bran and his brother Macsen had long been rivals, and had nearly come to armed conflict when their father died. Only Bran's alliance with Arthur and Arthur's power had prevented that war, and won Bran the election to the kingship which Macsen thought ought to be his. Now Bran was dead, killed in a border skirmish with the Franks the previous autumn, and Macsen had been chosen king in his place by the royal clan of Less Britain. He was understandably hostile to Arthur, and the whole web of law and custom that bound Britain and Less Britain together was all under challenge. We had sent Gwalchmai as an emissary to Macsen as soon as the weather permitted the voyage, and he had listened to Macsen's claims and justifications for two weeks before sailing back to consult us on the responses we were willing to make. Gwalchmai was invaluable as an emissary: he was of royal birth, and so must be received honourably anywhere; he had been brought up at a scheming court and could find his way through any maze of political intrigue without difficulty; he was literate and could speak good Latin, as well as British, Irish and Saxon, and he was an eloquent advocate in all four languages. None of this had been of any use with Macsen, and I could not help suspecting, as we again plodded over Macsen's claims and our possible responses, that on this mission as well Gwalchmai would achieve a limited success at best. Macsen was unlikely to risk war with us, but he would undoubtedly try every trick short of it to have his way. And if Gwalchmai was forced to return for more consultations, the accusation against him would grow and gain strength, and with it the question: 'Why does Arthur do nothing?' and its insidious answer:

38

'Arthur is deceived, a fool; Arthur is partial and blind.' I shivered.

The conference ended. It was agreed that Gwalchmai would leave again for Less Britain in two days' time, and he and Bedwyr took their leave, allowing Arthur and me to prepare for that night's feast. I began to take my hair down, as it was to be a formal feast for which I must look impressive and tie my hair up with gold. Arthur looked at me wearily.

'So much for King Macsen,' he said. 'Though, indeed, I think we have no more seen the end of our troubles with him than we have of our troubles with that fox King Maelgwn of Gwynedd. Gwynhwyfar, my heart, I am sick to death of these kings.'

I looked for my comb, found it. 'Unfortunately, these kings cannot be abolished.'

He snorted 'Any attempt would abolish us instead. And they have their rights to their kingdoms.' He stood and moved restlessly about the room, then stopped, leaning his hands on the table, and asked the air, 'What am I to do?'

I knew that he was no longer thinking of Macsen of Less Britain, or of any king. I had heard that note of pain before. More and more often over the past year he had woken at night rigid and soaked with sweat, crying 'Morgawse!' It was always Morgawse, always his dead half-sister who filled his nightmares, and never the waking cause of them, her son Medraut. But there was a reason for that, and he had told it to me the night he had heard that Morgawse was dead. He had told no one else, not even Bedwyr. Gwalchmai knew, but that was because Morgawse had been his mother as well, and Arthur had once assumed that he knew already.

'What am I to do?' Arthur asked again, turning from the wall. 'I must prove things which ought to be obvious, prove that I trust Gwalchmai, whom the worst tyrant would not suspect of disloyalty. And if I can disprove one lie by some public gesture, disprove it without giving it the substance that acknowledging it would give it, I am no better off, for ten more have sprung up. And yet I cannot charge the source of them with anything, for he speaks no treason, and denies originating the rumours with a face of perfect innocence. He uses even my questions against me. If

I could sentence him with exile! But on what charge?'

'I thought we had decided to weather the storm as well as we could,' I said.

'I decided. Bedwyr agreed with me, you and Gwalchmai disagreed. Send him to the Islands, you said, even if it does seem a criminal breach of hospitality. But it is too late for that now. He has friends.'

'He has friends.' I set the comb down; it felt very heavy in my hand. 'Nor would it be safe to send him to the Islands. His brother is . . . ill.'

The eldest son of Morgawse, Agravain ap Lot, king of the Orcades since his father's death, was in fact a broken man. His act of matricide had destroyed him, and now, by all accounts, he was drinking himself to death. His father had had a large degree of control over Pictland and the Western Islands as well as the Orcades, but this was slipping through Agravain's lax fingers, and his clan and countrymen were not pleased. To send Medraut to the Islands when they were so ripe for intrigue would be at once dangerous to ourselves and cruel to Agravain, who had, after all, followed Arthur and fought bravely for him for many years, and who had suffered enough already.

'Even if it were safe, I could not exile him. I have nothing to charge him with. Gwynhwyfar, how did you know that this would happen? You warned me, the first night that he came.'

I thought of Medraut on that first night, sitting at the high table during the feast we had given to welcome his brother, the new king Agravain. He had worn a saffron cloak, and the torchlight caught and glowed in his fair hair. He was a beautiful young man – of average height, like his brother Gwalchmai, strong, graceful, a fine horseman and a skilled warrior. Most of his features were like Gwalchmai's – or, I suppose, like Morgawse's – the straight nose and finely moulded cheekbones, the same narrow long-fingered hands. But his wide-set grey eyes and square jaw were like Arthur's, and I had sensed in him the same passionate dedication I knew so well in my husband. But the dedication, I had been sure, had been to a very different end. And even when Medraut smiled I had been afraid.

I shook my head, then rose, went over to my husband and put my arms around him. He did not move; only his heart beat steadily against mine. 'I did not know,' I whispered into his shoulder. 'I was merely afraid. I do not know why. You and Bedwyr wanted reasons, and you were right. It would have been unjust to have condemned him untried.'

'You had reasons.' Arthur pulled away from me and sank into the chair. 'You have dealt with people enough; I ought to trust you when you say that someone is lying. And I should have listened to Gwalchmai – he knows Medraut better than any living. But I thought he was too close to his mother's death to think clearly yet, and I thought you were being over-cautious and perhaps jealous, and I determined to take the risk. I should not have. The stakes are too high.'

'You couldn't simply have rejected him. He is your son.'

Arthur flinched and looked away from me, leaning against the table and staring at the smoke stain left by the lamp upon the wall. Medraut was his son, born of incest committed twenty-six years before with his sister Morgawse. He had not known, then, that she was his sister; he had not known who his father was. She was a married woman, staying with her father the Emperor while her huband fought a war in the north of Britain. He was one of her father's warriors, a bastard raised at a monastery, who by skill and good luck had found himself a place in the imperial warband. She had paid attention to him, pursued him, told him that her husband was cruel, and eventually seduced him one night after a feast given in honour of his first victory. He had been eighteen at the time. Shortly afterwards, he had discovered that Uther was his father, and discovered from Morgawse that she had known all along. The black horror of that discovery had ridden him ever since.

Arthur had told me this when he heard that she was dead, speaking as though he tore the story from himself like a monstrous growth buried in his flesh. I had wept, but he had been dry-eyed, brutal with himself. 'I knew what she intended when I came out of the Hall and saw her waiting in the shadow,' he said, 'and I agreed to it. I agreed only to adultery, but that was enough, and that one instant of agreeing will extend for the whole of my life, and, if God is just, endure for all eternity. And she is dead, now, and I cannot confront her, cannot ... escape from her.' He picked up the letter that contained the news, stared at it, and said, quietly, so quietly I barely heard him, 'Her son – our son – adored her.'

And yet, when Medraut had appeared at Camlann, he had seemed more confused than hostile. We knew from Gwalchmai that Morgawse had told Medraut the secret of his birth, and Gwalchmai had insisted that his brother was now Arthur's deadly enemy. But Medraut seemed more bewildered than anything else: very bitter against his brothers, but uncertain what to do now that his adored mother was dead. This had given Arthur hope that we might win him over. Gwalchmai had told us that Medraut had once been a sweet-natured child, and that they had been very close. Gwalchmai himself had once worshipped Morgawse, but afterwards broken free of her hold on him. Arthur had hoped that Medraut might do the same. Perhaps he had even hoped to confront and escape the shadow of Morgawse through her son. At any rate, he had given Medraut a place at Camlann. And I could not blame him for hungering for this child of his enemy, this golden youth. I had given him no son, no child at all. There might even be some truth in his idea that I had feared Medraut because I was jealous of him. I could not believe it was so, but on such a matter I might easily lie to myself. Arthur's enemy had given him a son out of hatred, while I, who would have given up my eyes and hearing to bear a child, I was barren.

I sat on the edge of the table and caught Arthur's hand, held it in both of mine. My heart ached again for him, and I was very weary. 'My own,' I said, 'we have decided to try to weather this storm. We have endured worse. Do not torture yourself with it.'

'There will be fights soon. My men may begin to kill each other over Medraut. What am I to do then?'

I did not know. I could only hold his hand and press it until his dark reverie was troubled and he turned to look at me again. Then I kissed his hand, and kissed the ring on his finger, the signet carved with the imperial dragon.

He gave a deep sigh, and the tense muscles relaxed a little. He reached out and stroked my hair back from my face. 'My white hart,' he said. 'Yes, we may yet survive it. All may yet be well.' He rose, kissed me, and added, 'But now there is that feast for the emissaries. We must prepare for it.'

I nodded and went back to combing my hair. I felt as exhausted as though I had spent the entire day journeying, and that on bad roads.

The feast glittered with splendour, and the emissaries of the kings of Elmet and Powys were entertained as magnificently as befitted an imperial court. Our seven hundred warriors filled only half the Feast Hall, and the rest of the places were taken by the wives of the married men – we relaxed the custom which bars women from the Hall, on some occasions – by the entourage of the emissaries, and by priests and potentates and petitioners from all of Britain. Torches in brackets down the walls lit the Hall, and the two great firepits, one at either end, cast light and heat up to the high roof. The whitewashed shields along the wall shone, and the tables were full of the glitter of jewellery and arms and embroidered cloaks, while the collars of sleek warhounds here and there caught the light even under the tables. There were beef and venison, pork and lamb and wild birds to eat, and mead and wine imported from Less Britain to drink till the Hall seemed to whirl in circles. And there was music, songs by Arthur's chief bard Taliesin, who was called the finest poet in Britain, and by other singers as well, till the tables seemed to float in the strains of the harp.

Cei and Rhuawn made their reconciliation at the feast, quietly but publicly. Arthur granted three petitions, one for mercy by a criminal, one for a just settlement of a feud, and one that of the boy Gwyn, who had his place at Camlann confirmed. I had him called in, and he stood before the high table looking very thin and afraid. Arthur smiled at him gently.

'My lord,' Cei said, remembering his irritation from the afternoon, and on edge from the forced reconciliation, 'why not send this boy home and find the Empress a proper clerk instead? He is only a bastard from a monastery, and likely to be no use with either pen or sword.'

Arthur looked at Cei sharply, and the corner of his mouth twitched. The black mood of the afternoon might never have existed. 'Cei,' he said in an even tone, '*I* am a bastard from a monastery.'

43

'You are an emperor, and were never anything else,' Cei replied without so much as blinking. 'I knew you to be capable of Empire from the time you first came to Camlann, long before you claimed the purple.'

Arthur smiled. 'Spoken with uncustomary gallantry, old friend, but nonetheless a lie. Who was it that called me "the monk" when I first took service with Uther? Yes, and knocked me down when I took exception to the name! And yet, I thank the heart that can so overlook the past. Boy, you are welcome here. You are to help the Empress Gwynhwyfar as she sees fit, and may spend the rest of your time training with the other boys of the fortress. Take note, Lord Gereint, you will have to train him! They use the yard behind the stables in the morning; go and join them tomorrow, if the Empress has nothing for you to do.'

Gwyn flushed with pleasure and bowed very low, his eyes shining. He was a sweet boy, I decided, and I wished him all good fortune. Likely he would need it, for the other boys would hardly welcome a foreign intruder to their well-established circles.

I rose and poured more wine for the high table, as I did at every feast, even the ones most women were barred from – it confers honour, and the men love it. The emissaries smiled and bowed their heads when I poured for them. I knew what they saw – the purple-bordered gown of white silk I was wearing, the gold and the pearls, the confident smile, the lady of the glorious fortress that was the Empire's heart. A lie, and the glory of the feast also a lie, which we told them without speaking a word. The brittle splendour of ice, soon broken; frost on the grass that melts with the morning sun. And yet, the bitter truth of division, of foreign hostility and inner weakness, might fade away, and the glory would remain alone, and who could say then that it was a lie?

Yet that night when I returned to my own house and saw the ashes of Menw's letter in the firepit I grew sickened at myself. I wished desperately to be honest, to weep when I was grieved, to return openly love and hatred, to escape from riches, honour and the sword-edge of power. But Arthur was already in bed, asleep in the sleep of exhaustion. He bore a heavier burden than I, and needed his rest, so I crept into bed quietly so as not to wake him.

Two

I visited the lord Gwalchmai ap Lot the next day, before he set off for Gaul. He had a house to the east of the Hall, on the steep side of the hill but with a fine view towards Ynys Witrin and the marshes. When he was in Camlann – which because of his value as an emissary was seldom – Gwalchmai shared the house with Cei. When Gwalchmai was not there, Cei brought his mistress and her children into the house to live with him, as he disliked being alone. Warriors are used to close quarters, in the Hall or on campaigns, and never like solitude. Cei probably would have preferred to stay in the Hall most nights, but his rank and importance forbade it, just as it forbade his marrying his mistress. She was a fat, good-natured washerwoman named Maire and had been Cei's mistress for some years now. She was a widow with four children, the last two of whom were Cei's. She was at the house when I arrived, helping Gwalchmai's servant Rhys pack while Gwalchmai sat on the threshold sharpening a spear. Her third child, Cei's chubby two-year-old son, sat on the other side of the threshold sucking his thumb and staring at the whetstone as it glided rhythmically along the bright metal of the spear head.

Intent on his work, Gwalchmai did not notice me until I was almost at the door, but when the morning sun cast my shadow before him he looked up, then set down the whetstone and rose.

'My lady,' he said, 'a hundred welcomes to you.'

Cei's son grabbed the whetstone and began to pound it hopefully against the threshold. 'No!' Gwalchmai said, looking for a place to lean the spear. I knelt and took the whetstone away from the child.

'You mustn't do that,' I told him. 'It will break.'

The child gave a howl of outrage and tried to grab the stone back.

'Cilydd!' said his mother, emerging indignant from the house, 'you are a bad boy! Ach, many greetings to you, most noble lady – Cilydd, be quiet, do not disturb the lady.'

'Cilydd is like his father: he speaks his mind,' said Gwalchmai, smiling. 'Here.' He picked up another stone, a piece of ordinary flint, and tapped it against the threshold. Cilydd stopped howling and squinted at it. Gwalchmai offered him the stone, and the boy took it and began pounding the doorpost. The warrior straightened and dusted off his hands. 'Again, my lady, welcome,' he said, raising his voice to be heard over the pounding. 'But I am afraid my house is not fit to welcome you, at the minute.'

'Ach, great lord, we can leave,' said Maire cheerfully.

'It would not matter much if you did,' said Gwalchmai's servant Rhys, also emerging from the house, 'for the place would still be inside-out. You have moved in and out often enough, Maire. One would think you could do it better by now.' Maire grinned and bobbed her head, and Rhys, having dealt with her, bowed to me. 'Greetings, most noble lady.'

'I am sorry to have no better hospitality to offer you, my lady,' Gwalchmai said, 'but if you care to come in, there is probably some wine.'

'I thank you, no. Lord Gwalchmai, I wish to speak with you. Perhaps we could walk down to the walls – unless you need to prepare for your journey now, of course.'

'I am the last one needed to prepare for my journey; indeed, I am in the way – am I not, Rhys? It is a sweet morning, my lady. Let us walk.' He leaned the spear against the doorpost, then, looking at Cei's son and his flint hammer, handed the weapon to Rhys instead. I handed Rhys the whetstone, which I was still holding, and Gwalchmai and I set off down the hill. It was indeed a sweet morning. The previous day's clear weather continued, and the sun was bright in a soft sky, the air warm enough to make my spring cloak too heavy. Gwalchmai wore no cloak, and for once was without his mail shirt as well, and he walked lightly. His red tunic was loose, and I could see the end of a scar running up onto his collar bone. He had plenty of scars.

'You seem pleased today,' I said, to start the conversation, and because he did appear happy – a rare thing recently. 'And Rhys did as well. Are you glad to be leaving Camlann?'

'To be leaving Camlann – I am neither pleased nor displeased at that, lady. But I am glad, for Rhys's wife had her child last night, and she and the baby are both well.'

'Ach, good! I must visit them. Is it a girl or a boy?'

'A girl. And Rhys is pleased with that, as well, for now he has both a son and a daughter.'

'I am very glad of it. So, will Rhys be coming with you to Gaul now?'

He shook his head. 'I have told him to stay. He was meaning to stay until his wife was delivered, and there is no need to change the plans. He now says that he will go, because she is safe, but it is plain that his heart stays with her, and I would not wish to drag the rest of him away.'

I was a trifle disappointed. Rhys was a plain, honest, down-to-earth farmer's son, and in his way as great an idealist as Arthur. When he had become Gwalchmai's servant he had eased one trouble from my mind. Gwalchmai was otherworldly enough to forget to eat, and honourable enough that he thought it preferable to be cheated than to stand up for his rights against someone weaker. Without Rhys he would undoubtedly overwork himself. I wanted to order him to be gentle with himself, wanted to mother him, as I had ever since I first met him. Then he had been flat on his back and delirious among the other wounded whom Arthur had left in my father's cow-byre, the first time he came to my home. Gwalchmai had watched me then with the dark eyes of an injured animal, and flinched when I came near him. Most wounded men like having a woman to tend them. They are reminded of their mothers, and feel safer. Perhaps I had reminded Gwalchmai of his mother, and the thought of Morgawse had frightened him. At any rate, I had noticed him, shown him special warmth, until the wariness dissolved suddenly and absolutely into gratitude and friendship. But he was too proud to receive much from another. He would give his heart's blood, for me, or for any of his friends, but I could not tell him not to work too hard. So I said only, 'I hope your journey will not be too long.'

'It is not likely to be long.' His smile faded. He knew as well as I that Macsen would raise new questions for every one that we solved, and that he would have to return to Camlann for more consultations.

'That is what I wished to speak to you about,' I told him. 'You will probably be back in another month.'

He nodded, frowning a little, his eyes fixed on my face.

'Although officially you have heard nothing, you know of this new rumour. If the negotiations are protracted, it will grow. And as it grows it will turn into an attack on Arthur as well as on you. They have begun to move against him, these rumours: they hint more and more that he is a fool, that he listens to flattery, and is partial and unjust. Listen, I want you to bring up the subject of the negotiations tonight and in the hearing of those who believe the rumour. If one of them challenges you on it, appeal to Arthur and have it dismissed. I talked to him about it this morning, and we agreed that this might kill it.'

The frown grew deeper. 'I could speak of it tonight in the Hall. But I do not think I would be challenged. And if I were challenged – my lady, I do not wish to fight anyone. If I were challenged it might well be in such a way that it would be impossible to settle the matter by appeal, and I would have to fight.'

'You could always appeal. No one would suspect *you* of being afraid.'

'They will say that I am afraid to kill; or, more likely, that our lord Arthur prevented me from fighting so that I would not kill, because he did not trust what I would do in combat. And there would be some truth to that. I do not know what I might do, either.'

Gwalchmai was subject to a kind of madness in battle, which took his actions beyond his or anyone's control. He considered it a gift from Heaven. Medraut had made much of it, saying that his brother's mind was disturbed and that he was likely to go berserk at any time. I had never seen this famous madness, and certainly never seen any trace of insanity in Gwalchmai, but most of the Family had fought beside him and were more willing to listen to Medraut's stories.

'Are you really afraid of that?' I asked Gwalchmai. "Have you ever killed against your will – for instance, in a mock combat?'

He hesitated. 'No. No, I do not think I would kill . . . but even without killing, I do not wish to fight anyone of the Family.'

'Nor do I want you to fight anyone. But I want the matter brought into the open.'

'If it is, and if I can appeal, and Arthur then decrees for me, it will merely transfer the blame to him.'

'And that will help to bring the matter to a head. Gwalchmai, time is against us. Medraut has worked slowly. First he exclaimed against Agravain as a matricide, and then you. He found a faction of his own. Now there is a continual questioning of Arthur's judgement, and a mask of wronged innocence when it becomes apparent that Arthur suspects and disbelieves him. But if we push the pace, make him accuse Arthur now, before his followers have had their minds quite poisoned, we may force him further than his friends wish to go. We may even catch him in treason, and be able to exile him somewhere and reunite the Family. But if we let him take his own time, he will destroy us. Isn't that his goal?'

'It is. But you have omitted one of the things he has done, my lady. He knows that you are his enemy. He says that you are in league with me; perhaps he even says we are lovers – forgive me! I think he may have hinted that. If Arthur supports me, it will be said that it is your doing, that he is weak, a deceived husband ruled by his wife. It would be very ugly.'

'It will be ugly, and painful. But it will be worse if we delay. We must get it over with.'

'There is another thing Medraut may do,' Gwalchmai said, very quietly. He glanced about to see that no one was near enough to hear us. But we had reached the walls and were walking along them, with open space on one hand and only the rough mass of stone on the other. 'He may accuse my lord Arthur with the truth.'

'It will still take time for him to have the truth accepted,' I replied, after a pause. 'And he will not have the time if we succeed.'

Gwalchmai was quiet for a while, walking with his head down, staring at the grasses. Finally he nodded. 'Very well,' he said heavily. 'Since you think it likely to do good – and very probably, after all this, no one will challenge me.' He smiled apologetically.

'Thank you.' I caught his hand and pressed it. 'And you need not try to fight anyone. I agree that your killing a member of Medraut's faction would be the worst thing possible.'

He smiled again and bowed his head. I had known that he would do as I requested, and had known also that he would be reluctant. I had been the one to speak to him, rather than Arthur, because Arthur he would have obeyed at once, while he allowed me to argue him into it. It was easier for him so. But it was a hard thing to ask of him. He knew that, despite my reassurances, he might be required to fight a duel, and could only hope that he would not be forced to kill. I knew how bitter the thought of drawing his sword against a member of the Family must be to him. I looked at his worn face and wished I had not had to ask it of him. But that is another of the bitter facts of power: those who give freely must be asked to give again and again, till they have nothing left to give, while those misers who hoard every drop of their wealth and strength can escape rich and easy to the grave. Perhaps God will give fair justice to all, but they find none on Earth.

We came to one of the stairways built along the inner face of the wall, and climbed it to the ramparts. The walls were not guarded in time of peace, and the battlements stretched empty to either side, curving about the hill. We turned, and looked back at Camlann, rising lively and strong from the smoke of the morning fires.

I looked sideways at my companion. It was hard that Cei must be restrained from quarrels, when he took them lightly, and that Gwalchmai must be encouraged to court them. But it would do no good to have Cei quarrelling, while Gwalchmai might manage to resolve something . . . he looked like his brother Medraut, the cause of his grief. He was said to look even more like his mother Morgawse, the reputed witch. Blood is a strange thing, that can be so at odds with itself . . . I thought of my cousin Menw, and turned the thought quickly. 'Gwalchmai,' I said, because it was a bright morning and I could speak of such things, 'your mother – was she beautiful?'

He did not seem surprised at the question, but his hand slid to the hilt of his sword and his eyes widened a trifle, as they did whenever she was mentioned. At times like this he looked as though he had stepped from the hollow hills, and most people seeing him in such a mood crossed themselves.

'She was very dreadful,' he said, softly but quickly.

'But was she beautiful?'

He paused, his thumb idly rubbing the gold crosspiece of his sword's hilt. 'I do not know,' he said finally. "I always said, "She is beautiful", to explain what happened to those who beheld her. Yet when I confronted her – twice I confronted her, once when I left the Islands, and once before she died – then she did not seem beautiful. No. If the sea and the earth are beautiful, she could not have been. But to look at her troubled the soul, and no one who once saw her could forget her.'

'But why? Even now, even dead, she influences us. Arthur and Medraut both fear her still. And Agravian...' I stopped myself; it was not kind to remind Gwalchmai of his brother.

'It was the force of her hatred and the force of her will,' he said, slowly now, but still softly. 'Her sorcery. That was real, as I have cause to know. In her ... it was as though this world and the Otherworld met.'

'You speak as though she were a kind of demon.'

He looked away. 'Perhaps she was.'

I put out my hand to touch his, to call him back to the real world – then, again, stopped myself. Instead, I turned and looked out over the fields outside the wall, beyond the ring and bank defences of the fortress. The nearest field was brown and raw, newly furrowed by the plough; beyond it sheep grazed in a pasture and the new lambs were dancing in the sun. Far off rose the hill of Ynys Witrin, blue-green and mysterious above the deeper green of the marshes. It seemed to float above the cultivated land. I could see why it had its name, 'Isle of Glass'. But now that name made me think of the castles in the tales, the towers of glass which are said to revolve between this world and the next, surrounded by mist, torchlight and sea: gateways to either Yffern or the Kingdom of Summer, to Heaven or to Hell. The tales say that this world and the next penetrate each other. You can walk into a familiar field, they say, and suddenly find that it has grown strange; and turning, discover that all familiar things are gone. And they say that what the world is depends on the heart's intention, that reality is fluid as water, that one can put one's hand through its cool surface and touch some deeper reality, like a rock beneath the surface of a stream. And had Morgawse found some such reality, to trouble the current of the world by the power of her will and the power of her hatred?

I took a deep breath, feeling the wooden upper rampart of the wall warm and real beneath my hand. Too much poetry, too much listening to tales, I told myself. And yet, I was answered. Even dead, Morgawse's influence surrounded us; and perhaps I understood something of the reason. Perhaps I had known it for a long time.

'We must get Medraut away from Camlann,' I said, aloud, and Gwalchmai, turning to meet my eyes, nodded.

The immediate attempt to push the pace, however, failed. Gwalchmai brought up the subject of the negotiations in the Hall that night, and did all he could to rub it in the faces of Rhuawn and the rest of Medraut's faction, but they said nothing whatever to him in reply, merely whispered among themselves afterwards. And the next day Gwalchmai left for Gaul. He was the centre of the dispute, and we did not dare use anyone else to push the pace.

That same day I visited the wife of Gwalchmai's servant Rhys, bringing a gold charm for her new baby. I found Eivlin already on her feet again, with the ever-present Maire attending her. Maire had her own baby with her, but the rest of her children were not there, and had presumably been left in the care of her eldest, a girl of ten. Both women made me welcome, and showed me the new baby with great pride, as well they might, for she was a fine, healthy little girl.

'We named her Teleri, after a nun who was kind to us,' Eivlin explained, while I offered the baby my finger to clutch. 'Though, indeed, I hope this one will not be a nun, nor so strong-willed as her namesake – or as you, you good-for-nothing little fox!' – this to her son, her first child, who stuck his fingers in his mouth complacently, and smiled at her through them. 'Och, look at him! As though he had not drunk all the cream from the milk this morning, and then refused his dinner! Well, Sion, Mama is too tired to thrash you for it, but do you know what your father will say when he comes home?'

'He'll give me some nuts,' predicted the boy through his fingers. 'He promised.'

'Indeed he will, for he's a fool and spoils the boy,' said

Eivlin sorrowfully, 'as I do as well, more's the pity.'

Maire laughed. 'Ach, he's not spoiled; are you spoiled, Sion?'

Sion shook his head.

'You must be a good boy, and look after your little sister.'

Sion beamed at her, and nodded.

'He has been longing for a sister,' Eivlin explained. 'He would have preferred a brother, but now he only wants to play with Teleri. Indeed, it will be a task and a labour and a hard trouble to stop him strangling her with embraces.'

'Who did you name Sion after?' I asked, feeling clumsy and uncertain with these women. Most of my work had to do with administering Camlann, and with affairs of state, and hence with men; Eivlin and Maire inhabited a different world. I often found I had little to say to other women.

'Sion? He is named for Rhys's father, of course. Rhys is a Rhys ap Sion, and his father is a Sion ap Rhys, and *his* father was Rhys ap Sion.'

'Who was *his* father, then?'

'A Sion ap Huw,' she said regretfully. 'Still, *that* Huw's brother was called Rhys, so the name is old enough, and a good name, too. Hush, my love,' to the baby. 'See the pretty thing the gracious lady has brought you?' The baby's blank, unfocused gaze took no notice of the golden charm Eivlin suspended above her head. Eivlin set it in her hand, and the small red fingers half-folded around it, feebly, the way they clutched any object that touched them; then the blurred eyes closed and the child went back to sleep.

'You must be tired,' I said to Eivlin. 'I will go, and let you rest.'

'You are most gracious, most noble lady; indeed, it is fine, to receive visits from an empress! I thank you.'

I made myself smile and excused myself, declining Maire's offers of wine-cakes and new cheese, just made, which she would be delighted to present to the Empress. I walked back up the hill struggling with my soul. I did not want to be an empress, gracious and strong for her husband's subjects. I wanted at that moment, desperately, to be a plain man's wife and to have children of my own.

As I walked past the stables I saw Bedwyr training a horse, a two-year-old brown gelding he had been working on the lead rein. When he saw me he lopped the rein around one of the fence-posts and came towards me. I forced myself to smile.

'My lady! A fine day,' he called, coming up, the warmth of a smile in his eyes.

'A beautiful day,' I returned. I smiled again and began to walk off. I did not want to talk to anyone.

'What is the matter?' he asked, the warmth disappearing from his look and concern taking its place.

'Nothing, Lord Bedwyr; I am in a hurry, that is all. Will I see you in the Hall tonight?'

But he had reached me and caught my arm, looking at my face carefully. 'You are nearly in tears, my lady,' he observed, in the same tone he would have used to say, 'Your gown has a thread loose on the sleeve.' 'Lady Gwynhwyfar, can I be of any help?'

I shook my head, pulled my arm free and began to walk up the hill again. He came after me. 'If I can be of aid to you, do not hesitate to ask it,' he told me. 'If it is your cousin, if you should want help ... my lady, I could beg my lord Arthur's leave, ride north, and speak to him for you. I promise you, if it came to fighting in your name, I would not kill him.'

I stopped, astonished. 'Merciful Heaven, no! Lord Bedwyr, you are most generous, but ... indeed, I thank you, it is kind, it is more than kind! But do not bring up this matter of my cousin, I beg you, before Arthur and the world! And for you to speak for me ... it is noble, but not wise, for how could I speak to my kin after? I ...' I paused, overcome. 'I thank you. But it was not my cousin's letter that troubled me, lord. It was ... something else.'

'Come and have some wine,' he offered. 'You are weary, and it will be better if you rest a moment.'

I went with him to his house, and he poured me a cup of wine, adding an equal measure of water. His house was on the west side of the Feast Hall, near mine. Because he was warleader he had all three rooms to himself. It was much like my house, but plainer, suiting his taste. The only decoration was a rack of books on the desk, at which I sat while I drank the wine. He sat by the fireplace and looked at me.

'Thank you,' I said, managing to keep my voice even again. 'It was a foolish matter. I should never have allowed it to distress me.' I intended to say nothing more, to turn the conversation to the books or to politics, but under his calm, concerned eyes I suddenly found myself saying, 'Oh, Bedwyr, I wish to God I could have children!'

He jumped up, started towards me, then stopped, looking at me. I pressed my hands against my face, drew them down under my eyes to ease the pressure there. 'It is only that I am tired,' I said. 'One feels it, sometimes: all the wars and consultations and factions. And sometimes I wish I could be an ordinary woman – ach, I know, no doubt I would hate it if I were. Only . . . if I had a child, if Arthur had a son . . . he would never have trusted Medraut, if he had a son by me, and we would have a future, someone to inherit the Empire when we are gone . . . and I would so love to have a baby, my own child . . .'

'Hush,' he said, and then did cross the room to me and stooped clumsily over me, patting me awkwardly on the back with the stump of his shield arm. I burst into tears, and he put his arms around me while I leaned against his shoulder and sobbed, bitterly ashamed of myself all the time.

After a while I pulled away from Bedwyr and dried my eyes. He leaned back against the desk, his arm still around my shoulder, still watching me with concern. I fumbled for the wine glass, took another sip of wine, and managed to smile. 'Forgive me,' I said. 'It is very weak and foolish of me.'

'My lady!' he protested. 'God knows, you bear the weight of Camlann: is it strange that you grow weary now and then? I am honoured that you should choose me to speak to.' I laughed a little, wiping my eyes again. 'Truly, I am honoured!' he said, with some vehemence. 'Do not blame yourself, noble lady. There is not one of us who is not borne down by cares sometimes, and few who have as many cares as you.'

'But not all of us imitate a fountain because of it,' I replied.

'True. Most warriors asked to endure what you do would take a sword to one of their comrades over a trivial word or a joke. Fountains are safer.'

I laughed, wiped my face once more, and rubbed my hands dry on my gown. 'But not for your cloak, noble lord;

I can see that I have drenched it as well as any rainstorm.'

He glanced at the damp patch on his shoulder, then smiled, the smile that lit his face from the inside. I returned the smile, then rose shakily to my feet.

'I must be going, lord,' I told him. 'I am supposed to discuss next year's tribute with the emissary from Elmet this afternoon, and I have some petitioners to hear before then. So we must weep a while and part, like lovers in a ballad. I thank you for the wine and for the use of your shoulder.'

'I am your servant, my lady,' he returned seriously. He opened the door for me. As I paused outside it to take my leave he added, 'my lady, you should demand less of yourself, and work less hard.'

'More easily advised than done, Lord Bedwyr. Strange that that saying should apply to so much of your good advice! But I thank you. Truly.'

I felt his concerned gaze follow me all the way to the Hall. I was ashamed that I had broken before him. And yet, I felt better for it. It is useful to weep, sometimes: it frees one to concentrate on other things afterwards. And, as they say, a grief shared is a burden halved. But I wished I could have spoken to Arthur about it. Yet he had burdens enough and more than enough of his own; and I could never quite mention my childlessness to him. That, while it must be his grief as well as mine, was plainly my failure. In that at least Medraut gave true evidence.

The next day there was another almost-duel, but after that Camlann became comparatively quiet. This was not because anything was resolved, however, but because Arthur managed to send some of the most quarrelsome warriors off in opposite directions: one party escorting a supply train to the work on the dyke repairs in the Saxon kingdom of the East Angles, and the other to Dyfed, to enforce a settlement of some debated lands. Medraut himself was kept at Camlann. We could not trust him to leave it, either with his friends or with his enemies.

Gwalchmai returned from Less Britain in the second week of May, looking ill and worn to the bone. The negotiations with Macsen had gone exactly as I had expected: one or two claims were resolved, but five more had been raised in their place. Moreover, Gwalchmai had had to use all of his skill to prevent himself from becoming entangled in a duel with some of Macsen's warband, who had been deliberately provocative. If he had fought them, and won – and he would not have lost – Macsen would have had a legal charge against him, and through him, against us, which he could have used to block future negotiations. Arthur was angered by this, and, instead of sending Gwalchmai back, wrote Macsen a courteous letter requesting that he send an emissary of his own to negotiate the points which remained to be settled. He also commanded Gwalchmai to remain in Camlann and avoided giving him any work. He wanted to give the warrior a rest, but he wanted even more to bring out the smouldering tension in Camlann and resolve it. The plan worked, too, after a fashion, for the conflict burst into open fire soon after the quarrelsome parties returned from Dyfed and East Anglia: and yet still little was resolved.

I was taking an inventory of wool in the storerooms when Medraut came in to find me.

I had been walking along the stacked bales of different weights and dyes, checking them, while my clerk Gwyn trailed along behind me and noted down the amount of each kind on a wax tablet. The sheep of the region had been recently shorn, and I needed to know how much more wool I should buy for the fortress, and so needed to update my inventory. The storeroom was a long, narrow building, windowless, with the wool bales stacked up to the roof, and the sunlight coming through the eaves in dusty streaks. Many of the older bales had been sitting in storage for a long while, and were close-packed, compressed and thick with dust; I had to stoop over and prod them to find out what they were, and they covered my hands with their grease and filled my lungs with the dust. Then the door at the far end of the storeroom opened, letting in a flood of blinding sunlight, and Medraut paused in it like a statue of a Roman god. I stopped counting the bales and straightened.

'Noble lord?' I said, trying not to cough.

He strolled leisurely through the door, out of the sunlight, down the narrow building, and stopped before me. He gave a slight bow, then stood looking at me with Arthur's grey stare and the hint of a smile at the corners of his mouth. He was, as always, impeccably dressed, his short beard neatly trimmed, graceful, controlled, invulnerable. 'My lady,' he said, a dutiful concern in his soft, pleasant voice. 'The lord Goronwy has been hurt in a duel, and the Emperor wishes you to join him in attendence on him at once.'

'Oh God,' I said. I rubbed my filthy hands on the apron I was wearing, then pulled the thing off and tossed it onto one of the bales. Medraut glanced down, not quite quickly enough for me to miss the look of satisfaction in his eyes. 'How badly hurt? Who was he fighting?'

'Most noble lady, how would I know how badly he is hurt? I was not there. I was told he has been taken to the house of Gruffydd the surgeon; I pray he is not much hurt, for he is my friend.' He paused another moment, then added, 'The warleader, Lord Bedwyr, was the one that hurt him.'

'Bedwyr?' I asked, staring at him. I could not imagine Bedwyr embroiled in a duel. Yet Medraut would not fabricate such a thing. He nodded now, still with that faint hint of a smile. Goronwy was one of his followers, his supposed friends; but he was pleased that there was bloodshed, if I judged him right, and did not mind whose the blood – though no doubt he would have preferred Bedwyr's to Goronwy's. 'Where is Arthur?' I asked, suppressing my sudden loathing of him.

'With Goronwy, at Gruffydd the surgeon's house, noble queen. May I have the honour of attending you there?'

'I thank you, no. Undoubtedly the lord Goronwy should not be disturbed by many visitors. Gwyn, leave that now. Lord Medraut, your pardon.' I gave him a slight curtsy, the politest way I knew of saying, 'I want no more of your company', and hurried from the room. Gwyn gave one frightened look at Medraut and ran after me.

'You don't have to come,' I told the boy as we hurried through the hot, sullen afternoon sun. 'I won't need you again this afternoon. You can go to weapons practice – or is it riding this afternoon?'

'Riding, noble lady,' he said. He sounded utterly wretched.

'Why, what's the matter?' I asked him, registering his distress for the first time.

He stopped, fixing me with his oddly dark eyes. I had grown very fond of him in the short time he had been at

Camlann. He was a sweet-tempered boy, with a great deal of courage. He suffered the dislike or cruelty of the other boys at Camlann with patient persistence, and worked at his weapons with unflagging determination. I had once found him weeping in a corner of the stables, but he had at once dried his eyes and denied that he had cause to weep.

'Noble lady . . .' he said, then, in a rush, 'I know I am no one, no one at all, but you should not trust Lord Medraut. It is his fault that Bedwyr fought Goronwy.'

I looked at him in surprise. 'You seem very certain of that.'

'Everyone knows it,' he replied. 'Goronwy is the lord Medraut's friend, and the lord Bedwyr is the lord Gwalchmai's friend: why else would they fight?'

I put my hand on his shoulder, feeling the bones through the plain tunic. He had learned very quickly. But he was an intelligent boy. 'Why do you hate Medraut so?' I asked gently.

'He . . . once he hit my mother.'

'What? How could he? Was he on some expedition?'

'It was at the convent, in Gwynedd. I had nightmares about it for years.'

'But you said that your mother was at a convent in Elmet.'

He blushed. 'Oh.' He looked at his feet. 'I didn't want to say it was in Gwynedd because the monasteries there are so full of sedition. I was afraid you would not accept me here if I said I came from Gwynedd. Please, noble lady, don't tell anyone that it is really Gwynedd. The others will say . . . you won't tell them?'

'Of course not. But what happened?'

'He came to the convent, with some of his followers to . . . to take something which he had no right to. My mother tried to shame him out of it, but he hit her with the side of his sword and rode off without looking back. He hit her, and knocked her down, and she was bleeding. I saw that he had no honour and no shame, and I swore that one day I would become a warrior and challenge him. But when I came here, I found him, proud and powerful, and many of the warriors following after him like . . . like dogs looking for titbits. And he does nothing but engender quarrels and slander his brother Gwalchmai. I have heard people talking ... my lady, people talk in front of me because they think, "He is just a servant; he must be a fool". I know what Medraut says to his followers, and it is all lies. The lord Gwalchmai,' with a plain and desperate intensity, 'the lord Gwalchmai is a great and good warrior. He is the best, the very greatest warrior in Camlann. If I could be like any of them I would like to be like him. You must not believe what the lord Medraut says of him. I know that I am only a nun's bastard, as the lord Cei says, but please, please believe me, my lady. You must not trust Medraut.'

I thought over what Gwyn had said, and regretfully decided that there was nothing that would be useful. 'Hush,' I told him. 'We do not believe what Medraut says of Gwalchmai.' I turned and began to walk up the hill again.

'Then why do you let him stay here?' Gwyn cried out, running after me. '*He* says that you would send him away if what he says was false, and many people believe him. And he says that the Emperor is set about with flatterers, and does not know whom to trust, and he says that you, most noble lady, are the worst of the flatterers – oh, forgive me! I did not mean . . .'

'I know what Medraut says, Gwyn,' I told him, without looking at him. 'But you see, we cannot send him away. Rulers cannot send people away without charging them with some crime, and we have nothing to charge him with. And he has fought for Arthur for some years now. We must pretend to overlook him, and hope that we can weather whatever storm he manages to raise. But do not be afraid to tell me what Medraut says. If there is something important, I want you to tell me immediately. It would help me, and the Emperor as well. And we can hope that Medraut will find nothing to confirm his accusations, and they will eventually fail for lack of evidence, so that men will see him for what he is. But do not tell anyone what I have just told you, Gwyn. Officially, Medraut is one of us and trusted, and I cannot be reported to have said differently or many people will think Medraut is right and that I am his cunning enemy.'

'Yes, my lady,' he whispered. 'But the lord Gwalch-mai . . .'

'No one who knows Gwalchmai at all well will believe

Medraut's accusations. But come, why do you so admire him, Gwyn? You can scarcely have met him.' I looked back at the boy, managing to smile.

The distraction worked He flushed a little. 'I always admired him – from the songs, you know. And I saw him once in Gwynedd. I thought he looked like an angel of God. He rode by on his horse, looking like the Word of God in the Apocalypse ... there was a picture of that in a gospel I copied, my lady. But he is courteous, even to people like me, and he notices. The other day,' – the flush grew deeper – 'he told me how to use a spear from horse-back, and he showed me himself what I had been doing wrong, and was so kind! And he said I ride well.'

I smiled again, this time a real smile. I could imagine Gwyn seeing Gwalchmai, in Gwynedd: a small boy raised on songs and illuminated gospels transforming the great white stallion, the gold, crimson and glitter of arms into wings of light, something as much greater than the world as his own hopes. Well, he could have chosen worse men for his hero-worship. It said much for Gwyn that he admired gentleness and courtesy as well as strength of arms. 'Gereint the riding-master says you ride well, also,' I told him. 'And he thinks, as I do, that you will make an excellent warrior, if you continue to learn as quickly as you have done.'

'I . . . I thank you, most noble lady,' he stammered, his eyes shining. He was as transparent as spring water, that boy, and could not more hide his feelings than he could fly.

'Then go and practise riding, most noble warrior, and we will finish with the wool inventory tomorrow morning. Is it well?'

'Very well, my lady!' he replied and, seizing my hand, pressed it to his forehead before running off. I was able to smile again, really smile, as I hurried on to Gruffydd's house.

The surgeon lived on the north-west side of the Hall, half-way down the hill. He was by birth a townsman from Caer Ebrauc, and had received some education there, and some training in surgery from those in that city who remembered the skills of the long-vanished Roman legions. On coming of age he had joined a monastery and learned some physic to supplement his knowledge of surgery, but had quarrelled with his abbot and been forced to leave. He joined Arthur shortly after the death of the Emperor Uther, before Arthur himself claimed the purple. He was a sensible, hard-headed man who never had a good word or an unkind deed for anyone. When I entered his house he was pouring some sticky syrup into a cup of wine, scowling. Goronwy, the injured man, lay on a bed. His sword arm was bound across his bare chest and his side and shoulder were bandaged. His face above his black beard was pale and he was sweating.

Gruffydd nodded and grunted when he saw me, but did not greet me. He set the cup in Goronwy's left, uninjured hand: the wine wavered as his hand shook. He swallowed some of the potion and made a face.

'Drink it all,' Gruffydd advised him. 'It will dull the pain – no, here.'

'I can drink it by myself; I left my mother years ago. Why didn't you give it me before, if it dulls pain?'

'I did give you some before; I'm giving you more now. I wanted you to have some of your wits about you while I worked. It would be easy enough to cut through a nerve, cleaning a wound like that, and under a broken collar bone. *Gloria Deo!* Are you eager to lose the use of your arm? As if you hadn't already given enough proof of your foolishness by duelling!'

'My lady,' said Arthur, emerging from the shadows beside the bed. I had not noticed him till that moment, and my heart leapt suddenly. He took my hands a moment and pressed them. The lines about his mouth and eyes were very pronounced.

'Medraut told me you were here, and wanted me,' I said.

He nodded, letting go of my hands. 'I saw him on my way here, and sent him.'

'Medraut!' said Goronwy, trying to sit up. 'He knows of this, then? Already?'

'I imagine half the fortress knows that you and the lord Bedwyr fought, Lord Goronwy,' I replied, keeping my voice even.

'Ah.' Goronwy fell back on the bed again. 'Well. If you see him, tell him that I would welcome his company. It was for his sake that I fought, and, had he been present, he would himself have fought, so this matter concerns him.'

Gruffydd grunted. 'It is for me to say whether or not you are well enough to see visitors. And I say that you will see none, not until tomorrow.'

Goronwy tried to sit up again, groaned and fell back. Gruffydd took the cup from him, poured some more wine, and added some more syrup. 'Take it,' he ordered. 'It will put you to sleep.' Goronwy took it without argument.

'Why did you fight the lord Bedwyr?' Arthur asked, as soon as the cup was empty. His voice was quiet, calm. Only I, who knew him so well, could hear the tension in it.

Goronwy blinked at him. 'My lord, he ... damn his spear! He said I was a liar!'

'Did he so? Why?'

Goronwy blinked again. The drug was having its effect, as Arthur no doubt had calculated. 'He said I ... no, first we were talking about the lord Gwalchmai, my lord. Morfran ap Tegid, and Constans, and I. We were in the Hall. And I said that you did not send Gwalchmai back to Gaul because you suspected him of negotiating with King Macsen in bad faith. But Morfran said ... he said, "By Heaven, it was false," and that you did not send Gwalchmai because he was ill. And Constans said that he could well believe that, and that Gwalchmai was indeed ill – in his wits, from killing his mother. He has a quick tongue, Constans! And Morfran went very quiet and shifty-eyed, and asked whether it was Medraut who said this; and Constans asked why he wished to know – and it was then that the lord Bedwyr came up – he had been sitting down the Hall from us – and said that Gwalchmai was not ill, but that you, my lord, wished him to rest, and that no one doubted his loyalty. And I said that that was false, for there are plenty that doubt it, and with reason; and he called me a liar. How can an honourable man endure it? I challenged him to fight me then and there. He said nothing, merely nodded, and we went out to the stable yards and saddled our horses and set to it. But damn his spear! On the very first attack, before I can get in one good blow, he jabs me under the arm and pushes me off my horse, so I am unfit to fight anyone for months. And, my lord, it is true that you distrust Gwalchmai, is it not?'

'I trust Gwalchmai above my own shield-hand,' Arthur replied evenly. 'And Bedwyr I trust above my sword-hand. You have given too much belief to idle rumours, Goronwy.' He took the cup away from the warrior, gently. 'Listen, cousin. This quarrel within my Family grieves me as deeply as your wound does you. I wish you to end it.'

Goronwy looked up at him, still blinking sleepily, his lower lip caught between his teeth. 'But you would trust Gwalchmai, after all? To such a degree as that? He is a matricide!'

'Cousin, that too is false. Think a moment, of the form in which you first heard the tale of the death of Queen Morgawse of the Islands. At first, were not all agreed that she died at the hand of Lord Agravain? And you have heard why. Think also of Gwalchmai. You have known him as many years as I have, and fought beside him from here to Caledon. Think how often he has saved us in battle, and how well he has served us on embassies, and how slow he is to quarrel with anyone, even the lowest servant. Can you truly believe that he is mad, and worse, treacherous? And can you believe that I would not know or act if it were so? Am I a fool, Goronwy?'

Goronwy looked at me, suddenly, uneasily; then returned his eyes to Arthur with a look of bewilderment. Arthur leaned forward and caught his hand, clasping it. 'Cousin,' he said, 'again, you think of wild rumours. But think of what you yourself have done and seen, what you know. You know who and what I am, and you know Gwalchmai, and Bedwyr.'

Goronwy continued to look at him in bewilderment.

'Will you be reconciled with Lord Bedwyr?' Arthur asked, after a silence.

'With Bedwyr? Yes, damn his spear. If he takes back the name of liar.'

'He will do so. But you must not stir up your friends against him.'

'If you desire it so, my lord, I will keep silent about this quarrel.'

'I do so desire it. Excellent, my cousin. Sleep now.' Arthur set Goronwy's hand down on the bed, where it clenched slowly and relaxed. My husband watched his warrior a moment, his face grim, then turned and left the room.

The neighbouring room was Gruffydd's kitchen, also

where he prepared his drugs. Arthur leaned wearily against the heavy table while Gruffydd closed the adjoining door, then asked, 'And Bedwyr is unharmed?'

'Entirely. It was he who brought Goronwy here. Nor is Goronwy hurt badly, besides the broken bone. He should mend quickly.'

Arthur nodded, then, in a low voice, said, 'He is not to see the lord Medraut. Prevent him any way that you can: tell Medraut that he is asleep, or is then too weak to see visitors. But allow Bedwyr to visit him.'

'I will do that, lord. And I will keep Rhuawn away as well, and all the rest of Medraut's faction, to give Goronwy a chance to regain his wits.' He met Arthur's steady eyes for a long moment, then added, 'It is what you wish, isn't it, my lord?'

Arthur nodded. 'It is. But do not be obvious in the doing of it.'

'Never fear. But I will work on him myself, and see if I can talk him out of his slanders.' As Arthur continued to fix him with his eyes, Gruffydd added defensively, 'Gwalchmai is my friend, and it sits ill with me to hear him called a traitor by some golden weasel such as Medraut.'

'The whole business is very ill, but Goronwy is a good man despite it. Whatever you say, do not begin any more quarrels! We can only hope that this will wear itself out with time, and that someone will challenge Gwalchmai directly.' After another moment, Gruffydd nodded, and Arthur sighed, rubbing his mouth. 'Good. If you need anything for Goronwy, or want him moved, the servants will have orders to help you. Gwynhwyfar, Bedwyr will be waiting at our house.'

Bedwyr was sitting on the edge of the desk, reading a book. He set it down quickly when we entered and stood still, waiting. There was blood on his tunic and cloak, Goronwy's blood, and his face was hard and bitter.

Arthur crosssed the room quickly and caught Bedwyr by the shoulders. 'It was well done,' he said, the grimness falling away from him suddenly. 'It was very well done, my brother. But do not risk yourself: I could afford to lose both Goronwy and Morfran more easily than I could afford to lose you.'

Bedwyr's expression relaxed, and he clasped Arthur's

arm. 'There was no other way to stop it,' he said. 'If I had not intervened, Morfran would have fought Goronwy, and one of them would have been killed.'

Arthur nodded, shook him very slightly, then let him go and sat at the desk. 'I have just told Goronwy that I trusted Gwalchmai above my left hand and you above my right, and I pray God that word of it gets around. And since it was you who fought Goronwy, perhaps that faction will begin to believe that their leader is attacking me, not Gwalchmai. But, God of Heaven! I trust nothing now. There is nothing that is beyond his powers to twist into something sinister.'

No one needed to ask who 'he' was.

'It would have been just as bad if you had sent Gwalchmai back to Gaul,' I said. 'He may not be the issue, but I think that Medraut hates him.'

Arthur nodded, heavily. 'And no one has challenged Gwalchmai directly. He has been back for two weeks and courting trouble, and still no one has challenged him.'

Bedwyr shook his head. He pulled out a chair by the fire for me, then reseated himself on the edge of the desk.

'Rhuawn said some violent things to Gwalchmai two days ago,' I said. 'But there was nothing that Gwalchmai could have appealed to us to refute. He would not say what they were, merely that he would have had to fight Rhuawn if he had taken note of them. So he twisted their meaning into a joke and excused himself.'

'This is still the old trouble, only more blatant, more immediate.' Arthur stood, walked over to the hearth and leaned against the wall, staring back into the dead ashes of the firepit. 'Yet there must be something more to it, or someone would have challenged Gwalchmai.'

'It will be easier for a few days now,' Bedwyr said.

Arthur did not stir. His wide grey stare fixed itself on nothing, and I knew, with a sudden rush of grief, what he was considering now.

'Perhaps you should send Gwalchmai somewhere,' I suggested, to distract him from the nightmare. 'You could send him on an embassy, to Ebrauc – or, better still, to the Islands, with an escort of some of Medraut's followers and some of his own friends. He might be able to resolve something then.'

Arthur shook his head, without looking at me. 'No. If

anyone did challenge him on the journey, he would be unble to appeal to us for judgement: he would have to fight. And if there were killing the rest of Medraut's faction would be out for his blood – God forbid it, but there might even be full combat on the road. No. I do not like this reluctance to challenge Gwalchmai in anything that I might be judge of. It suggests that already they distrust my judgement. Perhaps ... perhaps already they believe other rumours. It is working quickly now, this sickness. More quickly than I had believed. I must send Medraut away ... in God's name, where? I dare not send him on an embassy.'

'Send him to Gwynedd, to discuss the latest tribute problems with Maelgwn,' suggested Bedwyr. 'He will not dare to deceive us in something we can check, like tribute, and he can hardly make Maelgwn more our enemy than he is already. Indeed, if he presses Maelgwn too hard, the king may begin to distrust him, and he will have one ally the less.'

Arthur's hand, resting against the wall, clenched slowly. 'If I send him to Maelgwn ... He is ready to tell the secret. he will tell Maelgwn.' His stare went far beyond the grey heap of ashes, off into a deep darkness, and his face was lined, old. His voice had sunk to a whisper.

'My lord?' asked Bedwyr, also in a whisper, looking at Arthur intently. He did not know 'the secret', but he had known Arthur for many years, too long not to be aware of that shadow on him, or fail to recognize that stare into the blind dark.

Arthur looked up at him abruptly, bitterly. 'My wife knows.'

I looked down at my hands, folded in my lap; at the purple glint in the amethyst of the signet ring I wore, the carving of the imperial dragon. I would not meet Bedwyr's dark, questioning eyes. But I could feel it when he turned them back to Arthur.

'Now?' Arthur said, very softly, to himself, then, 'You should know. You are my warleader.'

'I am your friend,' replied Bedwyr, very quietly. 'And your servant.'

The two pairs of eyes met, held: Bedwyr's solemn in a straightforward humility, contented with whatever Arthur might say to him; Arthur's hard and cold, as he himself was cold, twisted with the pain of a memory.

Then Arthur sighed, opening his hands in a gesture of surrender. 'You are my friend and brother. And I know that, even knowing this, you will follow me. But I tell you now that I do not think it just that you should. I will accept it because I must, but it is not justice, and it was not just of me to have so long concealed this. Medraut...' he stopped, caught a deep, sobbing breath, 'Medraut is my son.'

Bedwyr stared at him. I watched the realization of what it meant creep over him slowly, first darkening his eyes with shock, then gradually draining the blood from his face. He rose, tried to speak; stopped, the fingertips of his one hand resting against the surface of the desk. 'Your sister?' he asked, at last.

'Yes.' Arthur stood perfectly still, almost calm, only his eyes alive, brilliant and terrible. 'Did you never notice that he resembles me?'

'I . . . he is your nephew. I thought that accounted for it.'

'He is my nephew, and my son. He is born of the incest I committed with my sister Morgawse. By all the traditions of the Church I am eternally damned.'

'He didn't know' I burst out, unable to be quiet longer. 'He did not know who his father was. She planned this to destroy us.'

'Silence, silence,' Arthur said, half closing his eyes in pain, and then, turning on me with sudden ferocity, cried, 'Do you think that makes a difference?'

The colour returned to Bedwyr's face all at once. 'My lord, there is no reason to shout at the Lady Gwynhwyfar.'

Arthur nodded, then sat down abruptly by the fire, as though his strength had at last given out. He covered his face with his hands. I jumped up and went over to him, knelt beside him, held him, but he was motionless in my arms. Morgawse had wounded him more deeply than I could heal. Bedwyr stood by the desk, watching us, saying nothing.

After a long minute, Arthur lowered his hands and again met the eyes of his warleader. 'So,' he said, his voice flat with exhaustion, 'now I have told you. But the tale will be current soon. You ought to know that it is true. Ach, if you like, add to that knowledge this, which Gwynhwyfar told you: I did not know. It was . . . a long time ago.'

Bedwyr bowed his head in assent, a movement which began a deeper bow, for he sank to his knees, drawing his sword. He offered it, hilt first, to Arthur. 'My lord,' he said, his tone as quiet and expressionless as Arthur's, 'I gave you this many years ago. Had I known then what you have told me, I would have done no differently.'

Arthur stared at him, then rose, pulling away from me, and touched the hilt of the sword. I thought he would help Bedwyr to his feet and embrace him, but he did not, only stood, looking at the warrior. 'I thank you,' he said at last. 'Sit down.'

He returned to his place beside me, and Bedwyr rose shakily, sheathed his sword, and sat down. Arthur took another deep breath and renewed the conference in a calm voice. 'So you see: I fear that Medraut will begin to spread the story soon. Therefore I will not send him to Gwynedd, or to any king who, like Maelgwn, would be able to use such a tale as a weapon against us.'

'Medraut could tell Maelgwn himself, without leaving Camlann,' I said, into the silence. 'By letter.'

Arthur turned his head and looked at me. His face was scarcely a foot from mine, but his eyes seemed to regard me from a great distance.

'Send him to Gwynedd,' I said. 'My dear lord, some of the men will doubt him now. If he is absent, no matter where, his spell will wane. And if he tells the tale to Maelgwn it will do less damage than told to some king who is our friend.'

'But he will wish to go to Gwynedd. He has spoken with Maelgwn before; we know that. He would not trust a tale like that to a letter. He will want to tell it in his own fashion, preparing his way with hints and rumours, and ending with a pretence of injury to the king himself. Dear God, I can almost hear him.'

'My dearest . . .' I began again, reaching out to touch him.

But he jumped up, strode to the door, turned and looked back at me. 'The best thing would be for me to abdicate. No, be silent. If there were another man in my place, someone untainted by any of this, all would be well. And why should Camlann, and you, and all Britain, pay for my sin? Why should anyone suffer for it but me? It is because I am Emperor, because I seized the purple, usurped it. If I could abdicate—'

'My lord!' exclaimed Bedwyr and I together.

He shook his head, angrily. 'It would be best. But there is no one I could appoint to succeed me who would be accepted by all, and the end would be war, another war, and things would end as they were when I seized power, and no doubt I should seize power again.' He struck his hand against the wall, hard, then stopped, cradling it in the other hand. 'There is nothing to do but go on.'

'Arthur!' I cried, rising from my stiff knees, pained to the heart because he would receive no comfort and no hope, and yet had set himself to struggle on.

'No! Gwynhwyfar, your pity is a reproach to me; can't you see that? Must I speak so plainly? This is my fault, mine! Leave me be for a while. I will go riding – indeed, I will take Medraut and Rhuawn with me as escort, and try to see if I can gather anything of their plans. Bedwyr, you will have to visit Goronwy. Take back the name of liar which you gave him and he will be reconciled and keep silence about the quarrel. Should anything else come up, I will be back by dusk.' He opened the house door, then stopped, looking back once more. 'Forgive me,' he said, very quietly, and was gone. Bedwyr and I looked at each other in the deep silence, and saw the desolation in each other's eyes.

'You have known – how long?' Bedwyr asked at last.

'Just four years,' I replied.

'And no one else knows?'

I shook my head, looked about, and sat in the chair by the fire which Arthur had just left. It still held the warmth of his body, and I wanted him, suddenly and terribly. 'Only Gwalchmai,' I said to Bedwyr. 'Arthur told him before Gwalchmai swore him fealty. Arthur thought he knew already, and had treated him badly because of it.'

'So that was the reason.' Bedwyr traced the line of his sword's hilt, then picked up a fold of his cloak, staring at the bloodstain on it. 'If I had known . . .'

'What?'

He dropped the stained material. 'Nothing. What could I have done? My lady, I would not fight for any man living but Arthur; I would have hung up my sword years ago, if I were called to serve any lord but him. What he has done is nothing less than a miracle. He has fought for the Light, when every other man fought for himself alone. No god would punish him for this thing he committed in ignorance; it is some work of Hell to weaken us all.'

'Gwalchmai,' I said tiredly, 'thinks the Queen Morgawse was a kind of demon.'

'By Heaven, her heart must have been blacker than any mortal's, to have done this thing. Does he really imagine that anyone could rule better than he does? Even now, even with him as Emperor, we are scarcely able to hold to what the old Empire was; what would we do without him?'

I shook my head, my hand clenching, feeling the line of the signet ring against my palm. 'I think that all we have done to this day has been to build a thornbrake against the wind,' I said, 'and since the peace we have been trying to light a fire behind it. But I thought we had the substance of a fire to light the world, here in Camlann, given time. Only Medraut will tear our thornbrake down, if we let him. Arthur knows, and he thinks it his fault. By you are right, without him we have nothing but the darkness and the winds, the kings of Britain fighting among themselve over a purple cloak. He will not let that happen.'

'I pray God it does not.' Bedwyr looked at me again, then crossed to me, knelt before me and took my hands clumsily. He kissed them. 'Most noble lady . . . you do not need me to tell you that he loves you beyond any other. If anyone can comfort him, it is you.'

'I have tried. But he does not want comfort. He will hold the fortress, but he will punish himself for this, and I cannot stop him.'

'Try again, my lady.' His expression was earnest and tender. 'You are no coward; I know you would fight on even if the fight were hopeless, and it is far from hopeless now'

My longing, his kindness, Arthur's pain: I was stunned with too much feeling, and could not feel. 'I am . . . justly rebuked, lord,' I managed to say. 'Very well. And for yourself, you deserve the trust he gives you, and deserve it as much from myself as from my lord. If I were to thank you as your kindness merits, I would never have done with thanking you.'

He looked at me earnestly a moment longer, then again, hurriedly, kissed my hands. He stood, looking at me, then bowed. 'I must go and find Gwalchmai, and tell him what has happened. God keep you, my lady.'

And you, noble lord.'

When he was gone, and I had the house to myself, I put my face in my hands and strove to calm myself. Be still, still . . . I could hear the breeze in the thatch and the hollow sound it made under the eaves; distant, indistinguishable voices shouting far off down the hill. There. My skin felt hot, and I stood up and went into the next room and found a pitcher of water. I splashed it against my forehead and cheeks. But calm eluded me. I felt as though a fire had begun below my heart in that web of grief and helplessness, and I could not extinguish it so easily. Though I was glad of Bedwyr; he had been kind . . .

I stopped, staring into the water pitcher. Bedwyr. What had I felt when he kissed my hands? What shape was it that he had made on the air before me, to draw my heart out after him, as Arthur did?

'Oh God,' I whispered, and the lips of my reflection moved in the water, horrified. Not this, not now, not when I had so much else to do! How had this danger crept up on me, that I had not even noticed it until now? I had been secure in my love for Arthur. Oh, to be sure, some men are attractive and the body finds them so, but that is a thing easily laughed away and not to be taken seriously. I had never loved any man but Arthur, never thought I could. There were many I counted as close friends, and Bedwyr had been among them, but now I was surprised, trapped into another feeling, one that bit more deeply into the heart.

I thought again of how he had looked at me, so tenderly and earnestly; of the hurried touch of his lips against my fingers . . . I could feel it still, like a ring of invisible gold. I clenched my hands to fists, pressed them against my eyes. The thought of that look in his eyes, of his rare, warm smile, melted my soul away within me. And it had struck him, it had trapped him as well, of that I was certain.

'Oh God,' I said again. My voice sounded strange to me. I wiped my dripping hands on my gown and went back to the conference room. The book Bedwyr had been reading when I came into the house was still on the desk: I picked it up to put it away – anything, to distract myself from the turmoil within me. It was the *Aeneid,* and when I lifted it it fell open at the beginning of book four:

At regina gravi iamdudum saucia cura
vulnus alit venis et caeco carpitur igni . . .

But meanwhile the queen, wounded with a heavy grief
Feeds the wound with her blood and is seized by a blind fire . . .

I threw the book down on the floor and stared at it. Unhappy Dido, in love with Aeneas, who was bound for Rome. In love, in love, in love. I had not noticed it coming, and now that I saw and understood it was too late: love seized me savagely, bitter-sweet, irresistible. And adulterous, treacherous, ruinous.

With trembling hands I picked the book up again. I smoothed the bent pages and set it back in its place in the bookcase, then stood a moment, my palms flat against the cool, scarred wood of the desk. 'Very well,' I said, aloud, feeling the beat of blood in my ears. It had happened; I loved Bedwyr. But still, Arthur . . . I closed my eyes, thinking of my husband: the eyes that could enforce silence with a glance or glow with pure delight; the confident step, the strength of his hands; the passionate force of his vision. My husband, my own, and if sometimes, burdened with Empire, he would not hear me – well, I had always expected that. But Bedwyr – no, I would not feed this wound with my blood. Nor would I even speak to the warleader, unless circumstances demanded it.

I turned and staggered from the room, stopped in the doorway. The day had grown dark, and clouds spat a few small drops of rain. I must . . . I must speak to the servants, and see that a few of them knew what Arthur had said regarding Gwalchmai, so that the rumour of his words would spread quietly, naturally, together with the tale of the quarrel. Yes. And as for Bedwyr . . .

Best not to think of him at all.

Three

I was finishing the inventory of wools with Gwyn the next morning when Gwalchmai came into the storeroom looking for me. He smiled when he saw us, nodded to Gwyn, and gave me a slight bow. 'My lady, I would like to speak with you, if you are free.'

'Is it urgent?' I asked, with wearied anxiety.

'Indeed not. I can wait – when will you be done here?'

'We're almost finished now. If you wish me to come to the Hall when I'm done, or to your house . . .'

'Do not trouble yourself. I will wait here, if I am not in the way. Can I be of any assistance?'

'None whatsoever.'

'A pity. I feel like a horse let out to pasture, with nothing to do but graze and watch his fellows working. I had not thought thirty so old as all that . . . Hai, Gwyn! How goes the riding?'

Gwyn, who had been watching Gwalchmai with shining eyes, stammered his reply eagerly. 'I c-can hit the target from a gallop now, since you showed me, noble lord. But I can't pick up the ring, and the others told me I should be able to. I tried it yesterday, and fell off, and the horse didn't like it.'

Gwalchmai laughed. 'You were riding that chestnut three-year-old again? The beast's half pony and has no more withers than a mule, and less training. One cannot throw all one's weight onto one side of a horse unless he is used to it. What did that one do when you leaned over his neck? Stop suddenly and look surprised?'

Gwyn laughed back. 'Like a hen with her tail-feathers plucked. He stopped as soon as I had my left leg round the cantle, and then I fell off. He sniffed at me when I was on the ground, and looked very puzzled. But the others had all told me I should try it.'

'They probably wanted to see you fall off – and with that beast, there's nothing to hold to if you do begin to fall. But if you could accustom him to the action, and train him to keep running while you do it, you might repeat the move and surprise them.'

'That would be splendid! How do you ... oh. I am sorry, my lady. It was three bales of green, wasn't it?'

'Three green single-weight, two double-weight. Perhaps the lord Gwalchmai could teach you how to pick a ring up from the ground from horseback this afternoon. Whyever do you want to do such a thing anyway?'

'If one can do that, one can deal with an adversary who has fallen, or pick up a dropped sword,' Gwalchmai answered at once.

'And if you can ride entirely on one side of the horse,' Gwyn supplemented eagerly, 'you can use the horse to shield you during a charge. The enemy may not even see you, or might not cast anyway, if he wants your horse.' He looked at Gwalchmai earnestly, received a nod of assent, then sobered and said, 'But I could not trouble the lord Gwalchmai. Truly, noble lord, I know you have much greater matters of concern than that.'

'I have just told the Empress that I have no matters of concern, great or small. And I have a new roan mare that I wish to train for battle. I will take her onto the field behind the stables. Come, if you wish to – that is, if the lady Gwynhwyfar has nothing else for you to do.'

'Nothing this afternoon,' I replied at once, pleased that Gwyn should learn riding from his hero. 'I need that list of women who will be doing the weaving for us, and the quantities of each colour that they want, but you can write that out for me tonight. Very well, Gwyn, three green single-weight, two double; and...' I counted quickly, 'five black, natural, single-weight...'

Gwyn hastily scratched down the amounts with his stylus, self-consciously competent, carefully not looking at Gwalchmai. We finished the inventory, checked through the result, and I told Gwyn to make a fair copy of it and sent him off to do so. Gwalchmai watched him go, smiling.

'That is a clever boy,' he told me, 'and a daring one.'

'He thinks very highly of you.'

That drew a quick glance. 'Does he? He is in love with songs, I suppose. It was a brave deed to come here, and braver still to stay. Most of the other lads in the fortress are cruel to him, though I suppose it is only to be expected.'

'He bears up to it very well. They will tire of teasing him

soon, and he will be able to make friends. But I am glad you will spend some time teaching him.'

'Och, that. That is a pleasure. I remember still what it is like to be despised by other children, and it atones for something, teaching him. Though Gwyn is a quicker learner than ever I was – but this is not what I wished to speak to you about.'

I gestured towards the door, and he opened it for me, following me out into the sunny morning air. 'Cei is in my house, in a black temper,' Gwalchmai told me. 'Shall we walk down to the walls again?'

We did so. It was a lovely day, the perfection of early June. The larks were singing above Camlann, and children played about the houses where women were hanging their washing on the thatch and discussing their neighbours' affairs. We walked down the hill without speaking, for the day was too fine to burden it with cares so soon. When we climbed the wall and looked out over the fields, the land that had before been raw mud was green – silver with wheat, shimmering with the wind. Gwalchmai stopped, leaning on the battlements, and I stopped beside him. It seemed to me that the breeze must draw away the cramped and manifold care from my mind and scatter it over the rich land. It would not be so dreadful: the worst would not happen. Camlann had survived civil war and Saxon wars; endured poverty and enmity and envy, and it was strong. Its life continued, steady as a pulse-beat, through all the doubts and turmoils of its rulers. Whomever I loved or hated, it would always provide me with work to be done, and new, small cares to destroy the great ones. Perhaps – no, certainly – in the end it would save us.

'Yesterday I spoke with my brother Medraut,' Gwalchmai said without preamble.

My instant of peace vanished as suddenly as a trout does, glimpsed in the shadows of a calm pond. 'You talked with him about Goronwy's duel? You were alone with him?'

'We were alone, yes. And we talked about the duel and . . . other things. You, and me, and my lord the High King.' Gwalchmai always said 'High King' for 'Emperor': it was his Irish upbringing.

'Did he tell you much?'

'Very little. He reviled us.'

'Oh, indeed! Did you expect more?' I turned from him bitterly and leaned over the battlements.

'I suppose not. But I had to speak with him. I have long known what he meant to do, but it is truly beginning now; he has achieved bloodshed. So, I went to his and Rhuawn's house, and when they returned from riding with my lord Arthur I greeted him and asked him what he intended to do next.' Gwalchmai shrugged. 'Rhuawn protested and said certain angry words, but Medraut sent him away. Then he himself spoke to me, very bitterly.' He looked down at the bank and ditch below the battlements, the green grasses bent in the wind. The feyness came over him, and I could tell that he did not see what was before his eyes, but looked into something deeper and stranger. 'He has no joy of the Darkness he serves. He walks in a blind horror, like a man in a dark sea where there is neither foothold nor breathing space, but he does not care. He cares only to destroy what he hates, and he lives by hatred, alone.' He paused, then said, 'He was different once. When we were both children – But this is no matter to concern you, my lady. When he had done cursing me and cursing the Family, he told me that he wishes to spread the story of his birth. He did not say as much, but I think he plans to whisper hints of it to emissaries of the kings of Britain, and, when the rumour is well established outside Camlann, answer the questions of his friends and followers with more hints. Moreover he is now devising slanders against Bedwyr as well, since it was Bedwyr who fought Goronwy. My lady, he must be stopped.'

'He told you all of this?'

He looked up at me, human again, and smiled apologetically. 'He makes no pretence with me, my lady. We know each other too well, and have too much in common. And he hates me very badly, because he thinks that I betrayed him and our mother. He wished to taunt me with the names he has been trying to give me, the names of traitor and madman and matricide, and when he saw that these had no effect, he fell to boasting of what he meant to destroy. My lady, I have urged this before, and now urge it again: he mut be sent away.'

'Where would you have him sent? He can write letters wherever he is.'

'They will have less effect if he is far away. Send him back to the Islands.'

I stared down at the wall. 'Arthur also wished to have him gone from Camlann. But he will not send him anywhere. He suspects that Medraut is ready to tell that story.'

'He suspects? How can he?'

I shook my head. 'His feelings for that tale are more sensitive than the horns of a snail, or the tentacles of the sea anemone. And the time is ripe. Medraut could easily lose ground after this duel, for Arthur has refuted the grounds which Goronwy was defending. Medraut needs something new. But he does not dare tell his tale openly, in the Family, or he will be disbelieved. Hence he will tell it first outside Camlann. How could we send him back to the Islands? To sentence him to exile when he is charged with no crime, and without warning, would open a rift in the Family which we might well be unable ever to close again.'

'I don't know,' said Gwalchmai, wearily. 'I have no answers. I merely know that I am afraid for us all if Medraut continues as he has begun. Let him go back to Dun Fionn and see what has become of Agravain. Perhaps it will trouble him: it troubles me.'

Gwalchmai had sailed to the Orcades after completing an embassy in the North the summer before, and had returned to Camlann still brooding over his elder brother's fate. It seemed that Agravain was drunk most of the time, had fearful nightmares if he went to bed sober, and had aged rapidly in the few years since Morgawse's death. He was becoming a figure of derision to the northern kings, and bitter with the knowledge of it. Now Gwalchmai looked up again, saw the expression on my face, and shook his head.

'Do not mind it,' he told me. 'There is nothing anyone can do. I knew when he killed her that it would happen.' Again he looked out over the fields, speaking in a low voice. 'As I knew that Medraut would be driven by her to destroy those who had been her enemies. Strange how her shadow endures among us. Agravain and Medraut, both devoured by it . . . and Arthur. And now it lives in the midst of Camlann and feeds on us all. How I wish . . .' his words trailed off, and he continued to brood over the field like the hawk of his name.

I put my hand on his shoulder. 'Wish what?' I asked softly.

He smiled ruefully, breaking from his abstraction. 'I wish that I had married my lady Elidan, and that there was something more to my life than battles and embassies. I wish I had even a little of ordinary life to turn to, to rest in. I swear the oath of my people, I envy Rhys and Cei their children.'

'And I,' I replied in a low tone. He looked at me sharply, then took my hand from his shoulder and kissed it.

'Forgive me, my lady. I know that you endure more than I, and I intended no complaint.'

'My brother,' I said, 'you complain less than a saint, and certainly less than I do.'

In fact, he suddenly made me feel ashamed. His relationship to his clan had long been as tense as mine, first because he served their traditional enemy Arthur, and secondly because four years before he had been forced to kill one of his cousins who had fought for Queen Morgawse. That was a crime for which he could be disowned by his clan, kin-wrecked, but since his brother Agravain was king the matter had been passed over with a few expiatory rites. But he was never welcome in the Islands. For the rest – I had Arthur, at least. Gwalchmai had had one passionate love affair with the sister of a northern king: the girl's brother rebelled against Arthur and Gwalchmai killed him. The lady Elidan, daughter of Caw, was of royal birth: she would never forgive her brother's murderer, and told him so. Even years after her brother's death, when Gwalchmai had sought her out at the convent in Gwynedd which she had joined, she had held resolutely to her word and refused either to pardon Gwalchmai or to have anything more to do with him. He blamed himself bitterly for what had happened, and in fact he had been to blame: he had lain with her while he was her brother's guest and Arthur's emissary, and he had sworn her an oath not to hurt her brother and broken it. But he had been very young, and quite desperately in love; her brother had been killed in battle; and he loved her still: I think most women would have pardoned him. Unforgiven, he paid little attention to other women's attempts to attract him. It was not only that he still loved Elidan, but that he had hurt her, and was afraid of hurting someone else. So he was left with nothing: no parents, no clan, no wife, no children, and even his comrades in the Family quarrelling about whether he was mad and treacherous. In comparison, I was lucky, very lucky.

'It would be better if you complained more,' I told him, still ashamed of my own weakness. 'We have worked you too hard, my friend; you have more than deserved this rest we are giving you.'

He smiled, gently and ironically. 'So then, I am a worn-out charger, put out to pasture before my time. Well, I cannot say that it is not sweet to have little to do now, even with the fortress on a sword-edge, and half of those who were my friends . . .' he checked himself from another 'complaint' about the effects of Medraut's slanders, and instead concluded, 'Enough of that. I wished to tell Arthur what Medraut had said, but I found him sitting in one of the gate-towers, staring into the west, and I thought it better not to disturb him. And if he suspects already what Medraut will do, it is not surprising that he is lost in thought. But you can tell my lord Arthur what I have told you, and tell him that I am willing to serve him in any way, if he should wish to send me to watch Medraut, either in the Islands or anywhere else. And I am sorry to have spoken so grimly on so sweet a morning.'

'Gwalchmai my friend, you know that it was necessary, so do not trouble to apologize for it. I will tell Arthur when he is free. And now, lord, weren't you going to train a horse?'

There was nothing much for me to do that afternoon: the spring planting and trading was largely done with, and the summer's business had not yet properly begun. Gwalchmai walked me back up the hill to the Hall, trying to discuss neutral matters, then left to find something to eat before working with his horse. I was not hungry. I wandered restlessly about the fortress, giving unnecessary advice to the servants, then visited a friend. This was one of my few women friends, Enid, Gereint ab Erbin's wife. There were so few women I could talk to that I usually enjoyed our conversations. But now she was in one of her duller moods, able to do nothing but gossip, and I was tense and sharp-tongued. we were both relieved when I excused myself.

I went back to my own house, into the bedroom to be

private, and sat on the bed. Camlann is strong, I had thought that morning, before Gwalchmai had given me his news. But the day before I had told Bedwyr that it was only a thornbrake against the wind, a fragile protection for the weak little fire we had set alight: and that image held the greater truth. Twenty years before, what had Camlann been? The fortress of the Emperor of Britain, a man emperor in name only, with only a shadow more authority than any petty king. And a hundred years before?

A hill overgrown with the grasses, inhabited by foxes and the bright-eyed rabbits and hares. The great cities of the area then were Baddon and Searisbyrig-Aquae Sulis and Sorviodunum. Young men and women still would have been able to remember the Roman legions departing finally from the south, and perhaps they had believed that Rome was still strong. It had still stood, then: Rome, 'the eternal city', as its lovers had called it, not knowing how close they were to the dark. I thought of the ruined Wall in the North, and bare hills behind it. That wall had been the reality: Camlann was only its shadow, attempting to protect the few small fragments that remained. It was not strong. Medraut was raising a storm that would tear it to fragments.

We were trapped. Medraut had set snares for us on every side, and Time pressed close behind us like a huntsman with his dogs. I could see no way out, any more than could Arthur, with his wide stare into the unyielding future, or Bedwyr with his call for courage and another blind battle. No way but one – and that one was not something I could admit. I had thought of it several times over the four years since Medraut had come to Camlann, and always I had thrust the thought from me in disgust, knowing that it was wrong.

And yet, I thought, *this cannot go on.* Medraut would destroy us with these quarrels. He had brought about bloodshed within the Family, and only Bedwyr's quick action prevented killing. What he planned was more: strife between my husband and his realm. Dishonour for Arthur, disaffection in the Family, and rebellion and civil war throughout Britain. The bloodiest kind of war, and the cruellest. Perhaps we could live down the slanders; perhaps we could force Medraut into some mistake – but that possibility grew more remote with every day that passed. Medraut had facts, and knew how to persuade, and to win followers. I was afraid, as I had been since first he came to Camlann. All of us, we were all worn out by the strife, the tension, the constant plotting to protect our future. And it could all end so simply, so easily, if Medraut should quietly die.

I remembered with uncomfortable vividness an incident years before, when I had been helping Gruffydd the surgeon tend a man with a fever. Gruffydd had been keeping that man in his own house, as he kept Goronwy now. I remembered him stooping over the man, taking his pulse and muttering in discontent. He went to his medicine cabinet and took down from the shelf one jar, a blue-glazed earthenware jar with a ragged 'H' scratched onto it. He poured some of the dark liquid it contained into a cup of water and gave it to the patient, explaining meanwhile to me that it would slow the heart and lower the fever.

'What is it, then?' I had asked.

'Hemlock,' he replied shortly.

'But that is a poison!'

He nodded, snorting. 'So are many things: so is mead, in large quantities. But this much,' he laid one finger sideways against the jar, 'this much is a fit dose for a large man stricken with fever, like our friend here, and can save lives. Half of that amount for a small man or a woman. This much, now,' and he laid a second finger beside the first, 'brings sleep, and even death, to some. More than that,' he picked up the jar and set it back on the shelf, 'four or more measures, at any rate, will kill anyone, and many have died by it. But those that have used it subtly have to smother it in mead or strong wine, for it has a bitter taste.'

'How cheerful,' I said. 'What about toad's blood, then, if one wishes to poison someone subtly?'

He snorted again, smothering a laugh, and replied, 'An old wives' tale. Toad's blood will poison no one, and I think it must have spoiled the taste of many a dinner.'

I would have to visit Goronwy soon, to see how well he was recovering, and to show a just concern for him. I could be as free of Gruffydd's house as of my own. It would be easy, so easy, to slip that jar from the shelf, and pour out four finger-measures into a flask – a flask like the empty scent jar of Italian glass I kept under the bed. Then, the next time I poured for the high table at a feast, I could mix it with a skin of mead and give it to Medraut. No, not a skin of mead. I would have to throw the rest out, and that would be dangerously obvious. Better to wait until there was only enough mead left in the pitcher for one person, and then add the drug and pour for Medraut. When it was late in the evening, and he had drunk well enough not to notice the taste. When the fires were low, and the torches flickering, and the others also had drunk well and would not notice if I had to pour in the wrong order. No one would suspect poisoning, if everyone had drunk mead at the feast. And Medraut would go home as though he had drunk too much, staggering a little, and next morning would be found to have died – in his sleep, painlessly. And no one would be able to say whether he had simply drunk too much mead for a hot night, or died from a sudden failure of the heart (as can happen, even to young men), or from some rapid disease. He would have a magnificent funeral, with all the fortress in mourning, and never trouble anyone again. His tale would rest forever untold, and his faction and his slanders at last would be stilled. We could heal the breach in the Family; we could restore the Empire. It would be the pitch of foolish absurdity to let all that we had suffered and bled for, the one last light of the dark West, won with toil and anguish from the collapse of our civilization, to allow all this to slip bloodily away into nothingness because of one sole man.

I jumped up, pressing my hands to my mouth. 'That is damnation,' I whispered through them, hearing the distorted sound of the words in the still air of the empty room. Damned. It was evil. 'You shall not commit murder. No murderer has eternal life,' proclaimed the scriptures.

Arthur called murder 'the tyrants' trick'. Bedwyr said that no expediency, or even necessity, could justify the commission of a mortal sin. Both of them, and Gwalchmai as well, sometimes doubted whether it was justified to kill even in battle. Yet they had all killed . . . but no, none of them would ever poison a man at a feast. Such an action would not only carry eternal damnation, but temporal condemnation from all those whom I loved most, whose opinions I most valued. And they were right. How could anyone – how could *I* – poison a man under the cloak of hospitality, charging him with no crime, giving him no warning, no chance for self-defence or for repentance? It was base, cruel, dishonourable, treacherous, abominable: how could I?

And yet . . . what other course was there?

It was the vulnerability of what I loved that tortured me. My husband, my friends were suffering now, and it was only beginning. And that was not the worst; it was not only that we would suffer, but that the future would suffer as well. Or did my fears exaggerate the danger? What did Medraut want? Power for himself? Probably. He had wanted to be king of the Orcades, and resented his brother's election. No doubt he would like to be emperor instead. That bleak stare I had noticed in him when he thought no one was watching sometimes fixed itself on the gold dragon standard in the Hall. But no, that was not what I feared. There were many others in Britain who would like to be emperor. What I feared from Medraut was something more, something that I had at first been unable to name, even to myself. It was the wind out of the darkness, the pure power of destruction undertaken for destruction's sake. I had never seen Queen Morgawse of Orcade, but I knew what she had done to the lives of those she touched. And I was certain that Medraut was still devoted to her, and loyal to her hatred. One understands who and what a man is in many ways, and few of them have to do with what he says. There are actions – small actions of little consequence, often, as trivial as a harsh word to a servant; there are friendships and ways of pursuing friendships; and choices of words, gestures, looks: all things unimportant in themselves but which taken together create suspicion and eventually certainty. I was certain that Medraut meant to break us, to destroy us, in vengeance for his mother. And I knew that his hold on us was strong, and we could not render him either friendly or harmless.

I was sick of carefully weighed reasons and precise justice. Our position was not reasonable, nor was Medraut's. And the need I had to protect was not reasonable, but I knew that my horror of murder would not stand against its force. Whether or not it was right, whether or not I would suffer for it, I knew with cold certainty that I would do it: I would try to destroy Medraut.

How I managed to continue to work, continue to smile during the next three weeks I do not know. Only the force of long habit kept me upright: my heart cowered within me, like a hare when the hounds are searching for it. My intention to murder was a cold, black weight within me. I stole the poison, but then tried to pretend to myself that I would not use it – yet I could not throw it away. As for Bedwyr, it hurt me to look at him, and I avoided him as much as I could. After the first few days, his look of puzzlement vanished and he began to avoid me as well. He understood. How long, I wondered, had he known what he felt? I suspected that it was longer than I had known. I wanted him to talk to, many times; kept thinking of things to say to him, and then remembering that I must say nothing, so that my thoughts were tormented. Arthur would have noticed, but had other concerns. Goronwy, recovering from the duel, wavered in his allegiance, and some other warriors with him. Arthur saw much of them, hoping to restore their loyalty, and for a time thought he had won Goronwy at least. Then we were unable to keep Medraut from seeing him, and found him once again uneasy, once again listening to the rumours. And there were more rumours than ever, now linking Gwalchmai, Bedwyr and me in a conspiracy against Medraut, slandering him to Arthur and trying to murder Goronwy. Arthur decided to send Medraut to Less Britain as part of an escort for Macsen's emissary when he returned to his lord.

This emissary arrived in Camlann in the third week of June. He was a low-ranking, ignobly born warrior of the king's warband, whose status was almost as direct an insult to Arthur as his words and manner. Nonetheless, we played our part correctly and feasted this emissary with the usual magnificence. It was to that feast that I carried my flask of stolen hemlock.

Macsen's emissary, such as he was, had the place on Arthur's left (it would have been an excess of courtesy to put him on Arthur's right; he was embarrassed enough as it was) and Medraut sat beside him. The emissary called for wine during the second course. It was a formal feast, and there were no women present in the Hall, so I entered only then, and poured wine for the high table. I sat down next to Arthur, on his right. I had bound the glass phial of hemlock under my belt, which was a wide, high one, and stitched with gold: the poison was quite invisible. But I could feel it against my side like a piece of ice, slowly chilling me through. I had a savage headache.

'You are pale, my lady,' Bedwyr said, moving over to let me sit down.

'It is my head,' I told him. 'It feels near to splitting.'

'What?' asked Arthur, breaking off a conversation with the emissary. The emissary looked confused, pugnaciously embarrassed, so I left off rubbing my temples, smiled, and raised my glass to the man.

'You are indeed pale,' Arthur said to me in a low voice. 'You have been overstrained lately, my heart. Go to bed now, if you wish; I will make your excuses.'

'No, no,' I protested. 'It will probably go away after a glass of wine, and we should do things twice as graciously if Macsen is ungracious.'

He looked at me steadily a moment, then took my hand under the table, pressed it, and turned back to the emissary. I glanced at Bedwyr, who was still watching me with grave concern, then hastily and resolutely turned to the emissary as well.

The Family was on edge from all the rumours, and many of the men were drinking too heavily while some remained sullen and sober. Medraut did not drink much: when I came to refill his glass the third time, I saw that he had barely touched the second cup I had poured for him. He smiled at me when I stared at it, a very knowing, bitter smile. the pupils of his eyes were contracted into points of hard, cold blackness. It frightened me, though I pretended to smile and passed on. His eyes followed me, still with that cold and knowing look.

It was impossible, I told myself as I sat down again. he could not possibly know. Somehow I must rein in my leaping imagination. Somehow ... I endeavoured to laugh, felt as though for a very little I might begin to scream. If only the night would pass! Here I sat, waiting to murder a man who sat three places from me at the table, feeling the phial of hemlock burn icily into my ribs, while from time to time my intended victim gave me a cold and knowing smile. I could give up the intention ... the wave of relief that swept me at the thought was greater than I had supposed possible. But no, no, I could not go back now. It was my imagination, I told myself again. And it was imagination that made the torches burn so redly, and made the half glass of wine I had drunk seem more intoxicating than the strongest mead, so that the room swam about my pounding head and I had to gasp for breath. I redoubled my efforts at witty gaiety, felt some of the edginess around me dissolve as I laughed and again poured the wine, but all the while I felt Medraut's eyes watching me until I wished to fling myself from the Hall.

At last the meal was finished and the singing began. Our chief poet, Taliesin, began by singing of some ancient battle, the conquests of the emperor Constantine, and the Hall fell silent, drinking its mead and listening. He paused when he had told how Constantine won the purple and was acclaimed emperor in Rome, and asked for wine. The emissary called for more mead at the high table. I rose and had another cask brought to the back of the Hall; when I filled my pitcher Taliesin was singing again, this time of a battle in our Saxon wars, a lament for Owein ab Urien, son of an allied king. It was one of Taliesin's own songs and the Hall was silent as the snow, with everyone wrapped in it, the fast uneasy circles of melody, violent grief chained in words. The torches were low, as I had foreseen they would be. Medraut still was not drinking heavily, but I judged he had drunk enough. It was time.

Beginning at the far end of the table I poured out the pungent yellow mead until there was only a cupful left in the pitcher, and then, standing out of the torchlight, I fumbled under my belt.

'His spears were swifter than the wings of dawn...' sang Taliesin.

The flask which had seemed so cold was warm under my fingers. I fumbled the stopper out and quickly poured the hemlock into the pitcher, then stopped the phial again and put it back in its place. I came forward with the music around me, smiling, and found that Medraut's glass was empty.

Taliesin was singing:

'For Owein to kill Fflamddwyn,
Was easy as to sleep:
Sleeps now the host of Lloegyr
With the red dawn on their eyes
And those who would not flee
Were bolder than was wise . . .'

I filled Medraut's cup, draining the last drop from the pitcher, then, as though in a dream, went back to the servants for more mead. I poured for the rest of the table quite carefully, not spilling a drop, but when I sat down again I found that I was trembling, and feared to pick up my cup lest it show how my hand shook. But Bedwyr was arguing philosophy with Gwalchmai, and Arthur was discussing politics with the emissary, and no one noticed. It remained only to wait. I felt as though I would burst into tears at any moment, and wished desperately that it was over, that it were already the morning, and that they were coming to tell us that Medraut was . . .

'My lord,' said Medraut, standing and smiling at Arthur, the poisoned cup in his hand.

Arthur looked up from his conversation with the emissary, then nodded to Taliesin. The music stopped, and the Hall, suddenly bereft of it, was very silent. I could hear the fires burning, the crackle of torches, and the dull pounding of the blood in my ears. I held the edge of the table, staring at Medraut, unable to feel much. Medraut stood straight and slender, the light glinting off his fair hair and beard, shadows caught in the folds of his purple-edged cloak. The cup he held was of bronze, inlaid with silver, and it seemed to burn in his hand, like the sun at noon.

'My lord,' he repeated, still in the same easy tone, his clear voice carrying through the stillness of the Hall.

'Lord Medraut,' responded Arthur, in the same tone, his voice deeper and rougher from the use it had had. 'What do you wish to say?'

Medraut smiled again. 'Many things, in the course of my life, if it is allowed me. Ah, but surely, my lord, one of the best things would be to toast you, for your health, long life and long reign. But I would be reluctant to do so with this cup.' He raised it slightly. 'Though I agree that to wish health and long life to the Emperor is a fitting use for one's last breath, it would not be fitting to drink to them in poison.'

A gasp, a murmur ran around the Hall, stopped. I closed my eyes, aware how beside me Arthur went tense, feeling his grey stare fixing on Medraut, knowing the uncertainty and doubt leaping in his mind. *Dear God,* I thought, *let me die now, here; do not let me see my disgrace . . .*

'I do not see the point of your joke,' Arthur said, his voice quiet but carrying. 'The mead is not so bad as all that.'

This brought a titter of nervous laughter, and abrupt silence again. My eyes opened of themselves, and I saw Medraut still standing, the cup still raised, and the bitterness growing in his face.

'The mead, my lord, is excellent, but the hemlock has a bitter taste. It is hemlock, is it not, Lady Gwynhwyfar?'

Arthur leapt to his feet, his hands braced against the table. 'You are serious! What are you saying, man, to accuse the Empress in this way?'

'She is trying to poison me!' Medraut shouted it. 'She is a jealous, a scheming, faithless woman!' Slamming the cup down on the table, 'A woman whose hand has been against me since first I came here, who has plotted against me with my mad brother. Look to yourself, Lord Pendragon, or she will plot with him against you as well! This cup is black with poison, which she with her own hand just now poured into it.'

'By the King of Heaven, you lie,' Arthur said, not raising his voice, but using it like the edge of a sword. 'I do not know whether what you say is slander or some madman's joke, Medraut ap Lot, but I will have you know that it is treasonous, and I will hear none of it, nor will any here who know the kindness of the Empress.' There was a ragged cheer, my friends leaping to their feet; and in response shouts of anger. Arthur lifted his hand, standing above me, tall and coldly furious, and silence, imposed by the long habit of obedience, ebbed back. 'You joke is in bad taste, Medraut: sit down and be silent.'

'It is not a joke, my lord, it is a matter of murder. Look at the Empress, the most noble lady, the most kind and excellent Gwynhwyfar: look at her, if you doubt me! *She* knows that I speak the truth!'

'Be silent!' shouted Arthur, and even Medraut flinched. 'The Lady Gwynhwyfar has been ill all the evening, and what woman would not be shocked to hear herself slandered thus? Do you say that that cup is poisoned? Give it to me.'

'My lord!' I croaked, finding no air, reaching up to catch at him.

'It is no matter, my heart, I do not believe him,' he said, pushing me aside. 'That is the cup, Medraut, "black with poison"?'

'My lord,' said Medraut, now disconcerted and off balance, 'do you mean to risk...'

'I am taking no risk. Give it to me. As I am your lord and emperor, give it here.'

Slowly, staring at him in amazement, Medraut gave him the cup. Arthur stood a moment holding it, his eyes terrifying, the amethyst on his finger burning deep purple against the bronze.

'My lord,' I said again, trying to stop him. But his foot moved under the table and stepped on mine, hard, though he did not look at me.

'Your cup of poison, Medraut,' he said, 'is nothing but a cup of lies and cheap gossip. And I put no more credence in it than I do in any of the tales told here in Camlann, by which your brother is made to be a traitor, and I a weak fool led about by my scheming wife. So!' He set the cup to his lips. I tried to scream, found all sound frozen in my throat. Arthur drank slowly, his hand completely enveloping the bronze; he raised his other hand to the cup as well, as though he found it heavy, but he drained it and set it empty down on the table. I clutched the table's edge until my fingers ached.

'There is nothing whatever wrong, Medraut,' Arthur said in a level voice, smiling into Medraut's fury and confusion, 'neither with the mead nor with my wife's honour. Your joke was savage and not at all amusing. You have my leave to go. Taliesin!' The chief poet bowed. 'Some music. I do not care what, anything to keep these drunken fools quiet.'

Taliesin struck his harp and Arthur resumed his seat, still watching Medraut with a cold smile. Medraut continued to stare back, pale with shock, for a moment – then began to laugh, loudly, over the music. Still laughing, he bowed low and left the Hall. Arthur snapped his fingers and handed the empty cup to a servant. 'Some more mead,' he ordered, and the servant bowed and hurried off.

'My lord,' I whispered.

'Silence!' he hissed, under his breath.

'Arthur, it was poisoned. I poisoned it. Get Gruffydd, quickly, and some emetics. It's not too late . . .'

'I didn't drink it. Do you understand? I only swallowed a mouthful or so; the rest I poured up my sleeve. Look!' He turned his right arm over, under the table, and I saw that the inner sleeve of his tunic was soaked with the sweet mead. Then I remembered a trick he had showed me once, a way to avoid drunkeness at some other ruler's feast: a trick of holding the cup high along the rim and pouring most of its contents over the palm and up one's sleeve.

I could feel the tears beginning, and I coughed to control them and the choking in my throat. 'But . . .'

'For God's sake, smile, pretend it was only a vicious joke. Eternal God, you don't want them to suspect, do you? Come, now pretend that you are giggling against my shoulder with relief . . . there.'

I pressed against him. The mead on his tunic sleeve was soaking into my gown, and I made a mental note to check that it did not show before I stood. I knew that Arthur was smiling, but as I pressed by head against his shoulder I could feel the bitter rage in him, the anger at betrayal, and I had to fight even harder to control the waves of hysterical relief and of grief.

I saw that the remains of the feast were disposed of before I went back to our house that evening. The feast went on till late, so it was very late when I returned to the house. Clouds skidded over the stars, and the fortress was very silent, except for the rustling of the wind in the thatch. The house was an oasis of lamplight: gold spilled over the swept hearth with its bright tiles, the smoke-stained wall; the inner door, then the bed with its yellow and white woollen coverlet, and the worn hanging oil lamp of red clay. Arthur was waiting, standing by the book rack, still wearing his purple cloak. The dragons worked onto its collar gleamed. His face was closed to me as it had never been closed before, and his eyes were bitterly cold.

'Sit down,' he commanded, indicating the bed. I sat, too tired and grieved to speak. 'You tried to murder my son.'

I swallowed, swallowed again. I could not reply.

'Was it hemlock?' he asked. 'Where did you get it? Purchased from some townsman? Or did you brew it yourself?'

'Gruffydd the surgeon keeps it to treat fevers,' I told him, finding my voice low and unexcited. 'I stole some from him.'

'Then he knows nothing of it? Good. Did you tell anyone else?'

'No one.'

Arthur sat down on the other end of the bed. I saw that he was shivering. I longed desperately to go to him and hold him, but I could not. Again, it was a question of sitting and waiting. 'Good,' he repeated. 'How he knew the cup was poisoned must be a mystery, then, for I would never have noticed the taste. At least he cannot produce anyone to confirm his story. We will not be publicly disgraced, and he has been made ridiculous. I can even send him away now. I could charge him with treason – but that would cause more problems that it would solve.' He stopped, stared at me again, and then the coldness broke and his face twisted with pain. 'In God's name, Gwynhwyfar, why?'

'You know why!' I cried back, as though I were pleading with him. But I would not plead, I would not say, 'I did it for you and for Camlann' – that would make it no less evil, and be shameless begging.

'But it is infamous, it is tyrannical! It is the act of a coward, a sorcerer, a scheming woman; it dishonours all of us.'

'It only dishonours me. And I am a woman, Arthur. I knew what I was doing, and what you would think of it. Perhaps I believe the same myself: nonetheless I thought it worth it, and still I wish I had succeeded.'

Just for an instant something leapt behind his eyes, and I saw that I had misjudged his anger. It was not that he was angry that such a thing had been attempted in his Hall, but that he also wished it had succeeded, and the recognition of that wish in himself was a bitter shame to him. He saw that I saw, and we stared at each other for a long moment in complete, tortured understanding. Then Arthur stood again and drew his cloak more closely around him, still shivering. 'You,'he said slowly, 'you, a would-be murderess. A wicked stepmother. Oh, they will tell tales of this, to be sure.' His teeth began to chatter, and he struck the wall with his fist, then knocked over the pot of wild roses on the bedside table, spilling water and flowers onto the polished wood. He struck them, again and again, crushing the roses and driving their thorns into his hand. I watched, horrified, unable to speak. He stopped and looked back at me, his fingers tightening and loosening in the water on the desk top. 'I almost drank it. I could not believe such a thing of you. Of anyone else, yes, but not of you. Oh, the devil take this chill!'

I realized what the chill was and jumped up abruptly. 'Arthur, it is the hemlock. How much did you drink?'

'I told you. No more than one or two mouthfuls. Enough to feel the cold, but not enough to do harm ... stay away.' I stopped in the middle of the floor. 'I have had enough of your tender care for tonight, my lady.'

'Arthur,' I said. The tears I had checked earlier leapt into my eyes; I could not stop them. 'Arthur, forgive ... I can't ask that. I am sorry, I wish I had drunk that cup. You are cold; please let me help. Oh, it was evil, I know it was, only, please ... you know I love you.'

He did not answer. He turned away, cradling his bruised hand and still shivering. 'Go to sleep,' he commanded in a harsh voice. 'We must not give them one shred of confirmation of their tale. Medraut may hint that I did not drink it, but we will not give him any evidence. Go to bed. I wish to God I had drunk that cup. It would make the world very much easier to endure. Got to sleep! And for God's sake, stop crying.'

I undressed silently, swallowing the tears. Only when I had climbed into the bed did he turn back, put out the lamp, take off his boots and climb in beside me, still fully clothed. He lay with his back to me, shivering, and I lay looking up at the thatch, trying not to cry. The night hours crept by more slowly than sails creep along the far horizon of the world; more slowly than a slug crawling across the petals of a rose.

After an eternity of misery I judged by Arthur's breathing that he was asleep, and slid close to him, putting my arms about him to warm him. In sleep he did not pull away, but moved his head against my shoulder. But when the grey dawn came in under the eaves, and I was at last beginning to drowse, Arthur woke, threw off my arms, and stamped off into the outer day. Then I curled up in the empty bed, with my head against my knees, and wept, wept bitterly because I had hurt Arthur where no one else could comfort him, forfeited my title to his love and my soul's salvation, and had, after all of it, gained nothing at all.

Four

I was determined to act just as usual the day after the feast, since to do anything else would give an occasion for more rumours; I therefore kept to the schedule I had set, leaving the house at midmorning to speak with some freeholders of the fortress about the crops they were growing in the surrounding fields. I had Gwyn called to make notes of the amounts of grain the farmers expected. The boy was anxious, inattentive and distressed throughout the interview, and I was probably not much better. I had a bitter headache all that day – it comes of too much weeping. But I had long years of experience behind me which Gwyn lacked: I did not have to think hard to ask all the appropriate questions and give all the appropriate congratulations and condolences. I may even have smiled at the farmers, though my heart was far away from any such mask-like smile.

I finished the business with the freeholders and dismissed them and Gwyn as well, telling the boy to make a fair copy of the amount of grain expected that harvest and to put it in one of my account books. The farmers bowed and filed off, but Gwyn hesitated. He began to walk away, then turned and ran back. He dropped to his knees beside my chair and clasped my hand.

'It was a foul lie, noble lady, and no one of any sense believed it,' he told me fiercely. 'And everyone expects that Medraut will be charged with defaming the imperial majesty and exiled. Is he going to be exiled?'

'The Emperor will probably dismiss him from Camlann,' I said stolidly, then, forcing a rather wan smile, 'thank you, Gwyn.'

He pressed my hand to his forehead, then again walked off, swinging his wax tablet and scowling savagely. I felt worse than ever at his misplaced trust. It deepened the shame. And yet the words of false comfort were echoed by others. Goronwy, now recovered from the duel, came up to me at the midday meal on some pretext and explained in a loud voice how nasty the joke was and how he hoped that Medraut would be charged with treason. I was glad that he seemed finally to have broken from Medraut and his faction, but I wished he'd had better cause.

But in the afternoon I saw Gwalchmai, and the conversation was a rather different one.

I wished to check the amounts of grain which Gwyn had noted down that morning against some other accounts, and discovered that the boy had not finished his fair copy. I went in search of him to get from him the original wax tablets, and found him in the yard behind the stables. He and Gwalchmai were teaching Gwalchmai's roan mare how to behave in battle and Gwalchmai was teaching Gwyn the same. This had somehow become a regular pattern of affairs, and seemed to give a great deal of pleasure to both Gwalchmai and Gwyn, though some of the other boys in the fortress objected to Gwyn all the more strongly for having a friend among the great warriors. Nonetheless Gereint as a riding-master and the mule-like chestnut gelding as mount had gradually been superseded for Gwyn by Gwalchmai and the roan mare. When I came up, Gwyn was standing in the middle of the yard holding a whip, while Gwalchmai rode the mare around him in a wide circle. They had finally arrived at the stage of picking up the ring.

'Now,' Gwalchmai was saying, 'this time I will keep her at the canter. If she falters while I'm out of the saddle, don't use the whip unless you have to. Shout at her first: she knows now what that means.'

Gwyn nodded gravely, and Gwalchmai touched the horse to a canter. She was a beautiful animal, the offspring of one of Gereint's horses by Gwalchmai's war stallion Ceincaled, and she could run as lightly as a deer. Gwalchmai rode her about the circle once, Gwyn turning on his heel to follow them, then dropped his head down beside the mare's neck, his weight shifting to his right side, one hand clasping at once the reins and her mane. Her ears flicked back as he whispered something to her, but she did not break her pace. Gwalchmai drew his left leg up, hooking his knee around the cantle of the saddle, and seemed abruptly to fall. The mare faltered; Gwyn shouted and she recovered. Gwalchmai, suspended upside-down, snatched at the ground with his right arm, his fingers trailing a moment in the grass, then, somehow, miraculously, he

96

was upright in the saddle again, laughing and holding between thumb and middle finger a gold ring. He tossed it in the air, checked the mare and rode over to Gwyn at a trot.

"So much for what my brother Agravain used to call a trick fit only for tumblers at a fair.'

'My lord, it is beautiful!' Gwyn said warmly. 'Gereint has to try two or three times at the least, and he can't do it so ... so ...'

'Can't he? He must be growing old. He used to do better than that. Here, you try it now.' He jumped from the saddle, taking the bridle and handing Gwyn the ring. Gwyn took it, stood a moment patting the mare's shoulder and whispering to her, then vaulted into the saddle. He gathered the reins and looked about, and only then saw me. His face fell.

'Noble lady,' he called. 'Do you want me now?'

I hesitated. I did not want to stand about telling lies to Gwalchmai, but I could not find it in myself to drag Gwyn away at that moment. 'You can come when you've finished with the ring,' I returned. 'It's only the list of crops.'

Gwyn nodded, happy again, but Gwalchmai looked at me seriously. 'My lady,' he said, 'perhaps you would care to stay a moment and watch?'

Again I hesitated, then, because the uncertainty looked ill, came across the yard and joined them, though I wished I could put off the lying until tomorrow or the next day or week. 'Will I be in your way here?' I asked.

'Indeed not,' replied Gwalchmai, 'but stand on my left, for I may need to use the whip if Seagull here forgets to keep her pace steady.' He clucked his tongue to the horse, who pricked her ears forward, then flicked them back again to listen to Gwalchmai. The boy smiled proudly and turned the horse, walking her to the circle already worn into the grass of the yard.

'Shall I put the ring down here?' he called to us.

'Even so. But take your time, and be certain that it is the most comfortable distance.'

Gwyn nodded, and, after a moment's solemn concentration, turned the mare and walked her around the circle to see if the distance was indeed agreeable.

'My lady,' said Gwalchmai in a low voice, 'Last

night . . .' he hesitated, looking at me, his dark eyes unreadable.

'It was a vicious joke,' I said, steeling myself.

He looked away again quickly. 'So Medraut himself now says, and so the fortress repeats, if uncertainly. Medraut hints at deeper things even while he denies them. And yet Arthur drank the cup and is unharmed, though some claim it for a miracle that he is so.'

'Medraut among them?'

'No, my lady.' Gwalchmai looked back to me. 'I heard that from Gruffydd the surgeon. He said it in secrecy, to me only.'

'Gruffydd? But he . . . I thought him Medraut's enemy.' I stopped myself, turning away and struggling for composure. Gwyn had completed the circle, and now was hooking his knee about the cantle and carefully practising the first stages of the drop, the ring clasped in his hand.

'He is Medraut's enemy. He thinks that to poison my brother would be an honourable, even a heroic action. He told me that if such had indeed been your plan, it was a sensible and a courageous one, and he wished it had succeeded. And he told me that he'd noticed some hemlock missing from his stores. All this was in strict privacy, of course. Gruffydd knows how to hold his tongue.'

Gwyn made the drop from the saddle, set the ring down on the grass, then rose again in a movement already filed smooth by practice. He turned to Gwalchmai, beaming, and Gwalchmai nodded. Gwyn touched the mare to a trot.

"Take your time," Gwalchmai shouted to him. 'If you hurry or hesitate from uncertainty the move is ruined.' Gwyn nodded.

'Why are you telling me this?' I asked in a whisper.

'My lady . . . my lady, I pity my brother Medraut. Once . . . once he was something like Gwyn. It has cut deep to see him so twisted, and living in such hatred. If I knew that one of my friends had felt compelled to poison him, I would . . . it would grieve me. And yet, I can understand it. Perhaps it is even what Gruffydd said, sensible and courageous. I am not a ruler: I cannot say.'

'Gwalchmai . . .' I began, and could think of nothing to add. He looked at me, waiting, the same grave look in his eyes, and finally I recognized the expression as compassion.

'My lady, I know that you would not resolve on such a thing lightly, or without anguish, or desire it from any but the purest motives. Now that it has failed ... Hai! Back, there!' – for Gwyn had tried the move, and the mare had slowed to a trot when he dropped from the saddle. She broke into a canter again, and the boy struggled upright, looking glum.

'I didn't get the ring,' he told Gwalchmai.

'On the first try. You yourself, cousin, said that Gereint must try two and three times at the least, and would you, scarcely more than a puppy, be a finer rider than he? Come, try again ... my lady,' lowering his voice again, 'whatever has happened, I am your friend and servant, as ever.'

'My brother and lord,' I replied, 'Gwalchmai, that I am not Medraut's murderess is due only to your brother's fore-knowledge and Arthur's quick thinking, for the one refused the cup and the other poured it down his sleeve. But at heart I am as guilty as I would be if I had succeeded in killing your brother, and still, I wish I had. I am sorry. I deserve nothing from you, not your friendship or your service, and certainly not this kindness.'

'You have deserved my love and obedience for many years and many things done. And I said that I understood why you should wish it. I do not bear the responsibility of Empire, so it is not mine to judge whether the plan was just. I would have opposed it if I had known of it, even to warning Medraut – though probably he has inherited sorcery enough to have foreseen it on his own. And he is well acquainted with poisons, able to protect himself from them. As it is, the attempt failed, and you do not bear the guilt of it.' He stopped, watching, as Gwyn again dropped for the ring, got his timing wrong and snatched at it too late, almost fell as he twisted around reaching for it, and rose unsteadily back into the saddle empty-handed. 'No matter, cousin,' Gwalchmai called. 'She is running better now. Try again!' – then, in the low voice, 'My lady, do not feed on the darkness and grief. Your strength is needed now. The very greatest of rulers have planned worse things, and carried them out as well. Think of the Roman High Kings our lord Arthur so admires ... what does Arthur say of this?'

'He knew nothing of it,' I said quietly. 'I never dared to

tell him. I knew he would oppose it.'

He looked at me evenly for a moment, and I had to continue, 'I have hurt him. Perhaps he will never love me again.'

He still looked at me, in open disbelief.

'He has reason! I plotted murder behind his back. I betrayed him – I betrayed his trust in my honour. And I have dishonoured him in his own eyes, forcing him into lies and empty gestures, trying to carry out something he half wished done but would never have attempted.'

'I cannot believe he hates you. His first thought was to protect your name.'

'No,' I replied, wearily, my dry eyes aching again at the thought. 'He wished to refute Medraut and to preserve us – Camlann, the Empire. Not me. And that is as it should be.'

'I do not think . . . och, well done, *mo chara*!' for Gwyn had dropped triumphantly upon the ring, and now turned the mare back holding it glowing and victorious in his hand. He slid from the sweating horse and gave it to Gwalchmai with a bow.

'Did you see me, noble lady?' Gwyn asked hopefully.

'Indeed I did. It was beautifully done, Gwyn.'

He smiled with delight, stood for a moment as though bursting with something to say or shout, then restrained himself and asked, 'Shall I fetch the lists now, noble lady, and the account books?'

He had his eyes fastened on me, and Gwalchmai gave me the same questioning look, one hand on the mare's bridle; the two sets of eyes equally dark.

'You can stable the horse first,' I told Gwyn, knowing that this was what they wanted. 'Even I know that is a rider's first concern. When you're finished, bring the list and the books to my room.'

Gwalchmai smiled very gently, then took my hand and touched it to his forehead, the same gesture that Gwyn had used, but used far differently, filling me with a terror of it: knowing what he knew, and still subjecting himself to me. That he knew set me free, that he remained my friend . . . but I had never had any right to friendship, his or anyone else's; no one can have. That was freedom too, if a bitter freedom where I ceased to matter and existed only in another's nobility. I was grateful, more than I could say.

'Many thanks for your kindness, lady,' said Gwalchmai. 'If you wish to speak further, I am your servant, as ever.'

I nodded and left the two of them to discuss the mare and Gwyn's riding, the fair head and the dark bent over the horse's sleek back.

Arthur that day gave Medraut the command to leave Camlann. He did not charge him with anything, but simply wrote out a letter to the effect that Medraut was relegated to the Orcades, and that all persons reading this letter were to offer him assistance to his journey. Arthur then took Bedwyr and Cei to Medraut at his house and presented him with this document. Medraut greeted them with smiling courtesy, unrolled and read the letter, and pretended astonishment. Cei told me of it afterwards. 'He said, "For what crime am I being exiled?" as though he'd never heard of such a sentence and couldn't think of anything he might have done, except perhaps it was throwing stones at cattle. But our lord would have none of it. "Because of your royal blood and your position," he says, "you have not been charged with any crime, although you have read enough history to remember that defaming the majesty of the emperor is a capital charge, and that offering deliberate insult to the emperor's wife is defaming the imperial majesty. However, I am bringing no charges. Moreover, you are not being exiled, but relegated: your property and your rank in Britain are secure, together with all your rights and privileges except that of staying here. You may leave tomorrow. Take as many horses as you want, and if you need fresh mounts, you can request them from the kings of Britain." Medraut began to protest his shining innocence, but our lord Arthur went on and said, "Cei will go with you," and I grinned at him, and he went quiet. My lord Arthur had just told me the same, my lady, and much as I dislike that eel Medraut, I'll be glad enough to be able to keep my eye on him. And it will be good to see Agravain again, however much he has changed these last years. But, my lady, you should see to it that Medraut cannot take all that Arthur has offered him for travelling expenses. He has poured out the gold as though Medraut were an allied king, and not the next thing to a criminal.'

'Of course,' I replied, 'Medraut's friends are angry enough that their leader is sent away without a trial. If he has been obviously well treated, he can claim less indignation from them and from the kings of Britain. And with you beside him, he cannot use the journey to further his intrigues.'

Cei grunted.

The two did indeed leave the next morning, with an escort of three others who would accompany them as far as Ebrauc, where Medraut and Cei would take ship for the Islands. I worried continuously until we heard that they had actually arrived: worried whether Medraut would start some trouble along the way; whether he would goad Cei into a fighting a duel; whether Cei would start a duel on his own – he was a lover of fighting – and, killing some northern nobleman, be killed by some northern king. But the journey passed apparently without incident, and a short note in Cei's own laborious lettering informed us that the pair had reached Dun Fionn in the Islands. By then, though, I had other things to worry about.

The first few weeks after the attempted murder were even worse than the weeks before it. Arthur, though in public as attentive to me as ever, in private could not bring himself even to speak with me. Silence grew between us; at night in bed we lay side by side as though we had the full half of the world parting us. In the morning I would wake and find Arthur watching me with a set, haggard face, and when I sat down at my mirror I would find the answering expression of guilt and misery still fixed on me. I had to smooth it away carefully before I could face the world. I hated the pretence of innocence, hated it more and more as the days went by and the wild speculations of the fortress gradually gave way to fresh affairs and new gossip. At first, of course, every possible explanation was put forward by someone or other: I had poisoned the cup, but Arthur was miraculously preserved; Medraut had poisoned the cup, to incriminate me, but Arthur either cunningly disposed of the poison or was miraculously . . . or the cup was unpoisoned, but I, or Medraut, had been deceived into thinking otherwise by Arthur, or Medraut, or some other party. Some people even believed our official explanation, that it was a joke with treasonous overtones. Some friends of Medraut's even guessed the truth. And all the interpretations of what had happened were endlessly discussed and argued, while I went about my business, trying to appear unconscious of it all, as though nothing whatever had happened. At times I wanted to stand up in the Hall and shout the truth at them, simply to be free of the endless, unspoken questions. But eventually all possible explanations had been searched out and found, and the frenzied questioning calmed. Medraut's departure had lessened much of the tension. Without his presence there to inspire them, many of his former followers began to think for themselves, and to decide that he had gone beyond the limit. This became apparent when, despite all the initial questioning and arguing, there were no more duels, and fewer quarrels. I worked very hard at convincing some of Medraut's waverers to distrust their exiled leader, and the more successful I was, the more I hated myself afterwards. My life was a lie, like my smiles, and I wished heartily that I had never come to Camlann, but married instead some fat farmer in the North and died bearing him fat babies. The heroines of songs are fortunate, able to die from grief or shame. In reality one is able to bear much more misery and suffering than would seem even likely. When one cares nothing for life, when all the world seems one great, corrupting falsehood, and even love seems shallow and pointless – still the hours grind steadily on and one continues to arrange their details. The most I could manage was a fever.

We had heavy rains in July, but at the end of the month a period of hot, sunny weather, which filled the air with fevers. I came down with one, lay in bed for a day or so, then, feeling better, got up and tried to begin the preparations for the harvest. This, of course, brought the fever on again, and more fiercely, and I was forced to go back to bed. As soon as I was able I had Gwyn called and dictated letters and accounts to him – the harvest season takes no account of human infirmity. Near the end of the second week of August Bedwyr came, asking what supplies of grain would be available for feeding the cavalry horses that winter.

I had not spoken to him since that feast. I had learned from Gwalchmai that Bedwyr knew the true story. He had been close enough to notice Arthur's trick with the cup, and had afterwards spoken to Arthur about it. What Arthur had said to him and he to Arthur was something I did not like to think about: it made me ashamed before both of them. I wished, more than ever, to avoid Bedwyr, but as warleader his responsibilities overlapped with mine in many areas, and I could not avoid him for ever.

At that time I was able to sit up in bed, and in fact felt recovered, though I did not dare go out for fear of bringing the fever on again. But I had dressed, and even had the bed moved so as to get the best light for reading. I was checking through some accounts Gwyn had left for me when I heard the muffled sound of a knock at the outer door. I called 'Come in,' and, after the inevitable pause, 'in here!' But I was surprised when it was Bedwyr who opened the inner door and stood in the threshold, pausing to allow his eyes to adjust to the light.

'Noble lord,' I said in greeting. Despite my desire to avoid him I was glad to see him standing there, looking as he always did, plain and sombre. He looked away from my gaze, however, and at this I became embarrassed as well, tense, uncertain how to receive him.

He turned the sideways look to a bow an instant too late for it to be convincing, and closed the door behind him. 'My lady. I am sorry to trouble you while you are ill, but no one else seems able to tell me how much grain we are likely to have this winter, or how many horses we can feed on it.'

'Oh,' I said. 'Oh yes.' I fumbled through the accounts, hoping to find the answer and be rid of him, then realized that I did not have any of the necessary lists by me, and struggled to remember what they said.

Bedwyr noticed my confusion and added quickly, 'It is not urgent. I need to know soon, for next week I wish to send the horses we will not keep here up to the winter pasturage. But I do not have to know today.'

'I think we will have enough for two thousand horses,' I told him. 'Or a little more: say, three horses for each member of the warband. But I cannot be more specific than that just now. I can probably send you some slightly better estimate by tomorrow afternoon.'

He nodded, but, instead of taking his leave, stood looking at me. 'God speed your recovery, my lady,' he said after a moment. 'You are much missed.'

'I am nearly recovered now,' I said, trying to smile. But the smile was a failure. Bedwyr was not a stranger, not someone to be easily fooled by tensing a few muscles in the face. Indeed, it was easier to conceal a grief from Arthur than from his steady eyes. I felt worn and wretched, and I could see that he knew it, and felt my face growing hot for shame at my lies, my many lies. But I could not bear speaking with him honestly, tasting his anger and bitterness as well as Arthur's. 'I may be up and about tomorrow,' I finished hurriedly.

'Do not press yourself too hard, my lady. Much depends on you.'

There was another minute of silence while we looked at each other and I wished desperately that he would go and leave me to my misery. Then he added, deliberately, 'Our lord Arthur misses your help.'

I looked away hastily. This gentleness where I had expected scorn confused me. 'Does he?' I asked, trying for a tone of uninterested inquiry but sounding merely flat and bitter. This additional piece of stupidity, my lack of self-control, disgusted me. I bit my lip, having to blink at tears: they come far too easily after a sickness.

At this Bedwyr took two rapid strides towards me and caught my hand. 'Lady Gwynhwyfar.' He dropped to his knees so as not to stoop over me, 'Forgive my presumption in speaking thus to you, but I must speak. Your husband loves you deeply, even if now he is bitter against you. We have spoken together since Medraut's exile, and it is as plain to see as the wide heavens. He longs for some words which would reconcile him to you again, but he does not know what to say. I beg you, my lady, do not grieve yourself so. Speak to him, make the reconciliation. You have more skill at such things then he does, and it will console you both.'

I pulled my hand away, biting my lip until I tasted blood.

'Why are you saying this to me? I have broken all the laws that you and Arthur live by in the name of your own goal, and thus betrayed you. And I can repent neither to Arthur nor even to God, because I still wish I had succeeded and that Medraut were safe in Hell. So how can I make a reconciliation with Arthur? And you, you must despise me as well. Do not lie to me, Bedwyr. I am sick of lies; I would prefer your hatred to more of them.'

He met my eyes a moment with an expression of shock,

then bowed his head almost to the bed. 'My lady,' he whispered, 'how could I hate or despise you? If what you had done had been a hundred times worse, still your grace and goodness would force me to love you, even against my will, and . . .' he broke off abruptly, staring at the coverlet, his hand clenching among its folds. I touched his shoulder in wonder and he looked up, and my heart came into my throat at that look.

'Do not,' he resumed after a pause, 'do not believe that your lord despises you. He is the more troubled because he so loves and honours you – and because he fears Medraut, and is himself ashamed because he begot Medraut and now wishes him dead. He is as bitter with himself as with you. Believe me, for I would not lie about this even to please you.'

I began to cry in earnest at this, and then sneezed and had a coughing fit, for my fever had left me with a cold. Bedwyr handed me one of the cloths by the bedside, sitting down on the bed as he did so. I wiped my face and blew my nose, managed to check the tears.

'I am sorry, Bedwyr. I always seem to cry when you are kind to me. If Arthur feels as you say he does, why doesn't he tell me so himself? No, you said that he hopes for some miracle to reconcile us. To console us both. And I am to produce this reconciliation? Lord God of Heaven, must I really lie to him, and say that I repent when I have not, and tell him I am glad that Medraut lives?' I called on God, but I was looking at Bedwyr, at his dark, compassionate eyes.

'You need only say that it would have been wrong, my lady. That I know you do believe. He cares more to have you back than to prove the rights and wrongs of the case.'

I laughed bitterly, coughed, found another cloth. 'Ah, is that all? And do you think it will be that simple, that I can simply say a few words and make all well again? No, I am sorry. Your advice is, as always, good, true, and difficult to follow. My friend, my heart, I thank you. But can you justify even to yourself this crime I have attempted – although you treat me with such kindness?'

His face was tense and strained, but his eyes were alight, intense, very warming to me after so much cold misery. 'I do not much care for such justifications. You acted from excess of love, to protect the realm at all costs. How can I say you were wrong? To be sure, I know it is evil to poison a man. But to justify or to condemn you – that is beyond me. And the thing was not done. Moreover, it has been bitter to me to watch you, seeing you conceal your grief and knowing that it devours you within.' He reached out for my hand again, touched it to his lips. 'Gwynhwyfar, I know that you have condemned yourself, but no one has the right to condemn but God, who alone can weigh the heart. Sweet lady, be merciful to yourself also.'

'Go on as though I had done nothing, as though it were unimportant, complacently awaiting the Last Judgement?'

'What else is there to do, except die? We must live with our sins. One chooses between evils and endures that choice. I . . . I once decided that it was evil to kill, even in battle. Arthur showed me that it can be evil not to act, when action might save something of value, even if the action includes killing. I agreed. But they are still there, all those deaths; I can clean the blood from my sword, but from my heart, never. All those men I have killed for the sake of the Empire, for the sake of the Light, are as dead as if I had killed only for hatred or to prove myself a better warrior than them. But you have never killed anyone.'

I shook my head, staring at him. His soberness was gone. For once the passion was on the surface, and with it the pain. He leaned forward, clutching my hand hard, leaning upon the stump of his shield-hand. 'It is easier than you would expect. It makes little impression, at the time. Afterwards, afterwards, one remembers it and feels differently about it. But the only alternative we have had is to allow others to be killed, and if that leaves no blood on a sword, it must leave more on the soul before God. What you have done – what you meant to do – must count for less in Heaven than the crimes I know I have committed, the deaths and the maimings and pain, the widows and children starving after their men's deaths, the burned fields and plundered towns – all done with this hand.' He pulled it from my fingers and held it before me: his sword hand, calloused from the sword, the spear and the reins, scarred on the back from practice matches and the hazards of war. He regarded it with a degree of pain and horror that tore my heart. I caught the hand and kissed it. He looked at me as though he had forgotten I was there, as though he had never seen me before. He drew his fingers along my lips, touched the tears that were still on my cheek, smoothed back my hair; caught hold of my shoulder. He leaned forward and kissed me.

I meant, at every moment of the next hour, to stop it: to say, 'No more.' But I did not. It was sweet, so very sweet that I wished always just one more minute of it, before returning to the cold and the loneliness and the futile longing for Arthur, the shame and tension and approaching dark. No doubt Bedwyr meant to stop it, also, but he too said nothing. Neither of us said anything until it was over and we lay side by side, knowing we had betrayed Arthur and everything we lived for. Then I turned towards the wall and began to weep again.

Bedwyr raised himself on his elbow and stroked my hair and shoulder, whispering, 'Hush. It is my fault, all my fault. Hush.'

'No, no. Mine. Oh, why did we?'

'My lady, my most sweet lady, I love you. I have always loved you. I told myself otherwise when I saw that my lord also loved you, but I could not believe that for ever. I have wanted this for such a long time . . . I should never have come here. You were sick and grieving and could not help it. It is my fault.' The gentle hand slipped lower and I shivered. I sat up abruptly and looked at him.

'It does not matter whose fault it was. Arthur must not know. It would hurt him too much. And we must never do this again.'

He stared at me for a moment, then turned away. He sat up and swung his legs over the side of the bed. 'You are right. Oh, Heavenly God!' He bent over with pain, clasping the stump of his shield arm. 'What have I done? My lord's wife, in his own bed – '

'We must not do it again!' I said, more urgently. 'You must go somewhere far away, until we have forgotten this a little, and until I am reconciled with Arthur.'

He nodded, keeping his back to me, still bent over double. The grey light through the eaves fell along his back, picking out a long scar which ran up from his right side. Arthur had similar scars. All cavalry fighters have them ; they cannot fight and defend themselves at the same time.

'It is my fault, too,' I told Bedwyr.

He shook his head, still without looking round.

'I love you,' I said. The words seemed meaningless. 'I love Arthur, but you, as well.'

He reached down, fumbled about for the breeches thrown aside not long before. He pulled them on, then, standing again, turned and looked at me. He had to hold them up because he could not fasten his belt with one hand; in a tale it would have made me laugh. But his eyes were very dark with the pain, and the skin drawn tight around his mouth.

'You must go to Arthur,' I said, thinking desperately. 'Ask him to send you to Less Britain, to talk to King Macsen. He needs to send someone, and he is determined not to send Gwalchmai again.'

Some of the pain ebbed. 'Yes,' he said, after a minute. 'I knew Macsen when I served his brother Bran; I could talk to him. Though my lord might be reluctant to allow me to leave for any length of time . ... but I could urge business, a desire to see my family and look to the estates. He will certainly give me leave to spend time on that.' He looked around for his tunic, picked it up, pulled it over his head with his shield arm. I got up and fastened his belt for him, then tied the fastenings of his tunic, carefully repeating the knots his servant customarily used. He let me finish, then caught my wrist.

'Gwynhwyfar.' His voice was resuming its usual quiet tone, but shock and confusion gave it still an edge of harshness. 'My lady, you know now that I love you, and am ruined. I have betrayed my lord. I do not even know that I can repent, for I still desire you – but enough of that. If ever this should be discovered, let me suffer for it. It would be a plain case of treason, but my lord would probably commute the sentence from death to exile. I could endure that. I could not endure it if you were made to suffer for my crime, for it is my fault – no, it is true! I swear I would feel your disgrace more than my own. I know that if this is ever discovered you will not escape punishment altogether, but you might escape lightly, if you did not try to intercede for me or shift the blame onto yourself. We would both suffer more if you did. And do not grieve yourself for it; it is my fault.' His struggle for calm failed for an instant and he kissed me once more, hard.

When he released me I said nothing, merely found his sword for him and buckled it on, and helped him on with his boots. Only when he stood in the doorway did I whisper, 'God keep you.' He bowed his head and was gone. I looked at the door for a long minute, then collapsed back onto the bed. I crawled under the blanket and lay there, trembling, remembering, until evening when I fell asleep.

Bedwyr spoke with Arthur that same evening, and set out for Less Britain within the week, despite the fact that he had, by then, come down with my cold. I stayed in the house until he had gone, and by then was recovered enough to get back to work on the harvest.

I worked also on reconciling myself with Arthur. Despite what had happened afterwards, I decided, Bedwyr had been right. I was punishing my husband as well as myself by continuing to wallow in guilt and grief. And it did no one any good at all. A few days after Bedwyr left, I came back from supervising the disposal of a feast's remnants, resolved to speak.

The house was dark when I entered it, carrying the dim rushlight that had shown me the path round the Hall. When I entered the bedroom I saw that Arthur was already in bed, but he flinched as the light fell across him and I knew he was still awake, though he lay with his back to me and did not otherwise move. I knew that he was trying to avoid the pain of the silence between us, and was afraid. I set the light in its holder beside the bed and undressed in silence, wondering what to say, wishing to put it off. Almost, I extinguished the light without speaking. But I sat on the bed a moment, looking at Arthur, and touched his shoulder. 'I am sorry,' I managed to say, hearing how rough and uncertain my voice was. 'It was an evil intention. I am very sorry.' And suddenly I was not thinking of Medraut, but of Bedwyr, lying where Arthur lay now: of the betrayal that was greater than Arthur knew.

He turned, looking up at me strangely – not coldly, but in puzzlement. He caught my hand from his shoulder and looked at it, studying the carving on the signet ring, then looked back at my face. The room was dark, for the rushlight was flickering, almost out. Arthur sighed.

'I am sorry,' I whispered again.

'I know,' he replied. 'But don't you see that it needs more than that? This thing . . . Medraut has crippled us.'

'I wanted us to escape from him.'

He touched my hand to his lips, his eyes seeking mine. 'Oh, my white hart, if only we could! But that, that degrades you. I know you would accept that, for the Empire, but I cannot. And he is mine, my son, my fault.'

'Please,' I said. I could not reason with him; reason meant nothing to what was between us.

He touched my face and stroked back my hair. 'You are cold,' he said, after a moment. 'Here, get into bed and go to sleep.'

He put his arms round me when I was under the coverlet, and I lay very still, not daring to move. My heart was crying for him, but it was a beginning.

The silence vanished slowly. But the harvest is a busy season, and, with Bedwyr away, Arthur and I had to consult each other more than usual. We had first learned to trust each other from the affairs of the Empire: from tribute received and dispatched, from the supplying of a warband, from the plans of kings. These restored our trust. Eventually, even in private, we could speak to each other freely, and even laugh. The last barrier dropped early in December, when Cei returned from the Orcades with the news of Agravain's death.

Perhaps we should have expected it. We had long known that Agravain was unwell, and in my heart I had always been afraid of what Medraut might do in the Islands. Nonetheless, the news came as a shock. Cei brought it fresh: he had sailed from the Islands with the first tide the day Agravain died, and posted from Ebrauc at a pace that must have left a trail of foundered horses behind him. The winds were from the north, very good for the voyage, and so he had made the whole journey in a week and six days. He arrived about midnight on a cold December Saturday and burst into our house at once, shouting that it was urgent. It was snowing a little outside, wet flakes mixed with rain. Cei had ridden from Caer Ceri that morning, changing horses at Baddon, and he was grey-faced with exhaustion and shivering with cold. As soon as Arthur had thrown his over-tunic and cloak on he began building up the fire in the conference room, while I poured Cei some wine and put more on to heat. Cei, however, did not wait to take off his wet cloak or take more than one swallow from the cup before he burst out, 'Agravain is dead. *He* murdered him. That honey-mouthed bastard murdered his brother.'

I almost dropped the pitcher of wine. Arthur froze for a moment, kneeling by the hearth, a piece of firewood in his hand. I know that the fire must have been roaring, the water dripping from the thatch: there must have been sound, but I can remember none, only a great stillness. Then Arthur set the piece of wood on the fire, stood, and pulled a chair closer to it, gesturing for Cei to sit down. Cei did so, unfastening his cloak and hanging it over the back of the chair to dry.

'Now, what happened?' Arthur asked quietly. 'Agravain ap Lot is dead?'

'Near two weeks ago. He was found cold in his bed one morning, with no mark on him. But Medraut had been drinking with him the night before, and Medraut is a devil and a follower of devils, and knows ways of killing men which leave no mark. I'm not the only one that thinks so, my lord: the royal warband of the Islands has always thought as much. They're dogs, those Irish warriors, a pack of curs that will lick the hand of any man that can beat them. They began cringing up to Medraut the moment he arrived, though when Agravain was present they pretended differently.'

'Then the warband supports Medraut, now?'

'Yes, the dogs! Medraut used to lead them, and might have been made king before, had his mother lived, for they were all in terror of their very souls from that witch. They loved Argravain better, for he was his father's son and a man who had fought beside them, but Agravain . . . was no longer his old self.' The furious indignation dropped for a moment, and Cei went on in a strange, hurt voice, unlike his own. 'And what was the worst of it, my lord. It was wormwood to the heart to look at him. He was not himself. I extended my stay to help him – you had that second letter – I tried to warn him against what was happening. He was too drunk, most of the time, to take any notice, and when he was sober he never really cared. That a warrior, a king and a king's son, should be so broken, so terrified and unsure! And he was my friend, a man who was a shield to me in battle, and like a brother to me. Poisoned, in his own home, by a smooth-speaking witch's bastard! God in Heaven! We must have justice for him; we must . . .'

'Hush,' I said.' Tell the full tale, and then rest, for you are overtired. Here, the wine is hot now.'

He set his cup down and I filled it with steaming honeyed wine. He sipped a little, cautious because of the heat, and curled his cold-reddened hands about the sides. 'There is not much more to the tale,' he said, wearily now. 'Agravain was found dead, as I said, the morning after he had been drinking late with Medraut. I woke up to hear them keening and wailing. Some of the royal clan, who hate Medraut though they do not dare say so openly, came to me and told me the news before Medraut did, and helped me to the port and a ship before the day was old. They wished to know what you would do; I said that I was certain that this murder would anger you. They say that they cannot oppose the election of Medraut to the kingship, but that if you wish to contact them you must send a message to Eoghan the shipwright in northern Pictland – I think he is one of their spies. I was glad of their help, my lord, for I had no wish to be on that island when Medraut was king.'

'Is it certain that he will be made king?' asked Arthur.

'No one dares to oppose him. He can have the kingship if he wants it, and it is certain that he does want it. My lord, Emperor of Britain, do we declare war?'

'No.'

When Cei leapt from his chair in anger, Arthur lifted his hand, looking at him. It was the calm look I knew so well, the look with which he commanded something that he hated but considered essential – an execution, a task which would cost the lives of those who did it. Cei also recognized the look and, though he loomed above Arthur, he seemed to shrink before it. Slowly he sat down.

'On what grounds can we declare war?' Arthur asked him. 'Medraut will doubtless give his brother a splendid funeral and mourn extravagantly, then hasten south to swear an alliance with me. We can prove nothing. And if I contact these enemies of Medraut, who neither dare to oppose him openly nor even to be known to have received messages from me, what am I to say? "Murder him, and I will reward you"? That is more shameful than poison, and far less likely to succeed. No. We must prepare, and be ready for whatever Medraut plans next.' He paused, then added in a gentler voice, 'Go to bed, Cei. I will need your strength.'

Cei nodded. He set down his empty cup, stood slowly. Then he stopped, remembering something, and his remembering touched mine.

'He shares a house with Gwalchmai,' I said. 'He should not have to tell this tale to Agravain's brother tonight.'

Cei nodded. 'You have it, my lady; it is bitter news to bring. I sent for Gwalchmai when I arrived, so as to speak only once. I do not know where . . .'

The door opened suddenly and Gwalchmai came in. His face was very calm, but for a moment I could not recognize him, he looked so unearthly and remote. He had plainly been outside for some time, for the snow was melting in his hair and had soaked the shoulders of his cloak. 'Your pardon,' he said, in a voice only slightly roughened, bowing to me and Arthur. 'I have been outside. I was listening. But I guessed what had happened when your messenger woke me, Cei, and I feared to come in. Cousin, it is a long way to the islands, and you had better sleep. No more words. My lord and lady, good night.' He held the door for Cei. Cei, after staring at him for a minute, crossed himself, picked up his own cloak and pulled it over his shoulders, walked out. Gwalchmai gave one more slight bow and slipped back out into the night; there was the faint clunk of the bolt of the door falling back into its place, then silence.

Arthur tore his eyes from the door, then sat heavily in Cei's empty chair and stared at the fire for a long time. I came and sat on the floor beside him. After a while he put his arm around me, and I leaned my head against his thigh. The fire crackled, and the smoke which the snow trapped in the room stung our eyes. 'My heart,' Arthur said at last, 'perhaps you were right, even then.'

'It is evil to poison.'

'But now Medraut has poisoned his brother, my warrior.'

114

'Perhaps it was not so. Agravain had long been ill.'

'And do you believe it was a natural death?'

'No.'

Arthur ran his hand through my hair, then turned my face towards him. 'I am sorry,' he said, in a very low voice. 'And yet, still, it must have been evil; we are no better than our enemies if we do such things. Only I am bitterly grieved for Agravain, and for Gwalchmai, and for us all. Gwynhwyfar, my white hart, it would have been better for you if you had never met me. Then the way of virtue would have been a Roman road, while now ... now we draw furrows on the pathless waves. My joy, I am sorry.'

After that we had to hold each other, for around us was only the silence, the darkness and the wind.

Five

Gwalchmai had loved his brother Agravain. He would have been much afflicted by his death in any circumstances, and that the death was probably caused by his other brother made it worse. I remembered Agravain and Gwalchmai sitting together at table in Camlann, years ago, talking rapidly in Irish: Agravain gold-haired with hot blue eyes, angry, excited over something someone had said to him; Gwalchmai calmer, regarding his brother with patient affection and a touch of amusement. Agravain had always taken a kind of proprietary pleasure in his brother's achievements, and was enormously proud of him; Gwalchmai treated Agravain almost as he might a sensitive child, protectively, defending the occasional outbursts of bad temper and violence – for Agravain always had been quickly moved to anger, overly-sensitive to insult. Yet I had gathered from a few things each had said that once the closeness had been between Gwalchmai and Medraut, with Agravain an outsider, a potential enemy. What Gwalchmai thought now was anyone's guess: he behaved as he always did when troubled, politely refusing to speak of it to anyone and spending most of his time riding his horse or playing the harp and brooding. But when Medraut sent a letter from the Orcades, lamenting Agravain's death and promising to pledge his new kingship to an alliance with Arthur, Gwalchmai asked to be sent to the Islands as an emissary. Arthur sensibly refused. There was no need of it, and Gwalchmai was the last person we could trust to Medraut's good faith. Instead, Arthur replied by letter that the King of the Orcades was welcome to visit Camlann peacefully.

Even before he could have received this letter, Medraut sent another letter saying that he hoped to come to Camlann in the spring or early summer, when he had established his realm in greater security and when it would be easier to travel. Arthur was content to wait until then. He sent a message to Eoghan the shipwright in northern Pictland, to be sent to those of Medraut's cousins who were displeased with their new king. In this he said that he grieved for Agravain, but that Medraut was his nephew and would be received as such. This letter was so worded that it would cause no difficulty if it fell into Medraut's hands, but equally made it plain that, if Medraut were overthrown, there would be no reprisals.

The sentence of relegation which Arthur had passed on Medraut was allowed to sink into oblivion. It had been passed against a private individual, and could not be allowed to obstruct relations with an important allied kingdom. So we waited, knowing that in the spring or early summer the contest would begin again.

It was a strange, bitter-sweet winter. The year was a wet one, with much snow and more rain: the thatching of the Hall and houses grew dark and heavy, and the rooms filled with smoke even with a hot dry fire. But a kind of truce was established in the Family. Medraut as an allied king far away in Dun Fionn was a different man from Medraut a warrior in Camlann, even to his friends. Foreign kings were no concern of the Family, unless they were inclined towards war with us; Medraut had no further claim on anyone's loyalty. Oh, things were not as they had been once, not as they were back in the days of the war, or the first years of the peace, when Camlann had seemed almost a new Rome. Then we knew that we had set ourselves a battle that all the world had lost, and which we were winning. We had fought as no one else had fought, not for power, gold or glory, but to preserve the Light, the Empire: knowledge and justice, law and peace. It had given a kind of exaltation to our lives, even amid hardship, violence and grief. Now the peace was old, familiar, taken for granted, and the battles were all fought; and now hatred and distrust had crept in among us. Yet there were times when it seemed we were still innocent, and all things were possible to us. We held festivals in the Hall, celebrating Christmas and the New Year for days on end. The splendour was greater than it had been during or soon after the war: everything glowed and glittered, and it seemed that the benches even of the lower Hall were afire with jewels. Taliesin sang of great things accomplished, by us and by others, until the men were as dizzy with music as with mead, stunned by the glory of the past and eager to emulate it.

And there were times, too, apart from the great festivals, when Camlann seemed apart from the rest of world, halfway to Heaven: clear winter days when the snow lay thick on the ground, and from my doorway I could see the fields stretching out and away, further even than Ynys Witrin, shining like glass and silver in the light. The children of the fortress would run about shouting and throwing snowballs, and sometimes the warriors would ride their horses about the hill at full gallop for the sheer joy of running, a splendour of plunging hooves, white breath and backflung snow, the jingle of harness and the flash of the rider's smile in passing. Indoors by the smoky fires women sang at the loom, craftsmen at their workbench – or else, gathered together, friends and families laughed and argued. There was not much for me to do; I could join any party gathered for talk or music. Winter is a quiet season: the harvest is gathered and stored, everything checked and inventoried; the tribute all delivered. It is difficult to travel, so there are few petitioners for justice, and any emissaries sent out generally wait until the spring thaws the roads and calms the seas before returning. So I had time, time to spend with Arthur, to listen to songs, to read books purchased from travelling merchants the summer before and lying on the shelf since, waiting my attention. I felt even in the midst of it that this quiet winter was the calm before the storm – but I was resolved nonetheless to make the best of it. And, I told myself, we can very likely weather the storm when it does come. We have some strength here yet.

One of the things that continued to grieve me was Gwalchmai. The festivals of December and January passed, and he remained courteous and remote, brooding over his brother's death. He only seemed to cheer up when he gave lessons to Gwyn.

The boy was now doing very well at Camlann. He had caught up with the other boys of the fortress in knowledge of weapons, and he was beginning to be accepted by them. He was now growing rapidly and always seemed too large for his clothes, but did not, like many boys, lose his sweet temper together with his treble voice.

However, one day in early February, when Gwyn and I were going over the preceding month's accounts in the

Hall, a monk came into the building and looked about as though searching for someone. Gwyn recognized the man at once.

'It's Father Gilla, from Opergelei monastery, near my mother's abbey!' he told me in great excitement, as I eyed the monk dubiously – monastics tended to disapprove of Arthur quite strongly, and it was rare to see one in Camlann on any errand but complaint. 'He must be bringing me some news. Hai! Father Gilla, here I am!'

Gwyn wrote to his mother whenever he could find some trader or traveller who would be going to Gwynedd and could carry the letter. Most travellers were willing to do so, as such a letter would assure them of a night's lodging and provision from the grateful mother. Gwyn had once had a letter back, but that had also been carried by some casual traveller. I had gathered that the boy's mother was angry with her son for running off to learn war against her wishes, and it was because of this that she had not written more often. Never had a messenger been especially sent, and I was suddenly afraid for the boy, the more so when the monk came nearer and I saw his face. Good news goes on two feet, they say, but bad news has wings – and, moreover, good news does not wear an expression like Gilla's.

Gwyn also realized this as the monk came up to us, and his first excitement was replaced by apprehension. 'Why . . . what is the matter?' he asked.

The man looked at me nervously, then let his eyes slide over Gwyn and away. He was a small, fair, wispy man whose plain black robe was worn through at the elbows and patched. He seemed unwilling to speak.

'Has something happened?' Gwyn demanded. 'Is Mama sick? Father, tell me. What is wrong?'

The little man finally looked at the boy directly, then embraced him. 'My child,' he stammered, then, proceeding in a rush, as though to get it over with, 'Gwyn my boy, I have bad news, bad indeed. Your mother . . . she wished me to come, she said, if she . . . she grew sick, three weeks ago, with a fever, and at first she wished you were with her – but you know how it grieved her, that you ran off here, when she meant you for the priesthood – but she said she forgave you, and that it was better, indeed, those were her words, that it was good that you were here . . .'

'Father, what has happened?' Gwyn interrupted. 'She had a fever – is she better?' Gilla blinked at him miserably. 'She . . . she didn't . . . she's not . . .'

'She is dead, child,' the monk said. 'She died a week and five days ago, on a Friday. She gives you her blessing.'

'Oh no,' Gwyn said. He turned from the monk, ignored my outstretched hand, and sat down on one of the benches, leaning his head against his hands.

'It was a rapid fever,' the monk went on, after a moment. 'She stayed up, the first few days, and then she fell down, at dinner, on Epiphany, and took to her bed, and died a few days later. She died very peacefully, after she had written the letter. She was willing to leave this world, and hurry to the next. She blessed you, and wished you all joy . . .' he trailed off again, uncertainly, staring miserably at Gwyn.

'Where is the letter?' Gwyn asked.

'What?'

The boy raised his head. His eyes were too bright, but there were no tears on his face. 'The letter. You said she wrote me a letter.'

Father Gilla flushed. 'No, no, she didn't. That is, she wrote a letter, but not to you. She wrote a letter to the lord Gwalchmai ap Lot, that you said had been kind to you. She sealed it and gave it to me. Perhaps there is another letter with it, inside the seal. We can give it to him now, and see.'

'Oh,' said Gwyn. 'To the lord Gwalchmai. So that he will protect me. No. I . . . I don't want to see anyone now. My lady . . .'

'Gwyn.' I started towards him, longing to put my arms about him, but he threw his hands up between us.

'My lady,' he repeated, 'please look after Father Gilla, and see that he receives hospitality: he is a good man, and not seditious, and notable in his own monastery, and he was always kind to me. Father, please, I will talk with you later, only now . . .' He turned suddenly and ran from the building.

Gilla looked after him, still blinking. 'Poor boy,' he said, 'poor orphaned child. And I cannot go after him, he would never let me, even when he was little.'

'He will want to talk to you later,' I said. 'Father, let me find you a place to rest, and see that you have food and drink. You must be tired after your journey.'

'Indeed, though my poor horse is in greater need of care. Lady, I thank you for your kindness – I do not know your name . . .'

'Gwynhwyfar, daughter of Ogyrfan,' I said and, when he stared, I smiled and went on, 'so you see, I have authority to see that you receive hospitality here, and that your horse is well treated.'

He bowed very low. 'I had not thought it was you, noble queen. I thought queens wore purple and gold; though Gwyn spoke of you often in his letters. I thank your grace. But first I must see the lord Gwalchmai ap Lot, to give him the letter of the lady abbess.'

'Gwyn's mother was an abbess?' I asked, surprised, 'He never mentioned that.'

'But she was a very great abbess! A noblewoman, wise and courageous. She came first to St Elena's fourteen years ago, near her time of bearing Gwyn, and stayed, and took her vows there. She has been abbess four years now, and never was there a finer one.' He paused, recollected himself, and added, 'I must give her letter to the lord Gwalchmai ap Lot. Could you graciously tell me, most noble lady, whether that lord is here now, and where he might be?'

I had happened to notice Gwalchmai practising spear-casting in the yard behind the stables, and I told Gilla as much. I escorted him – and his horse, which he had left tied to a post outside the Hall – to the stables, where I saw that the horse would be cared for; and then to the yard, where I pointed Gwalchmai out to him. Though, indeed, Gwalchmai needed little pointing out. He was casting his spears from horseback, and his white war stallion, famous from a hundred songs, stood out among the other horses like a swan among a flock of geese. Gilla walked out into the yard, waving and calling faintly, then stopped and waited while Gwalchmai threw a few more spears at the target. I began talking with one of the other warriors who happened to be there, telling him about Gwyn, and watching idly while Gwalchmai threw his last spear, turned his horse, cantered over to Gilla and reined in. They talked, I saw from the corner of my eye. I knew that Gwyn's mother had chosen well in deciding to write to Gwalchmai. The warrior would have done much for Gwyn in any circumstances, and the letter would incline him to do more. Still, it hurt me to think of the boy, suffering so, when grief is still new and one is unused to the thought of death. And he was like Gwalchmai in his refusal to accept comfort . . . Gilla had given Gwalchmai the letter, and he was reading it.

Suddenly, the distinct figure on the white horse whirled about and galloped off, leaving Gilla gesticulating wildly. I stared, surprised, for such discourtesy was unlike Gwalchmai. I had not have much time to stare, for the warrior galloped over, the snow flying in great wet lumps from the shining hooves of his stallion. He reined in sharply, and the horse danced, arching its neck and tugging at the bit.

"My lady,' said Gwalchmai, shouting to be heard over the horse's impatience, 'where is Gwyn?'

'Let him be for now,' I returned, 'He has just had the news of his mother's death, and he will no more wish to speak of it than you would.'

'Och, Ard Rígh Mor, I know, I know, but where is he?'

'What is the matter?' I demanded, for Gwalchmai was as agitated as I had ever seen him.

He flourished a roll of parchment. 'This letter . . . for the love of God, my lady, if you know where he is, tell me!'

This frightened me. I don't know what I thought – perhaps that the letter being sent to someone else was a sign to Gwyn that his mother had not, after all, forgiven him for leaving her, and that he might do something dreadful in his despair, and that his mother knew it – I do not know. 'He . . . he sometimes goes to a place in the stables . . . here, I will show you.'

Gwalchmai at once leapt off his horse, helped me up, and jumped up behind me. He touched his heels to the beast and we went flying up the hill, leaving the other warriors, and Father Gilla, gaping after us.

We slid off the horse in the middle of the stables, and Gwalchmai caught the stallion's bridle, then paused and unrolled the letter again. He stared at it, reading a few lines under his breath, then lowered it and looked up at nothing. His horse snorted and nuzzled his hair, and he patted the sleek neck absently.

'What is the matter?' I asked again, less frightened now that I had time to think.

He shook his head. 'This letter . . . my lady, I am glad of your company.' His agitation was less, but he seemed almost afraid. 'For he might hate me, and it might not be true, after all, and almost I fear to ask the question. Where do you think Gwyn is?'

I took the other side of the stallion's bridle and led the horse towards its own stall. Gwalchmai released his hold and followed, clutching the letter. The horse had a box by the west wall of the stables, by one of the ladders that led up into the hay loft, and I opened the door of the stall and let the horse go in and investigate its manger. Gwalchmai closed the door and leaned over the top of it, looking at me expectantly.

'Gwyn comes here, sometimes,' I said in an undertone. 'I've had him summoned from the hayloft, once or twice. Gwyn! Gwyn, are you here?'

There was a rustling noise above us.

'I must speak with you,' Gwalchmai said loudly.

Another rustling, and then Gwyn climbed down the ladder from the loft and stood at its foot. His eyes were red and swollen, and he looked at us with a wordless resentment. I was very glad to see him.

'Please, noble lady, noble lord,' he said, 'I would rather be alone now. It is very kind of you, but I would.'

Gwalchmai stared at him as though fascinated. 'Gwyn,' he said, in a hurried, breathless fashion, 'This letter . . .' he took a few steps towards the boy and stopped, extending the roll of parchment.

'Does she ask you to protect me?' asked Gwyn. 'I am sorry, lord, I know it is presumptuous, and I know I am only a bastard, but I wrote to her about how kind you have been to me, and she must have thought . . . do you mind, then? It is only that she wants someone powerful to protect me. Mothers want that.'

Gwalchmai flushed. 'Yes. Of course. She . . . Gwyn, what was your mother's name?'

'Elidan. Doesn't she sign the letter? She is – was – abbess of St Elena's.'

I heard my own breath catch with a gasp as I at last understood what was happening.

Gwalchmai's hand closed on the parchment, crushed it. He closed his eyes a moment; opened them, looked at the letter. He smoothed it again carefully, as though afraid the parchment would dissolve into the air. "And she came from the North,' he whispered.

'Yes. Does she say that?'

'Not here. She was the daughter of Caw, sister of King Bran of Ebrauc. I knew that she had settled in an abbey in Gwynedd. I saw her there, once, and begged her forgiveness, which she refused me. I saw you as well, I think, but I did not realize that you were her son. Why did you tell me that your mother lived in Elmet?'

Gwyn stared back, thoroughly startled now. 'Because the monasteries in Gwynedd are so seditious, and I didn't want people to know. But my mother wasn't a king's sister.'

'She was. I . . . knew her, then. She has written to me. She wrote this, when she was dying. She forgives me. She says she regrets any pain she gave me – me! who lied to her, and murdered her brother! – and she commends . . . her son to me.' He stopped, his voice breaking on the last phrase. 'She never told me she had a son. I never knew that, Gwyn. You must know, I . . . loved your mother once. It was dishonourably, shamefully: I was sent on an embassy and seduced the sister of my host. Afterwards, when her brother rebelled against my lord, I swore to her that I would not harm him, and then killed him. And I asked her to marry me, but after that she could not. But she never told me that she . . . that we had a son. I am your father. Can you forgive me?'

Gwyn went as pale as the crumpled parchment. He stared at Gwalchmai. Gwalchmai returned the stare for a long moment, then dropped to one knee and lifted his hands in a slight, helpless gesture.

'Most noble lord! Don't!' Gwyn cried. He ran to Gwalchmai, and tried to pull him to his feet. 'Not to me, noble lord!'

Gwalchmai shook his head and stayed as he was. 'You have the right to forgive or condemn me.'

Gwyn fell back a pace, blinking, then said, in a newly calm voice, 'Let me see the letter.'

Gwalchmai handed it to him. The boy stood very straight in the grey light of the stable, reading the letter in a low, clear voice:

'"Elidan, daughter of Caw and Abbess of St Elena's, to Gwalchmai son of Lot. I am dying, it seems, and things which once seemed great to me seem less now. It will not matter to God that I am a noblewoman or that I was strong enough to be unforgiving. I forgive you now for the way in which you wronged me; forgive me also for the pain I have caused you. It would have been better if I had yielded before, and married you – but it is an ill world, and what might have been is only a torment. I commend to you now the child I bore, your son. He was christened after you Gwalchaved, but has all his life been called Gwyn. I wished him to be a priest, but Fate is stronger than I, and it is a year since he went to Camlann, and, so I know from his letters, met you and grows already to love you ..."' Gwyn faltered, flushing, then struggled on, '"Care for him and protect him with a peaceful heart, for I swear before the God I must soon meet that he is your own son and mine, and no one's else. And at last I can be glad that he went to you, for it is right that he know his father, and that you should know him. God's blessing be with you both. Believe that I loved you. Farewell."'

The boy lowered the letter and looked back at Gwalchmai. 'You?' he cried, the forced calm gone, passionate and disbelieving.

Gwalchmai nodded.

'But ... *you*! Anyone else ... did you love her?'

For the first time that I could remember, Gwalchmai's face was open and totally unguarded, vulnerable: drawn with pain and fear, with the bruised look about the eyes that comes from sudden grief. 'I loved her,' he said. 'When I loved her, I did not know how much I loved her. But it was shameful for all that.'

Gwyn looked again at the letter. He bit his lip and began to roll it up. It took a long time; his hands were shaking. 'You,' he said as he did so. 'I never dared even to dream that it might be you. I knew – well, for a long time, I guessed – that she loved ... my father. I remember her saying dreadful things about him when I was little, but she cried sometimes at night, and the other sisters used to whisper about it and say she was still in love. But she would never tell me anything about my father, even when I was older and asked her. I never understood why anyone would leave her. And yet, you didn't marry her.'

'She couldn't marry her brother's murderer. When it was too late I wished to marry her, and she said she would kill herself if I came near her again. And I never knew she had a son.' Silence. 'By the High King of Heaven, can you forgive me?'

Gwyn looked back at him furiously. 'Of *course*. I could forgive *you* anything; I would still forgive you if you hadn't really loved her, if you had done it all on purpose. I've thought you were like St Michael in the missals, treading down the dragons; don't you know that? Only this . . . and she is dead, my mother is dead, and I was not there. I abandoned her to be a warrior, and now she blesses and forgives me, but doesn't write to me. To you, she wrote to you, because . . . because it was you . . .' he broke off, panting for breath and trying to choke off the sobs. Gwalchmai jumped up and caught the boy, and Gwyn began to weep, leaning against his father. Gwalchmai also was in tears. I finally remembered myself, turned, and ran out. The grey outside blurred around me and I raised my hand to find my own face wet. It was wonderful, it was terrible, and still (selfish misery!) Gwalchmai had a son, and I was barren.

Gwalchmai quickly took steps to have Gwyn legitimatized. Unfortunately, his position in his own clan was more precarious than ever. The old charge of kin-murder, which had lain dormant while Agravain was king and chieftain of the royal clan of the Islands, might now at any moment be revived by Medraut. There had been no mention of it in the brief months since Medraut became king, but Gwalchmai could not try to have his son given royal status without risking, and probably losing, his own. However, since he was unmarried, he could declare Gwyn to be his legitimate heir under the laws of the Empire, and thus give him the legal position of his son and Arthur's grand-nephew. Accordingly, a few days after receiving the letter, Gwalchmai formally presented Gwyn to Arthur at a feast, swearing that this was his son, christened Gwalchaved by the mother, Elidan daughter of Caw, and petitioning Arthur to acknowledge him as Gwalchmai's legal son and heir. Arthur asked if any gainsaid this and, when no one did, called the Family to witness that Gwalchaved ap Gwalchmai was henceforward to be considered a nobleman and his own kinsman. In token of this last he cut some of Gwyn's hair, as a godfather would, then told the boy to sit beside his father at the high table. Father and son took their places amid cheers from Gwalchmai's friends, and I poured wine for all the high table. Arthur smiled during this ceremony, as I did, but Gwyn looked very grave. Gwalchmai appeared calm, but watched Gwyn as though afraid that the boy were one of the People of the Hills, and would vanish at cock-crow. Gwyn took a swallow of wine, which he was not used to, and began coughing. He set the glass down, going red, but when he saw how we smiled at him, suddenly smiled back, his whole face flooding with pure joy. He lifted his glass to Arthur and to me.

'He is the sort of son any man would want,' Arthur said that night when we were alone together in our house. 'Gwalchmai is fortunate.'

'Indeed,' I said, sitting by the fire and letting down my hair. 'I shall miss Gwyn's help.'

Arthur smiled, watching me. 'You mean you will miss his company. It will be easy enough to find you another clerk. Children are less easily come by.'

I stopped combing and twisted a lock of my hair about my fingers as though I had found a tangle in it. There were still not many strands of grey there, but a few. Children were certainly less easy to come by. And I suppose to a man a child lost in the sixth month is not really a child. I once felt my son move under my heart, before I lost him, and I knew it was real. But Arthur had been away on campaign then; he had come back as soon as he could afterwards, when I was still very sick, and had tried to comfort me, but even then I could see that he had not understood. Only now, did he understand now?

'Arthur,' I said, 'have you thought of taking another wife?'

He smiled at me. 'Have you died, my white hart? I thought even I would be likely to notice such an event as that.'

'I am not joking. There are other separations than death, and if the Church does not approve of them, still they are well known in custom and law. Many nobles divorce each other. And you are not too old to have a child.'

The smile had vanished altogether. He jumped up, came over and caught my shoulders, crouching so as to look into my face. 'Do not be foolish,' he said harshly. 'Do you want to divorce me?'

I knew his face better than my own: the wide-set grey eyes, the beak of a nose, thin lips in the grey-streaked short beard, the strong lines of it, the rapid changes of expression. I could not meet his eyes as honestly as he met mine, and I lowered my gaze, touching his hands with my own. The depth of thirteen years was between us, the weight of habit, of long trust, fulfilled and betrayed and forgiven; a thousand thousand tiny things, unimportant memories, the customary expectation of what the other would think, say, do, dream. 'No,' I said at last. 'No, of course not. But if there was any hope that I should bear you a son, after the war, there is none left, and has been none for a long while. And you need an heir. Another woman might give you one.'

'And what would you do? For that matter, what would I do? Do you think another woman could take your place? I am not lord of this fortress: it is you who rule it. I swear by the God of Heaven, that if any man had served me as you have done, and I set him aside as you would have me do to you, I would straightaway be called the most ungrateful king in all of Britain, and my men would all leave me to seek some other lord who would reward them better.'

'They would not say that, or do that, if you divorced me.'

'They would not, for a woman. But I would. And for that matter, what ... Gwynhwyfar, I do not want any other woman. I have not since I first came to love you. Would you have me marry some empty-headed king's daughter of seventeen, and be content with her, while you did ... what? Joined a convent? Married one of my warriors? I would kill any warrior who offered himself!' He was beginning to smile again, again beginning to treat the subject as a joke. I abruptly thought of Bedwyr and shivered.

'You need an heir. It is all very well to speak of you and of me, but you need an heir for the sake of the kingdom.'

'No. I do not need an heir. Ach, my white hart, you are right, I wish we had children, your children; but it is better

128

without them. Now my usurpation will die with me.' I began to protest, but he silenced me with a hard, deliberate kiss. 'When I die,' he said 'The *imperium* will return to my father's clan; and any successor from that clan will have a legal right to his power. And I can designate anyone within four generations of an emperor as my successor, and, if I conduct the affair correctly, have him recognized as such. I could choose Gereint ab Erbin or Constans, in the Family – and Maelgwn Gwynedd has a claim...'

'Maelgwn!' I exclaimed angrily.

He laughed, 'Not Maelgwn, I agree. He rules Gwynedd badly enough. I would not give him my Empire. And the others are not suited to holding great authority. Only now, now – who knows? Since Gwalchmai has declared Gwyn legitimate, Gwyn can be considered a member of the royal clan. He is descended from the eldest legitimate child of my father Uther. True, Morgawse married into another clan – but if Gwyn is not a member of the royal clan of the Orcades...' He let go of my shoulders and stood, his eyes brightening with excitement. 'My mother was not noble, but Gwyn's was a daughter of Caw, of the royal clan of Ebrauc. That could be very useful; it might finally settle their hostility.' He began pacing the room. 'True, he is a bastard from a monastery, just as I am, but my father had legitimate children, and could not legitimitize me. People will soon forget that the grandson of Caw, the great-grandson of Uther Pendragon, ever had anything irregular about his birth. If we did have him accepted, legally, by the royal clan of Britain, he would have a very good claim. Not many people would contest it. Did you know,' turning on me and asking a question apparently unconnected with what he had just been saying, 'the Emperor Augustus was the grand-nephew of Julius Caesar? The same relation as Gwyn is to me ... but this is all dreams and wild conjecture.' He came back to me, pulled me to my feet and held me against him. I was smiling, because he was glad, more hopeful than I had seen him for a long, long time, and I felt hope rising in my own heart like a bluebell pushing aside the dull earth in the spring.

'Let the future wait until tomorrow,' Arthur said, smiling at me the old smile of delight. 'And do not say any more about this foolish business of other wives.'

Gwyn was fourteen in March that year, and was accordingly given arms – the finest Gwalchmai could find – and swore the Threefold Oath of Allegiance to Arthur. He moved into the house which Gwalchmai shared with Cei, where there was plenty of space. Cei, who had originally given the boy the sharp edge of his tongue, told me that he now 'got on well with the lad', though Gwyn had been cold at first. The tension which Medraut had created in the Family had continued to ebb throughout the winter, and everyone was much more relaxed. The whispers against Gwalchmai were no longer heard, both because of the lack of evidence and because it is difficult to hate someone who is truly happy. For Gwalchmai was intensely happy, so much so that one had only to watch him ride his horse across a practice field to know it. He had a son, the child of his old and dear love Elidan; he had her forgiveness for the affair that had long tormented him; he had something more than 'battles and embassies' to live for. Gwyn, in turn, after he had with difficulty managed to accept that his hero was his father, became enormously proud of his father. And the two did in fact have a great deal in common, so there was no hindrance to the love and admiration. While it was not true that they were never apart, they were certainly often together. They would take out their horses for exercise, Gwalchmai on his white stallion, Gwyn on the roan mare which Gwalchmai had now officially bestowed upon him ('Though I was intending to give her to you,' Gwalchmai stated as he handed his son the bridle, 'even before the letter'). Riding about the hills the two would talk of books and battles, foreign lands and old or new songs. Once taught, Gwyn proved to have inherited his father's skill at harping, and had been attempting to learn Irish 'even before the letter'. But he was not only eager to learn Irish songs, but hoped, like his father, to visit many strange kingdoms. 'The next time I am sent somewhere, you must come as well,' Gwalchmai told him. 'Perhaps it will be to Gaul. Bedwyr has been there all winter, but I doubt that all the problems there are settled even now.'

They were not. We did not hear from Bedwyr from December until April, because of the harsh winter and the unwillingness of the traders to risk their ships on the rough seas. We had received one letter from him late in September, written in the first week of that month upon his arrival at Macsen's fortress; and another early in December which had reported that some of Macsen's claims were settled, but that others had been raised. When the spring brought calm seas we had another letter, which had in fact been written shortly after the second one we had received, but which had spent the winter with one of our agents in a Breton port, awaiting a ship. This contained bad news: Macsen remained obdurate on all the points under discussion, and had insistently pressed Bedwyr to forswear his allegiance to Arthur and remain instead in Less Britain as Macsen's warleader.

'When I refused the place he offered,' Bedwyr wrote, 'the king grew angry, and called me a traitor to my homeland. He would hear no arguments for the unity of the Empire; he said that the Empire was dead and ought to remain so. And he has grown very insistent on this, until I thought it better to leave him and spend the winter on my family's estates in the south-east, whither I will go tomorrow. I will return to Britain in the spring, as soon as the roads and the winds permit – unless you wish otherwise, my lord. But I see no point to remaining, for I cannot negotiate with Macsen.'

Arthur agreed that it would be best if Bedwyr did not encounter Macsen again, and wrote commanding his return. So Bedwyr came back to Camlann in May, and as soon as he arrived I realized that what had happened in that grey afternoon in August was not over, as I had believed.

It was a lovely spring afternoon; I came into the Hall on some other errand to find a knot of men standing about and welcoming our warleader in loud voices, and Arthur among them, clasping Bedwyr's hand. Bedwyr stood among them looking travel-worn, plain, and unhappy. I had missed him sometimes in the months he had been away, but I thought that the ruinous love had died, and I missed him only as one misses a sympathetic friend. But somehow he sensed my presence beyond the others, and looked up, searching for me with his eyes. He did not smile when he saw me, but something leapt between us, an idle string on a harp suddenly drawn tight, plucked and drowning out other tones in its sound. I realized from the leap my heart gave that I was still bound to him, and I knew with sudden horror that it was worse for him, that he had not forgotten me for an instant of his absence; knew it without any need for more communication than a look. So I began again to avoid him.

In early June we sent Gwalchmai and Gwyn to Less Britain in Bedwyr's place. We were forced to, for the unresolved claims were beginning to cause problems. Macsen had imposed a tariff on the wine his people exported which was high, the rate traditionally charged on trade with barbarian nations, not even that charged for another province of the Empire. This had drawn loud complaints from the various traders, as well as from the noblemen they supplied, and had encouraged smugglers. Some of these smugglers had been caught and executed by Macsen, and now their clans were besieging us with petitions for vengeance, justice and the blood-price. Several fugitives from justice in Britain had settled comfortably in Less Britain, in defiance of all previous treaties. This outraged the clans they had injured, who joined the smugglers' clans in their petitioning. So Gwalchmai and Gwyn departed with announcements of harsh counter-measures: a trade embargo and an offer of asylum to any and all Breton fugitives.

Gwalchmai's servant Rhys went as well, reluctantly parting from his wife and children. 'After all,' he told me as we arranged supplies for the journey, 'Gwalchmai doesn't need me now. He won't overwork himself this time, not with his son along.'

'You think not?' I asked dubiously. 'He might work twice as hard, to make Gwyn proud of him.'

Rhys snorted. 'He might – but he would never let Gwyn work so, and I don't see Gwyn leaving his father to work alone. And he will see to it that he is well-treated, so that Gwyn will be as well. An excellent thing, fatherhood, for making a man take notice of what he does.' Rhys grinned, and added wistfully, 'I wish I had seen his face when he found out' – for Rhys, strangely, had known about Gwyn for years. He had learned of the boy from the lady Elidan herself, but had been sworn by her to silence on the matter. 'Though I would have spoken out,' he told me, on the occasion that he informed me of his foreknowledge and asked for an account of what had happened, 'if I had thought that those two wouldn't find out on their own.'

'I think you will find that you are still needed,' I told Rhys. 'Macsen will not make things any easier for Gwalchmai than he did for Bedwyr, and he will need a servant he can trust.'

Rhys sighed, ran a hand through his hair. 'True enough. And it's not that I grudge going – only that Eivlin is due to have the baby in October, and I would like to be on hand. My lord would be certain to send me back before then, if the negotiations drag on as they did last time, but I would rather be here all the while. We've been lucky in two healthy children, and Eivlin is fine now, but still, there might be danger. Still, I always knew I would have to do a lot of travelling if I served Gwalchmai, and it's late to complain of it now – and maybe the matter will be settled soon.'

It was not. Faced with the trade embargo, Macsen rescinded the tariff, but would not agree on a blood-price for the smugglers he had had executed, and denied that the fugitives existed. Letters flowed back and forth across the ocean; our emissaries returned late in July to confer, then sailed back again, and still the negotiations dragged on, with Macsen giving way on one point and suddenly discovering five others to stick on. In September a rough and unsatisfactory settlement was achieved, and the party returned. We might well have sent them out again, but by then we had other things to think of.

That same spring Medraut wrote and postponed his proposed visit to Camlann, explaining that he had some domestic difficulties which could not endure his absence. At about the same time we learned from the disaffected members of his clan that Medraut suspected some of their number, and that they were afraid: they asked if Arthur would grant them asylum, and judge between themselves and their cousin Medraut. Arthur wrote to say that he was willing to judge their cause, but could not promise unconditional asylum. But before they could have received this letter, we had news that five members of the royal clan and some twenty others of different, noble clans of the Islands were accused of plotting against their king. The five were kin-wrecked and exiled, the twenty executed. The five exiles, with their servants, set off from the Orcades in a twenty-oar curragh laden with goods, but were scarcely out of sight of land when a violent storm arose, and the ship was wrecked on the cliffs of northern Pictland, and all but one of the passengers drowned. This man was one of the five. His name was Diuran Mac Brenainn, and he had been warleader for King Lot. Gwalchmai remembered him as a sensible and a just man, passionately loyal to the clan's welfare. He managed to cling to the keel of the ship and was eventually washed ashore. He made his way to the shipyard of Eoghan, where previously he had sent messages to be relayed to Arthur. Here he stayed with the clerk at the yard, and sent a message to Arthur: a miserable, semi-literate letter obviously dictated in haste. It accused Medraut of murdering Agravain and of killing the others in the ship, by sorcery, and it begged Arthur, 'by the faeth of the God yow worshippest', to send him aid, and to lend support to an army of Islanders who would 'redeem the Ercendy Islands from the son of Iffernus'.

Arthur despatched a courier northward with some gold to support the man in his destitution, and with it a cautiously worded letter, inviting Diuran to Camlann, and asking him to represent his cause to the other kings of Britain. But the courier returned with the gold, surprisingly untouched, and with it our letter, enclosed in a letter from the clerk of the shipyard. He was evidently the scribe of the first letter, for his style of bad Latin was the same, and he announced in it that Diuran had died of a fever the week before our letter arrived.

'I offered him the gold,' our messenger said, 'for he was a poor man, and had paid for the other's burial out of his own money. But he refused it. He was a strange little man.'

Despite this, Medraut's 'domestic difficulties' apparently continued, for he again postponed his visit, and put another group of noblemen to death. He then declared war on some of the Western Islands which had been part of King Lot's domain, but which had seceded under Agravain and claimed the protection of the King of Dalriada. Medraut sailed to them with a great army, fought several short, sharp encounters, and defeated them. Their ally, Aengus of Dalriada, made no move to help them. Medraut was allied to Arthur and related also to Aengus's foremost enemy, Urien of Rheged, and no doubt Aengus thought the

Western Islands not worth the risk of a war with the greatest powers of Britain. At any rate, Medraut had a free hand with the Islanders, and showed no mercy. He deposed their ruling clans, executing the men and giving most of the women to the new clans he raised in their place. The old ruling clans were, he said, guilty of treason to himself and to Agravain.

This successful campaign won Medraut more support within the Orcades, for his people admired his military prowess, and were pleased to have reclaimed the Western Islands and the fear of their neighbours. In August he wrote to us again, saying that he was now free to make his deferred visit, and that he would set out in September, after he had returned to his fortress of Dun Fionn and set it in order. But he sent this letter from the shipyard of Eoghan in northern Pictland, and added a note which disturbed us.

'The troubles engendered by the laxity of poor Agravain's reign are widely spread,' he wrote. 'In this very shipyard I found a clerk, one Padraig Mac Febail, probably the only lettered man in Pictland, who had used this very skill in aid of treachery. I had the man brought to me and, on questioning him, found that besides aiding my enemies he had left his monastery in Erin, doubtless for some crime. I therefore had him put to death, seeing that his viciousness was of long standing. Why do I recount this to your grace? Merely as an example of how I am placed: I am certain that you will understand my position, and forgive my long delay in coming to swear my oath to you.'

It troubled me to think of this clerk, who had carefully copied out the messages which the noblemen of the Orcades must have sent him by word of mouth, and put them into his clumsy Latin. He himself was an exile, yet had somehow managed to support Diuran after the shipwreck, and had sent back the gold without even using any to pay for the burial. I could imagine him discovered, dragged before Medraut by the king's warriors, questioned under that cool contemptuous smile, and finally put to death with a casual command intended not so much to punish him as to display to Arthur the extent of Medraut's knowledge.

'My mother ruled in this fashion,' Gwalchmai said, when he returned from Gaul and Arthur gave him this letter to read. 'The Islands were afraid when my father went away on campaigns, for her rule was heavy on them then. But she was more skilled. She had a sense of what could and could not be done, and the people were more afraid of her than they will ever be of Medraut.' He looked again at the letter from his brother, and lifted his eyes to us, frowning. 'This will not be the end of Medraut's troubles.'

Nor, I thought, of ours.

Six

At the beginning of October Medraut sailed into Caer Gwent with two ships and fifty men. Because he came peacefully and in the Emperor's name, he was offered hospitality by Cynyr, Lord of Caer Gwent, while he sent Arthur notice that he had arrived and requested an escort so as not to alarm the countryside by the size of his bodyguard. Arthur himself rode west to meet him and escort him to Camlann, also taking fifty men. He left me and Bedwyr together to keep the fortress.

It had grown difficult for me to avoid Bedwyr even before Arthur left. When the warleader first returned from Gaul he had tried as hard to avoid me as I him, but this effort had lapsed. By September he was actually looking for opportunities to see me. I reproached him for it, once; he looked away from me and whispered, 'I do not mean to,' then, slowly his eyes moved back to meet mine and he added, 'I cannot help it.' It made me ashamed. Bedwyr was serious by nature, not easily moved to love but faithful and constant after he had committed himself, and because of this he was suffering. Men suffer so in the songs all the time, but in reality most of them forget love more easily. But Bedwyr was really almost sick from it. He had returned from Less Britain looking thin and exhausted, and thin and exhausted he remained. He no longer spoke freely with Arthur, which puzzled my husband. 'I do not know what is the matter with Bedwyr,' he confided to me one night. 'Ever since he returned from Gaul he has been as grim and silent as a memorial column. Does he think I am angry because he failed, or because Macsen tried to persuade him to desert me? He ought to know better.'

I said nothing. I knew well enough that Bedwyr was tortured with guilt before Arthur, and perhaps by jealousy as well. But I could say nothing, even when Arthur grew angry. Every time I saw Bedwyr I remembered that sweet and terrible afternoon, and sometimes I lay awake at night, listening to Arthur's quiet breath beside me, aching and ashamed. Sometimes at a feast my eyes would meet Bedwyr's, and we would understand without a word spoken where our thoughts had turned, and I would feel my face grow hot, and would turn and pretend to talk to someone else, but feel his presence like a bright light which cast shadows all about me. So I tried to meet the warleader only in public. I was afraid when Arthur announced that he would meet Medraut at Caer Gwent, and urged him to send Bedwyr instead.

'You rush off to meet him as though you were champions out to fight single combat,' I said. 'But you are Emperor, and he is only ruler of a few islands on the edge of the world. Moreover, he is officially your subject ally. You have the position of greater strength. Let him feel that, and the rest of the world see it; let him come to you.'

But Arthur only stood in the doorway of the conference room, keeping his back to me, gazing into the west and fingering the hilt of his sword. 'Why should I allow Medraut to act the part of subject and ally when we both know that he is my competitor in Empire?' he demanded bitterly. 'Let him, and let the Family and all the rest of Britain, see that I am matching myself against him, and let them realize that it is a question of choosing. Besides, I wish to see for myself how he conducts himself with my subject lords. Perhaps he has told his tale to Cynyr of Caer Gwent now. I can see what Cynyr makes of it, and of me.'

'My dear lord, if he has told Cynyr we will know soon enough from our other sources. In seeing for yourself you will only hurt yourself.'

'I wish to know! In God's name, am I remain here like a statue in a niche, smiling at all comers while they whisper, "Ah, he looks fine, but really is a bastard, a begetter of bastards on his own sister, and a usurper"? No!'

'But Arthur . . .'

He whirled about and looked at me. 'I am leaving tomorrow for Caer Gwent, and that is the end of it.'

I looked away from the cold eyes and nodded.

I could feel the hardness leave the stare, and looked up again when I thought it was gone. He flinched, seemed to begin an apology, then stopped, awkwardly. He shrugged. 'I must arrange it, then. In a few hours . . .' he turned, looked again out over the walls westward, then started down the hill, his purple cloak flapping and his hand on his sword.

He was, in fact, impatient. All the summer he had been bracing himself for Medraut's arrival, for the gradual onset of the rumours that would disgrace and discredit him, and reveal his most painfully held secret to the scorn and hatred of the world. He could bear it, just, and hope to hold onto power long enough to find a suitable successor. But Medraut's constant deferral of his arrival, the postponing from week to week of the anticipated struggle, were wearing him out with expectation and fear. He gave little public sign of it; he could not afford to. But he grew increasingly hard to reach, and irritable. Sometimes he even uncharacteristically lost his temper, usually with me. I was the one who knew him best, the one he could afford to be honest with. But after he had broken and shouted at me, it was always harder still to draw near to him. Ashamed, he recoiled from me. And I wanted him more and more as the autumn continued. The harvest is always exhausting, always demands more than it seems possible to give. I would wake in the morning, feeling that I could scarcely muster enough energy to rise, and my husband would look at me wearily, not daring to apologize for some scene the night before and not touching me. And most of the day would be utter madness, dashing wildly about the fortress checking and making inventories of goods stored for the winter, arranging payments, receiving tribute, hearing petitions, organizing, ordering accounts, paying attention – and feeling Bedwyr's gaze now and then like a searing fire.

> Tell me, oh you learned ones,
> From what is Longing made?
> And what cloth is it woven from
> That with use it never fades?

> Gold wears out and silver,
> Silks and velvets tear,
> All adornment ages:
> Longing never wears.

> Longing, Longing, back a pace,
> Do not weigh on my breast so heavily,
> But move over from the bedside
> And let a brief sleep come to me.

It's a common song, but it ran through my brain for weeks on end, until I was heartily sick of it.

Oh, after Arthur left it happened in a way that was as obvious as the course of flood waters down a dry stream bed, and as irresistible. For two days Bedwyr and I held stiffly aloof, speaking to each other with stilted formality, hoping, making one last effort against the humiliating treachery we both knew was near. Then, on the third day, we were in the conference room, alone together. We were discussing what to do with the tribute.

'I can send another three hundred head of cattle, under guard, to the holding near Llefelys's Stone,' Bedwyr said, 'but we will be short then, will we not, noble lady? Maelgwyn Gwynedd sent us fifty fewer cows than he gave his word for.'

'I calculated that he would send us seventy fewer cows, noble lord, so we have a good margin of safety.'

He looked at me in surprise.

'Well, what is wonderful in that?' I asked. 'Maelgwn tries to cheat us on the tribute every year; it would be amazing if he did not. During the war, he often succeeded. In the spring we'll send him the usual party to correct his "unfortunate mistake" – and perhaps this time we'll make him pay their travelling expenses.'

'But you can calculate by how much he will cheat us?'

'Of course. We set the tribute by the size of the harvest. Maelgwyn's tribute is the size of the harvest less 15 or 20 per cent, and plus a factor of how difficult he's been that year. If he's guilty of too many other incidents, he grows nervous, and a trifle more honest.'

Bedwyr laughed, and I laughed as well. Then I saw that he was looking at me with that particular light in his eyes and I stopped laughing. He grew very serious, reached out and caught my hand. I turned away.

'But . . . but we must have another two hundred head of cattle nearby . . .' I began uncertainly. His hand against mine was like the warmth of a fire to a blind man, something more real than the vision of the eyes.

'My lady . . .' he whispered.

'You must have the sheep moved from the south pastures, with a guard or two over them to see that they reach . . .'

'Gwynhwyfar.'

I stopped trying, and looked at him. The pulse of my blood dizzied me: I could feel it over every inch of my body. 'We must not,' I said. 'It is treachery, and that is the worst of all sins.'

'Please,' he whispered. 'Just this once more.' He moved closer to me, his hand sliding up my arm.

I closed my eyes, trying to pray. 'But think what would happen if Medraut discovered this. Think how he could use it.'

'Just once more, only once. Please. I cannot live like this. I cannot think for thinking of you; I cannot sleep or rest. My most sweet lady, I cannot bear it.' He was beside me now, his arm around me, touching my breast.'

I meant to stand up. Instead, I only said faintly, 'But you must bear it.'

'Please. Only once more.' He kissed me. I could not think after that; when he pulled away and looked at me, I held to him and nodded, weeping.

When it was over with we again vowed that this was the end, that it must not happen again. But when one has twice been unable to keep a resolve, one begins to expect failure, and that expectation breeds failure. We held our resolve for less than a month, before breaking it in a new crisis and losing ourselves once again. After that we began to hope that desire would be satisfied by much loving, but only succeeded in becoming necessary to each other. And with repeated sins, the conscience, which is at first tender, grows gradually numbed, finds excuses, ceases much to be moved. After a time it was even possible to behave naturally to Arthur. But that came later; at first he might have noticed something, if he had not been himself too tense, too depressed, to speak naturally to his friends.

Arthur returned, with Medraut, on a golden October morning the week after he set out. One of the guards came from the gates an hour or so before noon to tell me that the party had been seen approaching, and I went with him back to the gate, and climbed the gate-tower to watch. Bedwyr was at the gate already, but stayed before them, mounted on his horse and waiting to welcome Arthur and relinquish the military command Arthur had temporarily given him. He nodded to me when I arrived, but no more. We could hold our resolve that long, at least.

The sky was cloudless and had a hard glow like blue enamel, and the trees at the edges of the fields seemed cast in bronze by sunlight. The fields themselves, though, were drab, for the harvest was in and the earth was stubble-marked and grey, or black from the annual burning, and hazed over with smoke from the fires. In the distance, Ynys Witrin rose tall and green over the dark marshes, seeming to float above the main road where a long column of horsemen trotted steadily forward. They were already near enough, when I climbed the tower, for me to pick out a few individual figures, and I saw that Arthur's fifty warriors were interspersed with Medraut's, for greater safety. Two figures rode side by side at the head of the column, one wearing a purple cloak, riding a familiar grey horse, the other in a cloak dyed with saffron and a gold collar, riding a fine bay: Arthur and Medraut. As they came nearer, I waited for the line to increase its speed, to sweep up to the gates at a canter with a jingle of harness and glitter of weapons and jewellery, as Arthur always did in the gladness of coming home. But the column maintained its slow, jolting trot, and, as it drew nearer still. I saw that Arthur's shoulders were hunched as though against the cold, while Medraut rode with his cloak tossed back over one shoulder, sitting his horse with easy grace. Already the shadow had fallen on us; already Medraut had set some chill upon the heart.

I climbed down from the tower and went back up the hill to the Hall. I had no extraordinary power in Arthur's absence, nothing to hand over at the gates, and no one would expect me to welcome Medraut to Camlann, not after the way he had left it. And I wished to postpone, even for a few hours, the inevitable grief.

I saw Medraut in the Hall for the midday meal of course. He bowed stiffly, and I nodded my head, equally stiffly. But I could see that his kingship agreed with him. He looked sleeker than ever, graceful and regal in the saffron cloak, gold about his neck, fastening his cloak, on his arms and fingers. He had the same easy, ingratiating smile as well; the smile I had long before been disturbed by, and which I had grown to hate. But he also looked more like Arthur than he had done, and I realized that he had cut his beard and hair in the same fashion that Arthur customarily used.

After the meal, while ostensibly resting from his journey, Arthur told me what had happened at Caer Gwent. 'Medraut has begun to spread his story, as I thought,' he said, very quietly. He looked older than his forty-three years, and hunched over the fire like an old man whose blood has grown thin. 'Cynyr of Caer Gwent has certainly heard it. No, he said nothing – but he looked at me, and looked at Medraut, and looked at me again, all the time I was there. And he was very quiet. Ordinarily he gossips like a barber, but this time he was quiet. And also – you know I was in Caer Gwent for Sunday? When we went to Mass, Cynyr made some excuse, and would not take communion. He looked at me then, as well. He is afraid of being tainted in God's eyes by taking communion after a man who slept with his sister.' Arthur laughed, very bitterly. 'And his men had heard, and my men will have heard it from them. And I could not tell whether Medraut has simply started the rumour there, now, or whether he has been spreading it for months and our spies simply have not heard it. But it is established, now, and he need not say anything, not himself, not directly. He can merely wait until someone asks him questions. Did you notice the way he has cut his hair? He is ready to begin the battle in earnest. But still he will not admit as much to me: when I met him he was all smiles and bows and courtesies. There is no winning through to anything real in him. I do not know how to fight him any more than I did before.' Arthur rubbed his hands, held them out to the fire. His signet ring gleamed. 'If the kings of Britain believe this rumour, they will have an excuse for a rebellion. A bastard emperor is bad enough, but an emperor guilty of incest – that will pollute the land, and draw down the wrath of God, or so my enemies and the Church will say. How long can we hold on?'

I shook my head. 'Medraut still cannot prove anything. We can still deny it, perhaps successfully. We might hold power till our lives' end.'

He looked up and smiled, a little half-smile of ironic amusement. 'Might we? Come, my white hart, you are wiser than that. Medraut is no fool, and has no lack of skill.

Perhaps when actually in power he is too heavy-handed, but he can play upon the discontents of Britain as skilfully as his brother does on the harp. And he has strings enough to hand: dissatisfied and revengeful kings, like Maelgwyn Gwynedd; the enmity of the Church; the boredom of my own warriors. Our wars with the invaders are finished, but the Empire is not entirely restored, as we promised, and the frustration of that is burning in Britain, like a stubble fire, waiting for fuel to blaze up. It only needs a skilful leader to direct it. Medraut can break us – or make us pay such a price for power that we would be better off dead. It's not worth ruling if one has to be a tyrant to do so, or if one has to destroy one's own people. No, we must hold on as long as we safely can, and then abdicate. The problem is still to find a man to give the power to, one I could trust to rule justly, who would be strong enough to hold his own against Medraut. And still, there is no one.'

'It would be very dangerous to abdicate,' I pointed out.

He gave the same tired smile. '"For this Empire which we have acquired is a kind of tyranny,"' he quoted – it was one of a collection of sayings of famous men, most of whom I had never heard of, which Arthur had brought from the monastery where he was raised – '"which it may be wrong to have taken up, but which it is certainly hazardous to let go." But what does that have to do with either of us? We did not take it up to be safe, and have risked death for it often enough.'

'I meant it would be dangerous for the Empire. The kings of Britain know you, and if they do not believe in your justice, they at least believe you are a skilled war-leader. They might be willing to fight a successor of yours, especially if he was young, where they would not fight you.'

He sighed and rested his head on his hands. 'You are right, of course. It might come to war before I could afford to abdicate. And if I were to be defeated, and if Medraut seized power – no, I must trust God that that, at least, he will not permit.' He looked into the fire again, and continued in a voice so low I could barely hear it. 'And yet, this darkness was of my getting. I myself am responsible for Medraut. The unrest in the kingdom, too, is my fault, for I got my power by strength of arms and contrary to the law, and it is not surprising that I have enemies. I thought I was doing right at the time, but perhaps, in God's eyes, it was as grave a sin as incest.'

'No,' I said, laying my hand on his.

He shook it off. 'The destruction is coming from within us, and from within me. The Saxons could not defeat us, but we ourselves are destroying the Empire; the faction in the Family, the flaw within. Once I thought that merely the shame and dishonour of being known to have loved my sister would be intolerable. Now that seems unimportant. That only affects me, while this, this is the ruin of the West, the Darkness coming upon us. Why must we love the Light so much when we are bound to work its destruction?' He looked up at me as he asked this, raising his voice, as though I might have the answer. The fire crackled softly on the hearth.

'My dearest, we have not lost yet,' I said at last. 'And you yourself said we must trust God: surely he will not permit the Darkness to conquer. We have too much to fight for to give way to despair.'

He sighed. 'I am tired.' He rubbed his face. 'I have been fighting for the better part of thirty years, and I begin not to believe even in victory. And to be responsible for it . . . but you are right. We have a great deal to fight for. Indeed, we are fortunate to have so much, to be able to love it and fight for it. It would be cowardly and ungracious to surrender before the battle is under way.' He rose and kissed me, then stood, holding me against him. He was still wearing his mail-coat, and I could feel the links under his tunic and feel the strength of his body under that. I thought of Bedwyr, and of my own desire to be weak, and was bitterly ashamed.

'Gwynhwyfar,' said Arthur, 'I do not deserve you. Forgive me that I have been angry with you – and that I undoubtedly will be again, for I am very tired, and most bitterly grieved at heart.'

'Oh, my heart's dearest,' I said, and could not think of anything more. But words were not really necessary.

That night, at the welcoming feast, Medraut swore the Threefold Oath to an alliance with Arthur. He knelt in the centre of the Hall, under the roof-tree with its golden dragon standard, offering his sword hilt-first to Arthur and swearing in a clear voice, with apparent solemnity, to hold his kingdom at peace with Arthur, to make no wars against him or his subjects and allies, to respect the laws of the Empire, and to offer no refuge to enemies of Britain. Arthur took the sword and vowed to keep peace with the kingdom of the Orcades, and so on. The Family cheered as Medraut rose again and, smiling, sheathed his sword, but Medraut's own men, brought from the Orcades, watched Arthur with a grim, unblinking stare.

Neither they nor Medraut ever returned to the Islands. Medraut had stayed at Camlann two weeks, and was preparing to leave again – after engendering the old tension in the Family – when a messenger came from the Orcades to say that the royal clan was deposed, and that the Islands would henceforth be ruled by a branch of that O'Niall family who ruled most of Erin. There had always been hostility between the O'Niall and the royal clan of the Islands: King Lot had originally left Erin when his clan lost its position in Ulaid to the O'Niall. The O'Niall had now been invited to Dun Fionn by one of the noble clans that Medraut had injured: this clan, and its allies, on a day previously arranged, took the port on the largest of the islands. A fleet from Erin put in, and the combined forces marched across the island to Dun Fionn. If Medraut had been present, the fortress would undoubtedly have been able to resist, but, as it was, half the inhabitants mutinied and opened the gates to the invaders. All the male members of the royal clan, with its staunchest allies, were then put to death, and the women distributed among the invaders in marriage or concubinage, usually the latter. All this had happened shortly after Medraut left the Orcades, probably before he even reached Caer Gwent; it had undoubtedly been arranged months before.

We gave this messenger – who was a member of the injured, revenging clan – an audience in the Hall. He had arrived in the middle of the afternoon, and there were not many people about when he took his place under the roof-tree and began to speak – we had had to send for Medraut. But more people came hurrying in as the man continued, telling his story with evident pleasure, colouring the details in favour of his new masters, the O'Niall. The Hall began to fill with whispers, explanations to newcomers, exclamations of horrors, demands to know what would be done, but the messenger did not look around, but faced Arthur steadily. When he had finished his narration of the events in the Islands he drew himself up, laid a hand on his sword, and addressed Arthur proudly in conclusion.

'Do not think,' he declared in his excellent British, 'that it will still be possible for you to have an unjustified and ruinous influence on our Islands. We are Irish, not British, and now – rightly! – are bound to Erin. We will swear no further peace with you, High King of Britain. The accursed line of Lot did so, and all our evils sprang from that, from his marriage with a British witch for your thrice-damned alliance, and from his sons – the drunkard and the sorcerous traitor, and the last and worst, the one not of *his* getting, that shamefully begotten bastard, the witch's son and curse of his people. If you, Pendragon, mean to send this tyrant back to rule us, there will be a thousand spears to meet you, and a thousand swords, and not easily will you win through them, nor easily hold the Islands if you do. This we have sworn by the Sun and the Wind, by the oath of our people and by the new God of Erin and the O'Niall, now our God. But if you,' and he spat this at Medraut, who had stood silent and unmoving on Arthur's right, 'presume to return to the Islands, know that you are sentenced to death, and no matter how many guards and warriors you set about yourself, or how many men you sorcerously seek out and kill, still someone, one day, will find a way through to you and make you pay for your tyranny. This also we have sworn.'

Medraut stared at him, his eyes bleak, frozen with hatred, though his face was still, unmoved. 'And perhaps,' he said, in a smooth, conversational tone, 'you also are sentenced to death, overly boastful messenger.'

The messenger laughed. 'You killed my father, though no one could prove it, though he was charged with nothing and no blood-price was paid for his death. My cousin you had publicly butchered in your Hall. I asked for this mission, Medraut son of no one, so that I could see you when you heard this message; and having seen, I am not afraid of death. Lennavair, daughter of Durtacht, whom you had contracted to marry, sleeps with Laeghaire of the O'Niall as his concubine, and is glad to be a true man's woman and not a bastard's wife.'

147

'Look well to your ship when you sail home,' Medraut said quietly.

'He came as an emissary,' Arthur said in a quiet, but carrying voice. 'And he will be permitted to leave in peace, according to law and custom. I do not know what you mean by telling him to look to his ship, son of Lot. Doubtless he is accustomed to sailing, even in autumn, and needs no such warning.' Medraut turned his cruel stare on Arthur; Arthur met it. After a moment, Arthur added very quietly, 'For if you wish ill to this man, I would have you recollect that sorcery is a capital crime.'

Medraut stared for another long moment, then dropped his eyes stealthily and bowed. 'Why do you mention sorcery, my lord? Do you believe the wild charges of those who have declared themselves your enemies, and who have deposed and murdered a clan allied to you by many oaths and much blood? I do not think you can or do believe such charges. I ask your leave, noble lord, to depart and to inform my kinsmen and followers of this calamity.'

Arthur nodded, and Medraut bowed and started from the dais. He paused by the messenger and gave him another cold, measuring stare, then smiled and walked out slowly down the length of the Hall, with everyone making way for him. Many of his friends trailed out after him.

The messenger, however, looked at Arthur with surprise. 'You preserve the tradition concerning emissaries,' he said, after a moment. 'It is well. What message shall I take from you to the lords O'Niall, the rulers of the Orcades?'·

Arthur leaned back in his chair and studied the messenger thoughtfully, until the man, up to then so bold, began to look uncertain and fidget with his sword.

"Tell your masters," Arthur said at last, still not speaking loudly, sounding tired, but causing a silence through the rest of the Hall, 'that I grieve for the Islands. Tell your cousins and their allies that I grieve for the royal clan, most savagely murdered. And tell your people that I grieve for them as well, that they destroyed the line that had always been their kings, and called in foreign masters to rule over them. Say to your masters, moreover, that it is easier to say that the Islands are bound to Erin than it is to rely upon Erin for aid. If the O'Niall trouble my subjects by raiding the coasts they will regret it; and I will follow that custom I have always followed, and put to death any raiders who are captured in Britain, and take no ransom for any of them. But if the O'Niall wish for British goods – and they will want wood, and tin, and iron, for they cannot get those in the Islands – then they will have to come to terms with me and swear oaths to respect my lands and my subjects.'

The emissary looked in the direction in which Medraut had gone. 'But the tyrant?'

'By birth he can be considered one of the royal clan of Britain. He has a place here, if he no longer has one in the Islands.' There was another moment's silence, then Arthur rose from his seat at the high table and walked down the steps from the dais until he was facing the messenger. 'I will not go to war with Erin for the sake of a tyrant, even if he is of the royal clan of Britain,' he said quietly. 'If you wish, you can have peace with me. I will arrange the terms for you to bring to your masters. Meanwhile, Camlann offers you the hospitality due to emissaries.'

The emissary stared at Arthur for another moment, not quite believing him; glanced about the Hall, back to Arthur. Then he bowed deeply. 'Lord High King, I thank you.'

When the messenger departed for the Orcades, Arthur had Medraut watched, gave the messenger a carefully picked escort back to his ship, which had been kept under a reliable guard, and finally sent money to the monastery at Ynys Witrin for a Mass to be said for those voyaging on the sea. Whether because of these precautions or because Medraut had decided to sacrifice his wishes to the need to make a good impression, the ship arrived safely back at Dun Fionn, and we presently heard that our arrangements for peace-oaths from the O'Niall to prevent piracy and raiding in return for some rights to trade in Britain – were acceptable. And Medraut stayed at Camlann.

Although it was plainly something he had not antici-pated or desired, Medraut's deposition worked in his favour. The fact that Arthur would not support him in a bid to reclaim his kingship gave him cause for complaint: he was Arthur's nephew, and had sworn the oath of alliance, but Arthur had made a peace with those who had murdered his kin and usurped his kingdom. It did not matter that the alliance had never extended to mutural defence – it was old, established, sealed by marriage in the previous generation, and it had been set aside in an instant. Even in the family there was strong feeling that Arthur should have supported Medraut. Medraut's actions while in power were not taken very seriously: Medraut himself blamed 'poor Agravain's laxness' for the fact that he had put so many noblemen to death, and men are never as concerned about tyranny in a foreign country as about some slight problem in their own. It did not help matters that Arthur arranged to have the sons of Morgawse formally recognized as members of the imperial clan of Britain, now that their father's clan was destroyed: this served only to strengthen Medraut's claim on British help.

The only bright spot for us among these calamities was the fact that, since Gwalchmai was now officially a member of the royal clan of Britain, Gwyn was as well. As Arthur had predicted, most of the warriors were already beginning to forget that Gwyn was not legitimate by birth. The boy had travelled with Gwlchmai to Gaul, and afterwards to the North – King Urien of Rheged had been having some disputes with his Saxon neighbours, and had requested arbitration from Arthur. Urien was a very powerful king, the strongest of all the northern rulers, and he was much impressed by Gwyn. He was apparently reminded of his own son, Owain, who after an unpromising childhood and youth had suddenly emerged glorious in a string of brilliant battles and expired winning victory in the last one. When Urien gave Gwalchmai the usual set of gifts – one for Gwalchmai himself as emissary, one for Arthur, in honour of his position, one for the Saxon King Gwalchmai had concluded the negotiations with – he bestowed one on Gwyn as well, and when the two left, he heartily wished the boy good fortune.

On concluding the negotiations between Urien and his Saxon neighbour, our embassy stopped in Ebrauc to break the journey back. King Ergyriad ap Caw made them welcome to his fortress, and at once claimed Gwyn as his kinsman, the son of his half-sister. This recognition enabled Gwalchmai to resolve some of the enmity between himself and the rest of the sons of Caw, who had hated him since he killed their brother Bran. Gwyn got on surprisingly well with some of them, and they too gave him gifts when he left Caer Ebrauc.

Arthur was very pleased when the two returned. He hoped, still, to have time enough in power to be able to appoint Gwyn as his successor. Urien's support in this would be invaluable, as would that of the sons of Caw. He made a point of talking to Gwyn about the different countries he had visited and came away persuaded that the boy was capable of considerable political insight – as he ought to be, with Gwalchmai to teach him. Gwalchmai himself would never have been acceptable as a successor, despite his political skill, both because of his foreign birth and because he was far too gentle and otherwordly to be suited to power; but Arthur thought that Gwyn might be capable of Empire. Perhaps Arthur was merely fascinated by the parallel between Gwyn's background and his own. But we both had hopes which we did not dare speak of much, and we hoped the more intensely as the situation grew steadily worse.

The fifty warriors that Medraut had brought with him from the islands soon began to cause problems. A few of these were of the royal clan and savagely indignant with Arthur; all were devoted solely to Medraut and completely obedient to him, while extremely hostile to everyone else. They formed a solid, self-contained group within Camlann, isolated from the rest of the warriors by the barriers of culture, language and religion, which they managed to breach enough only to carry out quarrels. After a few duels between them and some of our men, Arthur sent most of them back to Medraut's ships and had them patrol the western coast against raiders. In December it was discovered that one of these ships had engaged in some raiding of its own, and Arthur had the men responsible put to death. Unfortunately, this included two members of the royal clan, and their execution nearly brought on armed conflict with the others. For a long time afterwards the whispers circulated: 'The Pendragon wishes to finish what the O'Niall began.'

At the same time, the rumours Medraut had started about his own parentage were circulating widely, and our spies reported them from every corner of Britain. No king dared to ask Arthur if they were true, but we soon saw who believed them by the uneasiness of some who had to have dealings with us, and the reluctance of others to contact us at all. But the uneasiness the rumours caused was nowhere so marked as in Camlann. Medraut had managed to gather most of his faction under him yet again, and the quarrelling among the Family began anew. But there was a difference. Before, Medraut had attacked principally his brother Gwalchmai, and only questioned Arthur's judgement in his support of Gwalchmai, and hinted that my husband was subject to my partial whims. Now the attack was direct: Arthur had treated Medraut unjustly, because of a dreadful secret, a secret whispered about the fortress, searched out by hundreds of shocked or troubled eyes fastening on Arthur wherever he went.

Some of Medraut's followers grew uneasy as the direction of the attack grew plainer. Some had been lost after the poisoning attempt, and some after Agravain's death. But there was still a sizeable body of men whom Medraut could rely on, a hundred and six of them, with another fifty or so who were unsettled in their loyalties. This last group grew steadily smaller as the men decided gradually whom they chose to believe, and whom they would follow.

That winter was not quiet. Arthur drove himself as he had not done since the height of the war, rising before dawn and working all day, trying to keep the men occupied, to prevent quarrels, setting up half a hundred distractions for them to gain us time. He sent continuously to the kings of Britain on any pretext whatsoever so as to keep his authority before their eyes and maintain the contact so many of them were eager to break. He pretended that he had never heard the rumours, trying to act as though his energy and forcefulness were unimpaired by time, as though he were still moved by the old enthusiasm and delight. But in the evenings he collapsed on the bed in exhaustion, scarcely able to move. In the night he had dreams: he woke often, crying out the name of Morgawse. Then he would go to the desk, light the lamp, and read through our worn books or write furious letters for hours at a time. I would wake, and rise to see him bent over the desk in the adjoining room, the lamplight picking out the bones and hollows of his face until he seemed worn to a death's head. I would go over and try to persuade him to come back and rest, for he desperately needed sleep. For all his forced energy during the day, he could not hide that. The nightmare etched its record in his flesh, more and more deeply, and I could not smooth its carving away.

For my part I grew so exhausted that my main desire was to escape. I had as much to do as Arthur, and I felt that all our labour was to catch our own shadow. No matter how hard we worked, or what we said and did and what advantage we gained from it, still the rumours kept pace with us. Often we felt that we could do no more, only to find that we must do more, and, doing it, discover yet another thing, and another, till the days were whirling by like the blows of a hammer.

I had Bedwyr; I needed Bedwyr. He was my one refuge, a place of springtime in the midst of that dark winter. Though the nightmare surrounded him too, he did not live in the heart of it, and he had time, as Arthur did not, to talk and to breathe. I could rest with him, and find strength; I could, for a little while, lay my cares at his feet and forget them. Of course we were careful and very discreet. We had frequent legitimate causes to see one another, and could easily enough make arrangements for meeting somewhere in Camlann where we would not be disturbed. The sin of treachery became my solace – and still, even in consoling, a torment. Sometimes when Arthur had woken from a black dream and I lay in bed listening to the scratch of his pen I would wish that it was already over with, even if the end were defeat and if I myself should be eternally damned. In death there is at least some finality, and, after the unremitting struggle, rest. And the next day I might weep on Bedwyr's shoulder, because I had not been able to give comfort to Arthur, and ached for comfort myself.

But in fact the end did come soon – far too soon, I thought, when finally it was upon us.

In late March a new rumour began to circulate in Camlann. Arthur came back into our house one evening before a feast, tossed a bundle of dispatches onto the desk, collapsed into his chair and commented, 'My heart, there is a new rumour which you had best know of. You are now supposed to be sleeping with Bedwyr and plotting my downfall.'

'With Bedwyr?' I asked, feeling the coldness come over me, staring at Arthur.

But he merely remained slouched in the chair, his feet up on the grate. 'Indeed. One wonders why Medraut fixed on Bedwyr. One would think Gwalchmai the more likely candidate for such a tale. But he has tried that already. Besides, he has already called Gwalchmai matricide, traitor and madman, and has so far been unable to attach any stain to Bedwyr, so must invent this. Ach, I suppose it is clever enough, in its way. Bedwyr is not British, not of a royal or important clan, and yet he has power and influence. Medraut can use any resentment that causes to fuel belief in this tale, and can further blacken your name at the same time . . . ah, dear God, now Bedwyr as well. Now we have no one left who can mediate in a quarrel, or communicate with any of Medraut's faction. But a tale like this!'

I came over and sat down by his feet. I felt very tired, and rested my head against his knee. What if I should tell him, I thought suddenly, confess it all, escape the burden, take the consequences? But when I looked up into my husband's haggard face I knew that I could not speak, could not add to his pain or abandon him to suffer the ruin of his power alone. 'Do you want me to be cold with Bedwyr?' I asked. 'Avoid him during the next few weeks?'

Arthur laid one arm loosely around my shoulders. 'No. Do not trouble yourself. Medraut would only explain it to his followers as guilt fearing to be discovered. We can only hope that the thing will die out on its own. It must do so. It is too absurd for any thinking person to believe. You, and Bedwyr! My wife and my most loyal friend, the two people who care most for this realm, guilty of treason! No, my heart, leave it. It is sure to die out of itself.'

It did not, however, though it several times seemed likely to do so. Always as it was beginning to be laughed at it would rise again, with some new fabulous instance of proof. We could disprove or explain the instances – one was that I was seen wearing a hawthorn flower in my hair after Bedwyr wore one in his cloak-pin – Bedwyr and some six hundred others! – and yet still the tale persisted, and each time it faded it returned stronger and more pervasive.

Towards the end of April Bedwyr had a dispute with one of Medraut's Irish followers in the stable. This man, one of the royal clan, wanted some provision for a journey to his ship which Bedwyr thought excessive. The argument grew heated, and Bedwyr finally turned and began to walk off saying, 'I will speak to you again when you are cooler, Ruadh.'

'That is right!' the Irishman shouted after him, in the hearing of some dozen people (one of whom later recounted the whole incident to me indignantly). 'Run off to your lord's wife; do his business for him!' – and he made an obscene gesture.

Bedwyr stopped and looked back at the other. The man repeated the gesture, and Bedwyr turned and walked back to him. He looked the other up and down and said very quietly and very coldly. 'What foolishness is this? Are you drunk?'

The Irishman was completely unabashed. 'Must I be drunk to speak the truth? I am tired of your pretended virtue. Brave, loyal Bedwyr, the philosopher, the perfect warleader! All the West knows that you sleep with that whore-queen Gwynhwyfar, your lord's wife – much joy may you have of her!'

Bedwyr looked at him in silence for a moment, then still quietly but with a hard note under the quietness, said, 'You are guilty of defaming the majesty of our lord the Emperor. And you are lying.'

'Prove it,' said the other, eagerly. 'Prove it with your sword.'

"Gladly. Here and now."

The Irishman hesitated, then nodded. 'On horseback or on foot?'

'Whichever you wish.'

That created a stir among the onlookers, whose numbers were growing as the crowd drew together from nowhere, pulled by the expectation of blood. Bedwyr was no more than ordinarily skilled as an infantry fighter, but he was a brilliant horseman. Ruadh, however, was a very fine infantry fighter. Ruadh knew this and stared for a moment in disbelief before rapping out, 'On foot!'

At this one of the other members of the Family decided that Arthur should know of the duel, and ran off to find him. Arthur and I were together in the Hall, hearing petitions, and the warrior ran up and shouted loudly enough for all the world to hear, 'Bedwyr is fighting Ruadh, on foot!'

I did not consciously think of what could have happened;

I knew, at once, and I felt the colour go from the world. I rose without thinking and said to the petitioners, 'The hearing is suspended.' Arthur caught my arm and we started down the Hall.

'Where?' Arthur asked the messenger.

'The stables. They...' and the warrior gabbled out the whole story on the way.

We arrived to find a knot of men standing about and arguing. When they saw us they pulled apart and fell silent. In the centre of the knot was a space of trampled, bloody straw and a body: Ruadh.

'What has happened?' asked Arthur.

The first response was an indistinguishable babble, and Arthur raised his hand for silence, singled one man out of the crowd. 'Goronwy. What happened? Where is Bedwyr?'

Goronwy was very much excited, and ignored the second question. Having himself once fought Bedwyr, he had a great interest in the duel. 'It was a near contest, my lord,' he said, 'that dog Ruadh insulted her excellency the Lady Gwynhwyfar, and Lord Bedwyr fought him, on foot. Ruadh managed to get a thrust under his shield and stab in the thigh, so that he went down. Ach, but he was fast; Ruadh didn't expect that, came in to finish him, and found Bedwyr's sword up under his own shield, and into his stomach, quick as the lightnings of Heaven. Glory to God, it was a pretty stroke, and from his knees, too!'

'Pretty?' cried another warrior, one of Medraut's faction. 'God of Heaven, it is a man dead, a man of the royal clan of Britain!'

'Where is the lord Bedwyr?' Arthur demanded again, raising his voice over the renewed arguments of his warriors. They fell silent.

'We bound his leg up, and had him brought to Gruffydd the surgeon,' replied Goronway. 'Cei is with him now. Many of us would have gone, but he himself commanded us to remain here out of the way.'

I had not realized how my heart had been pressed, until that word freed it. Bedwyr was alive, and in control, commanding himself and the others. I felt Arthur relax beside me, though his face did not change from its set calm. 'Very well,' he said. He lifted his hand to hold the eyes of the crowd, and looked from one to another of them. 'It is enough, my cousins. No more quarrelling. Rhuawn, go and find Lord Medraut ap Lot, and tell him that his kinsman Ruadh is dead, and that he has my leave to do as he will with regard to the burial. The man was a member of the royal clan, and his body will be respected accordingly: four of you stay here to guard it. The rest of you are dismissed to go about your own business. I repeat, there has been blood enough shed for one day, and I wish no more. Gwynhwyfar, come.'

We hurried from the stables to Gruffydd's house, arrived to find the surgeon just wiping the blood off his hands. He nodded to us, then jerked his head towards the bed in the corner. Bedwyr was lying on it while Cei sat on the ground beside him, folding a bloodstained cloth. The warleader was very pale, sweating with pain, but conscious, self-controlled and, most important, alive.

'The worst of it was the loss of blood,' Gruffydd said, answering our unasked question. 'The wound was bound up at once, fortunately: otherwise the fool would now be chasing Ruadh to Hell. He should recover quickly, if there's no fever. Tell him to take the drug I have made him for the pain; he has refused it.'

Arthur went to the bed and grasped Bedwyr's hand. 'You fool,' he said angrily. 'Why, by all the saints, did you offer to fight him on foot?'

Bedwyr shrugged. 'I was angry,' he said, his voice hoarse from the pain, 'and I wished to kill him.'

Cei snorted angrily. 'You could have done that better from horseback.'

Bedwyr looked away. 'This way more of the men will believe his death is a sign of divine justice.'

'It was not worth the risk,' said Arthur. 'My friend, my brother, it was not.' The anger faded from his voice and he looked almost happy; Bedwyr was alive. He continued, with incongruous lightness, 'You have lost your philosophic detachment, old friend. What would your Victorinus say?' He released Bedwyr's hand, looked around, took the cup of drugged wine which Gruffydd was now holding ready for him. 'Here, drink this. There is no reason now for you to keep your head clear.'

Bedwyr did not offer to take it.

'I said the same,' Cei told us, 'but he seems to think he

157

must stay awake – as though none of us were fit to look after him.'

'Take it,' I said.

Bedwyr looked at me for the first time, and the bitter misery in his eyes shocked me. Then he looked at Arthur, nodded, and held out his hand for the cup.

'I was ashamed,' he told me, afterwards, when he was on his feet again. 'I killed Ruadh for a lie. He spoke the truth, and died for it. I could not have fought him from horseback, and given him so little chance. Yet I did wish to kill him. He had angered me, and I wished to see him dead and bloody before me. But after it, when I had killed him – then I wished to suffer.' He looked at the earth beneath his feet for a minute, then suddenly struck the half-healed wound on his thigh. He went white; I caught his arm, his shoulders, pulled him against me. We were alone for the first time since the duel, and I had thought during the two weeks he had been ill that I could not go on. My friends had all congratulated me, and attributed Ruadh's death to God's justice striking down a liar, and that hurt me even more than the insults of our enemies. And I had been afraid for Bedwyr, miserable at his misery, and still torn for Arthur, with no one to turn to who could make me whole again. I could talk freely only to Bedwyr.

I still thought about ending the relationship, sometimes. Once I meant to. I was in the Hall one morning, hearing complaints from some farmers and tradesmen, and sitting at the high table, when Gwalchmai came in. Since Gwyn was sitting over at one side of the Hall, playing the harp with some friends, I thought that Gwalchmai was looking for his son. I smiled and nodded and continued to listen to one old man's endless account of a strayed cow. I was disconcerted to look up a few minutes later and see the warrior standing in the circle of farmers, evidently waiting for me to finish. 'Is there anything the matter?' I asked.

'I would like to speak with you, my lady, when you are free,' he returned.

'Of course. Is it urgent? Then it may be a while.'

'I will wait.' He looked very serious, and there was no trace of his usual courteous smile. The old man coughed and proceeded with the cow, and I listened, feeling decidedly uneasy. Gwalchmai glanced at the numbers waiting for a hearing, then went over and joined Gwyn. Presently, over further details about cows, I heard him singing: someone must have passed him the harp.

'So-o,' went my old farmer, 'I saw her at the market, I did, at Baddon, last Sunday it was. It was my own cow, Strawberry, but this fellow – the lying dog' – he said it was his cow! But he must have found her on the road and taken her in, indeed he did, and...'

Gwalchmai was singing:

> 'The blackberry's white flower is she,
> The sweet flower of the raspberry,
> She's the best herb in the day's light
> And excellence of the eyes' sight.

'And this man's a fool, most noble lady, for claiming that my cow is his. Am I to blame that he can't keep his cows home? You know me well; I've farmed from Camlann twenty years, and I swear that it is my own cow, raised by me, and my kin and my neighbours can...'

> 'My pulse and my secret is she,
> The scented flower of the apple tree,
> She is summer and the sun's shine
> From Christmas to Easter, in the cold time.'

I pressed my hand to my head, feeling the headache coming. It was good, I reminded myself, that ordinary people such as these trusted us enough to come to us for justice – but I wished they would not do it just then, and not at such length. I recognized the tune of the song, though I had never heard the words. Bedwyr had been humming it for weeks.

Eventually I had the cow, and someone else's grazing rights, and someone else' frightened sheep all resolved, and was able to walk over to where Gwalchmai was sitting with the others. I smiled at them all, and Gwalchmai stood and bowed. Gwyn, who had the harp, just then, smiled and began to set it down to do likewise.

I motioned him to sit. 'Do not trouble yourself, Gwyn – I mean, Lord Gwalchaved. I only need to talk your father, if you can spare his company.'

By then, however, Gwyn was on his feet. He bowed. 'Couldn't you stay and talk here, my lady? If it is business, it would not disturb us, and we would be glad of your company when it is done. It is too long since anyone has heard you sing.'

'A mercy which all must be glad of,' I returned. 'But I believe that the business is confidential – fortunately for you. Otherwise I might accept your noble offer, and spoil your fine harping by trying to croak a melody.'

We walked down the Hall together, Gwalchmai and I; Gwalchmai paused in the doorway, listening as his son began to sing. Gwyn's voice had settled from its adolescent squeaking into a deep tenor. He was fifteen now, no longer a child, already as tall as his father. Gwalchmai smiled, glancing back into the Hall, then walked resolutely out into the sun, and I followed him.

It was one of those spring days which make one feel as though the barriers between worlds have dropped, and that Britain must have become the Kingdom of Summer. The air was soft and sweet, the grass impossibly green, and sky seemed alive with light. The larks were singing, and even the scattering of chickens about the fortress preened themselves and beat their wings as though they too wished to soar. My spirits lifted; perhaps I was wrong about what Gwalchmai meant to say to me. But when I hummed a bar of the song he had just played in the Hall, he looked at me sharply.

'Cei was in the Hall,' he said, 'so my house will be empty, my lady, if you have time for private speech.'

'Thank you, noble lord,' I said, trying to harden myself. 'We will go there.'

He offered me wine when we arrived, and I took some. He poured a cup for himself as well, but set it down untouched on the table by the fire, and sat a moment looking at me with that same dark, serious look.

'So,' I said, feeling entirely empty and almost uninterested in how it would actually happen, now that it came to the direct question from a friend. 'What is the matter?'

He looked away, quickly. 'My lady, last week, when my son and I returned from our embassy to Powys, we found that Camlann still repeated this new rumour. We were surprised to find that it was not yet discredited, especially after Bedwyr had fought for it.' He stopped, looking back to me and waiting. I said nothing, and, after a time, he resumed.

'Medraut came to me and spoke to me about it in private. He is very pleased with it. He says that it is true.'

'Everyone knows that Medraut begins all the rumours,' I said. 'Why should you pay special attention to this one?'

He stood up quickly and walked to the door, which was open for the sake of the light, and leaned against the frame, looking out at the walls and the distant fields. 'My lady,' he said, in a low, pained voice, 'do not play games with me. I know that half the tale is a lie. Medraut admitted as much. But he says that something of it is nothing less than the truth. And I have known Bedwyr many years, and I know . . . what might be possible. And Medraut cannot lie to me.'

I had lived through this discovery a thousand times in imagination, and the reality left me feeling merely tired, and, in a curious way, relieved. 'Why did he go to you and tell you all this?' I asked. 'And why should he be unable to lie to you?'

'He does come to speak to me sometimes, very rarely. You know that, my lady. I am the only one that he cannot lie to, and I think that gives him relief, of sorts. And I knew our mother as well as he did. My lady, is the story true?'

I was silent. He turned and looked at me. I felt my face go hot slowly, and stood. 'I will go,' I told him.

'No, I beg of you, wait. My lady, for the sake of any friendship there has been between us, sit down.'

I sat again, and he sat down opposite me. He looked very remote, tense with unhappiness, and I felt something in the emptiness within me: pity. Pity for him, and a deeper, agonizing pity for Arthur. 'It is true,' I told him in a low voice. I took a swallow of the wine. 'I have been sleeping with Bedwyr. The rest – the supposed plotting and treachery – the rest is false. But that much is true.'

He was silent for a long minute, then said, intensely, 'You must end it!'

'Oh God!' I said. 'If we could! But we – I am not strong enough. We have tried, but it is no use. We need each other.'

'But, my lady – my lord Arthur, your husband, do you know what it will mean to him if this is found out? And more, you must know that the Family will never believe that you were guilty in one thing but not in another: they will say, 'The Empress and the foreign warleader were

161

plotting the overthrow of the lawful Emperor!' taking the adultery and treason together. We will lose you, and Bedwyr, and our faith in everyone who remains, all at one stroke. My lady, how can you do this thing? This is the breach in the shield-wall, and Medraut knows it. He will attack here, and our defences will be gone like mist before the wind.'

I looked at the table, hunching my shoulders, feeling hot and cold at the same time. My wine glass was there, the cup bronze, chased with silver in the shape of birds; it had been given to Gwalchmai by some Irish king. I picked it up and drank some of the wine, too disgusted with myself to speak. I should end it. I should tell Gwalchmai that I would do it, tomorrow, and see . . . but I knew it was impossible. I could not do it. I could desire it, for the safety of the realm, for Arthur's happiness – but that was all. 'My friend,' I said 'love once made you an oathbreaker, and it has done nothing less to me. I cannot end it. Please try to understand.'

'My lady.' Gwalchmai reached out, touched my hand, and I looked up: the misery was plain on his face now, the remoteness vanished. 'What is to be done?'

'You must tell Arthur, of course,' I said, then swallowed and cleared my throat, for my voice was rough.

'I could not betray you.'

This surprised me, and I stared at him, saw that he meant it. It hurt. 'You must,' I repeated. 'It is your plain duty to your sworn lord. And it is better that Arthur learns of it from you than from Medraut and his friends, and better that he learns privately, and can take steps to ease the effect the news will have.' He continued to look at me without agreeing. 'Gwalchmai, the thing is certain to come out somehow, eventually, if not by you than by some other. You could not betray us any more than we have already betrayed ourselves.'

He shook his head. 'I have been your friend, I hope, and your friendship has meant much to me. My son adores you above the Blessed Virgin. And Bedwyr has been a brother to me since first I came to Camlann, for all that he has been afraid to speak with me, these past months. How can I betray you to disgrace, to exile or death? And how could I tell my lord that his wife and his closest friend are unfaithful to him? If this thing will be discovered anyway, let it be discovered without treachery from me. But I beg you, my lady, as you love your husband, your friends, and the kingdom, end this thing. I would plead with Bedwyr, but when you scarcely hear me, I know that he would not.'

He was so desperate, so caught with love for all of us, that I said, 'I will try,' and half believed I would. I wished that I were dead. In a way, I supposed it would be better if I were; it would certainly be a better end to our problems than discovery. But there were blind hopes and immediate needs to meet me every day, and I did not want to kill myself. Bedwyr and I might yet successfully deceive everyone, or the situation in Camlann might improve and we might end our relationship.

I finished the wine, trying to compose myself, then walked, with Gwalchmai, back to the Hall.

I had arranged a tryst with Bedwyr that afternoon. Camlann was large, and much land was enclosed within its walls. Some of this had not been built on, and a few stray trees, young oak, birch and alder, straggled up the slope on the east. I knew that no one was taking their pigs or cattle there that afternoon, and there was a storage shed built against the wall where I had arranged to meet Bedwyr. He was there before me. I heard him humming the tune Gwalchmai had played as I came down the hill, and my heart leapt.

Bedwyr was sitting on a tree-stump before the shed, holding in his hand the white wing-feather of some bird, turning it this way and that. He heard my feet among the remnant of last year's leaves, and stood, his face lighting with that warm smile. The wind was among the trees, and the sun danced through the branches, and I knew that it was hopeless: that I could not tell him that it was over, and go.

'Gwalchmai knows,' I said, coming up to him. 'But he will tell no one. He is unwilling to betray us. But he begs us to make an end of it.'

Bedwyr's smile vanished, but he had already put his arms around me. I leaned my hand against his shoulder, feeling the sun warm against my back, longing for a moment of light and joy among the shadows. 'We must end it,' I whispered.

'We must,' he returned, but neither of us moved.

Seven

Early in June Arthur left Camlann to visit the king of
Elmet, who was quarrelling with the king of the East
Angles but did not wish to bring the dispute to us for our
official judgement. Bedwyr and I were once again left in
charge of the fortress and, more surprisingly, Gwalchmai
remained there as well. Arthur wished to give the warrior a
rest, and hoped that Gwalchmai could keep an eye on his
brother.

The tension in the fortress became very great. Some of
Medraut's followers may even have suspected Bedwyr and
me of meaning to seize power while Arthur was away. At
any rate, there was a duel shortly after he left, and one of
our faction was killed. His opponent was badly injured,
and when we had him sent to Gruffydd for healing, further
violence almost erupted. Gruffydd's sympathies were well
known, and many of the men believed he would either
poison the wounded man or let him die of neglect. In the
end Bedwyr and I managed to settle the matter without
more fighting – we announced that Arthur would sentence
the man on his return; we forbade Medraut's faction's
setting up a guard; and we allowed the man's friends to stay
by him unofficially until he was well enough to be moved
to a friend's house. At least we did not have to keep him a
prisoner: he was far too sick to escape. But still there was
muttering in the fortress, and comments of 'cunning
whore' and 'upstart foreigner' behind our backs. There
were no more duels, but this was largely because the
tension had grown so great that the two factions no longer
insulted each other by ones and twos. The next quarrel, I
felt, would risk not a duel but armed conflict throughout
the fortress. But this was something I did not think
Medraut was quite ready for, so I waited, as he did, in
silence.

Some two weeks after Arthur left, shortly before he was
due to return, I ordered a feast. The tension had ebbed a
little, and I thought that a feast, full of songs about the old
war, might bring back some memory of the old comrade-

ship, and ease things further. Moreover, since it was a private feast, the women could share the tables with their men, and they unquestionably eased the tension.

It went very well, at first. Cei had asked my permission to bring his mistress Maire up to sit beside him, and she duly appeared in her best gown and some borrowed jewellery, as excited as a young child and laughing delightedly at the slightest excuse. Nearly everyone at the high table began laughing as well, and by the time the meal was over and we had heard several old eulogies from Taliesin, it seemed almost as though Medraut had never come to Camlann, even though he was sitting silent in our midst. The lower tables were full of laughter and joking and old battles refought. Taliesin came and sat at the end of the high table and smiling, passed his harp to Gwalchmai, saying that he was tired of singing and that it was someone else's turn. Gwalchmai laughed and played some Irish song about the spring which he had put into British some while before, then offered the harp to Bedwyr. Bedwyr was in an exceptionally good mood: he took it, smiling, and said, 'So I am to play first after you, and look a fool? Why don't you give it to Cei, and make him look a fool? But if I must . . .' and he played a one-handed setting of a a Latin poem I was fond of. He did not have a fine voice, but his harping was excellent: sparse, difficult, powerful. When he finished he offered the harp to me. But harping was one of the things I had neglected in favour of reading when I was young, so I declined to play, and instead offered the harp to Medraut, who sat on my left.

Medraut took it, smiling with all courtesy, and began to play the prelude to the tale of Blodeuwedd – a song about an adulteress. He ostentatiously caught my eye before he actually began to sing, however, looked disconcerted, paused just long enough for it to be noticeable to anyone who was listening – then began to play something else. It was very neatly done, an insinuation made perfectly plain without a word spoken, and all I could do was look calm, smile, and pretend that I was too innocent even to notice it.

But when Medraut finished his song and offered the harp to Gwyn, who sat next to him, Gwyn accepted it with a very grave look. He pulled at a few of the strings hesitantly, as though they were out of tune, then looked up resolutely.

'I do not see why you did not finish the first song you played,' he told Medraut in a clear, carrying voice. 'Was the harp tuned to the wrong mode?'

Medraut's smile was unchanged, but his eyes glittered. He had hated Gwyn passionately from the moment he learned that the youth was his brother's son, and so merited hatred rather than contempt. Dissembler as he was, he had obvious difficulty in disguising that hatred. Gwyn, of course, made no futile attempts to hide his loathing for Medraut, and a peculiar honesty prevailed between them.

'No,' said Medraut. 'But I thought the tale too long, and not suitable for the present company.'

Gwyn smiled, pulling a few more of the strings. 'Indeed, it would have bored us all – it has been sung so often that everyone knows it by heart. Nor is it suitable because of any great truth in it – I was talking to a priest, a learned man, the other week, and he said it is a pagan tale about the old gods, and is altogether false and wicked.' Maire giggled at this, and an instant later there was another ripple of laughter from everyone who had been following the talk. Gwyn looked at me, his smile changing into a look of wonderful and secret delight, sharing his pleasure at Medraut's discomfiture.

I smiled back, loving the boy. 'Play that song you were playing in the Hall the other day,' I suggested. 'It had a lovely tune, but I couldn't hear the words clearly.'

Gwyn flushed slightly. 'Oh, that song. It is of little value – but since it is you who ask for it, my lady, I will sing it.'

From this I gathered that the song was of his own composing, and tried to look serious and attentive again. Gwyn played a short prelude and sang,

'Where are you going? The whitethorn quickens
Up on the hill where the blackbird's singing,
While down the stream beds water wakens
As fresh from the sea the wind comes, bringing
The black-backed swallows from the blue south shaken:
Where are you going?

'I ride to the east where the streams are flowing
White with the snows and the haste of waters
Over the bright rocks and green weeds going

166

Into the swirl of the swollen river
That over the cloud-shadowed fields goes rolling
Off to the eastward.

'I ride east to war, and no more linger
For life is brief, gone sooner than spring-time,
Sooner than sun-glint goes from the river:
Why, then, delay till the coming of noon-tide
Or complain about death in the face of the winter?
Soon comes the cold, and no spring stays forever.'

It was, indeed, a lovely melody, with a curious lilt that ran through the mind unexpectedly when one thought it forgotten. Cei, however, who was sitting next to Gwyn, took the harp with a snort when the youth finished.

'You are a fine one to be singing about death, puppy,' he said. 'You've never ridden east to face the Saxons, and God send you'll never need to. It would be a cruel shame for a maker of sweet songs to die on a Saxon sword.'

Gwyn smiled. 'I hope that the Saxon would die, not me. Sing a sweet song yourself, most noble Cei.'

Just before Cei could strike up, Medraut leant forward across the table and interposed. 'There would be no fear of your being killed by a Saxon, nephew. I do not think you would see much of a battle.'

Cei responded to this before Gwyn could. 'What do you mean?' he asked, in the tone of polite inquiry which meant he wished a fight.

Medraut smiled contemptuously. 'Even if our young hero went to the battle, or took up some quarrel in a duel, do you think his father would allow him to risk his tender limbs among hostile swords? Oh no! Even in the grip of his famous battle madness, my brother would tremble with paternal fear, and chase glory from the field.'

Gwyn went pale and his eyes glinted, and Gwalchmai interrupted at once: 'You are much mistaken, brother. Neither would I command my son to be a coward, nor would he be so commanded if I did. I have seen my friends killed in battle, and know well enough that some griefs must be borne.' There was a pause, and Medraut and Gwalchmai watched each other in apparent calm but with a dark undercurrent of total understanding and irreconcilable

167

opposition. 'Of course,' Gwalchmai went on in a tone too casual for the tension, 'if my son were forced or tricked into some quarrel, or murdered by treachery, that would be altogether different. Death in an equal contention must be borne as one bears death by flood or fever, but the laws promote justice to those who have been wronged, and to obtain justice in such a cause I would go to the ends of the earth; I would take no blood-price, and spare no life in the world for pleading or claims upon me. And such is only right in cases of deceit or treachery – but in battle one must trust to one's own skill and the mercy of God.'

Medraut dropped his eyes, but Gwalchmai continued to stare unwaveringly. Gwyn also watched, uneasy, his hand looped through his baldric and resting beside the hilt of his sword. 'Of course,' Medraut said in a low voice. 'Everyone knows your passion for justice – even justice for an imagined evil, brother. And, of course, your son is able to defend himself. He takes after you in that – as in other things.' He looked up again, his pale eyes malignant.

'In what other things?' demanded Gwyn.

Medraut smiled cruelly. 'Why, you both abandoned your homes and kin, scorned your mothers as though they were strangers, and left them to die.'

Gwyn's hand closed about his sword, and he began to jump up. Medraut added at once, 'But, of course, I know nothing about that. And the law does not permit me to quarrel with my kinsmen, or fight duels with my own blood. My lords and lady, and I am grown unaccountably weary; I hope you will forgive any rough words that I may have spoken, and excuse me the rest of the feast. Good night.'

He stood and left the Hall. As he did so a number of other warriors rose, looking confused and surprised, and hurried out after him. Cei, still holding the harp, spat at their retreat. 'Lost his temper for once,' he observed of Medraut. 'We're well rid of them.' He struck up a harsh marching-song. Gwyn sat looking after Medraut, clenching and unclenching his grip on the hilt of his sword; then turned his head away. Gwalchmai watched him silently with concern.

When the feast was over, I was not at peace with Cei's conclusion that Medraut had simply lost his temper when

168

he came so near to offering to fight Gwyn. To be sure, he hated the youth, and could not conceal his hatred, but Medraut rarely did or said anything not dictated by policy. I could not quite believe this; I had never seen the face behind that gold mask, and I did not think I had seen it yet. If Arthur had been there we would have discussed what had happened for hours. In a way, I was glad he was absent and I did not have to talk about it, but the sheer habit of conversation kept me up. The house seemed very cold and empty, without my husband sitting at the desk waiting for me to come in. What with the tension and the extra work I had not spent much time in it recently, and the servant who had cleaned it had been the last person there, and had left it wiped clean of all character, like a guest house. I sat on the bed, took down my hair and combed it out, then found that I was too tense, and missed Arthur too much, to be able to lie down and rest. I went into the conference room and looked through some business at the desk, but could not concentrate. I sat and stared at the lamp until everything was black around the blue of its flame, and I thought upon the scene that had just passed, and on other scenes, and came to no conclusions. I put the lamp out, then went to the door. Outside the Hall loomed black and tall beside the house, blotting out the moon. Beyond its shadow the grass, the paths, the hunched shapes of the houses lay clear and plain, bleached colourless by the wan moonlight. But from Bedwyr's house came a warmer glow, the buttercup yellow light of a lamp. Bedwyr's servant would be asleep in his own house, at this hour, and no one else was about. I stood a moment, looking, then went out, closing the door behind me.

Bedwyr was sitting on the threshhold of his house, staring at the moon and singing, very softly,

> 'My pulse and my secret is she
> The scented flower of the apple tree . . .'

He saw me and stopped singing. He rose, stepped forward from the lamplight into the moonlight, and the moon made him pale as death. 'I wondered whether you would come,' he said. 'Welcome.'

The moon had laid a chill on my heart, and I pulled him

from the cold light into the house. He closed the door. The fire was burning brightly on the hearth, and the lamp cast a warm dim light over the plain room, over the rack of books and the silver wine pitcher with the two cups set on the table. Bedwyr smiled at me and poured some wine, saying, as he handed me the cup. 'I thought you might come, my lady. Your hair is very beautiful like that.'

I smiled back, brushing it away from my face. 'You know me too well, noble lord. What do you think Medraut hoped to gain just now?'

He smiled again, standing the other side of the table with the cup in his hand but only looking at me. 'Well guessed. I did think you would ask that. Ach, Gwynhwyfar, I do not know. I think for once he did simply lose his temper. He has as much cause to be tense as we have. He has failed to gain ground recently, now that the faction has become a plain matter of following him or following our lord the Emperor.'

'But his following is far more dedicated now.'

'True. But it is smaller than he had hoped.'

'Yet he wanted . . . something. I do not trust his loss of temper. He is too skilled to do that.'

'Perhaps. But Gwyn troubles and angers him, more even than Arthur, though he hates our lord more. And Gwalchmai says that he is honest with him. He might well lose his temper.'

I sat down at the desk, sipped the wine. The room was warm, and it was comforting to speak, to be understood, not to be alone. 'He might – yet now I am afraid for Gwyn. Ach, I know: Medraut cannot himself pick a quarrel with him, the law will not permit him to fight his own nephew. But he could persuade one of his followers to it. And Gwyn is hurt, and angry, and has been taunted with hiding behind his father. He could easily be provoked to fight. Does Medraut wish to destroy him? Does he fear the fact that Arthur favours him?'

Bedwyr shook his head. 'The boy is not altogether helpless, my lady. He is already a match for many men, on horseback. Moreover, he is popular. Such a quarrel would do Medraut little good. And Gwalchmai has made it plain how he would view such a quarrel, and I do not think anyone would care to have Gwalchmai as a dedicated enemy. Rest assured: I do not think Gwyn is in danger. And, bird of my heart, if there is more to the matter you will not find it by this scratching in the sand.'

'No,' I said. I found myself studying him in the warm lamplight: the dark brown hair, still untouched by grey; the grave eyes under the level brows; the remnants of a smile snared at the corner of his mouth. Love was a solid thing, hard-edged and painful, cutting into my breast. We had both known that I had not come just to talk about the terrors of the world, and labyrinths of plots and politics. We both wanted to break free of those for a little while, to be in another world private to ourselves; now that other world was flowering around us. Bedwyr set down his untouched cup of wine, came forward and bent over, kissing my eyelids. He twisted my hair around his fingers, kissed me again. I set down my own wine-cup and rose, pressing against him. One can lose oneself in love; forget identity, ties, responsibilities, everything. In love one can deny everything that one is and means, for everything else becomes nothing, another world, a dream. With Bedwyr I was simply Gwynhwyfar, not Lady or Empress, not old and trammelled with cares and bonds, and there was nothing outside the lamplit walls of his house. He loosened the laces of my gown and drew me down onto the bed.

And then our private world was broken into a thousand pieces.

The lamp and fire flared, leaping with a gust of sudden wind, and the cold smell of the night came in. There was a shout, more shouting; Bedwyr rolled off me and stood, seized his sword from beside the bed and crouched between me and the door. I sat up, trying to pull my dress straight, bewildered and hearing Medraut's voice crying triumphantly, 'She is here! Look!'

The light flickered madly. 'What are you doing here?' demanded Bedwyr. 'Get out! Or shall I kill you as I killed Ruadh?'

'Who is your woman?' yelled another voice, 'Why are you hiding her?'

Footsteps surged forward; Bedwyr backed against the bed, shaking the sheath off his sword; the flaring firelight caught the steel and made it blaze like the sun. 'Disharm him!' Medraut was shouting. 'He is guilty of treason!'

'Murderer! Usurper! Traitor!' came other yells. Steel flashed.

I threw off the cover and stood, pushing past Bedwyr. The room suddenly went very silent. I brushed my hair out of my eyes and pulled my gown up.

There were about a dozen men crowding in through the door, with Medraut in front of them, his face flushed with triumph and his sword drawn. I let my eyes run over him to his witnesses, and saw Gwyn in the front rank, white-faced with horror, a horror which abruptly struck me also so that I wished to sink under the earth. When my eyes met Gwyn's, he turned crimson, tried to back out through the press behind him, was unable to. I looked away, saw a few more shocked, agonized faces in the crowd, men who had been my friends, who had honoured me. Medraut had planned carefully. I had betrayed them, and now I could see it, I was so sick with shame that for a moment I could not speak. I looked back at Medraut.

'You challenged them that I would be here,' I said, and was amazed to find that I could hold my voice steady. 'And your faction clamoured of my guilt, and my friends of my innocence, until all agreed to put it to the test. And you proposed the test, as you had meant to, all along. Well, you have won. But,' looking to Gwyn and the others, 'not all of it was true, for all of this, not all of it.'

The flush had begun to fade from Medraut's face. He spat. 'You lying, perjured whore!' he said. 'Do you still pretend to innocence?'

Bedwyr moved beside me – just his sword arm, raising the weapon and angling it before himself, ready to attack. I caught his arm, pressed it. I felt his eyes on me, startled, but would not look at him. 'I am guilty of adultery,' I declared, to all of them. 'But before God, the Lord of Earth and Heaven, we are both innocent of the other treason with which rumour has charged us. We never wished any injury either to our lord Arthur, or to this Empire; and we never planned to gain power for ourselves. Now you may take us and punish us as you wish, for we deserve all that any of you would do to us, and I would not deny it. But, my friends, if ever you listened to me in your lives, listen now: Medraut ap Lot plans ruin for all of us, and if you distrusted him before, distrust him now even more. Now, let me out, to my house to await the judgement of my lord the Emperor.'

Medraut tried to rush forward and strike me, and one of his friends held him back. The grace and contemptuous smile were gone: he was red-faced, angry, excited, and a stranger to me. 'The liar, the adulterous traitress!' he hissed, spitting at us. 'Both of them, caught in the very act, panting in each other's arms and betraying their true lord, and still she reviles me!'

Medraut's friends gave a yell and surged forward. I dropped Bedwyr's arm and walked towards them. I did not dare look at Bedwyr. His passion had betrayed him again, and I knew he was eager to fight them, to die fighting them, no doubt. But that was the last thing we should do: we must stand trial, be convicted of what we had done, and let the fortress know the whole story so that they would know there was nothing more. I was myself again, what I was by nature, and also what chance and time and power had made me: I could think clearly. When I drew even with Medraut, his followers fell back a little, staring at me, hating me, but I knew that I could command and they would obey.

'I must become your prisoner,' I said, 'as must the lord Bedwyr. Where is Cei?'

A murmur. 'We take you prisoner!' insisted Medraut.

'Cei is the infantry commander, he is next in power after Bedwyr and myself, and now he is of necessity commander of this fortress, not you, Medraut ap Lot. Let him see to it that we are guarded – or do you think he is a traitor as well? Tell me, Medraut, am I sleeping with him as well? You have set so many lies around me that I cannot keep track of them.'

'You ... arrogant, brazen ... do you deny, can you deny what we have trapped you in?'

'I am guilty of one thing, one thing only. Or if there is more, that is for my lord to decide, and not for you. Let me go back to my own house, and wait for his return. I am willing to die, if he should desire it. But I swear again before you all that I never wished or hoped that any other should wear the purple in his place. I was weak, and desired comfort, which lord Bedwyr gave, and that was the whole of the matter. For now, you know as well as I that you may not judge us, or sentence us, or do anything but wait for the Emperor's return.' Behind me I heard a soft thud, and my knees almost gave with the relief: Bedwyr had thrown aside his sword. I went on more confidently, 'You, Rhuawn, and you, Goronwy: you can come and guard me, to make certain that I do not hang myself in despair before morning, as Medraut no doubt fears. Will someone fetch Cei?'

'I . . . I will,' Gwyn said. 'And I will fetch my father.' He turned, shoved his way through the rest, and was gone.

Medraut glared at me with passionate hatred. 'Still you give orders? That will change soon enough.'

I said nothing, merely walked towards the line of men, and they gave way before me. 'Gwynhwyfar,' Bedwyr said behind me. I looked back, saw him standing before the dark corner with the crumpled bed, his sword burning before his feet, his hand raised towards me, and a desperate horror in his eyes.

'We knew it would come,' I told him.

He nodded, lowering his hand. 'Remember what I said,' he whispered. 'It is my fault.'

I did not answer, but turned back towards the door. Rhuawn and Goronway separated themselves from the others and followed me out. I had picked them carefully to represent either party, and so content both. But the clarity of mind, the exaltation of finally speaking honestly to Medraut, departed as I passed the door and left Bedwyr to await what guard Cei would set. Then the depth of shame, of humiliation, anguish and terror for the future swallowed me, and I wished that I would die that night, and never see Arthur or the day again.

I did not see Arthur when he first returned to Camlann and heard what had happened. Gwalchmai and Cei met him at the gates and told him the news. At first he refused to believe it. But when he saw that it was plain and certain, and denied by no one, he ordered everyone to leave him. When they reluctantly obeyed, he turned his horse about and rode away from Camlann at a gallop. He did not return until noon the following day. Then he went to Gwalchmai, still covered with the dust of his riding, and consulted him on the situation and how best to contain it. He then, with Gwalchmai, visited Bedwyr, who was being kept under guard at his own house.

It was Gwalchmai who told me of all this. He had come at once when Gwyn informed him of the discovery, and had said no word of reproach, but instead immediately discussed with me how best to combat Medraut's allegations of treachery. He and Gwyn continued to visit me over the next week, informing me of events, helping me to plan for them, and bringing me accounts and papers I asked for – for I was determined to leave the affairs of the fortress in good order.

'Did Arthur speak with Bedwyr long?' I asked Gwalchmai anxiously.

The warrior shook his head. 'No, Indeed, he hardly spoke at all. He came into the house, and Bedwyr fell on his knees before him and bowed his head. Arthur said only, 'Tell me what happened, nothing more,' and Bedwyr said, "It was my fault, my lord, and I am most bitterly grieved at it." Arthur said, "Only the tale."'

'Was he angry?'

'Not angry. He looked at Bedwyr as though he had never seen him before. I have told you, my lady, how it is: he is like a man coming to himself after a great battle, stunned, knowing neither what he has done or what he will do. Bedwyr knelt before him with his fingers clenching in the dust of the floor, afraid to look up, and my lord Arthur merely watched him as he might watch an animal, trying to understand what it was and what it wished. Then Bedwyr told him that he had seduced you after … after you had made your attempt on my brother's life, when you were ill and unhappy. He said that he had loved you for a long while before that. And he said that you had often tried to end your relationship, but that he had always pressed you to continue – is it true, my lady?'

'He exaggerates to blame himself. Oh, the time is true, and perhaps the form of things as well, but he twists it to exonerate me.'

Gwalchmai looked at me closely for a minute, then shrugged. 'He told Arthur all of this without looking up. He did not look at him until the end. Then he raised his head, and they looked at each other for a long time. Then Bedwyr said, "But it was you that she loved. Only you asked more from her than anyone can give. No one can be always a ruler only, always strong, not even you or her. I pressed her to lean on me a little. That was my fault. Do not punish her for it. And, my lord, I have always been your servant in everything else, and this betrayal is bitter to me also." But Arthur said nothing, merely gestured to me to follow him, and left Bedwyr kneeling there.'

'Will Arthur come here as well?' I asked very quietly. I was afraid to raise my voice, afraid to find it twisted by hope or fear. I needed to remain calm.

Gwalchmai hesitated, then shook his head. 'I do not know, but I do not think he means to. He is sleeping in my house now, and he wishes you to stay here until the trial. He has told no one what he thinks of this, or what he plans to do. But I do not think that he wishes to see you.'

And he did not see me, not until the trial itself. This was held about a week after the discovery. It took place in the Hall, before all the inhabitants of Camlann and many outsiders.

The morning of the trial I dressed myself more carefully than I would have to attend a great feast, partly from bravado, and partly to make a point to the onlookers. I tore off the purple fringes of my best gown, the white silk kirtle that had travelled the long trade road from Rome and beyond; the silk was hard to tear, and left rough trailing threads of purple and gold along the edges. I wore no jewellery, and took the signet ring from my finger, wrapping it up in the strips of gold and purple silk. Then I put up my hair with a chain of Roman glass beads which as a girl I had found beside the Roman Wall, and which I had worn when I rode south to Camlann. I was surprised when my face in the mirror looked much the same as it had ever done. A week before the purple had been almost a part of me, and now I was less than what I had been when first I came to Camlann. I had no hope of power, and no clan to return to; even my clothing belonged to the Empress I would never be again. I had nothing more than the flesh I stood in, and whatever my lord's will would give me for a future.

My guards rapped on the door, and I set the mirror aside and went with them to the Hall.

It was full of men, almost overflowing: no women, for law is the affair of men. When I entered at the great door a murmur went up, and I could see those at the back craning their heads so as to look at me. I had resolved to bear my disgrace humbly, since it was deserved, but nonetheless I found myself proud and indignant now that it had come to the point, and I held myself very straight and walked the long way up towards the high table slowly. They had lit the torches, although it was day, and the beams of sunlight slanting under the eaves were blue in the smoke. It was hot, both from the warmth of the day, and from the tightly pressed bodies in the Hall, and as I walked I felt dizzy. The faces in the crowd were unfeatured, lost: I could see the glitter of armour and weapons, the white of the shields hung along the walls, but I recognized no friends. At the far end of the Hall, seated at the high table, was a figure like a statue, unmoving in the heat and smoky light. Arthur wore the purple and a collar of heavy gold, and his right hand rested on the scroll of evidence set on the table before him, the light burning purple in the jewel of his signet ring. His face was like a carving in stone, and as I approached his eyes looked beyond me, not meeting mine or answering any more than the eyes of an emperor pictured in a mosaic.

Bedwyr was already standing before Arthur, and I glanced at him as my guards helped me a place on his right. He looked exhausted, his face worn out around the hard pain in his eyes, and, in his dark clothing, without any badge of office or any weapon, he looked more like an impoverished monk than a warrior lord. His eyes met mine briefly, and something leapt in them – pity, apology or love, I could not tell, for he looked away again very quickly. Our guards struck the floor with the butts of their spears, and the trial began.

Arthur rose, picking up the scroll of evidence. 'Bedwyr son of Brendan, sometime warleader of this Family, and Gwynhwyfar daughter of Ogyrfan, are charged with defaming the imperial majesty, according to the laws of the Empire of the Romans and of Britain, by committing adultery. The charge is brought by Medraut son of Lot. Lord Medraut, repeat now before these witnesses the charge you have laid against these persons.'

Medraut rose from a place at the side of the dais and walked to stand before Arthur, on his left. He was not wearing his usual saffron cloak, but one bordered with purple, and a collar like Arthur's; he paused before beginning, to be certain that all the Hall could note the resemblance between Arthur and himself before being distracted by his words. Then, without looking at me or Bedwyr, he gave his own account of how he had discovered the adultery, speaking in a clear voice occasionally tinged with sorrow, as though he were grieved at such terrible events. I watched Arthur. My husband looked very tired, and still more haggard and grey, now that I was close enough to see it, but his face was expressionless. I had seen that look of set calm often enough before to understand what it meant, but I suppose most of the others thought him cold and unmoved.

It felt very strange to stand there before Arthur, listening to Medraut accusing me, when not long before I had sat in Arthur's place and given judgement for others. I clung to that sense of strangeness, of shock, because it was better than the hot shame and the unworthy rage against humiliation, the loathing of Medraut's smooth speech, which were the alternatives.

'There was a feast the night before these crimes were discovered,' Medraut said, finally approaching his conclusion, 'which I left early because of my indignation at the corruption of these two, and so as to keep a clear mind should there be any difficulties during my lord's absence . . .'

'Explain yourself,' said Arthur, for perhaps the twentieth time in that speech. Medraut had constantly tried to insinuate that Bedwyr and I had been plotting Arthur's overthrow, but had been stopped each time when Arthur demanded what he meant and what evidence he could cite for it. Since he had none he had been forced each time to back away from his hints.

'I wished to remain vigilant,' he said now, at once, 'in case some difficulty should arise in my lord's absence, which these criminals, in their preoccupation with a treacherous love, might have neglected.'

'You had reason to suspect these two persons of negligence?'

'No, my lord; but I thought it possible that they might be negligent, given the circumstances.'

'Ah? And perhaps you thought that they were untrustworthy on some point you opposed them on? I believe a friend of yours, Lord Llenleawc ap Creiddawl, was under arrest at the time, accused of defaming the imperial majesty; perhaps you suspected some ill might come to him?'

'My lord, I affirm nothing. And my friend Llenleawc merely said that these two persons were criminals, as the event has proved.'

'Indeed. It was reported to me that he had called me a criminal as well, and killed another member of the Family in a duel for defending my name.'

Medraut smiled, as though apologizing to the Hall for Arthur's bad taste. 'Indeed, my lord, I knew nothing of any accusations he made against you. As for this, let it suffice that I was concerned for the well-being of the fortress in your absence.'

'Your loyalty is welcome, Lord Medraut. You had no evidence of further crimes by the accused, then, or any reason to suspect them?'

Medraut hesitated, his smoothness finally marred by the merest hint of anger, then, apparently realizing that his hints would get him nowhere in court, finally responded, 'No.'

'I see,' said Arthur. 'You left the feast early, then – I believe after a quarrel with Lord Gwalchaved ap Gwalchmai.'

Medraut's irritation grew slightly plainer. 'Yes, my lord.'

'But you approached Lord Gwalchaved after the feast, and told him your suspicions concerning Lord Bedwyr and Lady Gwynhwyfar.'

'Yes, my lord.'

Arthur looked at the scroll in his hand, looked up at Medraut again. 'In your testimony you say merely that you were discussing the situation with a friend, when Lord Gwalchaved came out of the Hall and challenged you upon your statements. But now you agree with Lord Gwalchaved, and say that you approached him deliberately. What did you do, Lord Medraut?'

Medraut looked back at Arthur, hard; Arthur remained calm, mildly inquisitive. Medraut bowed his head. 'I believe I was speaking to a friend first, my lord, and, on seeing Lord Gwalchaved, addressed him as well.'

'Ah. And you suggested to him that the Lady Gwynhwyfar was with Lord Bedwyr?'

'I did, my lord. He denied it roundly, and I suggested that we test the suggestion. We went first to the lady's house, and received no answer when we knocked on the door; and then, on entering Lord Bedwyr's house, we found the two of them . . .' the anger surfaced suddenly, 'panting in each other's arms upon the bed.'

'So. And you arrested them?'

'Yes. Lord Bedwyr attempted at first to resist, but the lady insisted on his submitting to us.'

'And I believe the lady had you send for Lord Cei, who on her arrest must be head of the fortress.'

'I sent for Lord Cei, my lord, as soon as the crime became known.'

'Indeed? I have it here on the testimony of . . . four witnesses, that the lady demanded that Lord Cei be sent for, while you reviled her; and that Lord Cei was eventually brought by Lord Gwalchaved because of the lady's demand. It was, of course, entirely proper that Lord Cei be present, as you did not have the authority to arrest these two, and as your position was already irregular in that you had broken into Lord Bedwyr's house previous to accusing him.'

'My lord,' said Medraut, his eyes very cold, 'perhaps in the heat of the moment, and in my shock at seeing this crime of adultery virtually committed before my eyes, I used intemperate language, and acted in an irregular fashion, if so, set it down to my passion for your honour. I always meant to send for Lord Cei.'

'Indeed. I thank you, Lord Medraut, without you, this crime would never have come to light. Have you anything to add to your testimony?'

Medraut hesitated again, then apparently decided not to. 'No, my lord, expect my regret at this stain upon your name and honour.'

'I thank you. You may be seated. Lord Gwalchaved!'

Gwyn, Cei and several others were called upon to confirm Medraut's account, which they did as gently as they could. No further mention was made of plots and treason.

Finally, Bedwyr was called, and he took one step forward, went down on one knee to Arthur, and rose again. Arthur pushed the scroll aside and looked at him, as Gwalchmai had described, as though he were a strange and mysterious animal he could not understand. 'Do you admit the charge?' he asked Bedwyr.

Bedwyr bowed his head. 'Yes, my lord. I am guilty of adultery with the Lady Gwynhwyfar, and hence of treason against you.' Arthur watched him, waiting, and Bedwyr raised his head again before continuing, 'I loved the lady for a long time, perhaps almost as long as you yourself, though for long after you married her I would not speak with her. On one occasion, however, which I told you of, when you were absent and when she was lonely, over-burdened with care, and suffering a private grief, I persuaded her to confide in me, and seduced her. She tried often to turn from this crime, but I pressed her to continue, and she yielded, out of pity. For my part, my lord, I am certain that what Lord Gwalchaved ap Gwalchmai says of the events of that night is true, and I do not contest it. But I was driven by love, and not by any desire to do injury to the imperial majesty, which it has been my great joy to serve. My lord, in all but this my life has been at your command, and this was a madness that forced me out of myself. Believe that I have never otherwise betrayed you, and I am well content to die for this, as I should. And if you sentence me to exile instead of death, I will seek out some monastery and there undertake the harshest penance I can find, to punish myself for this grievous sin.'

Arthur looked at his hands, twisted the signet ring on his finger. I thought I saw a shadow of anger cross his face, but, if so, it was gone quickly. 'Have you anything to add?' he asked Bedwyr, quietly.

'No, my lord. I am content to await your sentence.'

Arthur nodded, then raised his head. 'Gwynhwyfar daughter of Ogyrfan,' he called, and finally met my eyes.

I stepped forward. I had meant to bow, but I was afraid he would look away if I did. My mouth was dry, and I had to keep swallowing. I forgot all the others packing that Hall, forgot the heat, forgot everything but him.

'You are changed with defaming the imperial majesty by committing adultery with this man. Do you admit the charges?'

'Yes, my lord.' I had to catch my breath, swallow again,

think whether I was going to correct Bedwyr's story or not, wonder how to tell Arthur that I still loved him. But after that sole reply he rose, and looked slowly about the Hall.

'Both the Lady Gwynhwyfar and Lord Bedwyr have admitted the charge of adultery brought by Medraut son of Lot. Is there any that would deny it?'

I stared at him, not believing that he was ending the proceedings without any more words from me than 'Yes, my lord'. But he stood still, holding the scroll of evidence, waiting. No one spoke. The Hall was so silent I could hear the swallows chirping in the thatch, and the children shouting outside, down the hill.

'Then I pronounce both Gwynhwyfar daughter of Ogyrfan and Bedwyr son of Brendan guilty of defaming the imperial majesty, for which the penalty is death. However, since both have given long and faithful service to the Empire, and since there is no evidence of any other treason, committed or intended, I here commute that sentence for both. Bedwyr ap Brendan.'

Bedwyr stepped forward.

'You I strip of all honours, ranks and privileges hitherto conferred on you, and sentence to exile in Less Britain, on pain of death if you are found in any other part of my realm after a week's time. You may take your horses, your arms, and sufficient goods to provide yourself and your servant with passage to Less Britain. You must leave this fortress before dusk this afternoon.' Bedwyr dropped again to his knee, bowing his head, and again rose. 'And you, Gwynhwyfar, daughter of Ogyrfan . . .'

The steady, ponderous words stopped as Arthur hesitated for the first time, looking at me. I almost cried out to him, begging him to give me a chance to speak; I wanted to rush forward and kneel at his feet, try to explain, let him know that, adultery notwithstanding, I loved him. But was there anything I could say that would alter the course of this irrevocable law? And his eyes were cold, bitterly cold. I could not move. The look was not the one with which he had regarded Bedwyr. I saw that he did not understand what I had done, could not understand, and was cut beyond healing by betrayal where he had most trusted. He did not want to look at me, I could tell. It hurt him, and I knew that he did not wish to hear me speak and to torture him with explanations. I bowed my head, and he looked over me down the Hall, once again as calm and distant as a statue.

'Gwynhwyfar, daughter of Ogyrfan, it is not fitting that a woman who has held the imperial dignity should go into exile, or suffer punishments from those who were her subjects. Considering this, and considering also that you were the less to blame than your seducer, I decree only that you shall be escorted back to your own clan, and returned to the protection of its chieftain, there to live out the rest of your life.

'The sentence is decreed; the trial is ended.'

'My lord!' exclaimed Bedwyr. I looked at him quickly and shook my head, and he fell silent, though he started towards me as though he wished to speak with me, and had to be checked by his guards. I bowed low to Arthur, as Bedwyr had. But I remembered, as Bedwyr evidently did, the letter of my cousin Menw. Exile would have been preferable to his 'protection'. It would mean more than simply hard words: I could expect beatings, and whatever else Menw could think of to humiliate and subdue me. Undoubtedly he would welcome the opportunity.

Arthur rose, and the crowd behind began to ease itself out of the Hall, talking in undertones. The set look was beginning to appear strained, as though his strength were failing and he could not hold it much longer. He did not mean to humiliate me, I knew. He knew very little of Menw, and had probably forgotten what he did know. The sentence — both sentences — were merciful, astonishingly merciful. And I would not plead with him, beg him to change his mind, explain. He wished no explanations, and I would not cling to his clemency and weep. I would not use the ties of love, of the fourteen years between us, to strengthen a plea, like a beggar flaunting a sore. I had wronged him, and he wanted nothing more to do with me. That was enough to keep me silent till death.

As Arthur was about to start down from the dais, Medraut intercepted him. 'My lord,' he said, 'I beg that you will allow me to display my devotion to your honour. Let me escort this woman back to her family.'

Arthur merely looked at him.

'I am most deeply moved, my lord,' Medraut went on,

not meeting the other's eyes, 'by the wrongs you have suffered, and I am eager to prevent more by seeing that this woman is kept securely, and is unable to slip her guards and run shamelessly after her lover.'

Arthur pulled away and began walking out with his long, firm stride. 'You speak very insolently of my wife, son of Lot,' he tossed back at Medraut without looking round, 'but please yourself. Cei, choose five others to accompany him – not Gwalchmai, and not yourself, for I will need you. They are to leave tomorrow morning.'

Cei, who had followed Arthur from the high table, looked after him as he departed through the crowd that melted before him; then himself looked round, scowling fiercely. Gwyn jumped off the dais and came over to him. 'Let me go with Lady Gwynhwyfar's escort,' he asked.

Medraut gave Gwyn a venomous look, but Cei nodded to him, grinned, and slapped him on the back. Gwyn smiled back and came over to me. He was still very confused about what had happened, but more inclined to blame Medraut (irrational, but kind) than me. 'At least I will have the pleasure of your company for another week or two, noble lady,' he said.

I smiled, found that my face was stiff, that it hurt to smile. I suddenly wanted to sit down somewhere, alone: not to cry, but simply to sit still until the pain diminished. 'Thank you, Gwyn,' I croaked. 'My lords, let me go back to my house, to prepare for the journey.'

Cei nodded, and I and my guards moved away.

I did not see Arthur when I left the next morning. It was the last day of June, and the light came early; the sun was high when I joined the rest of the party, my escort, at the stables, though the hour was still early. There were six warriors: Medraut, his friend Rhuawn, and Gwyn with three others of the loyal faction. There were also four servants, and our party had sixteen horses. I had my own horse waiting for me, my splendid, spirited little bay mare, and she whinnied eagerly when she saw me, and nuzzled my hand, looking for apples. Gwyn gave me his hand to help me into the saddle, and we set off under the clear pale sky, I riding in the middle, my escort flanking me, and the servants riding behind with the pack horses. The people of Camlann clustered thickly about the road down to the gate, watching. To my surprise, as soon as we left the stable someone called, 'Farewell, noble lady!' and many others took it up. A woman rushed out of the crowd, forcing the escort to stop, and gave me a bunch of roses and a parcel of sweet wine-cakes. 'Good fortune be with you, my lady,' she said, taking my hand and pressing it to her forehead. I recognized Eivlin, the wife of Gwalchmai's servant. 'Better fortune than you have had till now.'

'Thank you,' I returned. 'Farewell.'

Gwyn, who had let her through to me, smiled, but Medraut scowled and motioned the rest back, and spurred his horse to a canter, and the rest of us were forced to follow him, down along the road, past the houses, the open spaces, down to the gate and through it. I looked back at the fortress, rising behind its sheer wall from the gates to the distant thatch of the Hall; looked back again and again as we trotted on down the road, until I lost sight of it among the other hills. Still I rode looking back over my shoulder, unable to believe that I could no longer make it out, that I could leave so easily what I had loved so long.

Eight

The first night of our journey we stayed in a fortified villa some few miles south of Baddon, the holding of a local nobleman who was eager to offer hospitality to such notable or notorious figures, and who eyed me constantly with undisguised and insolent curiosity, so that I was glad to leave.

The next day we continued as far as Caer Ceri, and stayed with the local lord at the fortress there. This was a man I knew reasonably well, who had been useful during the war. He treated us with far greater courtesy, giving us a feast. From him I learned that Bedwyr had passed through Caer Ceri the day before. This circumstance might have gone unremarked, were it not that some half dozen of Bedwyr's friends, those Bretons who had followed him into Arthur's service, had chosen to follow him out of it, and had accompanied him in his departure from Camlann. Any party of armed men larger than half a dozen will be noted and inquired after in any town.

'But I do not understand,' I told the local lord. 'I did not think he was going to go this way. One would expect him to ride to Caer Uisc, or Caer Gwent, and take ship from there.'

'Like enough he will take ship from Caer Gloeu,' said the nobleman. 'The river port is large enough, and there's much traffic there from the upper Saefern, this time of year; one can find a ship quickly there. Perhaps he wished to avoid notice by avoiding the larger ports. Do not trouble yourself, noble lady. I would not have mentioned it, except that I thought he had been sent that way, and wondered at the reason.'

I agreed not to worry about it, though I was still surprised. But my mind felt numb and lethargic, and I did not think about it again.

The following day we took the north-east road that runs from Caer Ceri to Linnuis, where it joins the main road to Ebrauc. It was yet another fine summer day: the road was hazed with a light mist in the valleys, but the rising sun was dispersing it quickly. The damp woods glistened, the corn in the ploughed lands was beginning to turn silver-gilt, and the cattle in the pastures were sleek and shining with contentment. The bright day made my spirits heavier, and I rode staring at the sun on my horse's mane. Thus I could let my mind sink into the numbness, the fatigue that beset me, where every effort seemed too great; I could rest, and not feel much, instead of feeling all there was to feel for what had happened. I was almost dreaming when someone shouted, and the horse in front of mine stopped. I reined in my mare and looked up to see another party of horsemen approaching us at a trot, coming down the road from the opposite direction. With a shock, I recognized the foremost rider as Bedwyr.

'Lord Bedwyr!' said Gwyn at the same moment, stopping his horse beside mine. His dark eyes widened, as his father's did when he was tense, though Gwalchmai never showed that he was pained and nervous as clearly as Gwyn did. Gwyn was afraid of some scene, of harsh words, enmity between those he loved. 'What does he expect?' he asked me anxiously. 'Does he expect that . . .'

'He has come to steal the lady,' declared Medraut. He unslung his shield and strapped it to his arm. Some of the other warriors began to do the same.

'In the name of Eternal God!' I snapped, angry with them, and more angry with Bedwyr. 'There is no need to prepare to fight. If that is what Bedwyr has come to do, he will go off without having achieved it, for I will not go with him.'

Medraut paid no attention, but pulled his thrusting spear from its sling on his saddle, and started his horse forward. The other group stopped its advance, and Medraut reined in again, touching his horse with his heels to make it dance.

'You scheming traitor!' called Medraut. 'What have you come for?'

Bedwyr started forward again, then, clear of the others, stopped his horse. He too had strapped his shield to his arm, but held it away from his body at an angle, leaving himself unprotected. 'Let the lady Gwynhwyfar come with us,' he called to Medraut. 'I know that her cousin's house will be little to her liking and, as the Emperor said, it is not fitting for such a lady to be treated as a criminal.'

So that was indeed it. I remembered Bedwyr's attempt at

protesting when I was sentenced, and I cried out wordlessly in exasperation and anger. He should realize that I did not want to be rescued, that he could not protect me from the consequences of our crime; that it was not his task to protect me, that, though I had been weak with him, I was strong enough to endure suffering, and deserved it. Oh, he was kind, as always, but this was madness. I spurred my mare forward. 'Medraut!' I began.

He turned, and for just a moment I saw the triumph on his face, and then the butt end of his spear caught me on the side of the head and knocked me from the saddle. I was so astonished and horrified that I did not even cry out, and the ground seemed to leap at me. Above me I heard Medraut shouting, 'She plotted this with him! Guard her!' I tried to get up – I was sprawled in the dust of the road – but the breath had been knocked from me and I could not make my half-stunned limbs obey me. Hooves thundered past me, and ahead I heard shouting, a scream of rage or of pain. I tried again to shout, could not, managed to struggle to my feet, caught my mare's bridle to go after Medraut and stop him, for I saw that he meant there to be blood and I knew that I must stop him. My mare was unused to such commotion and she danced nervously, trying to turn about and go home, and I jumped after her stupidly. More hooves around me, and then Gwyn's horse was forced against mine, and Gwyn leaned from his saddle across mine, stretching out an arm to help me up. 'Stop them!' I shouted at him, not taking his hand, knowing that every second was precious and he could reach the others more quickly. 'Gwyn, Gwyn my heart, this is utter madness. Go tell Bedwyr that I will not go with him, make him leave; stop them! Oh God.'

Gwyn understood at once, and spurred his roan mare to a gallop. She leapt off like the seagull of her name, and I managed to scramble into my saddle, turn my horse about and gallop after her. Ahead of me was a whirling mêlée of men and horses and weapons: swords flashing, clouds of dust, and lime shaken from shields into the clear air, horses backing and turning. One of Bedwyr's men was lying very still in the dust of the road, soaking it with blood. Medraut was fighting another, trying to reach Bedwyr, who had engaged Rhuawn in combat. And Gwyn was galloping up to all of them, his fair hair streaming in the wind of his motion.

'Stop, stop!' Gwyn shouted, his voice breaking again with the urgency, going high like a child's. 'There is no need – the lady won't go; Bedwyr, Rhuawn, the lady will not go! Bedwyr! Listen!' He threw the shield down from his arm into the midst of the struggle, under the feet of Bedwyr's horse, and he flung wide his arms, 'Bedwyr!'

Rhuawn hesitated in the midst of a sword-stroke, and Bedwyr looked up. I was close enough then to see his face. He had a throwing spear in his hand; the light gleamed on that, and on his eyes. His arm was back, ready to hurl the spear, and, even as I watched, that arm came forward too quickly to follow, and something flashed. Gwyn, poised high in the saddle, perfectly balanced for each step of his horse, suddenly fell. Everything seemed to happen very slowly. I saw Gwyn fall onto the road as though he were falling through water, his horse plunging on past him, flicking her ears back, confused, not understanding what he was doing. Gwyn rolled over into the dust onto his side, rocked back; put out one hand and pushed himself up. He brought his knees under him and tried to stand, but fell back onto the road. Bewyr's spear jutted out from under his collarbone, very black except for the bronze sheathing on the butt of it, which stood out like some incongruous jewel. Gwyn opened his mouth, a look of astonishment on his face, but when he gasped only blood came out. One hand felt at the spear, pulled at it, then slid back down into the dust, palm upwards, and he lay relaxed, twisted on his side with the astonished look still printed on his face and the brilliance fading already from the dark eyes.

I was screaming, I realized, a horrifying loud, shrill sound; I dropped my mare's reins as she finally reached the group of men and stopped where the other horses had. I could scarcely hear someone's shriek of 'Murderer!' or the cry of a horse struck by another spear. I tried to stop screaming and could not. All around me now was the shouting and the confusion, and I thought *They will trample Gwyn*, and looked for him among the dust and the hooves, the shaken dust and the lime in the air and the blood on the road. I pushed my hands into my mouth, trying to stop myself from screaming, and some rider, some half-familiar face, dashed over and caught my mare's bridle, then spurred his horse to a gallop, dragging mine after him. I caught my mare's mane, trying to stop her, and she danced wildly and reared. Not sure what to do, and not even remembering which party this warrior fought for, I kicked my mount back into the gallop. The blood and sunlight of the road vanished behind trees; I realized I had been looking back. There was more shouting, and some other riders galloped after us, caught up with us and drew even.

'They are not following us,' Bedwyr's quiet voice said beside me. 'They are seeing to Gwyn, and to the wounded.'

I looked behind me, and already the road was lost in the trees. I did not know even in which direction our wild gallop was taking us. Branches whipped past us, tearing at me. 'Let me go back!' I cried.

Bedwyr nodded to his friend, and the other let go of my bridle. I gathered up the reins and slowed my mare to a walk. The others did the same.

'Do not go back,' Bedwyr said. 'I beg you, my lady, come with me.'

I stopped my horse. She stood still, her sides heaving and her eyes rolling back at me, ears laid flat against her head. Around us was only the sound of the wind in the leaves, the song of birds. I took a deep breath and looked up through the branches at the obscured sky. 'Gwyn,' I said, and my voice was almost gone. 'You killed Gwyn. You killed him.'

Bedwyr said nothing.

'But he was not even fighting; he had thrown away his shield! You *killed* him!'

I pulled my mare's head around, ready to force her back in the direction we had come, and Bedwyr leaned over and caught my hand. I finally looked at him, and saw his face for the first time. I have seen men dying in agony, from sickness or from wounds, and they have the same white, tortured face, and the same puzzled eyes.

'My lady,' he whispered. 'I beg you. Do not go.'

I let out my breath, found that it was in a sob.

'Your head is bleeding,' Bedwyr said, and the mask of pain faded a little, leaving his features more his own. 'Here, bind it up.'

I put my hand to my head, found a spot of pain, took my hand away sticky with blood from Medraut's blow. I shook my head. 'Let us put more distance between us and them first,' I told Bedwyr. 'I will go with you.'

We reached Caer Gloeu that evening by following one of the old roads through the forest, which joined the Roman road a few miles from the port. There was a ship in the harbour, ready to leave for Less Britain, and Bedwyr had already paid passage money for eight persons and their horses. In fact, there were only six of us, for two of his men had died in the fight on the road.

We tried not to attract attention in the town. We had stopped by a stream around noon and washed off the blood that bespattered us. Fortunately I was wearing only a plain green gown and dark travelling cloak, and there was nothing to mark me out from any woman in the port town; Bedwyr and his men might have been any party of noblemen off to buy horses.

All my things had been lost, and now I truly owned nothing but what was on my back. Bedwyr's passage had been all he had been allowed to take into exile, and though his friends were somewhat better off, we would have to travel some distance after we arrived in Less Britain, and we had little money to spare. Because of this, we did not stay in the town, but on the ship. I had a cabin to myself, and the five men shared the one other room the ship offered to passengers.

The captain showed me the room and I thanked him for it, and was glad to sit for a while on the tiny bed. But after a time I rose, found the captain again, and asked for vellum and ink. He grumbled at this, but eventually produced the ink, a pen, and a bill of lading which he told me I could easily write over. I found a pumice stone and rubbed at the parchment, and finally, though I had pressed so hard that it seemed more fit for a sieve than for a letter, I sat down with it. I sharpened the pen, dipped it in the ink – and sat, staring at that sheet full of holes. What could I say? 'My dearest joy, Bedwyr has murdered Gwyn, and therefore I must go with him, for he is grieved to the heart, and because you might have to have him re-tried, for murder; and me re-tried, for seeking to avoid the sentence you passed'? But I had not meant to go with Bedwyr. How could I say that and have it believed? And Gwalchmai would read this letter, and there were no words I could say to him. Indeed, there were no words I could say for myself. I had thought that discovery, disgrace, exile from Camlann and separation from both the men I loved, were catastrophes almost beyond my power to endure. Now I saw that one can never say that one has seen the worst. Even the ability to express grief failed, and words seemed altogether shallow and meaningless in the face of this reality.

The ink in my pen was dry. I cleaned it, re-sharpened it, and dipped it in the ink again. It was of the greatest importance that Arthur should know the true story. This calamity was a thing Medraut had seized on gladly, and I could not doubt that he would use it to create the greatest ruin he could. I was bound to do all I could to prevent further disaster.

There was a hasty knock, the door opened, and Bedwyr came in. I set the pen down.

He stood with his hand on the latch of the door, staring at me, at my sheet of vellum. 'You are writing to Arthur?' he asked, in a hoarse, uncertain voice.

I nodded. 'I thought we could leave the letter with the port officials.'

'Yes.' He came away from the door, stopped, staring at me hungrily. 'Say ... say that I did not mean to kill Gwyn.'

I took up the pen and wrote the superscription: '*Guinivara Artorio Augusto Imperatori domino salutatem vellit.*' I stared at it a moment, then continued, reading out what I wrote. The sharp marks on the Latin writing looked colder and more remote as I went on.

'My dearest lord, I beg you to believe that I knew nothing of the ambush, and neither planned nor desired that rescue. The lord Bedwyr, however, knowing that there was enmity between myself and the cousin to whose protection you committed me, met us on the road and asked Medraut to deliver me up. He himself used no violence until the lord Medraut attacked him. The lord Gwyn,' – I crossed the name out and wrote 'Gwalchaved' – 'endeavoured to make peace, and was killed by a spear cast by Bedwyr...'

'It was an accident,' said Bedwyr, coming nearer.

I looked up, putting the pen aside again. 'You saw him

before you cast the spear. I know that you saw him.'

'No! That is ... my arm moved quicker than my thoughts. Can you understand that? My lady, you must. One must move quickly in battle: if one pauses to consider whether or not to kill a man, one will die in his stead. I looked up, I saw a man who had left himself unprotected, and I threw the spear. Even as I threw I thought, "That is Gwyn; he is trying to make peace", but I could not stop my hand, or deflect the spear which I had already put into motion. I knew what I was doing, but still, my arm did it. I could scarcely believe that it had happened. My lady, I would rather that I had died than he! My worth is nothing, it has been nothing since first I betrayed my lord.' He paused, caught his breath, then insisted, 'You must believe me, my lady. I could not endure it if you also should think me a murderer.'

'I believe you,' I said after a moment. 'But when the escort arrives back in Camlann, they will say that you attacked us on the road, that Gwyn threw away his shield, and that you killed him. It will not sound well.'

'I know.' He sat on the floor at my feet, picked up the letter and looked at it. I touched his shoulder and he turned, caught me, hid his face against my thigh, shaking.

He suffered yes, certainly, but the image of Gwyn's astonished face rose between us, and I sat cold and silent. After a little while I said, 'Arthur had hoped that Gwyn would grow into a man he could appoint as his successor.'

Bedwyr moved his head from side to side in pain.

'And if Gwalchmai believes the story which the escort tells, he will plead for justice against you with any king on earth.'

Bedwyr lifted his head. 'Macsen has still not agreed to return fugitives. We should be safe in Less Britain.'

'Safe! We will be safe! Why did you ever plan such a mad ambush?'

'I did not think it would come to blows. My friends had resolved to follow me, and I thought that your escort would be unwilling to fight its comrades, men accused of no crime. I thought they might be half eager to release you. I could not bear the thought of what you might suffer from your cousin. I thought that even Arthur would not object, once he understood what you faced in Ebrauc. He is never vindictive, even when much injured. And I would not have fought, even with Medraut – only he struck you.'

'A meaningless blow, such as a woman might have given her husband with a broom handle! No, no, I believe you; never fear. And I believe you did not mean to kill Gwyn. Only there was so much that he might have done and been. He might have changed the world. There was no one else like him. And to die, at fifteen, by accident . . . by your hand . . .'

'He is well out of a bitter world.'

'Oh, doubtless he is; but the world now is bitterer yet. Very bitter. And your men fought my escort, and two of them are dead, with who knows how many of the escort. They were friends, comrades of many years, and they had barely a notion of why they were fighting!'

'I know. Once I led all of them. Gwynhwyfar, my life, do not thrust me deeper into my dishonour. I am nearly drowned in it already. I can scarcely endure myself, when I think of what I have meant to be, and have been, and then of what I am now – a traitor, false, perjured and murderous. Dear God, I had rather die than live so disfigured! But I fear damnation. I am afraid, afraid and in confusion. I cannot think. Nothing I have seen, or thought, or read; nothing I have hoped for or believed in; no philosophy or clarity is left to me, to heart or to mind. I am not myself. My lady, as you hope for salvation, be merciful to me! I did it for love of you, and if you turn against me all the world is drowned and empty.'

'Oh, dear heart,' I said, feeling something within me break, something too deep to overflow into tears, 'how can I turn against you? But I would rather we had both died before seeing this day, and what will come of it.'

He said nothing, only rose and put his arms around me, and I could not be cold to him still. For a little while we again inhabited a world confined to the two of us, where there was no past and no future. But afterwards we lay side by side in the dark, listening with open eyes to the creaking of the ship and the lapping of the waves, waiting for a morning endlessly deferred.

The next day I finished the letter to Arthur, sealed it carefully, and Bedwyr gave it to the port official, explaining that it was important information and must be sent directly to the Emperor or given only to one of the Emperor's known messengers. This request was not so unusual, for some of our agents had sent messages through Caer Gloeu before, and Bedwyr and I both knew the proper procedures.

While Bedwyr was off on this errand, the ship was checked over for sailing – the horses of our party tied tightly in their stalls, and the cargo of woollen and iron goods bound down. As soon as Bedwyr returned, the crew cast loose the moorings and the ship slipped out into the wide Saefern, starting down the river under a cloudy sky.

We followed the current of the Saefern through Mor Hafren, then made slow progress along the north coast of Dumnonia, working against unfavourable winds. I had never travelled by ship before, and was sick, which at least meant I was prevented from worrying. But when we reached the end of the Dumnonian peninsula and turned southwards the wind was behind us, and the ship ran smoothly. By the time we arrived at Bresta, in the north-west of Less Britain, I was beginning to believe that sea-travel was a reasonable proposition after all. And in spite of all that had happened, I was still excited when we caught sight of the coast of Gaul before us. In fact, it looked very much like the coast of Dumnonia, and had even been named after that part of Britain. But Bresta itself was a fine Roman town, with its lofty stone fortifications still intact, and a number of other ships moored in its harbour giving it a busy look.

We had intended to set out for Bedwyr's home as soon as we landed in Gaul, taking our horses out onto the south-east road and buying supplies along the way. But when our ship put in, and we disembarked onto the rain-soaked quay, we discovered that King Macsen had appointed harbour commissioners. This gave us a great deal of trouble. Macsen had been forced to rescind the high tax he had imposed on goods shipped to Britain, and was now apparently determined to lose nothing from the ordinary harbour dues – not for the flea on the cow's tail, as they say. Our ship's captain reported that he carried passengers, and accordingly two cold grey townsmen came up to us while our party was unloading the horses onto the dock, and demanded that we all come to the customs house. This was a Roman building, once very fine, but now half-ruined, and half-repaired in the British style. The conflict between the modes of building had made it uncomfortable: originally it must have had a Roman hypocaust for heating, but now had a hearth without the proper ventilation for one. It was filled with thick grey smoke from the damp wood fire, and filled also with confiscated British goods – sacks of tin ore, bundles of hides, wool and woollen cloths – piled nearly to the roof and threatening to collapse if one brushed against them, which it was hard to avoid doing. The two townsmen ushered us over to the fire, where they sat and kept us standing. They stared at us, peering through the smoke. One coughed, and the other asked Bedwyr, 'You are the leader of this party?'

Bedwyr nodded.

'You did not give your name to the captain of the ship you sailed in. You booked eight places; where are the other two?'

'They could not come.'

'What is your purpose in coming here?'

'I do not see,' Bedwyr said in his calm, level voice, 'why the purposes of private citizens coming into another province are of official concern.'

They blinked at him. The one who had spoken coughed and the one who had coughed said, 'We cannot have armed parties roving about wherever they please. We have bandits enough without importing more from Britain.'

'We are not bandits, but nobly-born Bretons.'

'He speaks like a Breton,' one of the officials conceded to the other. 'What is your purpose in coming here?'

We had no particular necessity to conceal our status. Arthur had written to King Macsen, informing him that Bedwyr had been exiled to Less Britain, though it was unlikely that the king had yet received the letter. Nonetheless, because the fight on the road had probably changed our situation, Bedwyr had thought it best to come unofficially and to avoid the king's notice as much as possible. Thus Macsen could truthfully tell Arthur that he did not know our whereabouts, which might ease any tension which might develop if another trial were demanded. Moreover, Bedwyr had not forgotten that Macsen had once attempted to persuade him to join his own warband, and been angry when Bedwyr refused. 'I do not think he would be angry enough to force us to return to Britain,' he had told me, 'but he might put obstacles between us and my home.'

Now Bedwyr tapped his sword's hilt idly, studying the two officials. 'I do not see that you have any right to question us so,' he said, at last, 'but I will tell you that I hope to return to my family's estates, and there settle peacefully. I trust that, if this does not violate any of your laws or your orders, you will permit us to continue our journey?'

One of the officials whispered to the other. I drew Bedwyr aside, and also whispered. 'If they press us, will you tell them who we are?'

He hesitated before answering. 'Macsen will discover soon that I am in Less Britain, and may send to me when he does. If I am found to have lied it will be the worse for us; I must tell the truth. But they have no right to act in this way, as though we were crossing the frontier into some land outside the Empire.'

One of the officials coughed again. 'You may be criminals,' he said. 'Tell us your names and your purpose in coming here.'

The other official pulled out a wax tablet and a stylus and sat, smug and confident, ready to take the information down.

Bedwyr sighed, took the letter Arthur had given him from his belt. It stated simply his name, the sentence, and a request that the reader render any assistance necessary in finding Bedwyr a ship and means of obeying the sentence. He gave the letter to the officials. They stared at the dragon on the seal, started, then broke the seal and unrolled it, holding it near the smoky fire so as to be able to read it in the dim light. Murmurs of astonishment; they glanced up at Bedwyr, at the rest of us, read on. They whispered together, and one rose and rapidly left the customs house.

'Noble lord,' said the other, 'your name is well known here. For what crime did Arthur of Britain exile his warleader?'

'For defaming the imperial majesty. I trust that we may go now?'

'Ah. Ah.' Coughing. 'Noble lord, perhaps you should stay here for the night. I know that Lord Hywel, lord of this city, would welcome a guest as famous as yourself.'

'I thank you, but I wish to comply with the sentence my lord the Emperor has decreed for me, and return to the estates of my family.'

'But you have already complied with that sentence, noble lord. See,' he tapped the letter. 'This says that you are exiled to the province of Less Britain: it does not specify a city.'

'Again, I thank you, but I have no wish to lengthen my journey. I feel my disgrace too keenly to take pleasure in the hospitality even of my countrymen.'

More coughing. 'Noble lord, the King will be offended if you ride south without first visiting his court and explaining yourself to him.'

Bedwyr was silent a moment, then bowed slightly. 'So be it. I would not wish to offend the King.'

Presently the other official returned, bringing with him some nine warriors and a plump middle-aged nobleman in a scarlet cloak covered with gold embroidery, whom the official welcomed, with a bow, as 'Lord Hywel'.

'Most noble lord,' this man said to Bedwyr, 'I am most honoured that you should come here, though, of course, deeely grieved that it should be on such an occasion as exile. Surely, it is an undeserved ruin, a tyrant's caprice. I beg you, accept my hospitality.'

Confronted by Hywel's warriors we were plainly to be either guests or prisoners, so we gave way as graciously as we could, collected our horses and luggage from the quay, and followed Hywel up through the town to the buildings he used to house his warband and himself. Hywel's own house was winged by the others, Roman-built, well-preserved and luxuriously furnished – finer, in fact, than anything at Camlann. Here our horses were taken from us, while servants carried away our luggage, and Hywel directed other servants to prepare the best guest room for Bedwyr. He then asked politely, 'And whose wife is the lady?'

At this there was an awkward silence, and Hywel looked at me sharply. Before I must have impressed him as a lady, and therefore a wife, but now I could see him taking into account my rough travelling gown and reconsidering. I realized that the tale would have to come out. We were plainly to be sent to King Macsen, so there was nothing more to hope for from concealment. Probably some rumour had reached Hywel already, and I could not disguise my northern British accent, which would set me apart from the others. For that matter, I was sure I could not submit to being treated like some sluttish serving maid.

'Lord Hywel,' I began, choosing my words at the cost of some pain to myself, 'I am not the wife of any of these men. Lord Bedwyr has graciously chosen to give me his protection, in consideration that it was through each other that we each lost our position. Since Bedwyr suffers exile because of the just anger of my husband, the Emperor, I thought it unfitting to escape more easily than he, and so have accepted his protection and his exile. If I also am welcome to your hospitality, I thank you. If not, I ask that you give me some trustworthy escort back to Britain.'

Hywel gaped at me, looked quickly at Bedwyr, was satisfied by his expression that I was not joking. He then looked thoughtful. The fact that he was thoughtful rather than shocked and amazed made me guess that I had been right, that he had heard the rumours but perhaps discounted them.

'Most, um, gracious Lady Gwynhwyfar,' he said, 'it is a pleasure, always, to offer hospitality to a beautiful woman: be welcome, lady. Um . . .' He glanced again at Bedwyr.

I quickly forestalled his next question by responding, 'I am grateful for your hospitality, Lord Hywel. And I would also be grateful if you could give me the use of some private room where I could rest. We have travelled very rough these past days, and I am fatigued.' That would ensure that he did not simply send me to Bedwyr's room. Unfaithful I might be, but I would not give the gossipmongers of Less Britain more material to cackle over, nor parade evidence of my shame about a foreign land.

We were kept at Hywel's fortress for two weeks before being given an escort to Macsen's court, and I grew to know Bresta and dislike it. My first impression of it as a rich and busy town proved false. The port was fairly busy, but the town, like most of the towns in Britain, was more than half empty, falling into decay within its splendid ramparts. It was, nonetheless, the chief city of the northwestern part of Less Britain, the region called Dumnonia after the part of Britain which it resembled. Most of the people were Armorican – that is, descended from those who had inhabited Less Britain before it was colonized from Britain. They spoke a peculiar dialect of Latin among themselves which I found totally unintelligible. Hywel and his warband, with most of the merchants and innkeepers, were within one or two generations of being British – Hywel himself had left Cawel in Gueid Guith in southern Britain when he was twelve, as he told me many times. He spent a great deal of time talking to me and to Bedwyr, generally with several of his warriors about him, though he was too polite to tell us in so many words that he was keeping us under surveillance. He always treated me especially with great courtesy, at least to my face. I knew, however, that he and the rest of the fortress all viewed me as Bedwyr's stolen woman, a show thing, a fine horse captured by a daring raider which they were eager to put through its paces and admire. They made jokes at Arthur's expense, some of the warriors actually laughing at these in my presence. There was nothing I could do about it. That was almost worse than the shame: I was useless and helpless. I had been accustomed to responsibility and authority, and I had become a piece of Bedwyr's luggage, the trophy of a battle. Bedwyr, of course, liked this no more than I did, and for him I was willing to endure a great deal. I told myself that things would have been no better in Britain; that with Menw they might have been considerably worse. Nonetheless, I grew to loathe Hywel, his fortress, his city and his kingdom, and I was even glad when he sent us off to Macsen.

We rode first north-east from Bresta: Bedwyr, his four followers, myself, and ten of Hywel's warriors. We followed the Elorn river towards the hills, then crossed it at Llandernoch and turned south towards Macsen's capital Car Aës. The Bretons all say 'Car' for 'Caer': they speak British in the back of their throats, so that it sounds strange, almost another language. Bedwyr's accent had been softened by years in Britain, and Hywel's and his men's were also gentler, but when we came to the older settlements of the interior the speech grew stranger. Less Britain is in fact several lands and several peoples. The earliest British colonies were made near the end of the Empire of the Romans, in the interior, carved out of the great forests which the original inhabitants had shunned. The coasts were only colonized from Britain later: Hywel's province of Dumnonia, and its neighbour Tregor, were comparatively new. Cernw, the central region, where Macsen ruled directly, was the oldest and strangest part. Bedwyr's family – it was not precisely a clan, for clans are less important among the Bretons – lived further east, near the city called Gwened in the province of Broerec. Macsen did not have uncontested authority so far east, for the eastern parts of Less Britain had partially submitted to a Saxon tribe called the Franks. Yet Macsen's authority was felt everywhere. He claimed his descent from the first lord of Less Britain, Conan Meriadec, and could demand obedience from whomever he pleased. We arrived at his court in the last week of July.

Hywel had, of course, informed his overlord of our arrival, and the King had also by then received Arthur's letter regarding Bedwyr's exile. Macsen himself came down to the gates of Car Aës to greet us – like Hywel, and like most of the Breton nobles, he had settled in a Roman town rather than a hill-fort. He treated us with greater courtesy than our present status merited, and rode with us through the town to his house, pointing out the sights to us. He was a man some few years older than Arthur, with a thin, hard face, lined with bitterness. The thing I chiefly noticed about him was his mouth, which had thick wet lips and strong white teeth that glinted through his heavy black beard. Sometimes he used to bite his upper lip and stare at someone or something with his cold black eyes, and I soon learned to recognize this as a sign of danger. But he was evidently doing his best to be charming.

Macsen's houses were in the centre of the town, the old Roman prefecture and public buildings, and they were in very good condition. He had us shown to very fine rooms, much finer than Hywel's, but he had me shown to the same room as Bedwyr, and the servants would not listen to my protests. It was a room very much in the Roman style, with a tiled floor, heavy, crimson-dyed hangings, and deep rugs by the bed, which was the only piece of furniture in the room. I would a thousand times rather have had a plain British room, clean and whitewashed, with a desk and tables and a case for books: this crimson luxury oppressed my spirits.

I argued with the servants, and Bedwyr stood by the wall watching me. He wanted me to stay, I knew, though he did not ask it. He was unhappy alone. I was as well, for that matter, yet still I feared to stay. I felt that I could not allow myself to be reduced to nothing, to an appendage, to a tool to use against Arthur. But the servants were sullen and insistent, and I had no authority.

Another servant arrived when I was beginning to despair, and requested Bedwyr to come immediately to speak with King Macsen. He hesitated, looking at me; then sighed and left. I sat down on the bed, exhausted, and the servants began showing me the things that Macsen had ordered brought there for my use, holding up silks and jewellery as though they expected me to clap my hands and squeal like a girl at the sight of such fine things. The finest piece was a gown they wished me to wear to a feast that night, 'a gift from the King'. It was of purple silk, heavy with gold. I refused to touch it. The servants would not listen to my refusal until I vowed to wear instead my plain green travelling dress, which was in none the better condition for having been worn for days on end along dusty roads. At this they sulkily left the room and went off to consult Macsen's steward, leaving me in a rage. I would not appear at Macsen's feast dressed as an Emperor's lawful wife, not to advertise my husband's disgrace and give Macsen and his followers a chance to gloat over Arthur's pain.

Bedwyr returned exhausted from his interview with the King, and sat down heavily on the bed. He noticed the gown, which the servants had left draped over the bedstead in the hope that I would change my mind, and gave me an inquiring look. I explained, with some vehemence.

'Yes,' he said, frowning. 'He wishes to make a display of us. To use us.'

My useless anger departed. The position was too hopeless and confined for it; it would merely break the heart, and achieve nothing. I came over and sat down beside the bed, near Bedwyr's feet. 'What did he say?' I asked quietly.

Bedwyr shrugged, rubbed his face. 'First ... first he asked for the details of our sentences, and of the fight on the road – he had heard of it. When I hesitated to tell him of the last, he insisted that, if I wished for his protection, I was bound to speak to him plainly. At this I was honest with him. Then he questioned me closely as to whether I had indeed plotted against my lord Arthur, which I denied on oath, and I think this displeased him. Then ... then he showed me a letter from Arthur, which he had received a few days ago.'

I looked up silently, afraid, and he nodded.

'It demands that he return us both to Britain. I am to be tried for attacking the Emperor's warriors upon the imperial roads, and for murdering one Gwalchaved ap Gwalchmai, of the royal clan. And you are to be tried for conspiracy and evasion of your sentence. The letter used very strong terms, my heart. It insisted that Macsen return us or he would be considered to have broken all his oaths and treaties of allegiance and begun a rebellion.'

'Oh, Heavenly God,' I whispered. It was worse than we had expected.

Bedwyr nodded. 'Yes. It was threat of war. I ... was deeply troubled by this letter. When Macsen saw that I had finished reading it, he chewed on his lip for a time, and watched me, then said, "You see what your lord commands me to do. Shall I obey him, or not?" And I replied, "You are King; it is your choice." And he smiled and said, "But it is you who will die if I send you back, since by your own account you are guilty: the matter concerns you rather nearly. And the Lady Gwynhwyfar may escape with some lighter penalty, if your tale is true and she is indeed innocent of conspiracy, but even so her punishment will be severe." And he talked of punishments for a time, and of ways in which we might be executed. When I said nothing, he folded the letter and put it away again. Then he took up the same tale I had refused to hear the year before last, when I came here as Arthur's emissary. First he said much concerning Less Britain, how it should be a separate nation, and no part of the Empire; then he said that he owed no obedience to Arthur, but had previously been forced to yield to the threats and demands of a tyrant. Then he said that I, as a Breton, and as a man wronged by the Emperor, ought to agree with him. To this he added much pointed flattery of how my quality as a warleader was well known, and how Arthur owed much to me, and ought to have at least given me wealth and lands when he dismissed me – as if any other king in the West would not have had me killed for such treachery! And then he recalled to me that he had before offered me a position as his warleader, and said that now he renewed the offer, if I would aid him in rebellion against Arthur: if not, he would send us back. "You know the Emperor's methods of fighting, his allies, his numbers and his strategies," he told me, "and my warband and the people know that you know them. They have already begun to make songs about you, how you stole the Emperor's wife, and took her away with you to your own homeland. If you are warleader, the people will follow me readily into war."' Bedwyr reported this speech in a tone of great bitterness, then caught the stump of his shield hand with his good hand and stared fixedly at the purple gown. 'What could I say?' he asked in a very low voice, after a long silence. 'Macsen has been awaiting his chance for rebellion since first he acceded to the kingship, for he has always hated Arthur. And he knows that I would be valuable to him. If I refuse, he is more likely to try us and kill us himself than to send us back to Arthur. Arthur might well spare you, and that would certainly be of less use to Macsen than killing you to impress his own people.'

'You cannot betray Arthur,' I said.

'I have already betrayed him. Betrayed his trust and my position, dishonoured him before his subjects, and murdered his followers. Does it matter if I add armed rebellion to my crimes?'

'Of course! How can you mean to lead an army against the men whom you yourself have led?'

'Less Britain has never been properly a part of the Empire. After a few battles Arthur might well make a new treaty with Macsen and withdraw. And the Family is finer than any force Macsen can raise, without Arthur's drawing on the forces of all the kings of Britain. Perhaps a foreign war would be useful to Arthur. Perhaps it would heal the Family. And if not, what does it matter? We are doomed as it is.'

I jumped up and caught Bedwyr's shoulders, forcing him to look at me directly. 'You did not tell Macsen that you would lead his army?'

Reluctantly, he shook his head. 'I told him that I would

consider it. He gave me until tomorrow morning to decide.'

'Until tomorrow morning.' I let him go and stepped back, thinking hard. 'We might escape tonight.'

Bedwyr shook his head impatiently. 'We could not. We are in the heart of Macsen's fortress, and have only as much liberty as Macsen allows us. And if we could escape, what then? Are we to run off and live among the Franks or the Saxons, or take to herding pigs, like the heroes of old wives' tales?'

'You cannot mean to fight, in cold blood, against Arthur and the Family.'

'I have already fought against Arthur and the Family! My dearest lady, we will both suffer if I refuse.'

'We have suffered already, and we are suffering, and we will suffer much more, whether you accept or whether you refuse; why, how, can you dream of adding yet more guilt to our suffering?'

Bedwyr stood, went to the bedstead and touched the glowing silk of the gown. 'We are damned upon the Earth already,' he said in a low voice. 'Must we hurry to be damned in Hell?'

'God is merciful,' I said, after a moment's silence. 'If we die because we would not break faith or betray our country and our lord, but give up our lives in sincere repentance, perhaps God will pardon us. But we know that traitors are damned to the lowest Hell.'

'If God were merciful,' Bedwyr returned, without looking away from the purple, 'then none of this could have happened. God is just. In justice I at least am damned, for I have betrayed my lord and all that I believed in. I think that in damnation one has destroyed the image of God within one's soul. Perhaps, perhaps if I live I can repair that a little. But in death the desolation would become fixed and everlasting. Perhaps it becomes impossible even to desire what is good, any more – though perhaps that can happen even to those living upon the earth. But eternal damnation... My lady, we are set about with crimes. If I accept Macsen's offer, that is a crime. But if we allow him to return us to Britain Macsen will still rebel, on some other occasion, and perhaps when Arthur is unprepared. And if we are tried again Medraut will have another opportunity to work at dividing the Family. So to return may give opportunity for more crimes than remaining here. And if we remain here and kill ourselves, that is also a crime. There is no escape. God is punishing us, and has given us over to our sins. Why not, then, take the easiest course, and live longer? At least then I can remain true to you, if to no other.'

I would have argued with him. I would have tried to talk him out of that extreme despair and convince him that he must refuse Macsen's offer, but at that moment two more of Macsen's servants entered.

'Lady,' said one, nervously, aware at least that the air was tense and that she interrupted, 'lady, have you decided to accept the King's gift, which he so generously made you?'

I looked at Bedwyr, who still stood fingering the gown, but he did not look back. If we were ruined and damned, I supposed a purple gown would make little difference to it. But I was not able, like Bedwyr, to view all the world as an expression of abstracts, so that one act of treachery must change my nature. I knew myself a criminal and dishonoured, but yet I could not bear to disgrace myself or my husband further, or take on one scruple of an ounce more of dishonour than I must.

'Give the King my apologies,' I said to the servant. 'The imperial purple is too noble a colour for me now, and it would not be fitting for me to wear it. Besides, it clashes with my hair.'

The servant sighed, nodded, picked up the gown, draping it over her arm. 'It is ungracious, lady, to reject a gift so generously given by so great a king. But, so that you will not shame him at the feast, the King has given you another gown.' She beckoned, and the other serving girl came into the room, carrying a blue-green gown and a great rope of gold strung with amber and blue enamel. I thanked them for this with the utmost courtesy, and asked them to convey my thanks to the King. When they were gone I looked again at Bedwyr, and could not endure the thought of being harsh to him in his despair. Since words would be no use I went over and put my arms about him, comforting him, holding him as a mother might hold an injured child.

Nine

Since Macsen had invited both Bedwyr and myself to the feast that night, I had assumed that it was an informal occasion, where men and women might eat together. But when I walked in holding Bedwyr's arm, I discovered that I was the only woman there. I stopped on the threshold, feeling my face grow hot under the stares of all the men. It was not the whole of Macsen's warband, for living in a Roman town he had no proper Feast Hall and could not accommodate them all – but it was enough of the band for their stares to be heavy. For a moment I considered turning around and walking out again. Then I forgot that, and forgot the stares, for sitting next to Macsen on the dais was Cei.

The entrance to the Roman state room which Macsen used as his Hall was behind the dais, so Cei had to twist about to see what everyone else was staring at. When he did turn his face went nearly as red as his beard and he jumped to his feet.

'What is this?' Cei demanded angrily of Macsen. 'You said when I gave you the letter that they were not in your fortress!'

'And they were not. They arrived this afternoon. I had them brought here.' Macsen returned smoothly. 'Sit down, Lord Cei.' And he looked at Cei in a considering fashion, biting his upper lip.

Cei remained standing. 'Do you intend to grant them sanctuary? They should be your prisoners, not your guests!'

'Perhaps they are. You will hear of that tomorrow, Lord Cei.'

'I am bound by my lord's commands,' Cei said sharply, 'and it would not be fitting for me to eat and drink with my lord's enemies.'

'I am lord here, not you,' Macsen said, more sharply now. 'Either remain here as my guest or leave the feast, but, as for these, they will stay.'

I let go of Bedwyr's arm and came over as Cei hesitated,

fuming. 'Cei,' I said, 'I did not know you were here, but it makes my heart sing to see you. If my lord's orders to you permit it, stay, and tell me what has happened at Camlann, for I am almost sick with longing to hear of it. But if you cannot stay ... Lord Macsen, I am willing to leave, and would sooner do so than cause you to take up, from your courtesy, such a dishonour as sending a guest and an emissary away from your feast.'

Macsen bit his lip and glared at me, for, put as I had just put it, to send Cei away would be a serious breach of hospitality. But Cei hunched his shoulders and gazed at me in confusion.

'My lady,' he began, then, in disgust, 'ach, to Yffern with it, I mean Lady Gwynhwyfar!' But he did not continue. I took his hand and clasped it. I was surprised at how glad I was to see his face; I felt as though some clinging layer of dust were washed away, as though I could be myself again. Cei still looked confused, but almost involuntarily caught my hand and clasped it with both of his. 'Well, then, my lady,' he said, more quietly. 'You have been my lady too many years for me to use another style of talking now, I suppose. And despite it all, we have been friends, you and Bedwyr and I. Perhaps I should walk out and let men say what they will of King Macsen's hospitality – but if he keeps faith, we'll travel together tomorrow on our journey back to Camlann.'

'And I would enjoy the journey, in such company,' I returned.

Cei smiled and helped me to a seat on his right – not the seat which Macsen had meant to give me – and Bedwyr sat down beside me at my right. He did not greet Cei, only stared at the table, and Cei said no word to him. But they had known each other better perhaps than I knew either of them; they had fought innumerable battles, saved each other's lives, camped side by side on numberless campaigns. That would make it more difficult to find anything to say now.

Cei looked at me closely as the meal began. 'Well, my lady,' he said, 'when you came in, I thought you looked the fairest queen since Elena the mother of Constantine, but now I see that you are pale. Have you been ill?'

'No, it is only the travelling, and the grief. But tell me,

how are things in Camlann? How is my lord Arthur? And Gwalchmai – I have been sick, thinking of him.'

Cei gave me a very odd look. Beyond him, Macsen glowered. His showpiece was not behaving itself as he would have wished. Probably he had hoped for a quarrel, and hoped that Cei would storm out, leaving Bedwyr and me to impress his men.

'You believe that I conspired with Bedwyr for my escape?' I asked, guessing the reason for the look. 'Cei, I swear to you I did not; I knew nothing about it until Bedwyr's party met us on the road.'

'And she only came with me,' Bedwyr added, in a low, hoarse, voice, 'because she knew that I was desperate with grief through what I had done.'

Cei did look at him, at that, and Bedwyr held his eyes for a moment, then looked away, out over the Hall. He had gone very pale, the skin around his eyes stiff from tension.

Cei's look of anger gave way to one of uncertainty. 'How did you come to kill Gwyn?' he asked Bedwyr, also speaking in an undertone.

Bedwyr shook his head, as though he were insisting on something he had said many times before. 'I killed him as one kills in battle, the hand moving more quickly than the mind that should guide it. I had no time to think.'

Cei gave a little whistle through his teeth. 'That was a black hour, cousin, when you planned to rescue the Empress, and a blacker one when you let fly the spear against your fellows. But I believe you. Indeed, I never thought that you would have killed our Gwyn, had you had murder on your mind. Not when that golden-tongued offspring of a fox and a devil, Medraut, was among your opponents.'

'But didn't you see my letter?' I asked, and, when Cei looked blank, added, 'The one we left at Caer Gloeu.'

Cei shook his head. 'We sent to Caer Gloeu when the news first came, to see whether you were still there and to find what ship you had sailed on, so we could be sure to follow you. But there was no letter there. Perhaps it was lost, or misplaced by the men you left it with.'

'Perhaps,' I said, but I was wondering whom Arthur had sent to Caer Gloeu. If not Medraut himself, then surely one of Medraut's friends, someone who could have taken the letter from the port officials and destroyed it privately.

I quickly told Cei what I had said in the letter, Bedwyr occasionally adding two or three words in a barely audible voice. When I had finished, Cei nodded.

'A grief to hear,' was his comment. 'One of your escort insisted that you had not gone willingly, and that you had offered to tell Bedwyr that you would not go, but we did not know what to believe. Now it seems that it is all Fortune's wheel turning against us, and even innocent intentions are turned towards ruin.'

'I pray that our Empire may yet escape it,' I replied quietly. 'But I beg you, tell me what has happened in Camlann!'

Cei looked at me with an expression I did not recognize at first, I had seen it on his face so rarely: pity. 'Nothing good, my lady. Indeed, there has been little enough that is good at Camlann since that witch's bastard came there.'

I said nothing, and eventually Cei went on, 'Very well then. Medraut and the rest of your escort returned to Camlann six days after they left it, and returned in sad condition, too. They had two men carried in stretchers slung between two horses and three wrapped in blankets and slung over other horses – and one of these horses was that sweet roan mare which Gwalchmai gave Gwyn. They rode up to the Hall without looking either to the right or to the left, and there they stopped. I happened to be sitting outside the Hall, enjoying the sunlight, but when I saw them coming I stood up and stared at them like any peasant staring at a fair. So Medraut dismounted before me and told me, "Bedwyr has stolen Gwynhwyfar. Where is the Emperor?" So I called for servants to come see to the wounded, and fetch Gruffydd the surgeon, and then went into the Hall with Medraut, for I knew that my lord would be there. Sure enough, he and Gwalchmai were sitting at the high table, talking politics, but they stopped and looked troubled when they saw Medraut come in.

'Medraut, with Rhuawn and all the others who could walk, went straight up the Hall, not hurrying at all, and then Medraut took his time in bowing to Arthur. "Why are you here?" Arthur asked him. "One cannot ride to Ebrauc and back within a week." "My lord," says Medraut, very cool and pretending he's trying not to give way to anger,

"Bedwyr ap Brendan and his friends attacked us on the road from Caer Ceri to Linnuis, and they have stolen away the Lady Gwynhwyfar." And Arthur just stared at him, and frowned. After a moment, Gwalchmai says to the Emperor, "My lord, if this is true, unless there has been bloodshed it is not a crime. You told the lady to return to her family but she has chosen exile, a more severe punishment. And Bedwyr has obeyed his sentence. But if there has been bloodshed we can claim the just blood-price and end it there." Arthur looked away and hid his face in his hand a moment. I think he was stunned by it, as I was. And I did not like the sound of it, for I knew that men had been killed, and even if they had not been, an Emperor cannot afford to have his wife living with another man in a foreign land. "She should enter some convent," says the Emperor. "She might prefer that to her family, my lord," Gwalchmai says, and Arthur nods, looking as tired as I've ever seen him, and I've seen him after all his great battles, in the midst of campaigns that last years and near kill a man with weariness. Then Gwalchmai turned and looked at the others and said, "But where is my son?" And Medraut says, "He is outside." And Gwalchmai smiled, God help him, and got up and began to walk out to see his son. I meant to stop him, but I was uncertain myself what Medraut mean, for Gwyn might have been one of the wounded. So Gwalchmai went out, and Arthur also, and Medraut and the rest. When we came out of the Hall we found the servants and Gruffydd looking at the wounded, and Arthur stops, and looks at Medraut, and says, "There was bloodshed, then." And Medraut bows again, to hide the fact that he's smiling (but I saw the smile first) and he says, "One killed and two wounded of our party, and two killed of Bedwyr's." And Gwalchmai looks around, and looks at the bodies wrapped in blankets, and sees his son's horse. And then he looks at that bastard Medraut and says, in a strange voice, "Where is my son?" And Medraut goes to the roan mare and cuts the ropes that tied the body to her back. And then the body falls onto the ground, and part of the blanket falls aside, and there is Gwyn, dead. And Medraut says, "There." And Gwalchmai stares a moment, and then he give this long, dreadful wail, and goes over to the body, and pulls off the rest of the blanket. And he puts one hand over the wound in the boy's chest, and the other under his shoulders, as though he were trying to help him stand up; but he stops like that, and kneels there, looking at him, and makes no further sound. So Medraut says, "He tried to make peace with Bedwyr when we were attacked. He threw aside his shield and called Bedwyr's name, and Bedwyr looked up, saw him, and put a spear through him." And he goes on to say that you, my lady, rode off with the others. Arthur looks at the other men, and they all agree to this, though one insists that you went unwillingly. But they were all angry. So Arthur asks who else is dead, and hears the names of those who rode off with you; and then he asks Gruffydd how the wounded are, and he tells him. Then he tells some of the servants to take away the bodies and wash them and prepare them for burial. And he goes over to Gwalchmai, and puts one hand on his shoulder, and Gwalchmai looks up at him, looking like a creature from the dark Otherworld. And Arthur says, "We must make arrangements to bury him," and calls the servants to take the body. And Gwalchmai says nothing, and lets them take it. Then he gets up, pulls his hood over his face and walks away without saying anything or looking at anyone, and no one wished to say anything to him.

'Well, Arthur had the wounded seen to, and they said Mass for the dead the next morning. Gwalchmai stood through the service without saying a word, and watched the burial with a face like a statue in a church. That afternoon he led the roan mare out of the stable, took her to the slaughter house and killed her. Then he went through our house, found all of Gwyn's things, and took them out to burn them. I came in as he was doing this; I had just been told about the mare. "What do you imagine you're doing?" I asked. "I do not want these things to remind me," he said, without looking round, "And I could not endure that another should use them." My lady, I cannot say what it meant to me; I was sickened by looking at him. It was the same for me when I saw poor Agravain before he died. One should not have to see such a thing done to a friend.

'That evening they had the funeral feast in the Hall. Gwalchmai came in late, walked up to the high table but did not sit down. Instead, he draws his sword and sets it down before Arthur, with the hilt towards his hand, and he himself goes down on both knees and bows his head. And Arthur says, "what do you wish?" At once Gwalchmai says, "Justice, my lord." Arthur says, "I will write to Macsen of Less Britain concerning Bedwyr. Will you agree to a blood-price?" But Gwalchmai says, "I once swore, in this very Hall, that I would go to the ends of the earth and spare no life in the world and accept no blood-price, if my son were murdered by treachery. And I will stand by that oath." Then Arthur looks very grim, but says, "I will write to Macsen." "Do, my lord," Gwalchmai says back, "but do not write to him as you have written before, or Macsen will pretend he knows nothing of any criminals, or say that we have not agreed to a repatriation treaty, and he will do nothing.'" (And Cei glanced at Macsen who was now listening enthralled, like the rest of the high table.) '"My lord," he says, "you must promise him war, if he does not give justice." Arthur says nothing to this. He was not eager for war, and I think he understood, lady, how it must have come about; he never believed Bedwyr meant to kill Gwyn. And he was never one to desire the blood of any who had ever done him service. But Gwalchmai remained kneeling and said, "My lord, for seventeen years I have fought for you, the full half of my life. In your service I have endured wounds and hardship, I have journeyed from one end of Britain to the other, crossed the seas, exiled myself from my own clan while I still had one. Never have I asked for any greater gift than that service in itself. And now I will not even demand it of you, but I will beg, like any suppliant, that you will give me justice against the murderer of my son." Then Arthur said, "It will probably mean war. I will give you letters and status as an emissary: go to Less Britain yourself, and ask Bedwyr for justice. I do not think he will refuse to fight you, or prevail against you." But Gwalchmai said, "I have not fought for the Empire and yourself all these years to wish for some private vengeance. No, my lord, let all the world see that you give me justice against this criminal, justice and the law." Then Arthur sighed and put out his hand, and took the hilt of Gwalchmai's sword. "You claim no more than is your due. You will have your justice, if we must devastate all Less Britain to obtain it."'

Cei stopped and took a deep drink of Macsen's wine.

'So,' said Macsen. 'It is Gwalchmai ap Lot who has stirred up this anger against me, on this private quarrel of his.'

'The Emperor is asking nothing more than due justice from one of his subject kings, who is bound by oath to render it,' Cei returned at once.

'But this Gwalchmai ap Lot is not even British, not from any part of the Empire. He is an Irish wolf, howling for vengeance.' Macsen spoke loudly, wanting his followers to hear him.

Cei slammed his glass down, glaring. 'Gwalchmai is a member of the royal clan, the Emperor's kinsman, and one of his finest and most loyal warriors! What king could ignore so just a plea, from such a servant? Certainly not my lord Arthur – as you will learn to your cost it you try to withhold what Arthur has demanded.'

'Which amounts to the life of this man, Bedwyr ap Brendan,' Macsen said. He looked at Cei for another long moment, and Cei looked uneasy and embarrassed. Macsen then looked beyond Cei to Bedwyr, but Bedwyr sat staring at his plate and said nothing.

'But what was the state of things when you left?' I asked Cei, to change the subject. I did not want to see the warrior involved in a quarrel here in Less Britain. Cei was an unusual choice for an emissary because he would gladly quarrel with anyone hostile to Arthur or to the Empire. Presumably Arthur had sent him to intimidate Macsen, and to put the ultimatum in the plainest terms.

Cei shrugged. 'Much the same. Arthur deals with the business of the Empire, the Family mutters and sharpens its swords, and Gwalchmai sits in the house and broods, or rides his horse half-way to Baddon for a day's exercise. Our servant Rhys and myself are the only ones who dare to talk to him, but he says little enough to us. He once spoke with Medraut for hours, but what they said no one knows.' Cei paused, glanced at Macsen again, and added, 'Medraut is as he usually is' – an uncustomary and rather late attempt at discretion.

'A very pretty report,' said Macsen sardonically. 'And that is enough of Camlann and intended vengeance for tonight. Come, let us have something more lively!' and he clapped his hands to summon his bards to sing for him.

Presently some of his men began a sword-dance.

Cei left the feast early, and Bedwyr requested leave to go shortly after Cei. I went back with him to our room, but he wished to speak neither of Cei's news nor of Macsen's offer, but only wished to hold me, and after lie still on the bed, awake and motionless, like a man dying of a fever.

The next morning I asked him what answer he would give to Macsen.

'None,' he replied.

'None? But he said that you must reply.'

'My lady, I have been trying to make up my mind to refuse his offer. Life is too dearly bought by treachery, especially after one has so injured one's friends. But I cannot simply refuse, I cannot. To stand trial by those I have injured, to see you punished – perhaps flogged, or even killed – to be so broken before my friends and before men I have commanded – I cannot do it. But how can I accept Macsen's offer, and commit yet further crimes against my comrades and my own lord? No, I will return no answer, and let Macsen choose for himself. In all proba-bility he will choose to send us back with Cei, and that will be the end of it, without my choosing.'

However, that was precisely what Macsen did not do. He summoned Bedwyr that morning and asked him what he had decided, and Bedwyr told him that he could not decide. So, after a time, he sent Bedwyr back, summoned Cei and commanded him to leave Less Britain as soon as possible, and to tell Arthur that he did not acknowledge Arthur's Empire over him, and would not accept Arthur's dictates respecting a man who was born his subject and not Arthur's. I only learned of this afterwards, or I would have written Arthur another letter for Cei to take with him to Camlann.

Macsen said nothing to us that day or the next, and we did not see him during all this time. We were closely kept, not allowed even to leave our room. I bribed one of the serving girls to find us some books, which helped to pass the time, but there is a limit to how much time one can spend reading.

On the third day after Cei left, Macsen again asked us to a feast. He seated Bedwyr on his right and me beside Bedwyr, and spoke graciously and casually about unimportant things, as though nothing had happened. Later in the evening he began to speak of Arthur's prospective invasion, but with his own warleader – a dour, thin man with prematurely grey hair – and not with Bedwyr. It was only when the meal was done and we were sitting drinking Macsen's excellent wine while one of Macsen's bards sang, that Macsen turned to Bedwyr and asked him about the subject he had just discussed with his warleader. 'What do you think?' he asked. 'Should we barricade the harbours?'

'Ach, it's no use barricading the harbours,' the warleader Lenleawc insisted. 'There are beaches enough, if he uses curraghs, and we cannot patrol the whole coast.'

'But if he uses small curraghs and beaches them he will have to make more trips to bring the army over,' replied Macsen, 'And then we would have warning and more time to move.'

'He will not bring a peasant army,' said Bedwyr.

'Why not?'

Bedwyr realized what he was saying, and hesitated.

'Come, this is not secret information! If you are as opposed to our war for independence as that, as disloyal to your own land as to scruple to give information at your host's table – if so, you should ride back to Camlann tomorrow.'

'Arthur will probably attack during the harvest time,' Bedwyr said, after another moment's silence. 'You will have difficulty in raising your own army at that time, and Arthur's advantage in trained warriors will be more effective. He will probably take a force of picked men, not more than a thousand in number, and strike directly at your fortress here, hoping to end the war quickly.

I stared at Bedwyr angrily, and Macsen noticed this, smiling to himself, but ignored me and put another question to Bedwyr. Bedwyr's reluctance to speak faded slowly as he became engrossed in Arthur's strategies, and I sat silent at his side, listening, and grew colder and colder at heart.

Macsen continued to consult Bedwyr in the days that followed, and the amount that Bedwyr yielded to him grew steadily greater. He knew now that his position was false. He had returned Macsen no answer, and Macsen had taken that silence for consent. Bedwyr could not accept the protection which Macsen had provided for us, which was the direct cause of the war, and still refuse to give Macsen any assistance. In a way he did believe that Less Britain was a separate kingdom from Britain, and that Macsen might do as he pleased in it. But the main reason he agreed to help Macsen in rebellion was the numb despair for which he seemed never to be free. He seemed no longer capable of making any moral decision, and Macsen continually pushed his indecision into agreement with himself. So, from giving advice, Bedwyr moved to setting up a system by which the army could be raised quickly, to helping to establish the coastal defences – barricading the harbours and proclaiming a reward to any peasant who reported a landing on the beaches – to helping to train the warband, and then, finally, in September, to officially accepting a military post under Macsen.

I argued with Bedwyr at each step. He would agree with my arguments, then say that he knew that this or that was wrong, but there was no way to be right, and he could not back out now. Eventually, since my arguments only deepened his despair, I gave them up. I tried to cheer Bedwyr, hoping to bring him to his senses that way. But he would not be cheered. His only escape seemed to be to throw himself into his work for Macsen, and I saw less and less of him as the days went by.

The restrictions we lived under were gradually relaxed as Bedwyr became cooperative. Presently even I was allowed to ride about the town when I pleased, though I was constantly watched in case I should attempt to leave the city. If fine gowns and jewellery had been a source of pleasure to me I would have been delighted, for these were showered on me. Macsen wished me to appear beautiful and valuable, so that his followers would be the more impressed by Bedwyr's having stolen me, and cheered by Arthur's disgrace. He also wanted me to keep Bedwyr happy. He soon realized that for my own part I was in complete opposition to him, but he was content that I had no power against him.

Well, I was at least glad to be able to ride my horse again, to go out into the open air, or ride under guard into the countryside and to the edge of the great forest. And I managed to find some books. But still the hours were wearisome and heartbreaking. Things were as they had been in Bresta, but worse. Sometimes when I walked along the walls of Car Aës I wanted to throw myself off. It was not even the desire to die, but only the soul-deep longing for freedom. Sometimes in dreams I could fly from the walls, but always the flight failed, even in sleep, and I would fall from the steep air into the darkness.

It was worse in late August, when Macsen and Bedwyr rode off to inspect the coastal defences. I was not allowed to leave the city, and two warriors followed me whenever I left Macsen's house. Macsen's steward approached me and suggested that he take Bedwyr's place while Bedwyr was gone. I had left my husband and was therefore shameless, he thought, and I must be eager for a man since my lover was absent. I struck the man and he grinned and tried to kiss me. I only shook him off by threatening to tell Bedwyr of his suggestion when the warleader returned. But of course I could not do that, when Bedwyr actually did return. It would simply have made more trouble for him, since he would undoubtedly have challenged the man. And it would have amused Macsen and his warband.

I grew angry and depressed, and could speak to no one without losing my temper. I spent hours on the wall near the town gates, looking out into the west and wondering when Arthur would come from Britain. From the gate-tower one could just see the end of the cultivated lands that surrounded Car Aës, and the edge of the great forest. The Bretons were afraid of the forest. They said that if you became lost in it you might never find your way back to the human earth, but wander in it for ever. All that was wonderful and terrible was said to inhabit the forest, devils and gods, castles of glass and enchanted springs, the finding of which meant the loss of all else. I wanted to visit the forest, but I was never allowed to ride so far.

Arthur came in September. He had known of the coastal defences – we had always had spies in Less Britain, and Bedwyr had not gone so far as to reveal their names to Macsen. Instead of trying to overcome the defences Arthur had chosen to avoid them. Some of his Saxon subjects had treaties of friendship with the Frankish kingdom to the north-east of Less Britain, and Arthur had agreed with the king of this land to pay a certain sum in gold for the right to use one of his ports and to cross his land into Less Britain.

The Frankish king was probably pleased that Less Britain was to be invaded, for the sum was quite moderate and he caused no trouble for Arthur. The Saxons and the Franks had been enemies of the British for so long that not even Bedwyr had expected this, and the invasion took him and Macsen by surprise after all. However, Macsen's warband was in readiness by the coast, and most of Macsen's nobles, with their warriors, had already been persuaded to join the king. With these forces Bedwyr and Macsen hurried from the coast, and managed to reach Car Aës before Arthur had done much more than cross the border. They had, of course, the advantage over Arthur in that they could requisition supplies from the country, while Arthur had to send out foraging parties or drag along baggage trains, which slowed him.

On reaching Car Aës from the coast, Macsen wished to remain in the fortress and allow Arthur to lay siege to it as much as he wished while Macsen called up his army. Bedwyr, however, persuaded him to abandon this plan and instead set out again from Car Aës the day after reaching it. Arthur, he said, would not waste his time in siege works, but instead would turn about and plunder the country, burning the grain which still stood unharvested in the fields. If Macsen sat securely in his fortress while this was being done, much of his army would not respond to his call to arms, and there was danger that he would be cut off from the rest of it. So instead they hurried north, planning to set an ambush for Arthur, then retreat towards the fortress, using delaying tactics to keep Arthur occupied until the harvest was in and the peasant army had joined them.

Arthur had crossed the border into Less Britain in late September. His forces first encountered Macsen's in the first week of October, and arrived before Car Aës by the end of that month. The delaying tactics Bedwyr had recommended had been partially successful: the harvest was in, with sufficient supplies stored in the fortress to last the winter, while the country people had hidden their goods and could feel secure that they would not starve that winter if they answered the King's summons. A part of the army had been raised. But the numbers Macsen had hoped for had never materialized. It seemed that the call to arms had been disrupted in the south-east by false reports (doubtless circulated by Arthur's spies) saying that the war had already ended. In Cernw and the north-west there was considerable reluctance to go to war against Arthur. If Less Britain had never been properly a part of the Empire of Britain, it had always been bound to it by the strongest ties, and many Bretons felt that Macsen's rebellion was undertaken only to gratify his own ambition and to support a notorious criminal. Many of the older warriors had come with Macsen's younger brother Bran, when he led them to Britain to aid Arthur when he first claimed the purple, and these supporters of Bran's had always disliked Macsen.

On the other hand, attempts to foment a counter-rebellion met with little success. The people were proud of Bedwyr, and respected Macsen's name and ancestry. Macsen therefore returned to Car Aës with the forces he had had in September – his own warband of four hundred men and another four hundred warriors from among his nobles – and an additional army of about a thousand ill-armed and ill-disciplined peasants, with vague hopes of a thousand more. Arthur had brought, as Bedwyr had predicted, about a thousand men: most of the Family and men from the warbands of King Constantius of British Dumnonia, of King Urien of Rheged, and of King Ergyriad ap Caw of Ebrauc. Though in numbers less than Macsen's forces, this was in fact a more dangerous power than Macsen's and, as was customary for Arthur, had an overwhelming advantage in cavalry. Macsen would have been soundly defeated within a week if he had not had Bedwyr. Arthur set half a hundred traps which Bedwyr foresaw or recognized and escaped. I think that for both Arthur and Bedwyr the campaign was like fighting with a mirror. Each knew the other's mind nearly as well as he knew his own.

Macsen and his forces rode into Car Aës one night at the end of October, entering the gates by torchlight. Behind them on the plain I could see other flecks of fire which brought my heart into my throat, for I knew the lights to be Arthur's.

Bedwyr saw me standing on the wall and watching when he rode in beside Macsen, and he raised his hand in salute, but was soon busied with seeing to the men – with the army and the warriors together there were more numbers than the town could easily hold. So I went back to Macsen's house alone – or rather, trailing my two guards – and Bedwyr came back to the room late, and lay down exhausted without taking off more than his boots and his mail shirt, only kissing me briefly in greeting. The following day, however, we went together onto the walls. We looked out over the bare fields and saw the Family encamped between us and the forest. My heart rose like an eagle on the wind when I saw the tents there, and caught, distant and heart-piercingly beautiful, the golden gleam of Arthur's standard.

'He cannot devastate the country now,' Bedwyr told me. 'But he can probably forage foodstuffs enough to support himself. Yet he dare not send parties out too widely, for fear that we should make a foray. It is a matter of time now, and he has the most to lose by waiting.'

I looked at Bedwyr as he said this, standing there in the early November sunlight. Something in his face had grown hard, and there were new lines of bitterness about his eyes and at the corners of his mouth. *He is destroying himself,* I thought. I remembered what he had said about damnation and looked away.

'It was bitter fighting,' he told me. 'We have lost many men.'

'And Arthur?'

'I do not know how many he has lost.' Something in the tone made me look at him again, and I saw that the new lines were not just from this new hardness, but from suffering, self-loathing, and despair.

Arthur did send foraging parties out a few days later, and Bedwyr did lead a foray of Macsen's cavalry out against the camp. Again, I watched from the walls.

Arthur's camp had plenty of time to see Bedwyr coming, and long before the force from the city reached them another column of horsemen was leaving the camp at a gallop, spreading out to weave across the plain. I stood straining my eyes. listening to the comments the guards around me made in their alien accents. I felt an agony of division. It was the first time I actually saw the war with my own eyes, actually witnessed my lovers setting out to kill one another, from despair and for justice.

The lines of cavalry met, and at once became indistinguishable from one another. I wondered how anyone could tell their own side from the enemy's in battle. Of course, it would be easier with Saxons, who tended to wear helmets and use a different style of dress; but when one blood makes war with itself, how can the beholder know where to strike? This war was like a madman in convulsions, beating himself and the bystanders without distinction, possessed solely by the violence itself. Madness, this, all madness: the divine madness that is sent on those doomed to destruction.

The line wavered back towards the camp. I thought I saw Gwalchmai, dreamed that I could pick out Arthur, Bedwyr, any of a hundred familiar forms. But the forces were small with distance, nothing but a glitter of arms and galloping of horses to and fro. Even the sounds were drowned by the wind along the plain, until they could not be heard above the comments of the guards around me. I sank to my knees, leaning my head against the wall, and wept bitterly. Then the guards came and took me back to my room.

I had to escape. I realized that as soon as I was alone again. This was my fault, my fault for being unfaithful, for putting my own happiness above the demands of the Empire. Other women might commit adultery and be guilty only of that, but I had committed treason as well, and I had known it. Perhaps others were also guilty, but I knew my own fault, knew it as I would know a rotting sore, which eats upon the whole flesh and consumes it away. I must die of this: only so could my life end free of that spreading corruption. Somehow I must escape, return to Arthur, and accept my sentence – which, after this rebellion, would have to be death.

In that case, it was no use sitting and weeping; I had done more than enough of that already. I must make plans.

I went to the silver mirror Macsen had provided and looked at my face. I had lost weight over the past months, and I looked pale, hollow-cheeked and sunken-eyed, old. Now my eyes were red as well. Abruptly, I felt ashamed at myself, for the long months of passive misery, for indecision, for weeping in front of Macsen's men. Enough, too much of that. Could I disguise myself and give my guards the slip?

I washed my face and went to see if I could find some cosmetics, or a wig.

I had to humiliate myself before the steward to get the cosmetics. He had resented his rebuff, and took advantage of my request to sneer at me for 'losing my looks' and to wonder pointedly if Bedwyr no longer wanted me. My position had taught me some patience, and I made no reply to him. Eventually I managed to extract from the stores some kohl, white lead, and carmine. When I came back to the room the door was locked. While I was unlocking it I heard, briefly, a sound of hammering. Bedwyr must be back.

When I opened the door I found Bedwyr standing near it with his back to it; he started violently and whirled about when I came in. He had taken off his mail coat and tunic, and his eyes as they met mine were guilty and alarmed. Some flash of insight told me what he had been doing before I realized it consciously, before I turned my eyes to the bed and saw his sword there, wedged carefully upright, ready to fall on.

'Gwynhwyfar,' Bedwyr said, idiotically apologetic, 'I did not expect . . .'

I went over to the bed and touched the sword. He had thrown the mattress off, wedged the weapon into the frame, and used one of the supporting leather thongs to bind it down, hammering the strip of leather back to the frame to secure it: that had been the hammering sound I had heard. I began to unfasten the piece of leather. My hands were quite steady; I felt a remote wonder that I felt so little, but that was all.

'Why did you think to do it this way?' I asked, without looking at him. 'Arthur might not have believed it when Macsen told him you fell on your own sword.'

'I did not think of that.' His voice was quiet, ordinary.

I had the sword free. I picked it up, holding the hilt with both hands. Though it was a cavalry sword, a cutting rather than a thrusting weapon, it still had a good point on it; it would have done what Bedwyr had meant it to do. I looked from it to Bedwyr, who still stood by the door, bare-chested, silent, ashamed. Out of the calmness, the ordinary words we used, I had suddenly a vision of him lying across the bed with the sword through him, twisting on it; I could almost smell the blood on the thick scarlet carpet. My hands did begin to shake. 'Why?' I asked.

Bedwyr began to turn away; saw the door; carefully closed it again and locked it. He came over to the bed and began to pick up the mattress. I set the sword down on the floor and helped him. When it was back in place he picked his tunic up off the floor and pulled it on – he was shivering a little, for the fire had burned low and the room was cold. Then he sat down on the bed and picked up the sword. He held it point upwards, looking at it. 'If I had two hands,' he said in an undertone, 'I could have held it firmly, and would already be dead.' He looked about, and I picked the baldric off the floor and handed it to him. He sheathed the sword.

'Why?' I asked again. 'Why now?'

He looked at me as though behind me he saw the gulf of death, as though that darkness were reflected and founded within him. 'I have killled Gwalchmai,' he whispered, and turned his head away.

For a moment the words meant nothing. I looked at him. Tentatively, I touched his shoulder. Then the meaning of what he had said washed over me. I remembered Gwyn and Gwalchmai bending together over the back of the roan mare, smiling; remembered Gwyn's astonished face, his blood on the road from Caer Ceri. And now? I leaned against Bedwyr, trembling. He put his arms around me.

'He . . . I sought him out,' he said, talking quickly now in a stammering, broken voice. 'I thought that he would kill me, and that would end it. I know I am no match for him on horseback. But when I rode up to him . . . he paid no attention. At first he paid no attention. Then I engaged him, but he held his hand. At the last minute he looked . . . he looked directly at me. He was in the grip of battle madness; probably he did not even recognize me. I was sure he would kill me then; he had his sword ready. I aimed a blow at his head. It would have been deflected, had he used his sword, but he would not, he did not, he only sat there, looking at me. My sword struck him and knocked him from his horse, and the horse reared and lashed out at me with its hooves. I had to turn and lead my men back, for the Family was too strong for us. Why didn't he strike? I meant him to. Oh God, God, I have lived too long!'

'We must go back,' I said.

He seemed to grow calm at once. He put his hand to the side of my face and looked at me, silent.

'We must go back,' I repeated. 'We have both lived too long. But it will do more good to put our lives in Arthur's hand than to take them with our own. If we are killed by the law we will give Gwalchmai what he wanted.'

Still he said nothing. I pulled away from him and stood. 'Listen, my heart. I decided that I would go after seeing you fighting this morning, and I will go. What is the watchword at the gates?'

'You . . . you cannot simply ride out through the gates.'

'You have put double watches on the walls to keep the men occupied and out of trouble at night. We cannot escape except through the gates.' I went to the cupboard, found my dark green dress and cut a wide strip off the hem with my own small knife. '*I* cannot ride out. But two men on horseback who know the watchword could. I know you have been sending men out to raise the army; you have sent messengers to every corner of the kingdom. If we give the watchword at the gates and leave at night there should be no questions asked.'

'No one would question two men, but a man and a woman would be questioned.'

'Look,' I said. I went back to the mirror and twined the strip of cloth over my head, under my chin and around my neck. It made my face look even thinner, and my hair would not stay under it neatly – but I could braid that and fasten it so that it would not be noticeable. 'I will wear this,' I told Bedwyr, 'and a cloak with the hood up. And I will paint my face so that, in the shadow, I will seem to have a beard. It would not do for daylight, I know, but at night it should pass.' In the mirror, I saw that he was looking at me dubiously. 'You have an armoured jerkin as well as your mail shirt, haven't you?' I asked his reflection. 'Well, I will wear that, and boots, and leggings. And I can ride well enough not to give myself away. Ach, I know it is a wild plan, but, if it comes to the worst they will think we are deserters and kill us if we resist arrest at the gates. They would not expect a woman and so would not see one.'

'If they killed us for deserters they would be right. I would be one,' said Bedwyr slowly.

I turned from the mirror, set it down. 'You would be returning to your true lord.'

'I have sworn an oath to Macsen as well.'

I stared at him, and he explained, 'You know he has appointed me cavalry commander; do you think I could escape swearing him an oath after such an appointment? I will not break that oath as well.'

'If you return to Arthur you will cancel out the first treachery.'

'No. Nothing can cancel that out. I have killed my friends.'

'And therefore you should return and suffer justice for them.'

He shook his head. 'Gwynhwyfar, I was born in this land, I was once sworn to serve its king – Macsen's brother. I was released from that oath to serve Arthur. But I have betrayed Arthur and perjured myself. Macsen may take reprisals against my family if I betray him also; and even if he did not, I will not twice perjure myself.'

'Yet you were willing to commit another mortal sin and die on your own sword, rather than continue to fight the Family.'

'That is different.' He looked at the sword he was still holding, put it down and clasped the stump of one hand with the other. 'I will not twice forswear myself. I would prefer to have died before being once a traitor, but I would rather be once a traitor than twice.'

'Oh, very fine! You would rather serve the devil, once fallen, than return to God!'

'Macsen is not the devil.'

I sat down, angrily untied the piece of cloth. I began to put my hair up again, plaiting it.

'But can you not see that it is worse to be a traitor twice than once?' asked Bedwyr, greatly distressed.

'All I see is that we have done evil to our lord, and more evil has come of it. We ought to go back and suffer the penalty for our crime, not skulk about like dogs that expect a whipping and wish to avoid it.'

'Gwynhwyfar, it is not your homeland, and you have not sworn an oath!'

'And I wish you had not, either. And though you have I do not see why you should weigh your oath to Macsen heavier than your oath to Arthur!'

'Because I have already broken my oath to Arthur.'

'Ach, damn your philosophy! Oaths are meaningless; it is the heart that swears, that binds itself to what a man is and what he stands for. You never meant in your heart to serve Macsen.'

'I cannot escape by asking what I meant in my heart. I swore to serve Macsen, and I must take the consequences. I have perjured myself once, and I know what came of that. I will not do so again, even with greater cause. I will die instead, if God, just or merciful, will grant me death.'

We glared at each other for a moment. Then I remembered what Bedwyr had meant to do, and went to him, knelt on the floor beside him, taking his hand. I could not understand why he refused to leave Macsen, but I had to believe that he acted in accordance with his conscience.

'Very well,' I whispered. 'Stay. But I have not sworn, and I will go. What is the watchword?'

He stared at me for a long moment, then dropped to his knees on the floor beside me and put his arms around me crushing me against himself. 'Do not go,' he cried. 'Do not go.'

'What is the watchword?' I demanded, fiercely because his plea tore my heart open.

He loosened his hold and looked at me again. 'You cannot mean to leave me as well.'

'I love you. You know that. And perhaps I only mean to go because I hate this land and this life. But I cannot endure this division any longer. If you will not help me, Bedwyr, I will find some way to escape on my own, I promise you. Though I love you, I will – must – go.'

As he continued to stare at me I wondered if he would kill himself if I left him. The thought made me shrink inside. But I couldn't let him live only for me, if it was for me in the ruin of all. And I thought he had prepared the sword on the impulse of immediate pain, and that his true hope was for death in battle. He knew that a private suicide would embarrass both Arthur and Macsen, and moreover was another mortal sin. And I hoped that he would die in battle. He had nothing to live for, and it was better than pouring out his blood in the smothering red luxury of that horrible room.

'The watchword of the fortress is "Liberty",' Bedwyr said in a low voice. 'But the guards at the gates have a special one. When they ask for the watchword, say "Liberty"; they will then ask, "Whose liberty?", to which you must reply, "The liberty of the will, and of this kingdom."'

'"The liberty of the will, and of this kingdom,"' I repeated, looking at him, feeling impossibly glad that he would understand, agree to at least this much. 'Was that your idea?'

'No, Macsen's. He gives a new watchword every day, but it is usually something to do with liberty. I will give you the clothing and the armour.'

'Not here. I am watched when I leave this room. Could you hide it somewhere – the stables? I think I could elude the guards when I leave the Feast Hall. They do not follow me when I am with you.'

'Very well,' he said, numbly.

I studied his face, wanting to memorize it. 'You can tell them afterwards that I said I wished to go back for something, and so gave you the slip.'

'No. They will know that you must have learned the watchword from me. I will tell them the truth, and I do not think the king will be overly angry. You are of no use to him, and he distrusts you. But he needs me, and will be content enough that I did not go with you. And if he does grow angry, and dismiss me from his service, all the better. He will either have me killed himself, or I will follow you and leave the execution to Arthur.'

Macsen gave a great feast that night, to celebrate the 'victory' of the foray that morning, and the 'success' of the war so far. Many of the men got drunk, and tried to congratulate Bedwyr for killing Gwalchmai. They had to be drunk to do so, for he looked so grim at any mention of it that the densest of warriors would notice it when sober. I said nothing all evening, only sat looking pale and remote, but this was nothing new and attracted no attention. Bedwyr and I left the feast as soon as we could, in courtesy, and went down to the stables.

It was dark, and the grooms were asleep. Bedwyr found a blackened lamp, and by its light we found the clothing he had left under a hay bale by my mare's stall. I dressed, and he saddled the horse. The clothes were too large, of course, but on horseback, at night with a cloak over them, it shouldn't show. I used some of the kohl I had borrowed to darken my cheeks and upper lip, then wrapped the scarf around my head and pulled the hood of my cloak up. Bedwyr lifted the lamp and looked at me critically.

'Your moustache is crooked.'

I put some more kohl on.

'That will do very well – the guards will have to look up to see your face, and that scarf hides a great deal.' He led my mare out of her stall and handed me the reins, then set down the lamp and kissed me, desperately and hard, several times. 'Good luck,' he said hoarsely.

I nodded. My throat was too choked for me to reply. I mounted the horse and took one last look at him standing there in the pool of dim light from the lamp. The kohl from my lip was smeared across his, and his face was almost as calm as it had been when he was Arthur's loyal and philosophic warleader. But it was a different calm, a calm such as comes to the sick when they are at last worn out by anguish, and can resist the pain no longer, but lie still and wait for the end.

'May God keep you, and be merciful,' I said, then, not trusting myself to say anything more touched my heels to my mare's sides and rode out of the stable.

I met the watch in the street, but gave them the watch-word in a voice as deep as I could make it, and was told to pass. I knew a quick way to the city gate, but on that ride it seemed to take a long time. My mare sensed my excitement and was inclined to be restive. She was a high-strung, nervous animal at the best of times, though she could run as lightly as a swallow flies, and had all the spirit in the world. But this unusual night departure from her comfortable stall made her bad-tempered, and I began to worry that she might cause a commotion at the gate, perhaps even rear so that my hood fell back and I was taken.

Reached at last, the gate was a blur of torchlight which I rode into boldly, my hare's hooves clattering on the cobblestones. Two guards before the massive oak door snapped to attention, and I could vaguely see others in the tower above.

'Watchword?' asked one of the two before me.

'Liberty.'

'Whose liberty?'

'The liberty of the will, and of this kingdom.'

The guard nodded to his fellow, who went to the postern gate beside the main one, and unbarred it. 'Be careful with that cold, friend,' said the first guard. 'And good luck. The enemy are closer than they were last night, for all of that fight this morning.'

I coughed. 'Thank you. Have a quiet watch.' I kicked my mare, took her through the gate at a trot, then spurred her to a canter. To my right Arthur's campfires glowed, but I held diagonally away from the wall until I was certain that I could not be seen by the watchers there. Then I doubled back and sent my mare galloping towards the fires as though I should die of cold for the lack of them.

I was still far from the fires when I heard another horse galloping on my left, still too distant to see in the cloudy night. I kept my mare at her pace, fearing that my escape had been discovered already, and that someone had been sent to find me. My horse was probably the faster one.

My pursuer realized this fairly promptly, as well, for after another minute at the gallop he called out, 'Halt! Halt, in the Emperor's name!' He had a British voice, a Northern voice like my own. I at once slowed my mare to a walk.

The other galloped up, looming out of the darkness, and drew rein near me. 'Watchword?' he asked.

I hesitated, said nothing.

'Whose man are you, and where are you going?' he demanded.

'I am British,' I told him, finding my voice still low, hoarse from tension. 'I am escaping from the city. I wish to see the Emperor.'

The sentry drew nearer, a dark shadow on a dark horse. 'Watchword?'

'Macsen's is "Liberty", but I do not know Arthur's.'

'A Northerner,' muttered the rider, evidently commenting on my voice, 'and only a boy. Eh, lad, it was well done to escape, if indeed you have. I will take you into the camp myself, for the Emperor has standing orders to bring anyone from the city to him. If you're telling the truth you'll find yourself fortunate. Give me your reins.'

I tossed the reins over my mare's neck and handed them to him. He took them with a nod, turned his horse about and rode back to call an explanation to another sentry before starting back toward the campfires.

'Watchword?' someone called as we passed the first picket line.

'*Lex victrix!*' called my captor, 'The law conquers', then added, to me, 'And now, boy, you do know our watchword. But hopefully you'll have no cause to use it tonight.'

A number of men were sitting about the main fire when we came up to it, drinking and passing a harp around. I recognized most of them, and the recognition came as a sharp pain to my heart, though I was glad.

'Halt!' called one of these men, standing lazily and brushing ashes off his leggings. 'Who are you and what do you want?'

'Morgant ap Casnar,' the sentry replied, 'of the warband of Ergyriad ap Caw of Ebrauc. I caught this lad riding out of the city. He is British, by his speech, and he says he's escaping. I have brought him here because I thought that the Emperor might wish to question him.'

'As well he might. Well, lad?'

'I am not a boy, Morfran,' I said, calling him by name. I tossed my hood back and untied the scarf. There was a profound stillness, in which the fire sounded very loud. More of the men rose to their feet. I rubbed at the kohl on my face with the scarf and asked, 'Where is my lord Arthur?'

The flap of the great imperial tent before the main fire was tossed open, and Arthur stood there. Over the fire our eyes met. I slid off my horse. 'Arthur,' I said; then, 'I have come back to accept my sentence.'

He looked at me for a long moment. 'Does Bedwyr know you have come?'

'Yes. He helped me to escape. Macsen had me kept under guard.'

'Come in here. Morfran, see to the lady's horse.'

I walked around the fire, awkward in the heavy boots. I felt keenly ridiculous in the outsized man's clothing, as though there were not more important things I should be feeling. Arthur held the tent flap open for me and I went in.

There were two torches and a lamp burning inside. Cei was sitting by the light table with a pile of maps; he jumped

231

up and stared in astonishment as I entered. Sitting on the bed, leaning against one of the tent posts, was Gwalchmai.

I cried out when I saw him, started forward and tripped over the boots. Arthur helped me back to my feet. 'Gwalchmai!' I exclaimed, feeling my face almost break with a smile such as I had not smiled for many weary months. 'Bedwyr told me he had killed you!'

'He almost did,' Arthur said, behind me. Gwalchmai stared at me as though he did not recognize me. He had aged since I had last seen him, and he was very pale and sick, his head bandaged. 'However,' Arthur continued drily, 'the blow was not a solid one. Gwalchmai, Cei, my wife escaped from the city with Bedwyr's help.'

'It alters nothing,' Gwalchmai said slowly, 'Bedwyr remains guilty.'

'Welcome, my lady,' said Cei, taking my hand and grinning. 'A hundred welcomes.'

'A hundred thousand thanks. Gwalchmai, I am very glad that you are alive. And Bedwyr will be glad, as well.' I glanced round at Arthur, decided to say it plainly, 'He meant to fall on his sword this morning, when he thought you were dead.'

'It alters nothing,' Gwalchmai repeated.

Arthur took my arm and directed me to another chair. I sat down, and he stood a moment looking at me. I could not read his expression, though I knew his face so well. 'What is that on your face?' he asked.

I rubbed at it, then took the scarf and rubbed with that again. 'A beard. I needed one to get through the gate,' I put the scarf down. 'If it is any use to you, Macsen's watchword tonight is "Liberty".'

'Ah!' exclaimed Cei.

'It may be,' said Arthur, still watching me.

'A night assault!' said Cei eagerly. 'Indeed, lady, that is an excellent idea. We might end it quickly. It would be better than more work on those siege engines' (to Arthur) 'which you took out of that book. Those will only waste time and lives.' He looked at Gwalchmai, seeming to challenge disagreement. Obviously I had interrupted some conference on how to take Car Aës, and Cei and Gwalchmai had had differing opinions. 'And I still say that if our night assault fails we should abandon this accursed city, move off

232

south, take all the plunder we can find and go home. We can come back again next summer. Macsen would be bound to tire of playing host to us and come to terms.'

'We will have to determine more about the defences before we can risk a night assault,' said Arthur, wearily and, to me, 'Will Bedwyr come?'

Everyone looked at me, and I looked down at my hands. I rubbed the finger where once I had worn the ring with the imperial seal, shook my head. I looked up at Arthur; he seemed tired, not at all angry. 'He has sworn Macsen an oath. He . . . I think he wishes to come. But he thinks that he is damned, and will not face you, and he says that he will not be twice forsworn.'

'I see. And Macsen, of course, will keep him as long as he can, for his own generalship is nothing in comparison with Bedwyr's. He will not make terms, not for a long while.' Arthur shook his head. 'Cei, you know that we do not dare stay long away from Britain.'

'What Bedwyr's reasons are changes nothing,' Gwalchmai repeated yet again. 'Justice requires that he die. Macsen is only incidental to that.' He took a deep breath. 'Try the night assault. Since we have the watchword it might work. If not, use the siege engines.'

'I still don't see why you didn't kill Bedwyr yourself this morning, since you are so eager for his death,' snapped Cei. 'You could have.'

'I tell you, the madness was on me!' Gwalchmai snapped back, trying to stand – then stopped short, went white with pain and closed his eyes.

Cei jumped up and took his shoulder. 'Lie down,' he urged, pushing .he other back gently. 'God in Heaven, you must keep still.'

'The madness was on me,' Gwalchmai insisted. 'It was as though we still fought the Saxons, and he still commanded me. I could not think clearly, or I would have killed him. But it would be best if he died after a trial, by the hand of the law, in Britain, before all the Family.'

Arthur raised his hand, nodding. 'We will try the night assault, tonight. Gwynhwyfar, what are their defences?'

I told him everything I knew, which my hours standing on the walls had made a good amount, though I had to admit that I knew less of what happened in Macsen's court than the servants did. 'I have been kept virtually a prisoner,' I explained, 'I was under guard whenever I left Macsen's house.'

'I know,' Arthur said, 'I had a man inside the fortress. He was killed a few weeks ago.' He was quiet a moment, still watching me. It was very different from our last meeting, when the sight of me had been painful to him. I wondered what it was that he felt now. 'Cei told me that you claimed to have known nothing about the attack on the road until it took place.'

'I knew nothing of it. But, afterwards . . . I went . . . I left with Bedwyr willingly, my heart. He was in such desperate grief that I could not abandon him.'

Gwalchmai laughed, then shuddered and closed his eyes again. The laughter must have jolted his wounded head.

'And yet, there was no conspiracy?' Arthur demanded, 'You can swear to that?'

'I, Gwynhwyfar daughter of Ogyrfan, swear in the name of the Father, the Son and the Holy Spirit, that I never conspired to escape with Bedwyr, and that I knew nothing of his plans until he encountered us on the road. Moreover, I swear that Bedwyr himself never meant to come to blows with anyone, and only drew his sword after Medraut had prevented me from telling him that I would not go, and incited the others to attack him. If I lie may the earth gape and swallow me, may the sea rise and drown me, may the sky break and fall on me.'

Arthur smiled very slightly and looked at Gwalchmai.

'Still it alters nothing,' Gwalchmai said wearily. 'We had heard that the lady was kept as a prisoner. We knew all along that she had the lesser share of guilt. But there has still been murder, Macsen still stands firm in rebellion, and there must still be justice for it.'

'You will have me tried again,' I told Arthur. 'I know that. And I am willing to accept my sentence. It is what I came for.' His eyes met mine, still without anger. The silence and the torchlight lay between us like a road, and I felt my blood begin to sing in my veins: he was not angry, he had forgiven me. 'I am grieved to the heart over what has happened,' I went on, uncertainly now, all my determination melting in the light of his eyes. 'I have deserved to die. And I would rather die than help to cause this division

234

among us for even one more day. I cannot live with it . . .'

Arthur began to speak, but fell silent again. He looked at Gwalchmai, then back at me. 'The war will still go on, my white hart,' he told me, very quietly. 'But I am glad that you are no longer part of it; I am glad you are back. And if you were stolen away by force, and kept a prisoner, there may be no need for a new sentence. Perhaps the old one could be altered, even suspended.' He was quiet another moment, then said, 'I received a letter from your cousin, the chieftain of your clan. If Bedwyr knew of him I am not surprised that he wished to rescue you. I do not think it would be well that you go there.' He glared around the room, suddenly, coldly angry, not so much with anyone there as with his kingdom and the purple. 'I do not wish her to die!' he cried, loudly. 'Let Bedwyr pay the penalty!'

Gwalchmai looked at me strangely but said nothing. Cei grinned. 'Why, she has paid her penalty already! She has been kept prisoner by a foreign king. Ach, my lord, my lady, it was a bold deed, escaping from Macsen's fortress dressed as a man: the warband will pardon her anything, after that. There will be songs made about it for years.'

I did not know what to say. I had not expected such a welcome. I was being received as though I had returned from an embassy, and not like an escaped criminal. But I was a criminal, and did not want Bedwyr to pay the penalty for my crime as well as his own. Yet my husband stood near me watching me, and I did not know what to say to him.

Arthur saw my confusion and shook his head. 'We must speak of it tomorrow. For now, my lady, rest. You look very tired.' He went to the entrance of his tent and gave orders for some servants to prepare me a tent to myself, then called various men and gave orders for the assault for that night. I leaned back in my place, looking at the familiar things and faces. I closed my eyes and listened to their voices: Cei's rumbling whisper to Gwalchmai; Arthur's strong voice giving orders outside; jokes, laughter, excited discussion from the men. It did not yet seem real. For a moment I was afraid that I would wake, and find myself back in that smothering red room in Car Aës. I opened my eyes again quickly.

Arthur came back in, went to his desk and checked a plan

235

he had made of Macsen's defences. Then he looked up at me again and smiled. I thought my heart would break to see him smile. He looked older even than before, worn into a greying shadow, but his smile was the same, and the direct honest force of his eyes. 'I cannot believe that you are here,' he told me. 'I wish – but you must rest, and there is work for me. Do you have any other clothing? Then I will have some found for you – though I doubt we have anything finer than some farm woman's festival dress in this whole encampment.' He helped me to my feet, ushered me to the entrance of the tent and snapped his fingers to summon a guard for me, then paused, still holding my arm. 'Wish me luck for tonight, my lady.'

I turned and caught his arms, looked up into his face. I thought of Bedwyr in the dark stable, and of Arthur decreeing my sentence at Camlann, things that had mattered, that still mattered. But beside this return they were unimportant; looking at him, I was home again. 'God defend you,' I said. 'And good luck.'

As I walked off to my own tent, escorted by a warrior I knew, I prayed that I would die there, among friends and not in humilitation among strangers. And I prayed also that Bedwyr would not be captured that night, not brought back and made to pay the penalty which I should have paid, but that somehow, somewhere, living or dying, he should escape.

Ten

The tent Arthur had ordered for me was a small one, but three men had been moved out of it to make room for me. It had a fire, and when I entered with my guard Gwalchmai's servant Rhys was heating water over this. When he saw me his face almost split with an enormous grin, and he bowed very low. 'Lady Gwynhwyfar! Welcome back. The news of your escape has swept the camp already.'

I took his hand, smiling back. 'Thank you, Rhys. I am glad to see you. How are Eivlin and the children?'

'When I left them, well. I am glad you have come back, my lady. It is a dead weight on the heart to make war against friends. Will the Lord Bedwyr come?'

I stopped smiling and shook my head.

Rhys sighed. 'Well.' He ran a hand through his hair. 'It will go on, then. God have mercy on us.' The guard muttered something and withdrew to stand watch outside, and Rhys bowed to him slightly, then checked the wood for the fire. 'Well, noble lady, you must wish to rest, and I must go back to my lord. He is wounded.'

'I know. He is at Arthur's tent, planning an assault.'

'What? Still?' Rhys stared. 'God in Heaven! He had to be carried there – can't walk, insisted on speaking to Arthur as soon as he realized where he was after the wounding. The surgeons didn't like that, only they liked the thought of exciting him even less. He only woke this afternoon, and he has obviously not yet recovered his senses. The stubborn, proud . . .' Rhys realized that this was an improper way to speak of his lord, so, instead of finishing, lifted the kettle of hot water from the fire and checked the bucket of cold water.

I sat down on the sleeping pallet and pulled off those absurd boots. 'Your lord is very bitter,' I said, tentatively. Rhys knew Gwalchmai as well as anyone did, and would know how things stood with him.

'And is it surprising that he should be? Why did Bedwyr kill that poor child? Excuse me, my lady. My tongue is more insolent than my intentions.'

'Do not apologize. You have been a part of this long

enough to have a right to ask such questions. Bedwyr threw a spear without thinking of whom he threw it at.'

'Ah. Almost, my lady, I could believe we were all under a curse. I could not believe that Bedwyr meant to kill my lord Gwyn, any more than the Emperor wants this war, or you ever meant any evil to the Emperor, and yet all goes wrong. My lady, my lord has been like a man in an enchantment, noticing nothing and caring for nothing. I can scarcely persuade him to eat or sleep, and he does not pay much attention even to his horse, and you know how he loves that animal. This war is bad for him. He has been worse since we arrived in this miserable kingdom. My lady, he does not really wish to kill Lord Bedwyr, but he cannot bear to think that Bedwyr can murder his son and escape unscathed. Well enough, but when today he met Bedwyr in the battle, he found for himself that he does not wish to kill him, and was almost killed himself. It is bad, that head wound. He cannot fight now, at least. God knows, he cannot even stand. The surgeons say that he must keep very quiet and avoid all excitement. But that is the one thing he will not possibly do, not while he is here and the war continues. My lady, the Emperor is sending some of the wounded home the day after tomorrow. Persuade him to send my lord with them.'

I looked at Rhys thoughtfully. 'I will tell Arthur what you say when I see him tomorrow. But why do you think I have any influence? I am a criminal awaiting my sentence.'

Rhys grinned again. 'Perhaps, my lady. But ever since we arrived in Less Britain, the rumour has run about that you were held a prisoner, and had been taken to Less Britain by force in the first place, and the Family has been burning to set you free again. It is strange what a war will do towards changing men's minds. They have almost forgotten the trial in all the excitement.' He coughed. 'Of course, things may be different in Britain. Medraut and his faction are all back there.'

'What?' I looked at Rhys sharply, saw that he was serious. 'Medraut and his faction, left back in Britain to keep Camlann safe for us, while Arthur and all our firmest allies are here? This is madness!'

'My lady, the Emperor could scarcely bring men whose loyalty he doubted here to Less Britain with him, not when he is taking such a small force. Any treachery here and Macsen would destroy us at once. But the Emperor is no fool, my lady. He has not taken all our firmest allies, only parts of their warbands. He has left Constantius of Dumnonia in Camlann to keep the fortress warm for him, and no doubt has told the king to keep a close eye on the lord Medraut. And he has left King Urien of Rheged, and Ergyriad of Ebrauc, prepared to warn him of any rebellion in the North. I would not trouble yourself, my lady.'

Rhys was probably right, though I still did not like the sound of it. I might have questioned him further, but another servant came in just then, carrying a plain dress and some blankets. I thanked him, thanked Rhys, and they both smiled, wished me a good night, and left me alone with the guard keeping watch outside.

I could not sleep. I lay awake, listening to the camp preparing its assault on Macsen's stronghold. I prayed for Arthur, for Bedwyr, lay tossing and turning after the last voices had vanished with the jingle of harness into the night. What would they achieve? Success? It would be good to have the nightmare over, but if Bedwyr were captured, brought back in chains, tried not only for his own crimes but for mine – then the nightmare would only have begun. It is hard, being a woman during a war, and worse when one does not even know what to hope for.

I rose, put on the dress, wrapped the blanket around my shoulders, and went out to talk to my guard. He had a leg wound, I had noticed earlier. Arthur would not set a skilled able-bodied man on an unnecessary guard duty. But the form of the thing was necessary, and I suppose it gave the warrior something to do. I knew the man from Camlann, and knew that he would be even more impatient than I at waiting for the outcome of an assault he could play no part in. We sat about and discussed the war, my imprisonment, his leg wound, Britain and the Empire until the dawn was grey over the forest at our backs.

The army returned very worn and tired, but in one group. The assault had failed. At first, we learned, the watchword and a diversionary attack had enabled them to take the gates, but afterwards the men had been trapped in the unfamiliar streets and forced to retreat again. Arthur was safe, we were told; Cei, Goronwy, Gereint, yes, safe;

239

others, safe; one or two dead, wounded. And Bedwyr, I was told, had commanded the defence, had not been fooled by the diversion at the north wall, but come straight to the gates and managed to foil Arthur's plans. Yes, Bedwyr too was still alive and unharmed.

Only after learning this did the sleep I had thrust aside suddenly present itself to me again, and I went back into the tent and was lost in oblivion as the sun rose over the tree-tops.

It was full light when I woke. I was still tired, and realized at once that I had woken because someone was watching me. I sat up and saw Arthur.

'Hush,' he said gently. 'It is only mid-morning. The guard told me that you were awake all night, and you must wish to sleep more.'

'So must you,' I pointed out, 'and I would wager that you have not slept at all. How long have you been here, my lord?'

'Not long. Come, if you will not sleep, have breakfast with me.'

We had breakfast in his tent, and it was like old times at Camlann, with people interrupting every five minutes. Arthur told me of the war, and I told him of the preceding months, and of Bedwyr.

When I told him of Bedwyr's suffering, Arthur nodded. 'I saw Bedwyr last night,' he told me.

'In Car Aës?' I asked, my throat constricting.

He nodded. 'He spared my life when he might have taken it. But that did not surprise me.' Someone came in with a question about horse fodder, and Arthur dealt with it, then resumed. 'We were trapped in a sidestreet, I and some others of the Family. I had miscalculated the width of the streets – or rather, I had not realized that horses would be so difficult to manage in such streets. We are too unaccustomed to siege warfare to be good at it. An organized body of spearmen has the advantage over cavalry in such a confined space, no matter how fine the cavalry. Bedwyr had troops near the gate, and when he appeared himself with additional troops we were forced to retreat. Only I led my men down a street which had no access to the gate, and the spearmen came after us. It was total chaos. We had set fire to the gate-house, and the fire was spreading widely; the horses were frightened, and there was no making oneself heard above the din. Then I saw Bedwyr over the heads of the other spearmen, and he saw me. He ordered his men back, and we advanced down the street and rejoined the others at the gate. We passed by him, very close, as we went to join the others. At one point I was not more than six paces from him. He is suffering.'

I looked at my hands, clenching them at each other.

'He will tell Macsen, of course, that it would have been foolish to kill me, that my men would have become ungovernable, ruthless and cruel were I killed, and so excuse himself for the orders he gave. It is doubtless true. Macsen owed much to Bedwyr. I have owed him much as well.'

'But you will have him put to death.'

He looked at me closely. 'You still love him.'

'Yes, of course. So do you.'

He shrugged, looking away from me, looking into nothing. 'He has been my friend for many years. He has been the half of my own soul. But I would cut off my own right hand, if it were necessary for the Empire, and it is necessary. Gwalchmai is right: Bedwyr must die as a matter of pure justice. Justice, and the continuance of the Empire. Only . . .'

'Only?'

He reached across the table and caught my wrist. 'Only I do not want that justice to extend to you.' After a moment of silence he went on, 'I expected to miss you. But it has been worse than I expected. And it is not because the fortress and the kingdom are almost ungovernable without you, because the affairs of the Empire are in disorder and the servants and farmers sigh whenever you are mentioned. I miss you. I could scarcely bear our house at Camlann, alone; I kept expecting to find you there, forgetting every morning that you were gone and discovering it again, to my sorrow. Shall I speak more plainly? Before the trial Bedwyr told me that I had demanded more from you than anyone can give. It was true, though I would not admit it at the time. I allowed myself to be weak, to lose my temper and make endless demands on you, but never allowed you the same. No, listen to me. I know well enough that the strongest need rest, at times. I have seen it in war: one can push any man so far, farther than he himself thinks he can be pushed, but in the end he will snap and kill a comrade or flee from the enemy, or forsake a trust. I should have realized what I was doing to you. Then I sat in judgement upon you. I myself have committed adultery, without the spur of love or loneliness, but only that of drunkenness and lust for the Queen Morgawse – how could I pass judgement on Bedwyr for loving you, or you for yielding to him? You would never have been unfaithful had it not been for me.'

'My own heart,' I said, 'you blame yourself overmuch. You committed no crime, and I did. And yet I love you, I loved you even when I was unfaithful. If you forgive me that is all I desire, and perhaps more than I deserve.'

He kissed my hand. 'It requires forgiveness on both sides, I think. My white hart, the people might accept you back now, as Empress, if it were proved at another trial that you had been taken from Britain by force and kept as a prisoner.'

'It is not true.'

'So you said. But Bedwyr must die. You see that, don't you? There is no way of avoiding it. Must you die as well? It would do no good, not to the kingdom, the Family, and least of all to me. We would all suffer for it. My heart, tell them that you were taken from Britain by force.'

'On trial? Under oath?'

'It is almost true. You would have prevented Bedwyr's attack if you had known of it, and you never meant to go with him.'

'But it would not do any good to spare me, either. The people will spit on me, and say that I am a whore who ran off with her lover, caused a war, and was reinstated to the purple by a deceived and doting husband. They will say you are weak and corrupt. Medraut will use it.'

He winced. 'We can bear that. But do not use such terms. Your cousin spoke so of you in his letter to me; he said that he accepted the charge of you and would see that you were fittingly punished. Why didn't you tell me of him? I would never have sent you to his house had I known. But I do not see fit to yield to the opinions of such as he, nor to suit all my actions to Medraut's judgement. I need you. Will you ... not so much lie, as distort the truth, when you are retried? Then I could impose nothing more than the penance which the Church proscribes for adultery, and keep you with me.'

'You . . . you risk much.'

'You do not understand. I need you.'

I had gone with Bedwyr against my better judgement because he needed me. Now, although Arthur was calmer than Bedwyr had been, I could tell that he was no less serious. But if I were dead he might find another wife, one that might bear him children, and be a better lady for him than I had been. To lie under oath and make another bear the punishment for my fault seemed to me monstrous . . . though I knew that if Bedwyr had been there he would have advised me as Arthur did.

'Let me think,' I pleaded. 'I was certain that I would die for my treachery if I came back. I never expected to be forgiven, I thought I would die honestly. Let me get used to the idea of living first.' After a moment in turmoil I asked, 'When would you hold this trial?'

A messenger came in with a question of ransoms, interrupting. Arthur dealt with him, turned back to me. 'It would be better if done at Camlann, after Bedwyr is taken or killed. I could send you back with the wounded tomorrow. Once in Britain you could begin the period of fasting and penance set by the Church, and also give me your opinion of the situation at home. This war should not last too much longer. I do not wish to follow Cei's plan and wear Macsen out with extended raids. It would cause too much division in the Empire and I cannot afford to leave Britain that long, or leave Medraut in Camlann, even under surveillance. Perhaps the siege engines will work. Will you do as I ask?'

'I . . . I will think of it. Give me until you are back in Britain.'

'You mean you will, unless Bedwyr is taken prisoner,' he said, smiling slightly.

'I do not know what I mean. I do not want him blamed for my crime. Rhys thinks you should send Gwalchmai away with the other wounded.'

Arthur smiled slightly more. 'I was planning to, if I can persuade him to go without over-exciting him and making him ill. My heart, do think of it. If we can hold our own against Medraut there is no reason why we cannot outface the kings of Britain.'

If stars were silver nails, I thought, *one could use them to shoe horses*. But I loved Arthur. Perhaps I would be willing to do even this to make him happy. But if Bedwyr were before my eyes and suffering for my crime, I did not know that I could.

I left the next day with the wounded. Arthur did not like having men in his camp who could not travel quickly, who might be endangered if Macsen did manage to call up the rest of his forces and Arthur had to retreat hastily. Gwalchmai, however, insisted that he was recovering quickly and that there was no point in sending him back to Britain. I went to talk to him myself the morning I left. Arthur hoped I could persuade the warrior to leave.

He was in a tent of his own, being looked after by Rhys. He was lying very still when I came in, looking at the blank wall of the tent.

'Gwalchmai,' I said, and he looked over at me, then at Rhys who was standing just behind me. He said nothing.

'Does it hurt you very much?' I asked.

'No. Do not trouble yourself. I need nothing.'

Rhys let out his breath between his teeth, irritably. 'My lord, the lady has come at the Emperor's request, to see if you will leave today.'

'I had thought as much. Do not trouble yourself, my lady. I shall be back on my feet in a few days – I would doubtless be able to ride back to the army before the wounded reach the ships, so there is no point in my leaving.'

Rhys snorted. 'My lady, reason with him,' he muttered to me. 'He should respect your opinion even now. I will go and pack.'

Gwalchmai watched Rhys leave, only his eyes moving. It was obviously painful to him to shift his head about.

'Rhys thinks the war is bad for you,' I said.

'Rhys is always meddling in things that are not his concern. He is supposed to be my servant, but he thinks himself my master.'

'I have never heard you tell him that.'

'What would be the point? Rhys means well.'

His dark stare troubled me. It was hard to see what he was looking at. I touched his forehead; it felt hot. 'You have the fever,' I told him. 'You would do better away from the

244

army.'

'Why do you show such concern for me, my lady?'

'I have always felt great concern for you,' I said, after another moment of silence. 'I have loved you as I would have loved a brother of my own blood.'

'All lies,' he muttered, so indistinctly that I barely caught the words.

I had been doubtful when Arthur asked me to talk to Gwalchmai, and I felt more than doubtful now, felt horror-stricken. 'Have some water,' I said at last. 'You will want it, with the fever.'

He laughed a little, bitterly, but took the cup of water I poured for him. 'It is worse in the morning,' he told me. 'But I am recovering . . . that is enough.'

'As you wish.' I looked at him closely, but he had leaned back into the pillow and looked past me at the low roof of the tent. 'Gwalchmai, you do not really believe that I lie when I say that I am concerned for you?'

'You may feel concern. But what do feelings and intentions matter? You and Bedwyr may have intended no evil, but still, between you you killed my son.' His eyes turned from the tent pole and met my gaze. 'Wasn't it enough for you that I held my tongue when I knew of your relationship, that I did all I could to help you, that Gwyn went gallantly to your aid, but still you must kill him?'

'It was an accident,' I said, but the words sounded empty.

'It may have been carelessness, not intent. But what does that matter? It is done.' Gwalchmai sat up straight abruptly, then gasped in pain and slumped over, holding his head in his hands.

'Don't!' I cried, trying to support him. 'You will hurt yourself.'

'What does it matter?' he asked, speaking like a man I had never met, and not like the friend I had loved for many years. 'What do I have to recover for? You and Rhys and the rest, they do not understand that. My lady, my lady, you had so much. You had a clan, and you were the jewel and the treasure of your father's house. He would not marry you to anyone, for long and long, though many desired it, for he could not find anyone good enough until he found the Emperor of all Britain. And then you became

245

the crown of the Empire, the lady whom all the kings and the peoples loved and admired – justly. I will admit that it was justly. Not content with your husband, you found a lover as well, a man worthy to be another Emperor. And you destroyed them, for all that you did not intend to; and, not content with destroying what was yours, you and yours destroyed my son as well – my son, who was all my clan to me, and all that was left to me of my lover or wife. And you still say that you have concern for me. You would have shown it better by killing me and leaving my son alive.'

Perhaps I might have spoken in answer, but the empty words dried in my throat and choked me. 'It grieves me,' I said at last.

He laughed the bitter laugh again. 'It grieves me, as well. Far worse.'

'Would Bedwyr's death, or mine, ease that grief?'

He sat looking at his feet. 'No. But at least it would be justice. There would remain some justice in the world.'

'Tell me, then. Shall I tell the plain truth when I am tried, say that I left Britain willingly, and die, condemned for treason? Would that please you?'

'You would lie if you said that. You did not leave willingly, but against your will, to comfort Bedwyr. Oh no, you are innocent in intention, and no doubt Bedwyr is as well. Only that alters nothing. And I cannot even wish that you or he should die. I have still some . . . concern for you. There is no justice, even in the heart.' He looked up and through me, remote and inhuman. 'Once I sailed to the Kingdom of Summer, the Otherworld. I thought then that the struggle between Light and Darkness is fought upon the earth, and that the intentions of our spirits reflect it, and bind Earth and the Otherworld. But now that world seems unconnected and remote from here, for even the best intentions of those devoted to Light can create Darkness. And so there is no justice, can be no justice. Perhaps we are wrong to act at all. Perhaps we are all damned perpetually to Yffern. Let me alone, my lady. Tell Arthur I will stay, unless he commands me otherwise.'

I nodded, left him and went back to my own tent, shaking and trying not to weep. It was true. All he had said to me was true. Ah God, God, why should the Earth ever have been created?

The carts with the wounded left around noon. There were three of them, long, covered over with a canopy against the rain and the sun, walled and packed with straw for the comfort of the men, of whom there were some dozen in each cart. There was also an escort of twenty men who would go only to the harbour where we were to embark. I had my mare to ride, but spent some time in the carts as well. I had assisted surgeons before, and knew how to care for the sick. There was plenty for me to do.

The carts jolted badly on the road, though we travelled fairly slowly, trying to keep the pace smooth. We drove north-east for some days, then followed the coast road due east into the region dominated by the Franks. We found Arthur's ships still secure in their Frankish harbour, and the harbour officials helped us to load the ship we were to use, trying to talk to us in bad Latin. They were delighted when they discovered that I spoke some Saxon – which differed only slightly from their own tongue – and attempted to inform me of various noxious remedies for wounds. When the ship was ready to sail they insisted upon providing a feast, for us and for the escort, which was to set out the next day on its return to Arthur. When the ship did set sail I wondered what Arthur's united Empire would be like. There was no reason for enmity with the Saxons, if they would keep the law. But I was not certain now that any such Empire would survive.

We had a shorter voyage than the one I had suffered on the way to Less Britain, crossing directly from Gaul to the south coast of Britain, and sailing along that coast to the port of Caer Uisc, where we put in and unloaded the ship again. The journey from Car Aës had taken the better part of three weeks. Three of the wounded men had died on the journey, but the rest were recovering well.

The journey to Camlann took two days. The night we spent in a small hill fort along the road – a mere clan holding, the name of which I forget. The lord of the place treated us very strangely, seeming perpetually about to burst into speech and never doing so. I judged that he was uncertain of my status, and wondered again what I would do.

We arrived at Camlann on the afternoon of the second

day, in the early dusk of winter. The green hill rose quiet from the drab fields and bare trees; smoke from the fortress drifted across the early stars, and we could see the glow of its fires against the dark east. Something within me began to sound 'Home, home!' like a clear-toned bell, but I was too heartsick and weary to give it much notice.

The gates of the fortress were locked when we came up to them, which surprised me, until I thought that our ally Constantius must have seen fit to take precautions. One of the guards called from the tower, asking our names and business.

'We are bringing the wounded home from Gaul,' the surgeon shouted – he was officially in charge of the party. 'You ought to have more torches here if you can't recognize your own comrades!'

The gates were unbarred and the carts rolled through. I was riding my mare, and again noticed that the guards looked at us strangely. I recognized them as some of Medraut's men. Two of them came from the guard tower and accompanied us up the hill.

The carts rumbled up to the Hall and there stopped. The guards who had come from the gate with us disappeared at once into the Hall and more warriors appeared to watch us as the surgeon went round the carts checking on the men, who were all sitting up and looking about, even the very sick ones. They laughed and joked about what they would do now that they were home. Soon a few more warriors came from the Hall, carrying torches.

'The Empress!' one of these men exclaimed, and at once the men at Camlann began babbling to each other, lifting their torches high so as to see me clearly.

'Why is she here? Has Macsen been defeated?' the first speaker asked the surgeon.

'Car Aës was still under siege when we left,' I said, and they all fell silent and stared at me. 'I escaped from his fortress and came to my lord Arthur for my sentence. He has commanded me to come here and here await trial. Where is King Constantius? We have some wounded here who need care.'

Some of the men laughed and the rest were uneasily silent. 'Where is King Constantius?' asked the first speaker. 'The lady wishes to know where King Constantius is.'

'She had better ask the Emperor – or the Church,' said another.

This mockery began to annoy me. 'The Emperor told me that Constantius was left in command here. Is that not so?'

'Constantius commands no one now. No one but worms.'

'No, the worms command him. They could command him to provide them a fine feast.'

'And, most noble lady, we have another Emperor now, a better one.'

The realization of what they meant seemed to turn the world upside-down, and I saw suddenly what our host of the night before had meant to tell us, realized why the gates were locked, why the guards had come up the hill with us from the gate. And even as I realised it Medraut came out of the Hall, wearing a cloak of the imperial purple. He was smiling pleasantly.

'Welcome to Camlann,' Medraut said to our party, which had grown suddenly silent, motionless. 'Your arrival is fortunate, for you now have a chance of joining our cause, a chance the tyrant Arthur the Bastard would have denied you. Those who will pledge themselves to follow me will be made welcome indeed, and can expect tokens of my gratitude. But how many of you are there?'

The surgeon, standing beside the foremost cart, only stared at him in bewilderment. Medraut strolled past the cart, looking at the men appraisingly. 'No able-bodied warriors? A pity. Still, most of you are much recovered, are you not?' He addressed these words to one man in particular, a fine infantry fighter who had lost his right leg at the knee. The man flushed when he heard himself spoken to, slid off the cart, clinging to the rim so as to be able to stand. 'I would never be sick enough to fight for a traitor,' he told Medraut, then, calling out to his fellows, 'see what this foreign bastard has done! He has used our lord's generosity as opportunity to usurp the purple! The perjured, murdering . . .'

Medraut's smile had vanished when the man first spoke, and he nodded now and stepped back. There was a flash, and the warrior suddenly coughed, bowed, and fell on his face, a spear jutting from his back. I cried out, leapt from my horse and ran over to the man, turned him over. He was dead already, his eyes set in his head. I touched the line of blood beside his mouth in horror, then fell back as Medraut kicked my hand aside, kicked the body back onto its face.

'Lady Gwynhwyfar,' Medraut said in a low, cold voice. 'How is it that you come here? I could scarcely believe the report. It is an honour I did not expect.'

I said nothing, only stared at Medraut. The cloak he wore was one of Arthur's, and its rich purple hem trailed on the ground.

'She said she fled Macsen and returned to Arthur for her sentence,' one of Medraut's warriors said.

'And we know what kind of sentence the Emperor would give her,' Medraut returned, his eyes narrowing, beginning to smile again. 'Ten minutes in his bed, and all would be forgiven!' His men laughed. 'Get up, my lady murderess. Justice is in my hands now.' I remained kneeling by the dead warrior, seeing how the torchlight caught in Medraut's hair, and on the gold of collar and cloak. His cold eyes glittered suddenly and he bent over, seized my arm and dragged me to my feet; held my arm, struck me twice across the face, and threw me at a guard. Someone cried out.

'The lady is the Empress, the lord Arthur's wife!' the surgeon cried, running over to Medraut, while I tried to gather my senses.

'I am the Emperor,' Medraut said. 'I may do as I please with this woman or with any of you. Anyone who wishes can pledge me fealty, and be welcome here. The rest are servants of my enemy, the usurping tyrant Arthur ab Uther: they are under arrest. Which of you will swear me the oath?'

Silence. Swearing of another kind of oath from some of the wounded.

'Take them away. Lock them in the storeroom,' Medraut commanded his warriors.

'But they are wounded, unarmed . . .' protested the surgeon.

'Then go with them and tend to them. No, do not take the Lady Gwynhwyfar with the others. Keep her . . . keep her in the warleader Bedwyr's house. Bind her and leave guards at the door. I will see to her later.'

Medraut's men poured in a mob about the carts, shouting and laughing. The wounded tried to struggle or protest, but the carts were quickly driven off. I saw this in a glance over my shoulder as my guards dragged me away, still half-stunned by the shock and by Medraut's blows, and led me stumbling to Bedwyr's house. They bound my hands in front of me with strips of the coverlet from the bed, took my own small knife away from me, then left, locking the door. I collapsed in a heap beside the bed and hid my face in the rough wool of the blanket. Outside, I could hear the guards joking and exclaiming excitedly.

Think, I told myself, trying to bite back the hysterical tears. You must think. You have been afraid of this all along; you need not be so surprised now that it has come about. Medraut has murdered Constantius and claimed the purple for himself. What has become of Constantius's warband?

I had seen none of the Dumnonian king's men, I realized. Medraut must have planned his move carefully: murdered Constantius, then had his followers take Constantius's men unawares, probably at night, when they were sleeping after a feast. Perhaps some of the men had sworn the oath to Medraut, and the rest? Death or imprisonment – unless some had escaped. Would Medraut have any allies?

Undoubtedly he had contacted Maelgwyn king of Gwynedd. Maelgwyn would support him in any move against Arthur. On the other hand, Medraut could not trust Maelgwyn very far. The king of Gwynedd wanted the purple for himself, and would not be eager to see Medraut wear it. Had Maelgwyn sent men to Camlann? No, I thought not. I had seen none. Though undoubtedly Maelgwyn had raised his army, and was probably hurrying even now to join Medraut.

Medraut, though, must have only his own followers in Camlann at the moment. Even if he had managed to enforce oaths from some of Constantius's men, and if he had been joined by some discontented nobles, he could not have much over two hundred warriors; three hundred at the most. Maelgwyn had another three hundred and an army of some two or three thousand peasants. When had Medraut acted, and seized power? Fairly recently – yet he had obviously had some time to organize the fortress to his own liking. A week before, two weeks? Someone must, even now, be travelling to Less Britain to warn Arthur. Arthur had plenty of spies and plenty of loyal followers: Medraut could not murder them all. And when Arthur heard, he would abandon the siege and return to Britain as fast as he could. Would he be able to match Medraut when he arrived?

Medraut, Maelgwn of Gwynedd. Who else? Dyfed, Powys, Elmet would probably remain officially neutral in the struggle. If they believed the rumours Medraut had been spreading and still remembered Arthur's violent seizure of power twenty years before, they might prove hostile and send some men to fight my husband. On the other hand, Medraut was a foreigner by birth and, by the same potent rumour, a child born of incest, accursed. The kings of Britain would not support him against Arthur, whose reign was at least familiar. And the kings would not support Maelgwn, either. They might rebel independently, but they would probably wait to see whether Maelgwn or Medraut or Arthur prevailed before doing that. Ebrauc, Rheged – they would support Arthur, if they heard in time, though half their royal warbands were off in Less Britain even now. The Saxon kingdoms?

They had a healthy respect for Arthur, who had defeated them against heavy odds. But a Britain torn by civil strife was much to their advantage. They might make common cause with Medraut for a time; betray him afterwards, of course, but support him against Arthur. Still, negotiations with the Saxons took time. Medraut could not have been negotiating directly before – Arthur and I would have heard of it. All in all, I decided, my husband and his son would be evenly matched in the war that lay ahead.

I sat up, wiping my face and feeling somewhat better. I had cut the inside of my lip against my teeth from one of Medraut's blows, and my face was smeared with blood. I stood up, looking around. There was no water in the room. The hearth was cold, even the ashes of the fire cleared away. The books were gone, and the lamp. Only the bed and a few musty-smelling blankets remained. No one had lived in the house since Bedwyr left it that summer, and the dust was thick over the desk. It was very cold, I realized. My bound hands had turned red, pale-mottled, and were numb. I flexed them, twisting them from side to side, trying to loosen the bonds. I went over to the coverlet, which the guards had thrown aside after cutting my bonds from it, and clumsily dragged it round me, then spat on a corner and wiped my face. My hair had come down on one side, but I could not fasten it up again. I sat huddled up against the bed, my hands between my knees for warmth. Medraut would doubtless send someone to care for me soon. Whatever he intended for me, he, he did not mean me to die from neglect.

What he intended ... punishment of some kind, no doubt. A public display of strength, a trial for the woman who had tried to murder him, and a public execution. Burning? Stoning? Torture? I began to feel a cold different from that of the chill, empty room. *Dear God*, I thought, *give me strength*. If I could not escape I must at least die bravely, as befitted an Empress of Britain.

Escape. My bonds were very tight. There were two guards outside – why had Medraut not posted one inside with me to watch me? He must be afraid I would try to kill myself, to have me bound. Whatever his reason, it worked to my advantage. If I could somehow escape – through the smoke-hole? – but then there was the rest of the fortress to cross, and after that the walls. It would be madness to try the gate. Here I would be recognized, and I did not know the password. Still, it should be possible to climb the walls on the inside. Medraut did not have enough men to patrol the whole circuit of the fortress very closely.

A servant girl came in, accompanied by a warrior. She looked about, saw me and went pale with fear. The warrior pushed her forward. 'Build up the fire,' he commanded, 'and see to the prisoner.' He leaned against the wall by the door, watching me. I remained sitting where I was. The girl built up and lit a fire, fetched water and swept the room without looking at me, although I had to stand and move when she came over to make the bed. She was plainly terrified. I suddenly thought to wonder about the servants at Camlann. If they were obedient, they should be safe – except for Cei's mistress, Maire, and the wife of Gwalchmai's servant. Medraut bore the latter woman especially an old grudge, for Eivlin had served his mother and betrayed her. He would be entirely capable of putting the woman and her children to death. And he could use Maire and her children against Cei.

'Eivlin, Rhys's wife,' I said to the serving girl, 'and Cei's Maire: are they at Camlann?'

The girl gave me a terrified glance, then shook her head. 'Quiet!' commanded the guard.

My hands were untied and I was allowed to wash, then was bound again, and this time my feet were tied as well. The servant and the guard left and I sat on the bed and stared at the new-made fire. Could I burn through the rag bindings with it?

They had just left. It was likely that I would now be left alone, for a little while at least. I did not know Medraut's plans, but the sooner I escaped the better. Where to go when I had escaped? Best to think of that later.

I rolled off the bed and crawled over to the fire. It was made of apple wood, and burned steadily. I thrust my hands over the flame, and realized as my skin scorched that this was unnecessarily painful. Taking a stick of loose wood I pushed a glowing coal from the fire and pressed my bonds against it. It hurt, and I bit my lip and closed my eyes, thinking of Arthur while the cloth smouldered. But soon I could flex my hands; the cloth loosened, tore – I dragged my hands back, free, clenching and unclenching my numb fingers. Thank God. I sat back and unbound my feet. Now – how to get out of the house? The smoke-hole over the main hearth could be seen by the guards outside. There was another hearth in the kitchen, an oven. If I pulled some of the thatch loose from the vent I might be able to climb out of it. Best to take the blankets from the bed and use them to make a rope to help in climbing the walls of the fortress. I dragged the blankets loose, looked around the room for something to cut them with. Nothing there. I went into the kitchen, came back, took another smouldering branch from the fire and used that and rough jerks to divide each blanket into three strips. They were old blankets, and it was easier than I had imagined. I tied the strips together. There. And now . . .

The door flew open and Medraut came in. Half-way into the kitchen, trapped, I saw him pause, smile, and close the door behind him. I dropped my armful of blanket rope.

'Most noble lady,' said Medraut. 'I had thought you

254

were bound and secure.' He glanced down, saw the fragments of charred coverlet by the hearth, stooped and picked one up. He looked at me and raised an eyebrow. 'Obvious, but quickly thought of and daring.' He came over and caught my hand, looked at the burns on my wrist, shook his head, smiling. 'I should have expected nothing less. And you have made a rope, too, to climb the wall! How fortunate that I came in just now. I think, most noble lady, you have mistaken my intentions towards you.'

'Do not play the fool, Medraut,' I said, keeping my voice level. 'You know that I am your enemy, and we both know that I am at your mercy now. And I expect no mercy, from you.'

Again the smooth smile, the ironically lifted eyebrow. 'You have always judged me hastily, my lady. What do you believe I mean to do with you, that you go to such lengths to escape?'

I stared at him, trying to penetrate the mask. I did not believe for an instant that he meant to be merciful, but I could not see what he wished me to believe, or what game he was playing now. 'You know that I tried to poison you,' I said at last. 'And I think you intend to have me tried for that, and for whatever crimes you can fabricate evidence for.'

'Ah, but the Emperor drank the poisoned cup, and was unharmed. Plainly, I must have been mistaken. What are you guilty of, my lady, but adultery? And that is no crime against me; indeed, if your husband is not Emperor – and I say he is not – it is not a political crime at all, and no concern of mine. Why should I treat you cruelly?'

I raised a hand to my jaw, still tender from the blow he had given me only a few hours before. 'What do you intend for me, Medraut?' I demanded. 'If you are trying to bargain with me, I will tell you plainly that I will not make peace with you on any conditions, nor give my support to you whatever you promise.'

'My intentions for you?' He laughed. 'This.' He seized me by the shoulders and kissed me violently.

For a moment I was so astonished that I could not react, and then I tried to tear away from him. He grabbed one of my wrists, held me, caught the other wrist, his grip agonizing on the burns.

'My father's wife,' he said through his teeth, 'my father's cunning wife, the wise and lovely daughter of Ogyrfan, the Empress Gwynhwyfar. Oh, you are beautiful, you are a queen indeed. This will hurt Arthur more than the loss of his kingdom; the Prince of Hell himself must have sent you here to me.'

'Let me go!' I said. 'You cannot do this!'

He laughed again, tightened his grip, dragging my hands up so that the tears of pain leapt to my eyes. 'I can, as you will see. I am going to have you, just as my father had my mother – by force.' He dragged me over to the bed, kicked my legs from under me, fell on top of me. I screamed as loudly as I could, got one of my hands free, found Medraut's knife in his belt. Medraut swore. I struck out, blindly, found his hand on my wrist again, smelled blood. My hand was forced back, and I could not hold the knife. It fell to the bed, slid onto the floor with a soft clunk. Medraut pressed against me, our breath mingling, trapping my arms with his right hand. His left hand moved slowly down my body, tearing apart the fastenings of my gown. His eyes stared directly into mine, savage, bitter, with a strange, agonized loneliness.

'He did not rape your mother!' I said, using the only weapon left to me – words. 'She seduced him. She did it deliberately, because she wished to bear you for his destruction. You are her tool, no more than a tool! Think of her! Oh God, God, help me!'

Medraut's body went slack against mine. 'Lies!' he screamed – screamed like a hurt child. Beneath the horror and the outrage, a little hope stirred in me. Everything Gwalchmai had ever said about his brother returned to me with burning clarity.

'She never loved you,' I told Medraut. 'She only loved destruction. Gwalchmai loves you, Arthur wanted to love you, but *she* never loved you. She . . . she only wanted to devour you. She has devoured your father, she devoured Lot, and Agravain, she devours everything. She has eaten away your soul, and left you alone in the night.'

'Lies!' he cried. He slid off the bed, kneeling beside it and struck out at me. I tried to cover my head and he struck frantic, hysterical blows at my head and shoulders without aiming them. 'She loved me! I will kill you . . . you witch!'

You proud whore! I ... I will ...'

He was sobbing. The blows stopped. I shook my head, lowered my hands and looked at him. His chest was labouring with the sobs, and his face was streaked with tears. When our eyes met he fell silent.

'She is dead,' I said. 'And she destroyed you as well.'

He moaned like a man in delirium when his wound is searched. He raised his hands to his face, then brought them down wet with tears. He stared at the tears for a moment uncomprehendingly, then looked up at me, anger growing behind his eyes. He wiped his face, turned, and without another word left the room.

'Tie her so that she cannot reach the fire,' I heard him order the guard as he left, and there was in his voice no trace of smoothness. I collapsed against the wall, trembling and weeping with relief. Thank God.

But would it work again? If he got himself drunk would he care how much I spoke to him of Morgawse? And if he gagged me – I must escape. I must escape from Camlann, if it was by death.

One of the guards came into the house with a strong rope, bound my wrists again, then tied them tightly to the outer post of the bedstead. As he turned to leave he paused, picked something up from the floor, and stood a moment turning it in the firelight. It was Medraut's knife, and it was streaked with blood. He looked directly at me for the first time, then spat on me deliberately. 'Murdering whore,' he said, and strode out.

I lay still, resting my head against my arms. Tied like that I could sit against the bedstead or lie flat with my arms above my head, but could neither stand straight nor move about. I could not have hurt Medraut badly with the knife. My blow had been wild and had not struck anything solid. It must have grazed him somewhere. He would come back and, bound like this, it would be very difficult to work free; difficult even to kill myself.

My thoughts leapt and ran among impossible escapes which grew wilder still as sleep came over me – one can sleep anywhere, if exhausted enough – till I lay moaning in a nightmare. I remember one dream in which I flew from Camlann on the back of the dragon of our standard, while Medraut, transformed to an eagle, flew behind me, drawing nearer and nearer. He reached me and I woke, screaming, feeling the cruel talons on my wrists – but the room was still and empty, and I had only twisted my burned hands against the rope. The grey dawn fell through the smoke-hole, and I lay motionless, staring at it while it brightened slowly into day.

I must have fallen asleep again, for when next I opened my eyes there were people in the room. I tried to sit up, caught my wrists against the rope, struggled about until I could swing my legs to the floor and sit leaning wearily against the bedstead. I could not see clearly. One of Medraut's blows had swollen an eye shut. My bruises ached, my wrists burned again, and my tongue seemed swollen in a scraped, dry mouth. I shook my head, trying to toss my hair out of my eyes, and managed to focus on the others in the room. One was the servant girl who had come the day before, and the other was Medraut's friend Rhuawn. He was staring at me, in horror or loathing, I could not tell which.

'Rhawn,' I said, my voice reduced to a croaking whisper.

He gestured to the girl, and she hurried over and untied my wrists, fumling with the stiff knots. 'Do you want some water, noble lady?' she asked in whisper.

'Thank you,' I replied. She had brought a jug of water, and she held it to my lips – my hands were too numb to grip anything, and there were, anyway, no cups in the room. The water was bitterly cold, and stung the raw places in my mouth, so that I could drink only a little of it. The girl set the jug down and built the fire up, then put the rest of the water on to heat.

'Noble lady . . .' Rhuawn began in a hoarse voice, then trailed off, still staring at me.

'What is it?' I asked coldly.

'I had heard that the lord Medraut meant to . . . marry you.'

I stared blankly for a moment, then shook my head. 'What Medraut told me of his intentions was rather less gentle than matrimony.' Though it might even be true; it would be an impressive public gesture for him to marry the Empress.

'He has beaten you!' Rhuawn's voice was suddenly loud again. The girl glanced up at him, terrified.

258

'I was fortunate to escape so.' I said evenly, then bit my lip, for the expression on Rhuawn's face was now plainly not loathing, but shock and horror. 'You do not support him in this!'

He looked away from me at once, and one hand fell to his sword, tightened about its hilt until the bones stood out. 'Medraut is my friend and my lord,' he whispered.

'You once swore an oath to Arthur,' I told him, my voice also low. 'You once told him that you would raid Yffern itself if he wished it. Now Medraut is your friend, your lord, and you are willing to make war against your friends and your comrades of many battles, to support a usurper to your sworn lord's kingdom, and stand by while his wife is raped in his own fortress. What real cause did Arthur give you, Rhuawn, for you to betray him? Do not tell me of those rumours and subtly devised slights Medraut has crammed your ears with. Did Arthur ever harm any of your clan or kindred, or stand by and fail to aid you when another injured them? Did he cheat you of your share of plunder? Did he steal your goods, or let them be stolen? Did he ask more of you in battle than he asked of himself?—Rhuawn said nothing. 'What cause has Arthur given you to perjure yourself and forsake him?'

'None,' Rhuawn returned in a whisper. 'My lady, I did not believe them when they said Medraut intended this . . . his crime against you. I did not believe it when they said he sought the purple. And now . . . now I no longer know what to believe. But Medraut was wronged, and he is my friend.'

I brushed my hair back from my face. The serving girl stared at us in fear, and I struggled to remember her, to try to determine whether she would report this conversation to Medraut. But even if she would repeat every word, I had nothing to lose by speaking.

'Why?' I demanded. 'What good has Medraut ever done for you? So, he told you that he did not desire the purple? Now you have learned that that was a lie.'

'He says that the Emperor would have him killed if he did not seize power to defend himself.'

'Arthur would do that? Arthur, who bore so patiently with the crime Bedwyr and I committed against him, and would still wish to spare us both, if he could? You know

Arthur better than that, Rhuawn. Let me speak plainly. I did try to poison your friend and your lord Medraut, because I feared this very thing that has now come to pass, this civil war, and would rather be damned myself than see the Empire broken by Medraut. But I did not tell my husband, and when he discovered it, he was very angry.'

Rhuawn watched me, white-faced, shaken. 'Medraut has lied to you all along. He always wanted power – think! Remember him when first he came here! And now that he has power, does he use it justly, mercifully? Does he even tell you his mind? You are afraid of him now, for yourself and for others.'

Rhuawn's face showed me plainly that I was right, and a desperate, almost overpowering hope leapt in me. I had never thought him evil, only greatly deceived. 'Rhuawn,' I whispered. 'Help me to escape.'

Abruptly the door opened, and another warrior stood in it, looking at Rhuawn grimly. Rhuawn's face at once became blank, guarded.

'Lord Rhuawn, you should not be here,' said the other.

'The lord Medraut wished the lady seen to,' Rhuawn stated. 'And Mabon on the earlier shift knew of no objections to my seeing to her.'

'You mean "the Emperor" wished her seen to,' the guard corrected, giving me a brief glare.

'The Emperor Medraut. I am just going to see him, to speak of her to him.' Rhuawn gave me one more unreadable glance, then left, leaving the other warrior to tie me up again.

The day passed with agonizing slowness. I was brought some food at mid-morning, and allowed to stand and wash myself. I welcomed the chance to stand, to tie together as best I might the tears in my gown and wash in the clear water, but had no appetite.

Some while after noon, more food was brought, but this I could not so much as look at, and none was brought that evening. I tried to work my hands free of the ropes, but could not get at the knots, though I twisted my hands about, fumbling at them until my wrists bled. The bed frame was all too solidly made, and could not be wrenched apart.

It grew dark. Rhuawn had not returned, and my brief hope seemed senseless. The fear and misery had grown so that I could no longer feel them, but only sit, leaning against the bedstead, forcing a numbed mind to think.

I was sitting like this when I heard voices at the door, and I looked away from the fire to that dark corner of the room which opened on the world.

'I have Medraut's permission to see her,' Rhuawn's voice said, protesting.

'The Emperor has said nothing about allowing you through,' one of the guards replied.

'I don't need permission. I have been his friend from the beginning.'

'An increasingly cold friend, Rhuawn ap Dorath, ever since he took the purple. Go away.'

'Very well.' There was a strange grunt.

'What?' came another voice – the other guard. 'Hueil – ai!' There was a brief clash of metal on metal, and a gasp. The door burst open and Rhuawn came in, his sword bare, but not shining in the firelight. There was blood on it. He hurried over to me and swung the sword hard against the rope around the bedstead, then caught my hands and dragged me to my feet. 'My lady,' he said, 'we must hurry.'

'Cut these,' I told him, for my wrists were still bound. He stared at me, and I put my hands against the sword. He saw what I wanted, jerked the blade down between my wrists. The cords parted. I turned back to the room, found the rope of blankets I had made the day before, then followed Rhuawn from the house.

The guards lay by the door, one sprawled across the threshold, staring upwards, face twisted in a grimace of pain. His open eyes stared into the darkness of the night, the few wet flakes of snow that drifted from the low sky. Rhuawn stared at him and shook his head. I hesitated, then stopped and unfastened the heavy winter cloak of the one who stared and pulled it loose. I would need it, and he would not feel the cold.

'Yes . . . good,' Rhuawn said, shaking himself. 'And the armlets, take those too. Here, take mine as well: you will need money. I must get your horse.'

'I could not ride her out of the gate, and you could not take her from the stables. But will they let you through the gate? Then take a horse – not mine – and say . . . say you have a message to Caer Uisc, and are taking a spare mount. Bring the horses round to Llary's field, on the other side of the wall, to the far end of it. I can climb over the wall there.'

'Yes. I will bring your horse . . . a horse.' Rhuawn drew a deep breath.

'And yours – do you have time, can you ride out through the gates?' I asked, for he seemed in such confusion that I was not sure he understood me.

'They will not stop me,' he replied.

'Then meet me at the far end of Llary's field, as soon as you can. At Llary's field.'

'Yes, yes . . . I will . . . fetch the horses.' He shook his head again, and said nothing as I pulled up the hood of my cloak and ran into the darkness.

The fortress was quiet at that time of night, and the few who were about saw me only as a figure hunched against the wind. The snow was falling thicker when I reached the grove where once I had trysted with Bedwyr. I stopped and watched. After a little while a sentry passed on the wall above, and, as soon as he was gone, I hurried over to the storage hut, clambered from the woodpile beside it onto the roof, and from there scrambled up onto the causeway that ran along the side of the wall. I paused, panting from the effort, then fastened my blanket rope to an embrasure, struggled over the top of the wall, climbed a little way down the rope, then fell – my hands were still too numb to grip properly. I twisted my ankle in the fall and sprawled in the mud of the field, but jumped up again and tried to shake the rope loose. It was no use; it would not come. I would simply have to hope that, in the snow, the sentry would not notice it. I stumbled away from the wall, down the ditch and up the bank, and started for the far end of the field, hoping that Rhuawn would manage to get the horses through the gate. I did not think I could walk very far.

I had not gone far when I saw the sentry outlined against the sky again, and I dropped to my knees in the mud of the ploughed field, huddled in my cloak, praying that he would not see the rope. He passed without giving me a glance: I was simply a dark patch in the black and white of the field and the snow. When I was certain he had gone, I jumped up, fell over again as my ankle gave under me. I sat up, feeling the tears of exhaustion in my eyes and wishing that I had eaten something that day after all. But I had no option but to stumble over to the far end of the field and wait. There I sat leaning against the fence. The wet snow fell from the heavy sky, and everything was very, very quiet.

After a dark age I heard hooves and the jingle of harness, and stood up. The sound became more distinct: two horses. I hobbled forward.

They loomed out of the dark, an indistinct figure on a dark mount, leading another horse. I called Rhuawn's name and they stopped.

'My lady?'

'Here,' I said. He came over, dismounted, and helped me into the saddle. I was ashamed to need his help.

'Yours is Constans's horse, Sword-dancer,' Rhuawn said. 'He is a war horse, and well-trained.' I nodded, gathering up the reins and patting the horse's neck: the animal flicked his ears back restlessly, uncertain about leaving his stall on such a night.

'My lady;' Rhuawn continued, speaking in a low voice. 'You recall Eivlin, the wife of Gwalchmai's servant?' I looked up at him, trying to make out his face in the dark. 'Medraut wished to kill her and her children, but I thought it dishonourable to make war on servants, women and children. I said nothing of it to Medraut, but I warned the woman when Medraut first seized power, and helped her to leave Camlann. Her husband's clan lives near Mor Hafren, and have a holding on a river called the Fromm: it is reached by the second turning east from the main road from Baddon to Caer Ceri. The chieftain of the clan is called . . . is called . . .'

'Sion ap Rhys,' I said, remembering.

'Yes. If you go there, my lady, I am certain that the woman will remember you, and see that you are concealed and kept safe from Medraut.'

Yes. Medraut would never know or remember a servant's clan.

'Good,' I said. 'But you will come with me, I hope.'

He laughed strangely. 'I think I will soon find a hiding place, my lady, if one not altogether to my liking. But perhaps not. My lady, by now they will know that you are gone. We must hurry, and hope that the snow hides our trail.'

He turned his horse, spurring it to a gallop, and I followed. Constans's horse Sword-dancer ran swiftly enough, though I had to set my teeth to stay on against the jolting.

We galloped a long way, until the horses were sweating heavily even in the cold; then trotted; then galloped again. The wind was bitter, and I bent low in the saddle, riding blind, content from the feeling of his gait that my horse kept to the road. The snow froze in my eyelashes.

Rhuawn's horse shied suddenly across my path, and I drew rein, saw, looking up at last, that the saddle was empty. I stared blankly for a moment, then guided my mount over to Rhuawn's, caught its bridle – not difficult to do, for the horses were both tired – and turned back down the road. We were on the main road by then, the north road; it was about midnight, and we might have come sixteen or seventeen miles from Camlann.

I found Rhuawn a few paces down the road, kneeling in the centre of it and vomiting convulsively. I jumped from my saddle. 'Rhuawn!' I said, and he looked up, his face a pale shadow in the dark. 'What has happened?'

Silence. 'I am sorry. It is so hot.'

The wind whipped the wet snow into our faces. The reins over my arm seemed frozen there. I went to Rhuawn, caught his arm, touched his forehead. Though the collar of his cloak was glazed with ice, his skin was burning hot. 'What has happened?' I whispered, suddenly very much afraid.

Rhuawn laughed, a laugh that ended in a sob. 'I went to Medraut this morning and pleaded for you. He asked me to dine with him that night, to discuss the matter. But he said nothing of it at table. Only . . . he looked at me. I remember that he looked at Constantius with those eyes, the last night that he dined with him. They say Constantius died in a burning fever. Medraut said it was a fever.' There was a long silence. The tired horses breathed heavily, champed their bits loudly in the stillness. 'It must have been in the wine,' Rhuawn said. 'I thought it tasted bitter. But Medraut complained of it and said it was because of the war with Less Britain that we had no good wine. So I did not suspect.'

'You should have told me!' I began – but what could I

have done if he had? Perhaps a surgeon might have helped Rhuawn if he acted at once, but no surgeon in Camlann would have been permitted to. And now it might be too late. 'You must have water,' I said, thinking rapidly. 'Eat some snow.'

'I will lose it.'

'That is the point. The poison makes you sick; if you lose enough of it, and if you can wash enough of it from your body, what is left may not be enough to kill you. Here.' I scooped up handfuls of the snow, and he took them, vomited again and again, began shaking. I helped him to his horse, managed somehow to get him into the saddle, and took some leather straps from the harness and tied Rhuawn in. 'We must hurry,' I told him. 'Perhaps we can find a place to stop.'

'No! We cannot risk stopping. Medraut will find us.'

I did not have anything to say to that, so only shook my head and spurred my horse to a gallop. Perhaps the whole flight was pointless. Medraut had many ways of learning things, by spies and by his private sorceries. I could only pray that neither means would serve him this time, and pray that Rhuawn had lost enough of the poison, and would recover.

The journey became a nightmare. The horses were now too tired to gallop, and we trotted and walked and trotted and walked, while the snow fell harder, and the world narrowed to the road directly before us, and to my horse and Rhuawn's. Presently Rhuawn's mount began to wander from side to side of the road and fall behind. I went over to it and took the reins from Rhuawn's hands. He was delirious and did not reply to my questions, merely muttering incoherently. I looked about for lights, for a place to stop, but there was no light. It was too late for that, and the snow swallowed everything into a white darkness.

Perhaps three hours after we stopped the first time, Rhuawn went into convulsions. I turned off the road, dragging the horse – which was terrified, despite its tiredness – and began to cross a field. The wind stopped, and I found that we had reached a patch of woodland. I followed the edge of this until I found a hollow of the ground, sheltered from the wind and clear of snow. Here I dragged Rhuawn from his horse, hobbled the animals, and collected some wood for a fire. Rhuawn had a tinderbox and a blanket in the pack behind his saddle, and by some miracle I managed to kindle some wood that was not too damp. I then moved Rhuawn closer to the fire, wrapping him in the blanket. I tried to feed him more snow, but his teeth were set and his body torn by the convusions, and he could not take it. His face in the firelight was almost unrecognizable: twisted, flecked with foam and vomit. The pupils of his eyes had dilated until it seemed that a living darkness boiled within his skull. I touched his forehead again, and still it was burning and dry. Standing by that fire off a road in Dumnonia, I remembered suddenly, as from another world, a conversation I had had with Gruffydd the surgeon, about, of all things, cosmetics. 'Nightshade,' he had said, 'is a deadly poison, but if you put it in your eyes it will make them bright. Dilates the pupils. Also causes fever, vomiting, delirium and convulsions. My lady, why do women tamper with such things? No sane *man* would employ them.' 'Men like bright eyes,' I had replied, 'but do not complain to me; I do not use nightshade. Can it even kill?' 'In the right dosage,' he said, snorting with disgust. 'Too much and it is lost in the vomiting. Not a poison for amateurs.'

But Medraut was not an amateur.

We could ride no further that night. The horses were nearly spent as it was. But I doubt that anyone could find us in the snow. I built the fire up, unharnessed the horses, and tried to construct some kind of shelter for Rhuawn.

Rhuawn died some two hours before dawn. He said nothing that whole while and did not regain consciousness. I realized, when he no longer breathed, that I had not thanked him for saving me. *Well*, I told myself, *it is an evil world. May God reward him.*

I sat for a long while looking at his body, then, because the night was cold though the snow had now stopped, I pulled the blanket from over him and wrapped it round me.

I had no way to bury him. I had neither the tools nor the strength to dig a grave. Nor could I load his horse with his body and continue down the road. It would attract too much attention. Alone, in my muddied peasant dress, I might pass unremarked as a farmer's wife who happened to have a fine horse, but leading another horse burdened with a warrior's body I would be noticed, remembered, found, and the whole escape would go for nothing. But I could not simply leave the body lying there for the scavengers: besides, Medraut's men, if they followed, might find it or hear of its finding, and know that I had taken this road. Moreover I had neither food for myself nor fodder for the horses, and could not travel another day without them.

I huddled near the fire, and must have drowsed a little, for when I looked up again the sun was above the fields. The snow glittered brightly, and the trees stood above fields slashed with their long blue shadows. Northeastward, and quite near, a plume of smoke rose white and thick into the morning air.

I rose, caught and saddled Rhuawn's horse, and managed to drag the body over and tie it there. Then I saddled my own horse, mounted, and rode towards the smoke, leading the other animal.

It was a small holding: a barn and two houses. When I rode into the yard a woman was crossing from the barn to one of the houses carrying two pails of milk. She looked at me, shrieked, dropped one of the pails, just caught the other one and clutched it to her.

'I mean you no harm,' I told her, as men ran out of the barn and the nearest house. 'Does your holding want a horse?'

It was a risk, but not too great a one. I knew that the countryside of Dumnonia was very hostile to Medraut – he had killed their king and unleased a struggle which would certainly harm their lands. And it was likely that they would be pleased with the gift of a fine horse like Rhuawn's and, if they took it, would fear to lose it by informing.

The men of the holding clustered around the woman, staring at me. I had a sudden vision of what I must look like, my face pinched and red with cold, blotched with bruises, my hair down in matted tangles, covered from head to foot with mud, riding a spent high-bred horse and leading another horse burdened with a corpse.

'Eeeeh,' said one of the men, then, 'You are from Camlann?'

'Yes.'

He came over to Rhuawn's horse, staring at the body. He touched it gingerly and felt that it was cold. He looked back at me. 'Your husband? Did the witch's bastard kill him?'

'Yes,' I replied, feeling too far removed from the world to add to either lie or truth. 'I will give you the horse if you will take care of the body, and give me some grain for my own horse. I still have far to ride.'

The man could, of course, take from me whatever he wished without bothering to pay me. But this was a Dumnonian holding, and near the road. Law ought to rule here if anywhere – and it did. The man nodded. 'It is a fine horse. And probably he was a fine man, as well. I am sorry for you, lady. Here, come inside and rest. I will see that your horse is cared for.'

'I must hurry.'

'Leave whenever you wish. But do not fear that we will betray you. Indeed, I think it would cost us our souls, to betray a lady to a sorcerer born out of incest.'

I stayed at the holding until the evening. I was lucky to have found the place: had I tried to ride on to Mor Hafren without pausing for food or rest, I believe I might have died. It was bitter weather, and I was already much weakened.

The people of the holding were cautiously friendly. They had heard tales of what had happened at Camlann, heard of executions, of their king's death; knew of a few servants who had fled the place. They treated my horse well and, at my request exchanged its silver-adorned, enamelled harness for one of inconspicuous plain leather, and gave me some clothing to make up the difference in value. They gave me hot food, hot water to wash in, exchanged my muddy clothing for clean, and gave me a warm bed to sleep in. They woke me in the late afternoon, saying that they were ready to bury 'my husband'. They laid Rhuawn in a grave behind their barn with a mingling of old superstitions and Christian prayers, and gave me his jewellery and his dagger – I told them to leave him his sword. I was grateful to them. But I knew that they believed me only a warrior's widow. What they might have done if they had known who I really was I did not know and did not wish to discover, so, when the burial was done with, I took my leave.

'But it will be cold tonight,' the head of the holding told me. 'You should not travel. And there have been many bandits about since the news came of the king's death and the Emperor's absence. It is not safe for a woman to travel alone.'

'It has never been safe for a woman to travel alone,' I replied. 'But it is not safe for me here, or for you while I am here, and it will be better if I travel at night. There are fewer bandits and . . . other dangers about.'

At this he nodded.

The previous night's rapid pace had brought me almost as far as Baddon, despite the snow. Now the snow was largely gone again, and I made good time, reaching the city wall of Baddon while it was still dusk. I circled this, not entering the gates, as Medraut had probably sent men there to watch for me. It was fully dark when I rejoined the road, the north road, and spurred my horse to a fast trot.

The second turning east on the road from Baddon to Caer Ceri, Rhuawn had said. I was afraid that either I remembered his directions wrongly or that he had been mistaken in them, and that I would find the wrong holding. And beyond that, I feared Medraut's sorceries, that he would somehow contrive to find me, and that death followed me, ready to strike down all from whom I hoped protection. But I had nowhere else to go.

The night was clear, and there was a bright half moon. The second turning which might be called a road came some seventeen miles from Baddon. My horse was still tired from the exhausting night before, and I let him slow to a walk, following the rutted, muddy path through the pasturelands. There were a number of holdings in the area, for at several points I saw smoke rising in the clear moonlight. But I judged that the holding I looked for, if it lay near the river Fromm, must be further east.

The stars wheeled about towards the dawn, and, half asleep, I came upon a holding very near the road. I hesitated, then turned and rode towards it.

When I drew nearer dogs began barking loudly, so I did not dismount, but rode close to the door of the largest house and there waited. The door opened a crack, and I could see lights being lit within. A man came out, carrying a hunting spear, and several others came out behind him, one hastily pulling on a tunic, the others bare-chested under their cloaks.

'Who are you and what do you want?' the leader demanded sharply.

'Is this the holding of Sion ap Rhys?' I asked.

'It's a woman!' one of the men exclaimed – as I was muffled in my cloak, they had been unable to tell this before. Now they visibly relaxed.

'I am Sion ap Rhys, of the clan of Huy ap Celyn,' said the leader. He was an older man, stocky, with a wide, strong-featured face: looking at him more closely I realized that I knew his son, who bore the same features, and I caught my breath.

'I seek Eivlin, the wife of Rhys ap Sion. I am a friend of hers.'

They looked at me a moment in silence. 'Are there no others with you?'

'I am alone.'

Sion ap Rhys sighed, handed his spear to one of the others, ran a hand through his hair. 'Dafydd, take her horse and look after it. Huw, check down the road that there is really no one else. Will you come in – is it "lady"?'

'Thank you,' I said, dismounting. I staggered and felt dizzy when my weight came onto my feet again, and I had to lean against the horse, but I recovered myself. The clan chieftain offered me his arm for support, I took it, and we went together into the house.

'She is looking for Eivlin,' Sion told the family, which was massed inside the door. There seemed to be a lot of them, and, almost at once, there were more, for Eivlin herself burst into the room.

'Most noble lady!' she cried. 'King of Heaven! What has happened to you?'

I tried to speak and began coughing. I was helped to the hearth and collapsed on a stool there, badly wanting to cry. Eivlin pulled my cloak from my shoulders, then saw the bruises on my face. She exclaimed again. 'What have they done to you, the murdering savages? Morfudd, fetch some water, the poor lady is ill. My lady, what has happened? Is Macsen dead? Is the Emperor back? Is my husband safe?'

'Rhys . . . was safe and well when last I saw him,' I said. 'I do not know the rest. I came to Camlann . . . was it four days ago? I had not heard of what Medraut had done. Rhuawn helped me to escape. He is dead. Medraut poisoned him – it was nightshade, I think. Medraut is seeking me. Rhuawn told me you might hide me.'

'And indeed we will. Och, Sion, my father, this is the Lady Gwynhwyfar, the Emperor's wife. Look how they have treated her! Medraut is a wolf, without shame or pity, and not a man at all!'

I began to laugh, weakly, while Sion and his clan stared at me in shock. Eivlin knew nothing of how bad it had really been.

But at least for the present I was safe.

Eleven

I stayed at Sion's holding for more than two weeks. Whether Medraut's sorceries did not work or whether he had no time or opportunity to employ them, I do not know, but I was not discovered.

From Eivlin I learned that Medraut had seized power a week and four days before I arrived in Camlann. The thing had happened much as I had guessed: there had been a feast, before which Medraut had advised his followers, in hints, to drink sparingly. That night Constantius came down with a 'fever', and Medraut told his followers that he would – most unfairly, of course – be suspected of poisoning. His men, alert and awakened, fell on Constantius's followers before the news reached them, and killed half of them. Some of the rest managed to escape in the confusion, and the remainder were locked into the storerooms. Constantius died the next day. 'Rhuawn came to me before morning, just after they had done murdering the King's followers,' Eivlin told me. 'He said that Medraut was to be Emperor, and that I must flee. And I was bewildered near to madness, for how could I flee, with the baby, and little Teleri not yet three? But Rhuawn said that Medraut had not yet made sure of the gates, and that there was great confusion, and he had seen some carts being harnessed by the stables. So I dragged the children out into the dark, with Sion and Teleri crying, and ran down to the gates, and God be praised, there was a cart there. Rhuawn helped me, carrying some goods to pay for the journey. I had wronged him in my thoughts, my lady, for I hated him as a traitor. Och ai, indeed no, not all Constantius's men were killed. I have heard that those that escaped rode across the country into the Saxon kingdoms, and from there took ship to Less Britain. It will not be long before the High King returns and peace will be restored again.'

I said nothing to that. I doubted, though, that anything could restore what had been broken. One might go some way towards piecing together a broken pot or a broom handle, but an Empire is a living thing, made of the hearts of men, and when it is broken, even if set well it may never grow straight again. The Family was at war with itself, and Britain divided in civil war as it had been twenty years before when Arthur seized power. Medraut apparently had had allies in the north: Ergyriad ap Caw, king of Ebrauc, had been forced by his own clan to abdicate and cede his title to his half-brother Hueil, one or two days before Medraut seized power in the south. Hueil was a trouble-maker, and hated Arthur, whom he blamed for the deaths of his father Caw and his brother Bran, and under his leadership Ebrauc rose in rebellion. Our ally, Urien of Rheged, had called up his army, and, with such of his warband as was left – the rest being in Gaul with Arthur – was trying to quell the rebellion. We could be grateful for that, for the timing clearly showed that Hueil was in league with Medraut, but, on the other hand, Urien had been our greatest hope of support on Arthur's return. Now I was not sure that Arthur could defeat Medraut and Maelgwn with the forces he had available to him.

For Maelgwn was, indeed, fighting beside Medraut. Two days after I arrived at the holding we heard that Maelgwn's army had crossed the Saefern river to our north and was hurrying southward to Camlann, and there was no united opposition to him. The middle kingdoms of Britain would fight for neither Arthur nor Medraut. Old differences and new rumours combined to make them unwilling to support their Emperor, though if Arthur died they would doubtless cry out against Medraut and go to war with him and with each other, trying to gain what advantage they could from anarchy. Only Dumnonia, of all the southern kingdoms, might have helped us, but Dumnonia was leaderless and powerless, her king dead, half the royal warband in Gaul with Arthur and the rest dead or starving slowly in the storerooms at Camlann.

If this were not bad enough, there was another cause of fear. Medraut's forces were growing steadily. Discontented noblemen, warriors tired of peace and hoping for profit and glory, debtors and criminals looking for a solution to their own problems in the collapse of the realm, all flocked to join Medraut. And Medraut was able to prevent a similar rally on Arthur's behalf. Almost every day there came some report of a nobleman of Arthur's party arrested or executed, of hostages taken from others, of goods confiscated and fortresses lost.

Yet the countryside about Mor Hafren, at least, seemed to support Arthur. A member of Sion's clan – usually his second son, Dafydd – went every day to Baddon, to learn the news in the market there. When the market was closed down by Medraut's order, there were gatherings at various places in the countryside where news and rumours circulated. And we had news from Baddon occasionally as well, for it seemed that Cei's mistress Maire had settled with some of her cousins there, escaping like Eivlin in the confusion that followed the taking of Camlann. One of these cousins came to the gathering places and gave mournful recitations of bad news, which Dafydd reported back to us. All the clans seemed to await the news that Arthur was back, that they could raise the peasant army and join him. Hunting spears were sharpened, and old war spears, daggers and swords brought from barns or hollows under the eaves, or even from graves; cleaned and polished and clumsily practised with for hours. Arthur had ruled long enough and well enough that the people trusted him and feared what his defeat might mean. They always had more to lose by civil war and anarchy than did the nobles, safe in their fortresses.

Twelve days after I arrived at the holding, Dafydd returned from news-gathering to say that Medraut and Maelgwn and their forces had left Camlann and were riding east. 'Echel Big-hip of Naf's clan says it is because the Emperor has landed in the east, and they ride to fight him,' he told us. 'But Cas ap Saidi says it is because they have made an alliance with the Saxons, and go to join them.'

Everyone in the clan looked at me, but I could only shake my head. I could not say which account might be the true one. I had not heard that the Saxons had taken sides, and had been uncertain that they would. Some of the Saxon leaders, as I believed, liked and respected Arthur. On the other hand, I knew that they resented their position as tributaries and wanted more land. If Medraut had promised them lands, they might have agreed to support him. But would they be willing to trust Medraut? But, again, could Arthur trust them, trust them well enough to risk landing at one of their ports after they knew that his people had risen in rebellion? He must know that the thing the Saxons were most likely to do under such circumstances was to entrap him by some trick, kill him, and then fight Medraut.

'I do not know,' I told Sion's clan wearily. 'We must wait.'

We waited. I could not sleep at nights, and the days seemed an endless succession of grey minutes, all exactly alike. It was difficult for me to stay in that smoky little holding. It was not fitting, the clan agreed unanimously, for the Empress of Britain to lift a finger towards housework; and it would have been discourteous of me to engage in the kind of work I was best used to, and run the holding. In the end I could only play with the children and pray for nightfall, and then pray for morning. Sion's clan was very good to me, and I owed them my life, but I longed for nothing more than to ride away from that holding and never see it again.

Three days later we had another piece of news: Sandde, the young lord of the fortress of Ynys Witrin, had risen in rebellion against Medraut, and declared himself for Arthur. I remembered Sandde from my many visits to Ynys Witrin: a tall, thin youth with the face of an angel and the manners of a frightened hare. His father had always followed the policy of the monastery of Ynys Witrin and been mildly hostile to Arthur; Sandde had become lord of the fortress on his father's death only three months before, and had had no reputation for supporting either side, and so had escaped Medraut's attention. He now sent men out throughout the Dumnonian countryside, a day's hard riding in all directions, announcing his rebellion and claiming that the rumour that Arthur had landed in the Saxon lands was true.

'Do we leave for Ynys Witrin tomorrow?' Dafydd asked eagerly, after delivering this news.

'Give it a few more days,' returned his father. 'This may be a trick.'

'Who would trick us into fighting for Arthur?' Dafydd demanded angrily.

'Sandde – or Medraut,' I told him, feeling very tired. 'Sandde may have no news about Arthur, and may be trying to win confidence in his cause by pretending to. But if that's the case, he has no chance of defeating Medraut and

275

Maelgwn on his own – he has only thirty warriors at Ynys Witrin, only his own cousins. It would be better to wait for Arthur. And it might be Medraut's plan to draw Arthur's followers into the open so that he can deal with them before Arthur arrives. We must wait until we know for certain that Arthur has come.' And, I added to myself, that might take a long time. The good sailing weather was now over. Arthur might have to wait until the spring before he could make the crossing from Gaul.

And yet three days later Dafydd rode back early in the afternoon, his horse foam-flecked and sweating from a hard gallop, and rushed into the house shouting that it was true, Arthur was back, and in league with Cerdic, King of the West Saxons. He had landed at Hamwih a week before, ridden north and met Cerdic who was riding south with his warband and some of his army to encounter him. He had spoken with Cerdic and instead of fighting him the Saxon king had agreed to support him as long as Arthur was in the boundaries of his kingdom. But there was more: Cerdic and Arthur had ridden west, and met Medraut and Maelgwn with their forces just west of the fortress of Sorviodunum, which the Saxons call Searisbyrig. There had been a fight between outriders of the two armies, developing into a cavalry skirmish which Arthur's cavalry, predictably, had won, forcing Medraut's to withdraw. That night, Medraut had sent a messenger to Cerdic. 'They say Medraut offered him half Dumnonia and a third of Elmet, and no tribute ever, if he would betray Arthur,' Dafydd said. 'Some say even more than that. But Cerdic offered a parley the next morning, and when Medraut rode up to it, he said, "Whatever enmity I may have borne the Emperor Arthur, and whatever grievances I may have yet, I will not betray him to a sorcerous, perjured, tyrannous bastard. If you come further east, Medraut son of No one, you will be invading my kingdom and you will suffer for it." And they say that Medraut is withdrawing!'

Sion ap Rhys began nodding, and Dafydd looked at him eagerly. 'Very well,' said Sion slowly. 'The army will be needed. We leave for Ynys Witrin tomorrow – and may God defend us!'

It was then the last week of December, but, after some snows, the weather had turned mild, and the roads were choked with mud. Sion had planned to take an oxcart full of supplies, but decided not to bring this because of the state of the roads, and instead loaded the two horses and the mule owned by the holding. There were nine men going, all the younger men of the clan, led by Sion himself; and there were also myself and Eivlin. Eivlin had been under some pressure to stay with her children, but in the end had decided not to. 'The noble lady will need an attendant,' she told Sion, 'and the Emperor's forces will doubtless be needing servants. And I wish to be with my husband.' So the children stayed with their grandmother and their aunts, and Eivlin walked in the mud beside the mule. Sion insisted that I ride the war horse I had brought from Camlann, as befitted a woman of my rank, but after the first few miles I dismounted and made him and Eivlin take turns with me. Sion was an old man, and Eivlin a young mother who had had no cause to walk far for years.

It was thirty-five miles to Ynys Witrin. We set out in the early morning, before the sun rose, and arrived after dusk. We met others on the road, bound on the same errand as ourselves, some by ones and twos, others in large clan gatherings like Sion's. They were armed with everything from ancient, rust-eaten Roman swords to pitchforks and ox goads. They all welcomed company, and even those who had never met one another on a market day were soon discussing taxes and the prices of cheese and ale since the markets closed. No one said anything about the war, which was strangely comforting. I did not speak much, but walked or rode among the others, listening to the steady voices and so longing for peace, for victory, that at times I thought I could not breathe.

When we arrived at the town of Ynys Witrin, Sion insisted that I remount Sword-dancer, so as to make myself known to the guards as stylishly as was possible for someone with as much mud over her as I had. So we went through the town of Ynys Witrin, in a party that had now grown to over thirty men, and began to climb the hill to the fortress. The night was already heavy over the marshes, and it was the dark of the moon, but even if it had been clear daylight it was, I knew, impossible to pick out Camlann from the hunched hills to the south-west. Impossible, though I looked again and again.

The fortress gates of Ynys Witrin were closed and bolted, but torches were set thickly about them, and our party was hailed long before we reached them.

'We are subjects of the Emperor Arthur,' Sion replied on behalf of the whole party, resting one hand against my horse's shoulder and breathing heavily from the climb. 'We have come to join Sandde, to fight against Medraut.' And the torchlight fractured on the makeshift weapons as the gates were opened.

I did not have even to tell the guards who I was. While I was yet riding through the gates I was recognized, hailed, and taken apart from the others. When I confirmed that I was, indeed, Gwynhwyfar daughter of Ogyrfan, and that I wished to speak with their lord, I was given little time to take leave of Sion before I was escorted to Sandde.

The lord of Ynys Witrin was worrying over accounts with his clerk when I was shown to his room, and when he saw me he leapt up, nearly knocking the inkwell over onto the parchment. 'Lady Gwynhwyfar!' he exclaimed, staring, then flushed, bowed, grabbed my hand and held it awkwardly, smiling. 'Most noble lady, I had heard of what that tyrant meant to do to you, and I had heard that you escaped; I am very glad, my lady, to see you. Cuall, fetch some wine! They say that your husband is near mad with fear for you, lady. But I am very glad to see you, I remember your grace well, even from when I was a boy. Cuall! Ah, here he is again. Have some wine, noble lady.'

Cuall, the clerk, poured me some wine and offered me his seat at the desk. 'There are another thirty-six just arrived with the lady,' he told his lord. 'A quarter of them have no supplies.'

'Oh. How many does that make?' asked Sandde. 'Numbers, I mean, not supplies.'

Cuall whisked the parchment off the desk. 'Three hundred and sixty-four today. Two hundred and twelve yesterday. One hundred and sixteen the day before. In total, including those that came the first days, before we made the proclamations, an army of seven hundred and forty. Your own forces, with the other noblemen who joined us, now amount to sixty-three.'

'Seven hundred and forty!' exclaimed Sandde. 'What shall we do? How many brought their own supplies? I wish

I had told them to bring their own supplies – how can we feed seven hundred and forty, to say nothing of sixty-three noblemen, and all the servants? Most noble lady,' Sandde abruptly fixed on me again, 'it is a miracle, it is the mercy of God that you have come. I have so often heard of your skill at managing fortresses and finding supplies; my father always cursed you for it. And I do not know what to do. Until three months ago I had never run anything, and this rebellion is more complicated than I expected, not at all like running a small fortress. My lady, if you came here to help – you did, didn't you? – please advise me how to feed this army!'

I began to laugh, and choked on the wine. 'I thank you, Lord Sandde,' I told him, when I finished coughing. 'Are you sure you want me to help?'

'Most noble lady, how could you doubt it? Why wouldn't I?'

'This war might be thought my fault,' I told him. 'For running off with the lord Bedwyr.'

He looked away from me, turning crimson. 'What does that matter?' asked Cuall the clerk. 'There is a war now – and from all I have heard, your loyalty to the Empire was never in question.'

'Exactly,' said Sandde, looking back. 'Exactly. And as to how to feed seven hundred and forty – the monks in the village have been helping, not much, but still, a little, which is a mercy, for Cuall here is the only one in the fortress who can read – but what supplies we have, and how to get more... Most noble lady ...' he took the piece of parchment from Cuall and gave it to me, looking at me eagerly. I pressed my hand against my forehead, feeling my skin hot, wondering whether what I felt was shame or fear at taking up authority again. But I looked at the figures on the sheet and tried to make sense of them, and, as I did so, felt a strange fierce gladness. The war had begun and I once more had a place in the struggle.

I stayed up till after midnight that night, trying to sort out Sandde's affairs, and might have stayed up later except that, tired as I was from the day's ride and the long waiting, after a time I began adding fifteen to twelve and getting fifty-two. At last Sandde noticed that I was weary and still mud-bespattered, leapt up with apologies, and had me shown to the house that had been his mother's. There I found Eivlin already installed and asleep, and I was too tired to even wash off more than a little of the mud before I followed her example. The next morning I found it more difficult than I had expected to get up, but it was essential to get back to work. I had learned from Sandde that Medraut's forces had retreated from their position near the Saxon border, though at the moment they did not seem to have gone far, and that they were expected to return to the neighbourhood of Camlann. It also appeared that Cerdic's support of Arthur would not extend beyond the boundaries of his own kingdom. Saxon and Briton had fought each other too often to feel confident about marching in company into British territory, and the Saxon warriors had only the haziest of loyalties to a British Emperor. If my husband wished to pursue Medraut, he would have to do so with nothing more than his forces from Gaul. He badly needed the army Sandde was raising. But by this time, Medraut must have heard of Sandde's rebellion. He would certainly wish to crush it before Arthur could join it. Indeed, I could not see why he was waiting near the border, and expected him at any minute.

Sandde, who had many surprisingly sensible ideas, if little experience, had sent messengers to Arthur as soon as he learned that Arthur was actually in Britain, but he had, as yet, received no reply. It was crucial that Arthur and Sandde should arrange some method of joining their forces, and Sandde was worried whether he should leave Ynys Witrin before Medraut arrived to besiege it. If he did so, however, it would be more difficult for Arthur to contact him, so he contented himself with my suggestion that he designate places for men who wished to join the army to meet, so that if Ynys Witrin were cut off by a siege, Arthur would not be entirely cut off from support. The problem of arranging for a possible siege was in fact more urgent than the problem of food supply for the army. That was quite easy to sort out, at least for the time being. I appointed Sion ap Rhys and some others as supervisors of food distribution, so that those clansmen who had brought supplies for themselves provided equably for those who had not. Appointing men like Sion was one of the better things I did, as the farmers were willing to accept measures from another farmer which they would have rejected from a noble. We had supplies to last for a while at least, and began to send messages to the meeting places which had replaced the markets, requesting more food – but we would not have enough to endure a siege.

As that first day passed, I continually expected to hear that Medraut's army was approaching. But no news arrived, and Sandde's scouts reported only that the countryside was quiet. Another five hundred men arrived to join the army, some coming from as far away as Elmet and Powys across Mor Hafren, and the number of our army was raised above a thousand. All the space within the fortress was filled, and most of those who had arrived the day before were already sleeping on the ground, under carts or shelters of firewood, straw and thatching. I had working parties sent down to the town to repair the old municipal defences as best they could, and billeted men on the town and in the monastery. And I had others cut reeds from the marshes, and others use them in constructing slightly better shelters for the army. And still there was no sign of Medraut.

The following day we heard wild rumours of Arthur: he had gone with Cerdic back to the Saxon royal fortress; he had ridden north of Medraut's army by night, and was hurrying towards Maelgwn's kingdom of Cwynedd; he had passed Medraut's army on the south, and was trying to make his way to Ynys Witrin or to Camlann. The only certain thing seemed to be that he was no longer by the Dumnonian border.

'Should we send men north?' Sandde asked me anxiously.

'He will have to pass through Caer Ceri if he is taking the road to Gwynedd,' I said. 'It is only a town, not a fortress, and there should be no warriors there. It would not take many men to hold it for a few days. Perhaps you should send a force there.'

Sandde agreed to this, and we discussed whether to send another force to Baddon. This city, however, was fortified and guarded, and we decided that we could not spare the men to take it, for if Arthur did come to Ynys Witrin we would need every man we had. This decided, I went down to the town to see if any of the monks were willing to work in the hospital I was establishing in the fortress. The monastery was, of course, a far more obvious place for a hospital, but I had little faith in the town's defences, and would not like to see our wounded come into Medraut's hands if the town fell in a siege.

Another five hundred or so men arrived that day. And still there was no sign of Medraut.

I went to rest late that night. I was very tired: more tired than I ought to be, I thought, as I combed out my hair. But I would be thirty-eight on my next birthday, in a few weeks. I was growing too old to run about like a girl. I remembered the girls I had played with when young, trying to imagine what they might be now. Married to landholders and farmers in the North, keeping a small house in order or a minor holding in peace. They had never walked the sword-edge of power. They would have children – I thought of one or two I knew who had died in childbirth. Perhaps their sons would fight, were fighting, in this war. But how would they have lived over the years? Arguing with a few servants, singing over the loom, spinning, cooking, gossiping with the neighbours – and now the war was howling like a black storm beyond their doors. They would be women grown wide-hipped and long-breasted from childbearing, and their faces would be worn and tightened by the land and its concerns, by time and by peace. I paused, then went over and picked up the mirror which lay on a table in the corner. The room was dim, lit only by one lamp. Eivlin and the two other girls whom the crowding of the fortress had pressed into the house were sleeping in the adjoining room; I could hear their quiet, even breathing. I lifted the mirror to catch the lamplight, and the soft flame hung in the polished silver, casting light back onto my face, making my eyes look very dark. My face was worn, but not by the land and certainly not by peace. My sick weariness seemed stamped upon the bone, and in that light I thought I might already be old.

I set the mirror down. God or Fate had chosen me from among those others to step from beside the loom to the heart of the storm. I had been caught in the lightning flash and the black wind. Once, I remembered, I had spoken to Bedwyr about our Empire being a thornbrake against the wind. And I had been the weak point in the barrier, the place where it had given: now all peace was broken, and the storm had come screaming in.

It was no time to think of such things. If I survived there would be time for repentance, but now . . . now there was much to do. I lay down, listening, before I fell asleep, to the girls' breathing and the wind outside in the eaves.

I was woken from a deep sleep by someone shaking my shoulder and saying softly, 'My lady! My lady!'

I struggled awake and sat up, and Eivlin dropped her hand. 'My lady,' she whispered, 'they say there is news – a messenger. They say to come quickly.'

I shook my hair out of my eyes, jumped up and pulled on my gown without putting on the under-tunic, then slipped on some shoes. 'Come quickly where?' I asked Eivlin.

She handed me my cloak. 'The hospital, my lady. They say that the messenger is dying.'

I had established the hospital in Sandde's guest house, which was large and well heated. At this time it was, of course, partly occupied, but it could be cleared, and it adjoined a storeroom which could be heated if more space became necessary.

'I will go, and stay as long as needs be. No, don't come: go back to sleep. The man who told you this is outside?'

He was, huddled against the door so that he had to stumble back hurriedly when I opened it. There was a fierce wind that left the stars blown brilliant and cold at mid-heaven, though the west was filled with a haze that promised snow. I judged that it was about four hours till dawn, and shivered. We hurried to the guest house, nearly running to keep warm.

Sandde was sitting in the dimly lit room on which the door of the house opened, while a few members of the army lay on pallets by the wall, trying to sleep. The lord of Ynys Witrin looked very glum, but leapt up in his usual fashion when I came in, waved at the door to one of the other rooms, stammered a greeting, then hurried to the indicated door and opened it. I stepped through into a glare of torches and saw Gwalchmai, lying very still on the one bed, his head wrapped in a bandage stained crimson with blood. A surgeon was bent over him.

I stopped, staring, filled with horror. 'What . . .' I began, then saw Rhys kneeling beside the surgeon; he had turned and was looking at me. 'Rhys. What has happened?'

He stood rapidly, looked down at Gwalchmai a moment very grimly. The surgeon nodded to him and he came over, urged me back through the door and into the other room, then closed the door behind him.

'My lady,' said Rhys, then caught my hand and held it very hard. He was pale, and his face and hand were damp with sweat. 'They said that you were here, and they would send for you. I could scarcely believe it. The surgeon here says that my lord is dying. Is he likely to know?'

'He . . . he is a monk from Ynys Witrin. They say he is very skilled. But what has happened? How . . . Arthur sent Gwalchmai here as a messenger?'

Rhys let go of my hand, rubbed his palms over his face and through his hair, stood with his face hidden a moment, then dropped his hands and nodded wearily. 'There was nothing else to be done with him. He would not rest, and he wished to ride into battle as soon as he was well enough recovered to ride at all. It was better while we were journeying back to Britain – he had to keep quiet on the ship. But since we arrived – my lady, the surgeons said that he must not become excited. So the Emperor sent him here with a message, to keep him out of the fighting. But today – yesterday – well, the country northwards is full of armed men, fighting for any lord you care to name, or simply for themselves. We met some who tried to kill us for our horses. Gwalchmai killed some of them, and the rest were frightened enough to let us ride off. But half a mile along the road he fell off his horse and went into a faint, just as he is now, and his head began bleeding. I couldn't wake him, and couldn't stop the bleeding. I tried to cauterize it; that helped a little, and your surgeon here has just done it again. Sometimes on the road he woke up enough to talk, but mostly to people who weren't there. So I brought him on here. But they have told me he will die, and probably in a few hours; that he is dead already from the waist down.'

After a pause Sandde asked, 'What is the message?'

Rhys stared at him. Sandde stared back, chewing his moustache and fidgeting with his baldric. After a moment, Rhys shook his head. 'You never knew him – and it is what we came for, after all.' He fumbled at his belt, drew out a letter. 'Here. I took it from him after he fell.'

Sandde took the letter eagerly, looked at the seal, then handed it to me so that I could read it to him. I stared at it numbly. It was sealed with tallow and lamp black, but Arthur's dragon seal was firmly imprinted on it.

'Please, my lady,' said Sandde. 'We must know what to do.'

I broke the seal, moved closer to the lamp to read. '"To Sandde, Lord of Ynys Witrin, from Arthur Augustus, Emperor of Britain: greetings,"' I read out, then stared at the bold familiar hand and lowered it. 'Sandde, Lord Gwalchmai ap Lot is my friend. Do you know why he is dying? Is there any hope?'

Sandde made an awkward gesture. 'They simply told me he was dying.'

'It is a splinter of bone,' Rhys replied. 'It broke when he was first wounded, but did not come loose; it might have grown together again – so your surgeon says. But now it is cutting the brain apart. The surgeon says it is too deep for him to get out. There is another wound, too, from the fight on the road, but your surgeon says that one does not matter. A few hours, he says. He did not wish even to try to help.' Rhys drew a deep breath and rubbed his face again.

'I see,' I said, then, not knowing what to do, lifted the letter again. '" – from Arthur Augustus, greetings. My friend, I do not know how to thank you. I beg you not to move from Ynys Witrin, but wait there and gather as large a force as you can. Send any messages to the places my emissary will inform you of. He is a man of great skill and experience, and you can trust his words as you would my own. He will inform you of my plans. If you can, send supplies, especially grain, to the places he will tell you of, for we may have to abandon our own supplies to gain speed. When next you hear from me, take all your forces to the place I will tell you of, and there conceal them, for I hope to set a trap for Medraut and Maelgwn. More I cannot trust to ink. God give you aid!"' I hesitated, noticed some additional words smudged across the end of the scroll. '"If . . ."' I began, then stopped.

'What?' demanded Sandde.

'If you have any news of me he wishes to know it. And he says to treat me honourably if I should come here. He says that you can trust me with authority, especially for finding supplies.'

Sandde smiled. 'Unneeded advice. You can write to him yourself, now. But what shall we do? He has trusted too little to ink and too much to his messenger's health.' He fixed his eyes on Rhys again, started, and demanded, 'Do you know what your lord was to have told me?'

Rhys shrugged, ran his hand through his hair again. 'Some of it.' He glanced round, then lowered his voice, 'When we left the Emperor the Family was already riding towards Gwynedd at a good pace. Our lord Arthur judges that Maelgwn will not consider fighting you worth the risk of having his own kingdom plundered, and will set out in hot pursuit. Medraut dare not risk fighting you with only his own followers – most of those who have joined him since the start of the rebellion are sure to stay with Maelgwn, for they wish to fight Arthur, and trust that the kingdom's ruined if they can kill him. But while they are following, the Emperor will send his men away in various groups, with spare horses and most of the supplies, and these will wait at assembly points southwards. Some time before he reaches the Saefern river, he will abandon the rest of his supplies, circle round his pursuers, and come south as fast as he can. He will pick up the rest of his men, and fresh horses, at the assembly points – and he may want supplies then, for, though we had goods from Cerdic, we could not transport enough to last long. Then, I think, he hopes that Maelgwn and Medraut will be following close behind him, and if he has your troops placed in an ambush, he doubtless hopes to lead the rebels directly into it.'

'Ach!' exclaimed Sandde. 'That is an excellent plan, and worthy of the Emperor. But these assembly points, where are they? I must find a place for an ambush, and tell the Emperor where I think would be best. Where shall I send the message?'

'I do not know,' Rhys said. 'Gwalchmai knows – that, and the watchwords, and the timing.'

Sandde exclaimed loudly and wordlessly, fell silent. 'Then what shall we do?' he demanded, after a minute. 'Is your lord likely to wake again?'

Rhys smiled bitterly. 'How should I know? Your surgeon couldn't tell me. He said only that my lord would die in a few hours.'

'Here,' I said. 'Find me some wax tablets and I will wait here and write the information down if Gwalchmai wakes.' I walked over to the door of the other room, and stepped again into the torchlight. After a moment Rhys followed me, then Sandde.

The surgeon was sitting on a sleeping pallet in the corner, taking his shoes off. He looked up at us with an expression of irritation, but stood, and bowed to Sandde.

Sandde walked over to the bed and looked at Gwalchmai, then at the surgeon. 'Is there nothing you can do?' he asked. 'Will he wake, before the end?'

The surgeon shrugged. 'Possibly. It depends how soon that is. Soon indeed, if there is noise and he is disturbed.'

'I will stay here, but be quiet,' I said, looking about for and finding a stool. I moved it to the bedside and sat down.

'As you please, noble lady,' said the surgeon. 'If your benignity does not object, I wish to sleep.' There was a tone of bitter irony in his voice. He must have long shared his monastery's hostility to Arthur, and doubtless found this alliance displeasing.

'Sleep while you can,' I told him. He bowed again, extinguished one of the torches, then lay down on his pallet, covered himself with his blanket, and turned his back on us.

'I will have someone bring you the writing materials,' Sandde whispered to me. 'I thank you, my lady. And I pray God he wakes!' He left, taking another of the torches to light his way back to the Hall.

Rhys sat down on the floor at the foot of the bed, leaned back against the bedpost, then covered his face with his hands.

'I am sorry,' I said, not knowing quite what I meant by it. 'Rhys, you have had a long journey, and must be very tired. Rest, and I will wake you if anything happens.'

Rhys shook his head. 'Thank you, my lady. But I will wait.'

We waited in a silence so deep that we could hear each flicker of the single remaining torch, hear the soft brush of ash falling to the floor, the breathing of each person in the room, and the loud wind outside the house. A servant arrived with the wax tablets, a stylus, and parchment, ink and pens, then left again.

I rested my head on my hands, looking at Gwalchmai. I had noticed first how gaunt his face had grown, eaten away by grief and sickness. But now in the torchlight he looked fearfully young, almost as he had looked when first I saw him, when he lay wounded in my father's house. He had always had a look of being haunted by something greater than the world; now he looked as though he were melting into it, balanced between Earth and the Otherworld. The red torchlight on his sweat-damp skin made it look hot, like metal in a fire, as though the bones beneath were melting into another shape. I touched his forehead lightly, but it was not hot. My hand brushed the bandage and it fell aside, for it had only been drawn across his head, and not fastened. I drew it back hurriedly: his head had been dented by Bedwyr's sword, bone very white in a ruin of red and black cauterized flesh, now crushed and broken by the fall and the surgery even to the shapeless grey of the brain.

I twisted my hands together to make myself keep still, thinking of him in the past, riding his stallion about the practice field at Camlann, dropping in a falcon's swoop upon the ring left on the ground. Then I thought of Gwyn trying the same move; of the way I had seen the boy most recently, crawling on his knees in the road to Caer Ceri, dragging in puzzlement at Bedwyr's spear. And I thought of Bedwyr standing in Macsen's stables, saying farewell to me – his calm face and the total, bleak despair in his eyes. Of such had been our Empire, so much it had meant, and now it was all come to this. I wanted to weep, but there were no tears in me, only a great blank horror of all that was. And around was only silence and, outside, the wind.

About the hour of dawn I glanced up from some momentary abstraction to find that Gwalchmai's eyes were open and he was watching me.

'Gwalchmai,' I said, my breath catching. I put my hand out to touch his, then remembered his last words to me and drew back. Doubtless I was the last person he wished to see – but perhaps not, and there was the message. 'Can you understand me?'

His lips formed the word 'yes', soundlessly. Rhys stood and hurried over. Gwalchmai's eyes focused on him, and he smiled very slightly. 'Rhys,' he said, in the faintest whisper. 'Is it real, then?'

'My lord? Eh, my lord, we are at Ynys Witrin. This is real.'

'And she . . . was she here, before? I talked to her before.'

'Ah, the Empress! Yes, she is really here, now. You were dreaming on the road, my lord, but she is here now.'

He closed his eyes, then opened them again and looked at me. 'My lady,' he said, still in that almost inaudible whisper. 'But, of course you are here. Of course. Medraut did not . . .'

'He did not harm me.'

'Good.' The eyes fixed on Rhys again. 'This time I am dying, cousin.'

The servant said nothing for a moment, then glanced down and muttered, 'They say so.'

Again the slight smile. 'It is true. Have they cut my legs off? No? I cannot feel anything. I had not thought . . . to die this way. Rhys, where is my horse?'

'In Sandde's stables. I told them they were to look after him well or they would need looking after themselves.'

'Good.' The smile, slow and painful. 'Thank you. You must let him go. No one must ride him after I am dead. Let him see . . . that I am dead. Then let him go.'

'Very well, my lord.'

'And my sword . . . fasten that to his saddle. Let them go together. I will give them back.'

Rhys swallowed a few times, nodded.

Gwalchmai looked back at me. 'I . . . am . . . glad you are here, my lady. I should . . . no, I must say that later. Arthur gave me a message for Sandde. It is important.'

I nodded and picked up the writing tablet, and Gwalchmai smiled again.

He had just begun telling of the movements Arthur planned when the surgeon woke and came over. He took the warrior's pulse and shook his head. Gwalchmai politely asked him to leave. 'Though you are a surgeon, I must speak of my lord's secrets, which you should not hear.'

'Very well,' said the surgeon. 'There is at any rate nothing more surgery can do for you. Yet I am also a monk, a man of God. You would do well to make a confession of your sins, and receive the sacrament.'

'Later, if there is time,' said Gwalchmai.

The monk gave us all a look of venomous displeasure.

'You would do better to go before God with a mind hallowed and absolved of sin, not one bound up in worldly concerns and the secret policies of kings.'

'I would not go to my lord God leaving obligations unfulfilled behind me, and that through selfishness,' returned Gwalchmai. 'I beg you, go. If there is time, when I am free of what I am yet bound to, you will be called.'

The monk snorted and stalked out, and Gwalchmai resumed Arthur's message, laboriously, but with careful steadiness.

Presently he stopped for the fourth or fifth time, and closed his eyes. He scarcely seemed to be breathing, and I thought *It is now*, and felt my heart in my throat. But he opened his eyes again and looked at me.

'That is all,' he said. 'The last act I will do in Arthur's service. You must . . . you must give him my greetings, and my thanks, and say . . . say that I regret nothing in my choice of a lord, except that I did not serve him better. So. My lady, I . . . I wish now to send a letter. Will you write it?'

'Of course. Speak. I have parchment.'

He watched while I sharpened the pen and dipped it in the ink, resting the parchment across my knees. Then he closed his eyes.

'Gwalchmai to Bedwyr son of Brendan, greetings,' he said, in a voice louder than any he had used yet. The tip of the pen I was using went through the parchment and broke. Gwalchmai opened his eyes at the sound, and I pulled the pen out and stared at him.

'To Bedwyr?' I asked in despair.

'You agreed. You must write it; I cannot. My lady, there is not much time. This is the greatest debt yet binding me, and I have not much time left to pay it.'

I resharpened the pen hurriedly. 'Speak then. I will write. Only . . . remember, I have loved him, and he has been your friend as well.'

'I have remembered it.' Gwalchmai closed his eyes again. 'I wished to . . . and now I do not know what to say. I dreamed I was speaking with Bedwyr. It must have been after I fell. "Greetings. My cousin, I am dying. I wished to write, because . . . because now . . ." – no, don't say "now", say, "Because I so desired your death. And now

290

bitterness seems pointless. I wished for justice with a longing greater than was just, and so ... so I brought ruin upon our lord, and all we fought for, greater ruin than any you caused. You said ..." but no, he cannot have said it. That was in the dream. "If the justice I desired were in the world, there would be none left living. How can a man be justly punished for a crime he did not intend? You were right when you said that mercy alone is just. I ... I forgive you my son's death. Forgive me my vengeance. I ..."' He stopped abruptly, looked puzzledly over my shoulder for a moment, then, suddenly, his dark eyes flooded with brilliant life and he smiled. 'You?' he asked.

I looked over my shoulder. There was no one there. I turned back, frightened, and caught his arm. Rhys had said that Gwalchmai had raved on the road, and had talked with people who were not there; it seemed now as though he might again. 'Gwalchmai, what is it?' I asked.

He looked back at me, puzzled. 'Can't you see? Och ai, then it is the end. But there is no more to the letter, only that I pray God's mercy for us all. Rhys ...' The servant caught his hand, 'Rhys, *mo chara*, farewell. My lady, farewell – and if you can, tell my brother I loved him. I am coming.' He looked again into the empty air, smiling like a child. Beneath my hand I felt the muscles of his arm tense, realized that he was trying to sit up, and seized him and leaned against him. I felt his heart beat against me, once, twice, pause ...

Stillness. I sat up, looking at him desperately for a sign that he lived yet. But the look he had had all his life, the haunted brilliance, had vanished, and the face was almost unknown, my friend's face and a stranger's.

Rhys crossed himself. He was weeping silently. 'Lord God have mercy,' he said, in British, then crossed himself again and added the accustomed form in the Latin of the Church, 'Grant him eternal rest.'

'And let light perpetual shine upon him,' I replied mechanically. But I thought all light in all the world was dead or dying, and my own heart plunged in the darkness.

We pulled the blanket over Gwalchmai's face, and I went over to the last, guttering torch and extinguished it. The day had broken, and the room was already streaked with new sunlight. When I opened the door into the adjoining room I saw that the morning fire had been lit, and a number of people were sitting about it, breakfasting on bread, cheese and warmed ale.

'He is dead,' I told them all.

The monk nodded, took a last bite of bread, and dusted off his fingers. He was beginning to speak when another figure leapt up from beside the fire and shouted, '*Rhys!*'

'Eivlin!' Rhys shouted from behind me, and pushed past roughly. He and his wife locked together like a latch fitting into its place, each holding the other fiercely and painfully. Only when I saw them so did I realize how much each must have feared for the other – and realize how much I myself now longed for Arthur.

'Och, Rhys,' Eivlin said, as I moved from the door, 'Rhys, it is your lord, it is the lord Gwalchmai, that is dead?'

Rhys nodded, tried to speak, and choked on the words.

'Yes,' I answered for him. 'You came here looking only for me, then, Eivlin? Well, see to your husband. Will one of you,' I looked at the men by the fire, the monk and those who had slept in the room over the night, 'tell Lord Sandde of this, and ask him to make arrangements for the burial. Tell him also that I have the message and that I will join him presently.' One of the men nodded, and went with me from the room, outside into the morning.

There was fresh snow upon the ground, and the sky was patched with clouds. While my messenger trudged up the hill I leaned against the outer wall of the house and swallowed the cold air in great gulps, crushing the letter and tablets against me. The pain about my heart seemed almost stifling. But I could not weep, and presently I started back up the hill to my own house, to wash and change before seeing Sandde. There was still much to be done that day.

I wrote letters all that morning to everyone I could think of who might be willing to provide additional supplies on credit – a desperately short list of names, but one very difficult to compile. In the afternoon, when I wrote to Arthur, the bulk of my letter was concerned only with the question of supplies. Only when I was done with it did I realize with a shock that I had not said that Gwalchmai was dead. After only a few hours, with the body yet waiting for burial, it seemed already a thing fixed. *You are tired*, I told myself, to still the wave of sickness that came over me then, and I dipped the pen in the ink and wrote out a full account. At the end, I ran out of space on the sheet of vellum, and had to end abruptly. Almost I added nothing more, but then, turning the page over I saw the amount of space I had left above the superscription, and I added, in my smallest lettering, 'I escaped before Medraut could harm me. I want only to see you again. My soul, my dearest life, tell me to come and join you with Sandde and the army. But in all events, God defend you.' There was no more space, and the cramped letters seemed meaningless, set against the thought of his presence, so I added no more, but folded the letter over, sealed it, and gave it to a messenger. I sat for a moment staring at Sandde's desk, wondering when Arthur would get the letter, of what he would be doing, and when we would see one another again. I wished then, and wished again many times afterwards, that I had demanded another page of parchment and crammed the margins with words. But perhaps I did say what was most important – and perhaps I could not have said more if I had meant to.

We buried Gwalchmai that evening in the grounds of the monastery of Ynys Witrin. While the procession of mourners moved to the grave, Rhys held Gwalchmai's horse, with the jewelled hilt of the sword gleaming beside the empty saddle. The stallion nickered earnestly when the body was brought out, recognizing it, but became increasingly uneasy as the monks prayed and chanted, and when the body was lowered into the ground, neighed loudly and fought to pull away from Rhys. When the burial was finished, Rhys slipped the bridle from the stallion's head, and the horse cantered over to the grave and stamped about over it, looking about and sniffing the air and the ground, and then threw its head back and neighed. The monks crossed themselves and whispered.

'Let him be,' Rhys said and, turning on his heel, started back up the hill. I followed, and the other mourners and the monks dispersed. But when I glanced back, I saw the stallion, very white and splendid in the dusk by the damp grave, tossing its head and neighing again, and again. But in the morning the horse was gone. I feared for a time that someone might have stolen it, it and the sword that was supposed to burn any hand that drew it against its owner's will. But such a horse, let alone such a sword, was too fine to be mistaken for another, or pass unremarked, and they were never heard of again, even in rumour. Gwalchmai had always claimed that the sword, and the horse, had come from the Otherworld. Perhaps the stallion did turn from that dark grave and run off through the night into a day that was now entirely separate from the Earth, to a place where no human grief could reach it, where no further love could hold it back. However that may be, it went, leaving only a few hoof marks around the new grave. And I did not have much time to worry about it.

Twelve

Gwalchmai had told us that Arthur planned to reach the Saefern three days after leaving Searisbyrig – two days after he himself came to Ynys Witrin. Arthur would turn and ride for Camlann very rapidly for the main part of a night, then proceed more slowly through the various assembly points, collecting his men, and arrive near Ynys Witrin about noon on the second day from the Saefern, four days after we received his message. It was on the evening of the day before this that we had our second letter from him. It was very brief, and obviously written in haste. It acknowledged the receipt of my letter, and said that some of the supplies had indeed reached him. It agreed to the place Sandde had recommended for the ambush, and told Sandde to leave Ynys Witrin before dawn the following day, and conceal his forces at that ambush, as Arthur hoped to arrive there about an hour before noon.

'Medraut and Maelgwn are no more than five miles behind me,' he wrote. 'I hope to keep them at that distance tomorrow. May you prosper!' then, written small, 'Gwynhwyfar, my heart, do not go with the army. We will have no camp, and I could not risk you if we should lose the battle. But if all goes well, I will see you tomorrow in the evening. If it goes ill, remember always that I loved you.'

I read all but the last lines to Sandde, then remained seated, staring at the lines I had not read aloud. I thought that the lamp was flickering, but when I looked up I saw that it was only the trembling of my hand.

'Tomorrow,' breathed Sandde. He took the letter from me and stared at it, as though he could wrestle out the meaning by looking at it hard enough. 'Tomorrow, before dawn! And by tomorrow evening, it will all be over.' He jumped up and strode across the room, stood on one foot looking at the fire, twisting his fingers in his baldric. 'How . . . how many men do we have now?' he asked.

'An army of two thousand, one hundred and seventeen,' I told him. I did not need to check the figures: they ran constantly through my mind. 'And ninety-eight warriors, including those we sent with the messages.'

'And Medraut and Maelgwn have how many?'

'Their army probably amounts to three thousand men. Their warbands, combined, and including those who have joined them since the beginning of the rebellion, probably amount to about a thousand trained warriors.'

'And the Emperor has a thousand.'

'Something less than that now. There were men lost in Gaul.'

'But won't some Saxons have joined him?' Sandde turned and studied my face anxiously. I shook my head – the Saxons would not trust the British in a British kingdom.

'We are outnumbered, then,' said Sandde, earnestly, forcing cheerfulness. 'Still, the numbers of trained warriors are evenly balanced, aren't they? And the Emperor, I have heard, is so accustomed to fighting against worse odds than this that this must seem nearly equal to him.'

'Arthur has fought against the Saxons at far worse odds, that is true,' I said, meeting his eyes. 'But Saxons usually rely more heavily on half-trained peasants, and almost never have any cavalry. Part of Medraut's army were members of the Family, and most of the other warriors will have profited by Arthur's example, and have training that nearly equals that of his men. This will not be the same as fighting the Saxons. The enemy's numbers will count.'

'Oh.' Sandde bit his lip, then came over and sat on the desk, still looking at me earnestly, his eyes very blue in the lamplight. 'I have never been in a battle,' he told me. 'I didn't know what I was doing when I raised this rebellion against Medraut. It was simply that . . . that Medraut had a friend of mine put to death for treason, and that I admired Arthur, and no one else was doing anything. But now everyone expects me to tell them what to do, and I do not *know* what to do. Most noble lady . . .' He clutched my hand suddenly. 'I know it is cowardly to speak this way, but you are like my mother, who understood. Please excuse it.'

I took his other hand. He was too young for it, I thought, far too young. I was indeed old enough to be his mother. 'Don't be afraid,' I told him, as quietly as I dared. 'You have not failed your men once, and you will not fail them tomorrow. Our numbers are nearly even with the enemy, our cause is more just, and, moreover, we will have the advantage of surprise. Trust to God for the victory.'

He kissed my hands and pressed his forehead against them. 'Lady Empress,' he whispered, then broke away, stood suddenly, fingering his sword. He straightened his shoulders and tried to smile. 'It will go well!' he announced.

'It will, as God is just,' I returned. 'And for you, at least, I need not fear, Lord Sandde. Indeed, I think that all in the battle will mistake you for an angel assisting the souls of the dead, and not a spear will be cast at you.' He tried to smile at this, feeble as the joke was. 'Here,' I went on, 'who shall we wake first tomorrow?'

I wondered, watching him as he settled to work at the business of moving the army, whether he would be living when the sun next set, and, if he lived, whether he would be able to stand so straight: whether he would come back blind, missing an arm, a leg, screaming on a stretcher. There would be plenty that would do so, and they would be brought to Ynys Witrin, for it was the nearest town to the battle where we had some control. I thought of my husband, wondering if he would come to me, and how.

Most of the army rose three hours after midnight, and marched out before dawn. Sandde went first, followed by the noble warriors who had joined him – a group which Medraut's oppression had made small – then by the common army, roughly grouped in clans. Eivlin had already said farewell to her husband and his kin, and now stood beside me at the gate, huddled silently in her cloak. When the last pair of feet had tramped past the walls we remained staring after the force a while, watching as they wound down the pale road into the town at the hill's foot, vanishing in the shadows of the dark marshes. Already the stars were pale, and the night air heavy with dew. When a cock crowed in the fortress I turned back and looked at the crowd of women, old men, children, scattered monks and servants, who all waited expectantly for my orders. I wondered briefly why the authority had fallen so plainly to me, and not to Sandde's clerk Cuall, who was waiting with the others. But I knew the reason. Cuall himself was bewildered with events, and no one else was willing and able to exercise the authority. In this crisis, no one cared what I had done, how much I might be to blame for what had happened. All that mattered was that I was the Emperor's wife, and used to riding the storm.

'Nothing will happen until noon,' I told them. 'Go back and rest while you can. When it is time to send out parties to help with the wounded, I will have you called – but you will have to hurry then, and hopefully most of you won't be needed.' And I smiled, trying to look as though I feared only that the victory would be too swift for us to get the carts out in time. It won a few smiles, a ragged cheer; an old man took my hand to his forehead as I walked back through the crowd, and exclaimed that I'd soon be Empress in Camlann again. I laughed, and said that he would soon be back on his farm. When I was back in my own house, and alone again, it was, of course, another matter. I sat on the bed waiting and waiting for the morning, twisting my hands together, rubbing the finger where once I wore the ring carved with the imperial dragon.

That morning seemed to have sprung free from the wheel of time, and hung off apart by itself, unmoving, unending. I had every vessel and water trough in the fortress filled with water, took inventory of our food supplies again and again, arranged again with the surgeons which of them would go to the battlefield and which stay in Ynys Witrin to treat those who were brought back; I went over the places we had cleared for the wounded, I found wood for the fires, and still the sun waited eastward of the zenith. The site of the ambush, I knew, was just by the turning of the main road onto the west road that led to Camlann. Arthur hoped that Medraut would think he was making for the fortress itself, and perhaps expect Sandde to meet him there. He could not help but know that Arthur meant to meet Sandde, and, since he had left Camlann under only a light guard, it might be expected that the Emperor would try to take the fortress itself, and meet his ally there. But still, Medraut might expect and be prepared for an ambush. But even if he did, there was no way of imposing formations on Maelgwn's peasant army, and the precise place and time would be unknown to him. He would have to hurry to catch Arthur before he could reach Camlann, so Arthur's plan should have some effect.

At noon I sent the carts out, with the surgeons and servants who could provide emergency treatment on the battlefield, and with some water, food and fuel. Winter is a bad time for a war. The casualties are higher, for the wounded die quickly unless they can be brought to shelter and kept warm. It would be very difficult for us to care for them properly, ten miles from the site of the battle, short of horses for the carts, and, assuming that Medraut's forces took the main road, with an enemy army between us and the battle. But we hoped that Arthur had brought some extra carts with supplies from the assembly points, and that some of those who were injured could be dragged free and sent off to us.

In the mid-afternoon a cart did arrive, not one of those we had sent out, but one of Arthur's. It was driven by a peasant with a crippling leg wound and filled with men mostly from Sandde's army, one of them dead, the rest needing attention. I saw to it that the cart was unloaded, and questioned the driver.

'Indeed, we reached the place in good time, noble lady,' he told me. He seemed to be in no pain, though his eyes were dark with shock. 'We had time to build the fires and warm ourselves, have a bite to eat and a rest, before the Emperor came and told us to put the fires out. The enemy came up before noon, soon after the Emperor. We ran at them.'

'Did they march into the ambush?' I asked. 'Did Arthur stay with you, or go up the road? Where were the cavalry?'

'I . . . I don't know. We ran at them, and when we reached them it was all shoving and shouting. They were Maelgwn's men, farmers like me, not warriors. One of them stabbed me, and I fell down, and my cousin Gwilym jumped over me and went on at them.'

'Where were the warriors, then?'

He waved his right hand vaguely. 'At the side. It was very confusing, noble lady, with the whole air shining with spears, and shouting on all sides, and men killing and screaming. I did not know what was happening. After I was hurt, I crawled away, in case the rest came and trampled me. When I got back to where the fires were, there were other hurt men there, and one or two cowards who had run away and sat crying, and someone told me to drive the cart here. I can drive the cart back, if you wish, my lady. I can't walk, but I can still drive.'

'You have done well,' I told him, despairing of learning more. 'Rest first; we have plenty who can see to the cart, and you must have your leg looked after.' And I doubted that he would be able to drive the cart after his leg was seen to, for he had bound it up so tightly and at such an angle that I suspected it would have to come off.

As he was being helped into the house we had prepared for the wounded, another cart drove up, this time one we had sent out earlier.

I had little time to question the men it carried, for they brought an urgent demand for fuel. It was beginning to snow, and the battle had still been raging when they left, and some of the men needed to rest and were freezing. I ran off to make arrangements to have the returning carts re-loaded with fuel, and when I returned to the sick houses, yet another cart had arrived. This one contained a trained warrior, a member of the Family, who lay quietly among the peasants, looking at them contemptuously if they moaned. When they moved him from the cart he flinched, clenching his teeth together, but made no noise. He was so covered in blood that it was hard to see where he had been hurt.

'Goronwy,' I said, and he looked up at me. His set face relaxed a little.

'They said you were here,' he told me. 'Good. I'll be well treated, then.'

'As well as we can manage. What is happening in the war? No, tell me when you are inside.'

Inside the house, we waited for a surgeon to finish with the others. Goronwy kissed my hand. 'Wise lady, who always knew that Medraut was treacherous,' he muttered. 'The lying dog, the weasel ... to think that I once trusted him.'

'He was good at lying,' I said. 'But what has happened? Did he enter the ambush?'

'No. We had no such good fortune. No, he stopped at the turning of the road, and began preparing his men in a hurry. He had his – Maelgwn's – army in the fore, to take the first onslaught, and all the trained men behind, and the cavalry behind them. He knew what he was doing. We ...

have you heard it? No? We'd sent our cavalry back north-wards, some distance, so that they were behind Medraut, and sent our infantry down the road towards Camlann, round the turn, so that they would not be seen until Medraut was into the ambush. Sandde's army was in the hills, just by the turning itself. When Lord Sandde saw that Medraut had realized we were there, he told his men to charge at once, and galloped down the hills straight into Medraut's army. A fine man, Sandde. I hope he lives through the day.'

'So do I. Did his charge carry, then?'

Goronwy began to shake his head, winced. 'No. They went deep into Maelgwn's army, with heavy losses on both sides, and then Medraut sent his infantry in, and Sandde's peasants were chased up the road, straight into the Family.' He smiled grimly. 'And that was the last I saw of them, for Medraut had ordered his cavalry about, suspecting that we were in the hills somewhere near, and we had to ride quickly to prevent their encircling our infantry. Oh, we met them, sure enough, and we were winning. It was a fierce fight; I'm sorry to be missing it.'

I clasped his hand briefly. 'What more is there? Is Arthur safe?'

'He was when . . . when that traitor Constans put his sword through me. A man that had been my friend, my brother . . . well, he is paid for it. The Emperor was with the cavalry. I tried to fight on, after Constans, but . . . I am going to die, my lady.'

'You don't know that. Ah, here is the surgeon.'

I stayed with Goronwy for a little while, as he was stripped and brought under the knife. But when he fainted I rushed off with a servant to see that another house was ready, for another cart had arrived, and there was no more room in the first house. From that time, for a long time, I had little opportunity to question or worry.

I was used to wounded men, but not in numbers like this. Partly this was simply because Arthur's battles had mostly in the past been fought in distant places: I had not seen such numbers brought directly from the slaughter before. But the battle of Camlann was the cruellest battle of the age, and the casualties were very high. When the two peasant armies met in that first onslaught, perhaps a thousand men were killed, and by the later afternoon the road must have been running with blood. The first carts brought only men who could crawl back to safety. By the later afternoon, the battle had moved up the road towards Camlann, and the carts could pick up the casualties of the first meeting, and carried as many new corpses as living men. The reports they also carried varied like the sea: Medraut, Maelgwn, Arthur or Sandde were dead; Maelgwn had fled; Maelgwn was taken prisoner; Medraut had killed Arthur in single combat; Arthur had killed Medraut – uncertain victory hovered over both. I had no time to be afraid for my husband or my friends. I was needed by the surgeons, by the dying, by the servants; needed to find fresh horses for the carts when there were no fresh horses; needed to say where the corpses should be piled, and whom the surgeons should treat first, and what use should be made of fuel, and who should rest. I was Empress, and I could not be a human woman.

Night came, and still there was no official report. The carts that arrived now had left the struggle in the last hour of daylight, and reported that still some fighting was going on, but that the forces had moved back down the road to the turning, and most of the peasants on both sides had fled or stopped fighting. I wished someone could be spared to bring me a message – for a horseman with a fresh horse it would only be an hour, perhaps less. But it seemed that all was complete confusion.

'Maelgwn is retreating,' I was told, again. 'The Emperor has won.' But how could anyone know?

'Where is the Emperor?' I asked at random, as one cart pulled up before the stables, where we were now bringing the wounded. It was a big cart, and full of indistinct forms.

'He is with the cavalry,' came one voice.

'He is dead,' a different one said.

'No, it was his horse; his horse was killed under him, but he got up again.'

'Was that a grey horse?'

'No, he was riding a bay.'

'That was the second horse, after the bay was killed.'

'He was alive . . . before that last cavalry charge,' came a strangely familiar voice from the back of the cart. I peered into it, trying to make out the face, and could not.

Then men unloading the cart dropped someone who

creamed horribly and began to sob. 'Be quiet!' shouted omeone else savagely. 'I can't bear it. Do you think you're ny worse off than the rest of us?'

'Can your horses make it back to the battlefield?' I asked he driver of the cart.

'No,' he said in a hoarse voice. He loomed over me, only is face visible as a pale shadow in the darkness, with the gleam of his eyes in the distant torchlight. 'The poor brutes ould hardly climb this last hill.'

'Wait here, then. Yours is a fine big cart. I will try to find resh beasts for you.' I summoned another servant over and old him to unharness the sweating team, and give the cart priority if any fresh horses, mules or oxen could be found. Then I went into the stable to check on the wounded. It seemed to me that inventories had become the substance of my life; always I was writing out lists of supplies, of suppliers, and now, of dying and dead. Perhaps I would one day keep inventories of the damned, forever writing out lists of names that my stupidity had helped to kill. But we would have to know who of our followers were yet living, nd be able to tell friends and kinsmen what had become of ur army.

Names: three peasants who could give them, two who ould not, one dead. Gwythyr ap Greidawl, one of the family. A northerner who had followed Arthur to Gaul. And the voice that had been familiar, but unexpectedly amiliar, not associated with these others?

I remembered it, placed it, just before I saw him lying in he far corner of the stable. No one else had recognized im, and he had been brought back in the cart with our own wounded – there had been others from the enemy's forces aken up so already, for friend and enemy lay together on he battlefield with nothing to distinguish between them. But I had never expected to see Medraut so.

I finished with my list and went over to him. He had been watching me from the time I entered, watching with old contemptuous eyes.

I stared down at him for a long time. He was lying flat on is back and did not move under my stare. Someone must ave stolen his purple cloak and golden jewellery, but there eemed to be little wrong with him.

'You need not concern yourself with how to finish me

off, noble lady,' he said at last. 'I will be dead within the hour. But it was not your precious husband and his men that did it; that honour they do not have.' He smiled savagely. 'When my loyal ally Maelgwn saw that my forces were defeated and my father's decimated, he took a dagger I had given him, a pretty thing steeped in poison, and put it in my back while I was trying to see where my men were. Thus, he has inherited my following, and become the strongest contender for the purple. I should have realized that I could never turn my back on him . . . yet at least I am spared having my father gloat over me.'

I went down on my knees beside him and looked at him. 'Are you pleased with what you have done?' I asked, hearing my voice very low and shaking.

He smiled, the grey eyes unfathomable with hatred. 'Yes. I am only sorry not to see it all fulfilled. My mother is revenged. And even if my father survives this ruin, your Empire is broken like glass. Maelgwn is going home to Gwynedd, but he will be back. The North is already tearing itself apart with war. Dumnonia is a wasteland. Whether it is my father or Maelgwn who ends up with a few purple rags, doesn't matter: the end result will be the same. Desolation. Think on it, noble lady. Tell my father to make songs about it at his victory feast, and tell my brother.'

'Your brother is dead,' I said sharply. 'He died here at Ynys Witrin four – no, five days ago.'

Medraut's eyes widened, and the stare changed from one of deep hatred to puzzlement. 'Gwalchmai? Dead?'

'From the wound he got from Bedwyr in Gaul, and from his own neglect of it. He never wanted to live after his son's death . . . I heard that you smiled when you told him of that.' Medraut continued to stare at me, and I wished to strike him as he lay there helpless, wished to give him pain. But I remembered what Gwalchmai had said and clenched my hands behind my back, forcing out the words like brittle ice, 'When Gwalchmai died, almost his last words were, "If you can, tell my brother I loved him."'

Medraut looked away. His right hand clenched into a fist, loosened, clenched and struck the ground violently. 'No,' he said, and gave a sob that seemed wrenched up from the heart. 'Not him, och, *mo brathair* . . .' I had never efore heard him cry out in his father's tongue, and I stared t him in amazement. He struck the ground again, shouted loud, in anger now, and heaved himself up so that he was itting. His back was soaked with blood. I jumped back as e tried to crawl onto his knees, but he fell over onto his ace and began to sob. A servant girl hurried over.

'Is he delirious?' she asked me in a whisper. 'Shall I help ie him down?'

'No,' I replied. I went back and knelt beside Medraut, in great confusion. For all that Gwalchmai had said about his rother, I had never expected that under his hatred and his nany masks Medraut might still love anyone. But there ould be no mistaking the look with which he had greeted ny news.

The pale eyes saw me again as I knelt, fixed on me, and he opened his mouth to speak, but only brought out blood. He ad injured himself in that attempt to rise. He shuddered iolently, coughed, went very still. After a moment I ouched the side of his neck, just under the jaw, and found hat the beat of blood had ceased. Arthur's son, his only hild, was dead. I took my hand away and looked up at the ervant.

'This was the enemy's leader, Medraut ap Lot,' I told ier. 'You can put the body outside by the south wall as oon as we need the space in here.' The girl's eyes widened nd she bobbed her head, staring at the corpse that lay there quiet and bloody, with the torchlight caught in its hair. I ressed my hands to my face a moment, brought them lown, saw that they were stained with blood. Medraut's, r someone else's? I couldn't tell. And I had another list of iames to make, and needed to find fresh horses.

About midnight, Cuall, Sandde's clerk, came and found ne. By that time we had been worrying for some while vhere to put the unscathed survivors of the battle, who had een returning in steadily growing numbers for some time, nd were badly in need of warm places to rest, warm food nd drink. We were also almost entirely without transport. f there were any more wounded on the battlefield they vould die of the cold before morning. Oh yes, by that time t was certain that Maelgwn Gwynedd had withdrawn with iis warband and the remnants of his army – all that had not cattered on their own account. And still I could get no clear report of Arthur.

'Noble lady,' said Cuall, as I tried to discover what a casualty's name had been, 'Lord Sandde has returned with the army. He begs you to come and speak with him.'

'Sandde?' I asked, straightening and brushing back my hair. 'What of my husband?'

But the clerk shook his head. 'I do not know.'

I closed my inventory book and followed Cuall up the hill from the stables. I was numb and blind with weariness of soul and body. Everything seemed a great distance away, and I little part of it.

We had filled all of Sandde's own rooms with the wounded, and the Lord of Ynys Witrin was sleeping in the Hall with his men. He was inside when I came up, and Cuall with an absurd sense of propriety stopped me from going into the Hall where the men were sleeping, and himself went in and fetched his master.

Sandde had taken off his mail coat and was wearing a torn and bloodstained cloak over his under-tunic. He had taken his boots off, and kept shifting his weight from one foot to the other because of the cold. He had that blank stunned expression that I had seen repeated endlessly mindlessly, on every face returning to the fortress; but he tried to smile, and took my hand. It was snowing, thick wet snow which melted in the thatch and dripped hissing into the torches he had brought out beside the Hall door.

'Lord Sandde,' I said. 'I am very glad you are unharmed.'

He patted my hand stupidly. 'It was as you said, my lady. Not a spear . . . oh God of Heaven, I am glad to see you, glad to be back!' He put his arms around me and clung, like a child, hurt, demanding comfort.

'Have you brought many men back?' I said after a few moments. 'How much more space do we need?'

He pulled away, nodded. 'I . . . I have been trying to make a list, with Cuall, of those we have. We have most of the Emperor's men . . . those that can still fight, that is. Maelgwn has withdrawn northwards. We don't know where Medraut is.'

'He is by the south wall of your stable, dead,' I said levelly. 'They brought him in with our own wounded.'

He stared at me in disbelief, then smiled, hesitantly. 'We have won, then?'

I closed my eyes, wanting to scream, to wail out grief and weep until I was blind and voiceless. 'If anyone has won, we have,' I said. 'But, noble lord . . .'

'Oh. Yes. The Emperor.'.

I opened my eyes again, fixing them on Sandde's face. It was terribly still after the heat and madness of the sick rooms. Sandde's left cheek was smeared with blood. The dripping of the water in the torches behind me was very loud. 'Is my husband dead?' I asked.

Sandde shook his head. 'I don't know.'

I turned away, and he reached out after me, touched my shoulder. 'My lady, he had three horses killed under him today, and yet he lived. I . . . I met him, near the end. The enemy were on the road eastwards, and in the hills. The Emperor was trying to gather and rally all the cavalry he had left. He was galloping up and down and shouting. He was so hoarse from shouting that no one could understand what he was saying. But we did rally, and made one last cavalry charge. After that Maelgwn began to retreat. We pursued them northwards for perhaps a mile, and then I called the men back, because it was dark, and snowing, and they were so tired that any bandit or pillager could finish them off, if the cold didn't, should they get lost. And then I realized that no one knew where the Emperor was. I had them all gather at one point, and sound horns to draw in the stragglers. We drew in a lot of men. But there was no more news of the Emperor. I . . . I took some men and went about, looking. Many men had seen him at the beginning of the charge, but none afterwards. We . . . perhaps he is wounded. Perhaps he took a party of his men after Maelgwn, and will come in later. We can search in the morning.'

'Yes,' I said, after a moment. 'Lord Sandde, do you have any horses that might be useful for drawing carts? There must be many on the battlefield who will die before the morning, and if my husband is there . . .'

'The horses are foundered,' Cuall told me. 'Not one in fifty could gallop to save its life. But what we have, we will send off.'

'Don't despair, noble lady,' said Sandde. 'He may well be unharmed.'

'He may be,' I agreed stupidly.

After a long silence, Cuall said, 'We do not have enough space for all the men, my lady. Which of the wounded can be moved?'

I bit my lip, trying to think, then realized from the expression of helplessness and confusion on Sandde's face that I must be weeping. I wiped my face, not caring if my hands smeared more blood onto it. 'I will show you who to move,' I said. 'Can you give orders about the horses?'

The labour, and the counting of names, went on all the night. When the sun rose pink and lovely over the snow-covered land next morning, the dead lay in tall stacks by the wall. By then some of the horses were rested enough to be harnessed again to the bloodstained carts and sent back down the road towards Camlann to pick up what remained.

Our scouts reported that Maelgwn had camped a few miles to the northward, and was burying some of his own dead, who were many. We sent him a messenger request-ing an official truce for the burial of the dead, and he at once agreed to this. We also sent a messenger to Camlann telling the men whom Medraut had left there to guard the fortress that we would permit them to follow Maelgwn home to Gwynedd if they would surrender Camlann without a struggle; they asked to be allowed to send to Maelgwn, which we permitted.

The carts began returning heavy laden with the dead, leading baffled war horses behind them like so many oxen. The horses, like the bodies of their masters, had already been mysteriously stripped of rich harness and ornament either by pillagers during the night or by the salvage parties themselves. Men and beasts seemed reduced to something unimportant, ordinary, broken and dishonoured. I had the corpses laid out in long lines by the wall for people to claim and always I looked for one particular body, but never saw it.

'Perhaps he took shelter at some holding for the night,' said Sandde. I nodded wearily and made inventories.

Names. Some of them were Medraut's followers, the traitors from the Family, men I had known, whose loyalty we had struggled to win: Iddawg and Constans and Cadarn and the rest. There were warriors from the North, who once had followed Urien of Rheged or Ergyriad of Ebrauc

308

and who now would never return to their masters and the other war. There were Constantius's men, who died leaving a kingdom kingless and in ruins. And there were members of the Family, many of them, too many, for they had borne the brunt of the battle. Cilydd and Cynddylig, Gwrhyr and Gwythyr ap Greidawl; Gereint ab Erbin, the skilled horseman with the patient smile. Goronwy, who had been called 'the Strong', had died from his wound in the night, unobserved. And Cei, stubborn, quarrelsone, loyal and courageous, was found lying at the far end of the field, where he had stood firm in resistance when Maelgwn's forces were about to break through. He was enormous in death, his features locked into a snarling mask, and his red hair was thickly caked with blood. Of that Family which six years before had numbered seven hundred of the finest warriors in the West, scarcely fifty were left alive.

There were many peasants dead as well, but their numbers were hard to determine. Many must have returned directly to their clan holdings after the battle, and many more left Ynys Witrin without waiting to be counted, as soon as they had collected their dead. Thus we were not certain who was dead and who was merely missing. Only one name among them, one still form, remained cut into my heart like the shape carved into a seal: Rhys ap Sion, found dead among the others at the road's turning, where he had fallen in the first onslaught, to be heaped anonymously with the other dead in the night following the battle, and only recognized the next morning by his wife. Dead, dead, dead: the whole of Ynys Witrin stank of death, and everything I touched, everything I saw, heard, felt, the air I breathed and the food I ate, seemed heavy with it.

In the afternoon Maelgwn Gwynedd sent us a messenger who bore an offer to extend the truce until the spring, and to return to his own kingdom for the time being. We agreed to this. The enemy garrison at Camlann also sent in a message, in which they agreed to our terms and promised to be gone from the fortress the following day, going north with Maelgwn.

'Good,' said Sandde, relieved. 'There is more space at Camlann. If we had this kind of crowding much longer we would have to fear the fever.'

And still there was no sign of Arthur.

The next day Maelgwn started north again, and Sandde sent men to all the cities of Dumnonia, proclaiming that we had a victory, peace was restored, and the markets were open again. I had wished in my heart to proclaim a reward to anyone with news of Arthur, or of his body, but I knew that it was unwise to tell the whole countryside that we also did not know if he were living or dead. There might be more risings, or Maelgwn might break his word and come back, and so much of our army was gone that we could risk no further struggle.

Sandde sent the men off to Camlann, where there was both space and supplies enough for them. On the first day he sent off all the uninjured men, then all the less severely wounded. I offered to stay at Ynys Witrin with the more severely injured until they could be moved without risk and, after some hesitation, Sandde agreed, and left me in charge of Ynys Witrin while he went to Camlann.

I waited. The peasant army did not trouble itself with moving to the imperial fortress, but went home in the days after the truce – those that had not gone before it. Sion ap Rhys and his kinsmen left five days after the battle. They would have gone sooner, but they had to send one of their number back to the holding to fetch the ox cart, for another of their number was wounded and could neither walk nor ride. They also wished to bury Rhys in the clan's lands. I guiltily gave them a few gifts, small return for their kindness to me, and perhaps shamefully like a payment for their kinsman's life, which was beyond price – yet the things might be useful. And I went down to the gates with them that morning to see them off.

Eivlin went with the others, leaving only one serving girl at my house. She had not said much to me or anyone else since her husband's death, but went about red-eyed, hard-faced, with the kind of callousness that springs from great grief.

'I am sorry,' I said to her, and to all of them.

Sion ap Rhys shrugged, staring at the long bundle in the back of the cart that had been his eldest son. 'We all knew we might die if we went to this war, my lady. We thought it worth the risk.' He picked up the ox goad. 'And Rhys believed in your Empire more than any of us, and set much of his life on it. Perhaps it is for the best that he does not see it now. We must all die some time.'

'It is not for the best!' Eivlin cried out sharply. 'Indeed, how can you say such things, a man to leave his three children fatherless, and they thinking him a finer man than the Emperor of Britain, and waiting yet for him to come home and bring them presents? Best? That such a man as my husband should . . . och, ochone!'

Sion set down the goad and covered his face a moment, then lowered his hands, ran one through his hair with a gesture that had been his son's also. 'The children still have their clan, daughter. And they have a mother. And she has them.'

'Indeed,' said Eivlin, more quietly, but looking at the bundle in the back of the cart. She looked up at me again, and saw something on my face I – I do not know what – that made her jump off the cart suddenly and put her arms around me. Something in my heart gave way and I embraced her, biting my tongue so as not to cry out. For a moment I forgot that I was Empress and ruler of the fortress, and we were only two women who had lost the men they loved. Then Eivlin drew away. 'I must look to my children, my lady,' she whispered, 'or I might stay, for you have not deceived me into thinking you do not feel it and need nothing, whatever the others may believe. God bless you, my lady.'

'And you, my cousin, and your children.'

Eivlin let go of me, nodded, bit her lip, climbed back into the cart and sat beside her father-in-law. Sion goaded the sullen oxen, and the cart lurched slowly out and down the hill, vanishing into the quiet farmland of Dumnonia. I never saw them again.

And still I waited.

About a week and a half later, Sandde sent me a messenger from Camlann, bringing more supplies and some trivial news. The news did not surprise me, but the messenger did, for he was Taliesin, who had been Arthur's chief bard and a sometime cavalry fighter, and of whom I had neither seen nor heard anything during the whole of this last war. When he arrived, and presented me with a list of the supplies he brought, I asked him up to my house and, when he was there, poured him some mead.

'I am glad to see you well,' I told him as he sipped the mead. 'I had assumed that you were dead.'

He made a face and shook his head. 'No. I was merely away from Camlann.'

He offered no further explanation; he never did. He was a mysterious man whom no one knew much about, and he rather enjoyed making himself yet more mysterious. Gwalchmai at least had been firmly convinced that Taliesin was from the Otherworld, and only stayed upon the Earth for some unknown purpose of his own. But many people had thought much the same about Gwalchmai himself.

'Oh?' I asked, impatient with mysteries. 'Where?'

Taliesin smiled, a quick acceptance of my impatience, amusement that became sad. 'Arthur sent me north to Urien King of Rheged when he left for Gaul, first as a messenger, and afterwards to reconcile Urien to the absence of half his warriors. The war between Rheged and Ebrauc broke out while I was there, so I stayed in the North until I heard that Arthur was back. I arrived at Camlann two days ago.'

'So you were in the North – when? Two weeks ago? What is happening there?'

He shrugged. 'Rheged raids Ebrauc, and Ebrauc raids Rheged and shouts forth bold defiance at the idea of being subject to an Emperor. There were no pitched battles and it is unlikely that there will be any, and neither side can take any clear advantage. If Arthur is indeed dead, and there is no Emperor for Ebrauc to rebel against, there may be a truce declared again – for a time.'

'If Arthur is dead,' I said. It was the first time anyone had spoken those words to me. 'What would you do then?'

He looked down at the desk and traced a pattern idly on its polished surface. 'What I have always done, my lady: make songs. I can play in the court of any king in Britain, even that of Maelgwn Gwynedd, and be welcome.'

'Songs about the fall of the Empire?' I asked, before I could stop myself.

He looked up. He had grey eyes, like Arthur or Medraut, but of a lighter shade. In the dim house they looked almost silver. 'Songs about the fall of the Empire, yes, and songs about the Emperor. There will be no more emperors now, not in the West. No one will claim the title, because everyone now is too weak for it, and none has a better claim than another. There will be many eager for songs about the Emperor Arthur and the Family.' He looked down again and hummed a bar of music softly; one of his new tunes, no doubt, for I did not recognize it as an old one. I felt a slow tide of anger and bitterness rising within me. 'The glory will not fade, my lady, because it will have no successors. And my songs will be remembered. The times that come will remember us. Something of you, and something of what we fought for, will survive.'

'Do you think,' I demanded, 'that we fought for *songs*?' He looked up again, mildly surprised, calm and unmoved, and the anger, the blind wild loss suddenly took possession of me. I jumped up, swept my hand over the desk, and the jug of mead crashed to the floor and broke. The serving girl came rushing in from the next room, but I waved her back. 'Do you think songs feed the hungry, or administer justice, or keep peace between kingdoms, or restore the ruins of the Empire of the Romans? Go and sing your songs to the Saxons; I am sure they will pay great attention to your melodies sung in an unknown tongue. Songs! They are no remedy. Glory is not a consolation. It's lost, don't you understand? It is all lost. The Light has gone, and the Darkness covers Britain as closely as the air, and there is nothing left of what we once dreamed and suffered for.

'And if you sing your songs, and if they are the greatest of songs, and able to move men to believe in an ideal, what sort of ideal will it become in a few years? An Emperor commits incest with his sister, and begets his own ruin in the person of a treacherous, malicious son; and an Empress divides the realm at the critical time by playing whore with the Emperor's best friend! What a beautiful story! What a theme for songs! Not only is it all lost, it was we who lost it, we who by our own stupidity and weakness allowed ourselves to be divided, and break like a pot flawed in the firing, that spills everything put into it. It is gone like smoke into the air, like mist before the wind. There is nothing left of the Empire, and nothing remaining from which we could build again, and nothing to show for our lives' effort but guilt, shame, and a few lying songs!'

My voice had grown shriller and shriller as I spoke, and

at last I screamed at Taliesin, who sat watching me silently. I had begun shaking, and tried to cover my face. The serving maid rushed out of the doorway again and caught my arm. 'My lady, my lady, sit down,' she said, and, to Taliesin, 'she is over-tired, poor lady, she works so hard. Here, noble lady, I will fetch some water and some more mead. Don't you fear, your husband will come back.'

I laughed, but sat down on the bed. 'My husband is dead,' I told the girl.

'Ach, noble lady, they never found his body; he cannot be dead.'

'He was lost in the cavalry charge,' I said, finally admitting what I had known for some time. 'I never recognized the body because the charge went over it, and it was mutilated beyond recognition. Arthur is dead, and even dead I cannot see him again, or bury him. I wish to the God of Heaven that I were dead as well.'

'Do not say such things!' exclaimed the girl. 'Here, here is some water.'

I drank a little, looked at the girl's shocked, miserable face. The anger was leaving me. 'Don't worry,' I told her. 'It is merely weariness.'

The girl smiled hesitantly and left to fetch the mead.

'I am sorry, noble lady,' said Taliesin. 'I did not mean to offend you.'

I pressed the heels of my hands to my eyes, feeling how the sobs were again locked within me. 'No, I am sorry,' I said. 'Forgive me. It is only that there has been too much death and, as the girl said, I am tired. You spoke to comfort me.'

Taliesin stood, took my hand, kissed it and touched it to his forehead. 'You have endured too much, noble lady.'

'Everyone endures too much.' I wiped my eyes, and the serving girl came back with the mead and gave me some. It was fresh from a storeroom, bitterly cold, and hurt in my tight throat. 'Thank you,' I said to the girl, trying to control my shaking. Then I thought of another thing, and added, 'Can you fetch me some fresh ink and some parchment, Olwen? Thank you.' She bobbed her head and left again, and I turned back to Taliesin.

'You say you can go to any king's court and be welcomed,' I said. It was true, of course: no British king will harm a bard. Law and custom do not permit it – and Taliesin was famous. 'Could you journey through Less Britain as well?'

He nodded, warily. 'You wish me to take a letter to the lord Bedwyr.'

'Two letters. One the lord Gwalchmai dictated to me as he was dying, and one I will write myself. It will only tell Bedwyr of the battle, and say that Arthur is dead and I will join a convent. You can read it first, if you like. You will compromise no one's honour by bearing it for me.'

'A convent?'

'What else does a noble widow do? It is that, or remarry, and I will not remarry.'

'Lord Sandde . . .'

'I am old enough to be his mother.'

'He would be willing to be your client king, not a husband. He admired you very greatly. He means to establish you in Camlann as Empress.'

'I would not last a year. We do not have the warband to enforce such a rule, and the kings of Britain would not permit the unfaithful wife of a usurper to claim the purple. You yourself said that there will be no more emperors. There is no longer an empire.' I felt as though I had been saying nothing else for a long time. 'To pretend that there is, when we have no real power, will only create more wars and factions than there are already. Let Sandde be king of Dumnonia – there is little doubt he will be recognized as that. I will go north and join a convent.' I rose and picked up one of the fragments of the broken mead jar. 'As a girl, I knew a girl who is now abbess of a convent near Caer Lugualid. I know I would be welcome there – perhaps I should write to her as well. If there is a truce proclaimed in the North, I will go there in the spring. I am sure that Sandde will give me some kind of escort.'

Taliesin bowed, and when he straightened again I saw to my astonishment that he was weeping. I had never seen him weep. 'Noble lady,' he said in a rough voice, 'I will carry your letters.' He bowed again and started from the room, then paused in the doorway and looked at me again. 'I dreamed, or foresaw in a vision, years and years ago, that this Empire would fall. I expected it, and watched, and waited, setting it out in my heart for a song. I had not thought to find such bitterness in seeing it. Even my songs seem nothing more than the wind in the reeds, hollow and without life. I am paid for . . .' He stopped, staring at me, his face working. 'For trying not to care. Have me called, lady, when you are done with the letters.' He gave one more bow and slipped out.

I picked up a few more pieces of the mead jug and weighed them in my hand. They were sticky, and the room was full of the sweet honey scent of the mead. I had already composed the letter to Bedwyr in thought, and it would not take long to write it. I cared enough still, I supposed, to want to let him know – but my heart was numb, and my only awareness of him was as another responsibility, another thing to mark off on some interminable list.

I set the broken fragments down, wiped my hands, and waited for the servant to come back with the ink.

Epilogue

It has now been some weeks since I finished this account of the past, set down my pen, and wondered what to do next. I began because one day I found that when I thought of the past only three things stood clear in my mind: the hour, with the water dripping from the thatch and sputtering in the torches, when Sandde told me that Arthur was gone; Bedwyr's face, dark-eyed, calm beyond any more anguish, when he said farewell; and Gwalchmai, innocent, dying in my arms in that hideous room at Ynys Witrin. And all these memories were bright and hard with such pain and bitterness that I grew afraid. I am old now. If I see my reflection, in water or a cup of wine – there are no mirrors in the convent – I can scarcely believe that I am that same Gwynhwyfar whom Arthur and Bedwyr loved. The face I see is an old woman's, lined with use. Much use: many tears, hour upon hour of a grief which can never be eradicated, never be forgotten. Lined with laughter, too. I have laughed in my life, thank God. But the laughter does not weigh even in the balance with the grief. My hair is white, and growing thin. My bones are stiff these days, and they ache deep within, the way the heart aches and is stiff after irreparable loss. Only my eyes still look as I remember them from the past: brown and steady. It is a terrible thing to have worked the ruin of all one loved best, but it is worse to survive that ruin, and grow old, forgetting.

I am abbess of this convent in the North, now, responsible for the well-being of nearly a hundred people, and I am – incredible word – respected again. The local people come to me with their problems, the sisters copy books and look after orphaned children, the world goes on. Bedwyr, I have heard, became a monk after hearing of Arthur's death. When Arthur lifted the siege of Car Aës to come to the aid of Britain, Macsen proclaimed it victory, and at the victory feast offered Bedwyr the title of warleader and various lands and powers as well, which Bedwyr refused. Despite the refusal, Macsen's old warleader was not pleased, and partly because of his displeasure Macsen acceded to Bedwyr's demand for release when the warrior received the news I sent him later that year. A few years ago I heard from an itinerant priest that Bedwyr has become famous throughout Less Britain for his asceticism – scourging himself and fasting, kneeling in icy streams before daybreak and reciting the psalms, and so on. The Breton monastics believe him very holy. Myself, I know he believes the opposite. Bedwyr would not believe he could persuade God to forgive him by torturing himself. And I do not think he will succeed in punishing his body enough to win his own forgiveness, either. But perhaps God is more merciful than Bedwyr. Perhaps.

Sandde became king of Dumnonia and ruled from its new capital, Camlann, until a few years after I left the South, when he died in one of the new wars against the Saxons. There are many wars now, small ones, and there is great uncertainty everywhere. The ships that used to come from Less Britain are more infrequent now, and they no longer bring news from the distant parts of the Empire. Rome now seems as distant and mysterious as Constantinople did in my youth. People live in the moment and are afraid for tomorrow, for the world grows steadily more dark.

A bard passed through this abbey not too long ago, and sang a new song about the death of a minor king, and the song has kept running through my head ever since. They say it was made by the dead man's sister.

> Cynddylan's Hall is dark tonight,
> Without a fire or bed for sleep:
> I will be silent after the hour I weep.

> Cynddylan's Hall is dark tonight,
> Without a fire or candle's shine:
> But God, what force will hold my mind?

> Cynddylan's Hall is dark tonight,
> With him who owned it gone away:
> Cruel death, why do you let me stay?

> From Gorwynnion's mound I looked upon
> A land lovely in summer ease.
> The sun's course is very long
> But longer are my memories.

My memories are long, but they will die with me, and soon no one living will remember our Empire. What remains, then, for all that blood and all that sorrow?

Sometimes I think that nothing remains. For a very long time I thought that the end of Camlann was the end of everything, and the bitterness swelled in me until I grew afraid, for it is not good, when one is old and shortly to come before God and answer to him for one's deeds, to be filled with a wordless bitterness. I began to tell myself that I ought to forget.

But I could not wish to forget, and the more I remembered, the less I wished to forget. I could not lose the memory of Camlann in the morning, the sun shining from the snow on the roof of the Feast Hall, the smoke of the morning fires; the feasts in the great dim building, the glitter of much gold, the strains of the harp. Whatever the bitterness that mingles with the memories, what we had in Camlann was the dream that the hearts of all men have ever longed for. '*O Oriens, splendor lucis aeterna*', 'O Dayspring, splendour of eternal Light and Sun of Justice, come, illumine those who sit in darkness and the shadow of Death.' We tasted on Earth the wine of the New Jerusalem that is forever to come. Of course the loss of that is bitter; more bitter than the loss of all the world. But I cannot wish to forget that it was there, for a few years. No, I wish to forget none of it: Arthur's smile and clear eyes, Bedwyr's warm gaze, the friendships and the loves and the astounding beauty of the world we were making anew.

I have digressed, and begun speaking like an abbess. Well, that is what I am, and it will colour my speech. We failed in Camlann; nothing of what we struggled to build remains, except the longing that drove us in the first place. But it was worth it, to have possessed that joy for a few years, and I cannot regret that we tried. And perhaps though we failed, God has not. Perhaps it is not the end.

Last year a new monastery was founded on an island to our north – founded by, of all people, the Irish. There is nothing so remarkable in that. The head of that settlement sent a few monks here, looking for books: that is remarkable. No one travels miles to look for books, in this age; I had begun to fear that the ability to read would die out and the world would truly be confined to the present. But this Irish abbot is wild for books; his reason for coming to Britain is trouble over one he stole. And these monks are setting about converting the Saxons; they have converted a king, and their influence already spreads like fire in the grass. Arthur and I always wanted the Saxons converted, brought into the Empire, but the British Church would neither undertake this task itself nor permit us to subsidize anyone to undertake it.

A handful of monks on a little island called Iona: it is not much. And they are not Roman, have no understanding of what Rome was and meant. Yet they are as set to change the world as I was when I rode south to Camlann many years ago. Perhaps I am mad to hope that they can achieve anything, succeed where Arthur and I failed. And yet everywhere in Britain the longing is there, the soul-deep desire, waiting for someone to touch it and shape it anew. It is as Taliesin predicted: Britain has not forgotten our Empire, and longs to hear more songs about it, because it is gone and its absence leaves a hole in the world which even its former enemies can feel. I have heard tales recently that Arthur did not die, but sleeps under some magic, to one day wake again. When first I heard these, I loathed them for their blind, deluding hope. But the hopes remain in this realm, more powerful than the spring when the sun circles round from the dark winter. Our failure cannot put out the sun. If someone were willing to offer light to those than sit in darkness and the shadow of death . . . if, if, if.

Those monks were very eager to.

Was I wrong to cling so tightly to the memory of Rome? Perhaps the lightning strikes not from the East and the old Empire, but from the West, the limit of the world. Who knows? Do I dare to believe that life indeed goes on, to trust God and human desires, and die in hope?

Today is Easter Sunday. While I write the birds are loud outside my window, and the sun pours clean gold over the margins of the page, like those intricate designs the Irish paint in their gospels. Outside the early apple trees and the hawthorn are in blossom, and the woods are carpeted with primroses and harebells. Strange how the Earth renews herself, like a snake shedding a skin stiff and dusty with age, and polishing its shining new coils over a sun-warmed path.

It is not the end. It never can be. The tree, stripped barren in last autumn's storm, stands green-gold with new leaves, and by some special miracle, some unexpected magic, life returns from the dead.